Christmas in New York

Jeannie Moon

Jolyse Barnett

Jennifer Gracen

Patty Blount

TULE
PUBLISHING

This Christmas
©Copyright 2014 Jeannie Moon

A Light in the Window
©Copyright 2014 Jolyse Barnett

All I Want for Christmas
©Copyright 2014 Jennifer Gracen

Goodness and Light
©Copyright 2014 Patty Blount

The Tule Publishing Group, LLC

ALL RIGHTS RESERVED

No part of this book may be used or reproduced in any manner whatsoever without written permission except in the case of brief quotations embodied in critical articles and reviews.

This is a work of fiction. Names, characters, places, and incidents are products of the author's imagination or are used fictitiously. Any resemblance to actual events, locales, organizations, or persons, living or dead, is entirely coincidental.

ISBN: 978-1-942240-04-4

Contents

This Christmas   1

A Light in the Window   147

All I Want for Christmas   295

Goodness and Light   435

This Christmas

A Christmas in New York Story

Jeannie Moon

Dedication

For my husband,
my love story.

Acknowledgements

I've always wanted to write a Christmas story and *This Christmas* has been an absolute joy for me to create. There are a number of people who had a hand in making it so special, and I wish I had a whole book to thank them.

First, to my partners in crime and my best friends, Patty Blount, Jolyse Barnett and Jennifer Gracen, who would have thought when we met through Long Island Romance Writers almost four years ago that we'd be doing this series together? You girls are amazing and I wouldn't be half the writer I am without you. #Fab4.

To the team at Tule Publishing, Meghan, Lee, and Talia, thank you for making this experience so rewarding. You three are miracle workers. Many thanks, and much love goes to Jane Porter. Not only are you a phenomenally talented author, you're one of the best people I have the privilege of knowing. That you thought I belonged in the Tule family is a gift I will never take for granted. Thank you.

This book would not be what it is without the guidance of my editor, Lilian Darcy. Your understanding of story, your creative spirit and your tireless work on our behalf has made all of the *Christmas in New York* books truly special.

My agent Stephany Evans has the most amazing knack for keeping things in perspective and thank goodness I have you in my corner. An author couldn't ask for a better advocate and personally, I couldn't ask for a more steadfast friend.

Finally, to my dear family, through all the ups and downs, life with all of you is a gift and because of that, every day is Christmas.

Prologue

THANKSGIVING ~ 10 YEARS AGO

"She's not coming out. Do you think it turned blue?" Cass paced around the room wondering what the hell was going on in Sabrina's bathroom. She looked at her friends who were perched on the window seat in Sabrina's bedroom, both gazing out the window at the Holly Point lighthouse in the distance.

"Well? She's been in there a lot longer than three minutes." Cass demanded when neither responded.

"What do you want us to do, Cass?" Jade was as cool as a cucumber—measured and calm as always. And right at that moment it annoyed the crap out of Cass.

Kara looked over, twirling a lock of blonde hair. It was a nervous habit, one she'd developed after her mother had died. "You could knock."

Cass stormed across the room, not understanding why she was the only one freaking out over this. What was wrong with them? Had their first year of business school sucked the souls out of her friends? Flinging her hair over her shoulder, Cass knocked as Kara suggested. The four of them... five if they counted Elena who was two years younger and currently brooding over some greasy drummer... were closer than siblings. Their mothers were sorority sisters who were best friends for over twenty-five years, and the girls had grown up together, sharing holidays, special events and—Cass looked at Kara, thought of Elena—they'd endured a tragedy beyond measure. Cass knocked again, harder, and she heard the lock flip on the door handle.

Sabrina emerged, the look on her waiflike face answering the question that hung over the room.

"It's positive, isn't it?" Jade's voice, soft and steady, cut through the stillness that had descended.

Bree didn't say anything. She went to her bed, lay on her side, and pulled her legs up to her chest in such a way that she looked small and fragile. Cass looked into Sabrina's olive colored eyes which were large and cat-like—there were no tears, but the fear was overwhelming. Sabrina was a powerhouse, just like her mother. She was sweet and smart, and Cass couldn't imagine who had gotten her to go off her well-planned path. She'd just turned nineteen, was a pre-med major at an Ivy League school and had planned to be a surgeon. Years of schooling, a career she really wanted, was all up in the air.

As far as they all knew, Sabrina didn't even have a boyfriend.

Kara lay down behind her, curling in while she stroked Bree's long, dark brown hair. "What are you going to do?"

"Hold on a second," Jade said, focused as always. "Who's the father?"

Sabrina's eyes widened and that was when the tears came. Big, fat drops that told everyone their friend's heart was broken. Jade immediately felt bad and sat on the edge of the bed, reaching out and touching Bree's leg in comfort. "Oh, no.

Don't cry. I'm sorry. I'm so sorry."

Before Cass could say anything, seventeen-year-old Elena threw open the door, and bolted into Bree's bathroom. In ten seconds she was back in the room holding the pregnancy test. "Okay, so who's preggers?"

Kara was mortified, grabbing at what was in her younger sister's hand. "You shouldn't be in here, Elena…"

"Why?" She held the pregnancy test out of Kara's reach. "Who's knocked up?"

Sabrina sat up, her eyes still flooded. "I am."

"Oh, my God." Elena plopped next to Bree and looped her arm around their distraught friend's shoulder. Kara and Jade hadn't moved, and Cass pressed her back against the wall. This wasn't supposed to happen. Not to Sabrina. She was the one who was most focused. The most innocent. What the hell had been going on?

"It's Jake's, isn't it?" Elena asked.

Once again, there was silence and Sabrina was the only one who reacted. The tears fell faster and her breath came in little gulps. "I… I… why would you say that?"

"Oh, come on. I was here almost the whole summer. I'm not blind or stupid. I saw the way you two acted around each other." Elena shook her head. "I guess I was the only one who saw you sneaking out of the house in the middle of the night."

Cass was a word person, but right then she didn't know what to say. Sabrina and Jake Killen? Hot, older, and now married hockey player, Jake Killen? Sabrina's brother's teammate?

Kara yanked on one of the chopped, hot pink locks on her sister's head. "You shouldn't be talking about this."

"Oh, for God's sake," Elena moaned. "It's not like I don't know where babies come from. I've had sex before."

Kara's face dropped. "What do you mean you've had sex?"

"Look, sissy, just because you're saving yourself for Mr. Right, doesn't mean everyone is. Keep your eyes on the ball. This is about Bree."

Cass finally approached and knelt down next to Bree who was sitting straight and unmoving. She took her friend's hand and hoped Bree would look up and make eye contact, but she didn't. She just continued to cry quietly.

"Honey, is Elena right? Is Jake the father?"

Bree nodded, her hair falling forward, a shaky breath escaping her lungs. "We got to be friends last spring at the end of the season. We talked a lot, spent some time together. And then he broke it off with his fiancée." She looked up, her eyes full, her lip trembling. "Nothing happened before that, though. I swear." She swallowed, sounded almost desperate. "He never touched me, never did anything."

"Maybe not," Elena declared. "But it was pretty obvious that you two liked each other."

It hurt Cass to watch her friend cry, but she still couldn't wrap her head around the chain of events. How had they all missed what was happening with Bree and Jake?

"How old is he?" Jade looped her arm around Bree's shoulder.

"He's twenty five."

"Is that why he was here so much last summer?" Cass was still holding Bree's hands, she wouldn't let go until Bree wouldn't stand for it anymore. "He was here for you?"

"Not exactly. Originally, he was waiting for a place to open up in the city, but there was a problem with the sub-let. So he stayed in the apartment over our garage. He and Ryan trained together all summer."

Jade piped in, "And there are worse places to be during the summer than here."

All the girls had spent summers at this house—sometimes

all at once. Bree's father's family had built it years ago as a summer retreat, before Holly Point became a summer destination, and added on to it over the past fifty years. It was immense with seven bedrooms and five bathrooms and good feelings all around. But last summer was different. Cass stayed at NYU for summer session. Jade and Kara had jobs that demanded all their time. Bree was here with Elena. And now they knew Jake was here, too.

But he wasn't here for the sun, sand, and surf. He was here for Sabrina.

"I don't know what to say." Jade stood and paced the room. "Why didn't you tell any of us?"

Bree wrapped her arms around her middle and shrugged. "I don't know. I should have. But there was something so special about keeping it to ourselves. Plus, I knew you guys would think I was crazy because he's so much older than me, and Ryan would go ballistic..."

"Was Jake trying to keep you a secret?" Cass had to ask. The guy had gotten married a month ago, so something had to have happened. "I mean, did he take you out or anything?"

"He did. We'd go into town, or to the beach. He was so sweet with me." Bree gave a weak smile and Cass wished she had a memory of any of this, but she didn't. Bree was one of her best friends and she didn't know anything.

"He loved me," her friend whispered. "And I loved him. I still do. I think I will forever."

"Was he your... was he your first?" Cass already knew the answer, but she was trying to get her head around what she'd missed. Bree didn't speak, she just nodded.

That admission brought on a wave of tears, deep painful sobs that tore at Cass. "Oh, God." Sabrina looked right at Cass. "What am I going to do? He's gone."

"Gone? Where is he?" Cass wrapped her arms around

Sabrina as her friend collapsed on her shoulder. And that was it right there. Bree was always quick with a smile, a joke, or a smart ass comment, but the truth of it was, her friend was sweet and sheltered. And now she was really, really scared.

Elena mouthed the word *"traded"* right as Bree responded.

"He's in Toronto. But it's not just that. He went back to Sydney."

Kara handed Bree tissues to mop her eyes. "Who's Sydney?"

"His ex-fiancée. Well, she's his wife now." The pain, the sorrow was evident with every word Bree uttered. "She told him she was pregnant."

Jade was fuming. She was stalking the room like a willowy blonde cat and making Cass nervous. "Well... well," she stuttered. "You'll just have to tell him *you're* pregnant. And then, and then..."

"Then what?" Sabrina asked, her voice so small it broke Cass's heart. "He's not coming back, so what happens? He has to choose?" Sabrina stood and walked to the window, folding her arms and resting her head against the wall, tears staining her cheeks. "What if he picks her? I don't know if I can handle that. I mean, really, if you think about it, he already did. He picked her."

Cass rose and went to her friend. The five of them were all close, but she and Bree saw each other more than the others since they both lived on Long Island. Bree stiffened when Cass placed a hand on her shoulder.

"Are you going to tell him anything?"

"No," she whispered. "He made his choice. I have to live with mine."

"Oh, Bree..."

Sabrina spun and the look on her face was more serious, more frightened than Cass had ever seen before. "You can't tell anyone, Cassie." Looking past her at the other girls, she told them the same thing. "No one can tell. This has to stay secret. Ryan would kill him."

They all looked at each other, knowing that keeping the secret would cause more problems down the road. But smart, sweet Sabrina was unwavering. Each one of them nodded, their promise to her as solemn as any vow, and Cass knew right then that none of them would breathe a word of the father's identity. This secret was too important and they all knew it. Bree was right. Her brother, Ryan, would go after Jake. And truth be told, while seeing Jake get the crap beat out of him by big, bad Ryan Gervais would have some appeal, Cass figured it was better for Bree to close that door completely. She didn't need Jake Killen in her life; he certainly didn't deserve to be there.

Chapter One

JAKE KILLEN WAS happy to be back in New York. Not many farm boys from the middle of Canada could be heard saying that, but he loved the buzz he got being around the city. He liked the action and enjoyed the busy life he lived when he was there during the season. He loved the beaches to the east, the mountains to his north, and Jake liked the people.

Yeah, he especially liked the people. They were straightforward, funny, and once they got to know someone, very loyal. He'd missed being here and there were a lot of reasons for that. One in particular was a green-eyed girl who had changed his life. One whom he'd loved. But, ten years ago he'd broken her heart, as well as his own in the process.

Funny things those broken hearts… they never let him forget a damn thing.

Jake walked into the practice rink and drew in a deep breath. He could smell the ice. Cool, crisp, clean. And just like when he was a kid again, the smell offered him comfort. This was always where he came when he needed to think, when he needed to decompress. The ice never judged, never picked on him, and never expected more than he could give.

Making his way toward the familiar sounds of the rink, Jake was more than ready to finish the rehab on his shoulder. He'd taken a wicked hit during the pre-season and had been on the sidelines since, rehabbing at a specialized clinic in Canada, but now, with the worst of his recovery behind him, Jake could be back playing in less than a month.

The best news was he was cleared to skate. He may not have had all his strength back, but he was allowed to condition. He didn't want to tell the doctor he also needed it for his sanity. He'd been going a little crazy not being able to get on the ice. It had been that way for as long as he could remember.

When he was a kid, skating was sometimes his only release. Long days in school when he was picked on for being short or skinny, when he didn't get that math problem, or he couldn't pay attention during reading, sent him out to the frozen pond behind his parent's farmhouse where he skated in circles. He'd skate until his legs burned and the cold air stung his lungs. He blew off steam, did his best thinking and most of all, he dreamed. Jake Killen dreamed of being the biggest kid out there, the fastest. He dreamed of being a hockey star.

And now he was—an aging hockey star, but still mixing it up. He was thirty-five, and he brought his "A" game every night. As soon as he couldn't do that, he'd pack it in, but walking into the rink made him smile. The place was a hive of activity because there was a youth clinic going on that day. It was exactly what he needed. The kids were off from school because of Thanksgiving and a day playing hockey could never be considered a bad one. At least they weren't being dragged around to the Black Friday sales. He wondered what kind of crazy person shopped on a day like today?

It didn't matter. The kids were here and anytime he was able to work with a group of developing players was a good day. Jake was one of those guys who always wanted a family.

He wanted the wife and children, but here he was in his mid-thirties, still single, still without kids, and he couldn't shake off the feeling that he'd missed his chance.

"Jake!" Looking to his left, Jake saw his old coach, George Lamiroult approaching. This was a blast from the past. George was the assistant coach of the Mariners hockey team when Jake arrived in New York twelve years ago. He made sure a homesick kid from a little town near Winnipeg didn't get swallowed by the big city, and the two had made sure to stay in touch over the years.

Now retired from full time coaching, George ran youth hockey clinics and today's was one of his most popular. The kids on the ice were all under twelve—Pee Wee, Squirt, and Bantam players from the tri-state area who'd shown a knack for the game and were recommended by their own coaches. Sure, they were all still learning the game, but a day with George would make them even better.

"You're looking good," the older man said in accented English. He hadn't lived in Quebec for years, but the French had never left him. "How is your shoulder?"

Jake rotated it for him, grinning. "Just need to get my conditioning back. Range of motion is perfect." George nodded and turned his head at the same time Jake saw a pint-sized streak of blue and orange go by, weaving in and out of the other players on the ice.

Damn, that kid was quick. "Jeez. Someone had their Wheaties for breakfast. Kid's like lightning."

"That's Charlie," George said. "Lots of talent." He looked Jake up and down. "Go get some warm ups on and lace up your skates. You and that big, fat, free agent contract can help me and Gervais with some drills.

"Ryan's here?" He hadn't seen Ryan Gervais, other than on the ice, since Jake was sent to Toronto ten years ago. Ryan was also on his second go round with New York, being picked up in a trade right after Jake hurt himself during pre-season. Ryan was a nice guy, easy going, and a smart hockey player. When George nodded toward the far corner, he saw his old friend working with a small group on shooting, including the little rocket ship that had gone by him at warp speed a few seconds ago. The kids were shuffling their skates, tapping their sticks, and hanging onto every one of Ryan's instructions.

George cleared his throat and nodded again toward the tunnel. "You've been out since before the season started, let's see you earn some of that money."

Grabbing his bag, Jake turned and headed for the locker room, but he looked back once more and noticed something. There was a name on the speed demon's jersey. *Gervais.* That explained some of the kid's talent. *Ryan's kid.* Jake really was out of the loop though, because he had no idea Ryan Gervais was married or had a kid. But he shouldn't be surprised. Most of the guys he knew when he broke into the league were married by now and had a couple of kids. That he was flying solo was his own damn fault. He'd walked away from the best thing that had ever happened to him and he'd wrecked someone he cared for in the process. His life was what he'd made it.

He had to stop dwelling on the past even though being back in New York meant it would kick him in the ass every now and then. Today was one of those days.

He got ready, absorbing the feel of the locker room after being away for the last two and a half months. It was surprisingly busy, considering there was no practice and it was an off day. A couple of guys were working with the trainer, and the equipment manager was prepping and organizing gear for tomorrow night's game.

He changed and got his skates on, before finding a stick in

the equipment room. Yeah, it all felt good.

Making his way to the ice, Jake welcomed the feel of his blades hitting the surface, which was a little soft for his liking, but after being abused by a couple of dozen pairs of skates all day, it was understandable. Ryan was teaching his charges how to shoot from the point, his specialty as a defenseman, and Jake couldn't resist the opportunity to bust on him.

"You trying to teach those kids hockey with your skating skills, Gervais?"

All the helmeted heads turned and it looked like a convention of mini storm troopers from Star Wars. Jake smiled and skated over, taking off his glove and shaking Ryan's hand. "How are you, man?"

Ryan looked the same as always, big, broad, and intimidating as hell. He was the nicest guy around, but there was no one more physical on the ice. Coming in contact with all 220 pounds of Gervais at center ice, or digging a puck out of the boards, could send a guy to the hospital.

"You are the last person I expected to see, Killen. Welcome back."

The kids started buzzing and looking at each other. They'd caught his name. "Guys," Ryan said. "You have one of the best centers in the game standing in front of you. You all know Jake Killen? He's going to do some drills with us for the last half hour."

The heads bobbed up and down and he heard the excitement in their voices. It was a buzz, no doubt about it when a kid was excited to meet him. He remembered how he felt about his favorite players. Some of the old time hockey guys weren't always so nice, though, so meeting them was a letdown. Jake vowed that would never happen with him, always making sure a kid felt happy they'd met. He looked over at Ryan and saw the speed demon tugging on his sleeve. He bent down and from the way his friend and the boy were looking over, the conversation was about him.

A pat on the back from Gervais sent the kid, Charlie George had said, back to his group to play. Jake took over after the shooting drills and worked with the players on skating. Balance drills, sprints, and power stops had everyone huffing, puffing, and laughing.

Even Jake was huffing and puffing, a sure sign he had a lot of work to do if he was going to be playing again by the January.

Parents were filtering in, watching the end of the drills and he wondered how that would feel—watching his kid grow up, do things. Once the clinic ended, Jake signed a bunch of helmets, sticks, and jerseys, got lots of high fives and thank yous, before the group dispersed. They were nice kids, Jake wished he gotten there earlier.

Ryan skated over and little Gervais, who proved to be the best skater on the ice, was right next to him. The kid stuck close to Ryan, helmet on, and head down. Jake wondered what was up. He couldn't imagine Ryan Gervais, the life of the locker room, having a shy kid.

"Jake, I want to introduce you to someone." He looked down. "Charlie, take off your helmet."

Charlie started working the straps and to Jake's surprise, when the headgear came off, a long, braided pony tail fell out. Charlie was a girl—a badass, super-fast, hockey-playing girl.

Ryan must have seen the shock on his face because his eyes flashed right before the corner of his mouth tipped up. "This is Charlotte. My niece."

Whoa. *His niece*? "Hi, Charlotte. Or did I hear you prefer Charlie?"

The kid looked up and Jake had to have stepped back. Dark brown hair, full lips and large green eyes dominated her pixie face. It hit him like a stick to the head. Charlie looked just like Sabrina. Jake nodded and smiled as best he could, having just received one of those kicks in the ass he'd been thinking about earlier. He was glad she'd found someone after he screwed up, but then he started to run numbers in his head and there was no way...

"So," he started. Not really wanting to ask, but not being able to stop himself. He had to know. "How old are you?"

She smiled shyly and Jake's heart lurched. "I'm nine," she said. "I'll be ten in May."

It didn't take long for Jake to do the math. Jesus, if what he thought...

"Ryan? How did it go?"

Jake's back tensed at the voice echoing through the arena.

"Mom!" Charlie took off toward the tunnel and Jake turned to see the love of his life, the woman he never thought he'd see again, hugging her nine-year-old daughter. Bree had just turned twenty-nine. Jake's eyes were locked on the scene and when Sabrina looked up, the happy expression dropped away and pure shock and fear washed across her face. Her reaction told him everything he needed to know.

Chapter Two

IT HADN'T BEEN easy for Sabrina Gervais. Giving up her dream, or at least modifying it, so she could raise her daughter, had tested her at every turn. Yet nothing prepared her for Jake. Nothing. But there he was. Large. Looming. And obviously connecting the dots.

"Whoa. Wait. Is that..." Her good friend Jade's words hung in the air as Sabrina hugged Charlie and stared into the eyes of the man she never thought she'd see again.

"Jake," Bree swallowed. "Oh, God."

"He helped with the clinic." Charlie turned her face up and Bree pushed a sweaty lock of hair away from her brow. "He knows Uncle Ryan."

"Yes, he does."

Bree looked back toward Jake and saw he was still staring. The man hadn't moved an inch. There was a twitching low in her belly, while her heart... her heart damn near beat out of her chest. Emotions she'd buried long ago washed through her, filling Bree from head to toe with grief, regret, and the oh-so-familiar longing she felt whenever Jake had been close by. How was it possible he was better looking than the last time she'd seen him?

But he was. He was bigger, more rugged than boyish—this Jake was all man. The ten years had made him broader, harder—and yes, hotter. His eyes still blazed a brilliant blue and his hair was shorter, a little darker. But at the core she could see in his gaze his passion, his drive, and the tightness in his jaw revealed his anger.

This was Sabrina's worst nightmare. The way he looked at her, and then looked back at Charlie, he knew. He knew she was his daughter and Sabrina had some serious explaining to do. Turning toward Jade, whose mouth was still hanging open, Bree needed help and she needed it fast.

"Can you help Charlie get changed?"

"I guess?" Poor Jade. She was making a major life change of her own; the last thing she'd expect when she decided to stay a couple of extra days after Thanksgiving was Bree's drama. And there would be drama. "I don't know how to undo all the stuff she's wearing."

"She knows how." Bree gave Charlie a hug. "Aunt Jade will take you back to change, sweetie. Okay?"

Charlie raised an eyebrow, skeptical, because if nothing else her daughter was bright. "Why?"

"I'll explain another time." At that point she saw Jake start to skate toward them. *Damn.* This would not happen here. It couldn't. "Take her now," she whispered to Jade, who also saw Jake coming.

Wrapping her arm around Charlie, Jade hustled her down the tunnel toward the changing rooms. Bree's eyes stayed locked on her daughter, whose face was awash with questions, and she was sure Charlie wasn't the only one. When they were out of sight, Bree turned back toward the ice and came face-to-face with the man who had changed her life.

Dear God. It was more like face to stomach, because in his

skates, Jake was at least six-four. Bree was barely five-one.

"You and I need to have a conversation," he growled.

Then, before she could respond, he left, walking into the dark area near the locker rooms, leaving her to think about the way this was going to turn her life, and more importantly Charlie's, upside down.

Her eyes were still focused on the tunnel, on the place Jake had been, wondering what he was going to do next.

"You want to tell me what that was all about?" Bree turned and looked up into her brother's eyes. "Killen looked like he saw a ghost. Tell me what he said to you."

"No." She wasn't going to say anything now. Bree had kept the identity of Charlie's father a secret for ten years. Other than Jade and the other girls who were with her on that Thanksgiving that felt like a lifetime ago, the only other person who knew was her mother. The last thing she needed was her brother going off half-cocked. More, it was the last thing Charlie needed.

"You're not going to tell me?"

"Tell you what?"

"Why I shouldn't kill that son of a bitch for leaving my baby sister pregnant?"

So much for a secret. The revelation dropped between them like a large weight. Bulky and immovable, there was no way for Bree to get around the truth, especially when Ryan already knew.

"I don't want you to do anything." The words caught in her throat as the emotion rushed to the surface. *Jake.* Jake was back and he knew about Charlie and now nothing would be easy. Bree had managed to put so much out of her head since he left. It was the only way she could survive.

Surprisingly, her brother stepped toward her and reached out. She didn't hesitate and walked into his waiting arms, and let the boy who'd taunted her turn into the man who would not only comfort her, but kick the ass of the person who made her cry—if that was what she needed. Ryan's hand patted her back in reassurance. "I really want to kill him."

"I know, but you can't. He has to meet Charlie."

"How do you think she's going to take it?"

Holding onto Ryan's warm up jacket, Bree buried her face again.

"I have no idea. I think she's going to hate me. A lot." Jake was one thing, but dealing with her ten-year-old was going to prove to be the real test.

"I don't think she'll hate you, him maybe, but not you."

"No, it's on me, Ry." She looked up. "I never told him."

He was quiet. Her big brother looked like a dangerous, dangerous man, but in truth he was a pussycat. "Damn. Why?"

She shrugged. "I didn't want to be hurt again. He left me to go back to Sydney, and what if he really just didn't want me."

"He's divorced, you know. He went back to Sydney, but they split two years later. The kid she was pregnant with wasn't his."

Bree knew the story. She knew all about his divorce and the baby belonging to some other guy. All she could think about was that Jake hadn't come back to her. He'd left to try and do the right thing, she got that, but he didn't come back when he was free.

And that was what had driven her decision. She couldn't want a man who didn't want her. Who hadn't come back. Jake would do the "right" thing and ask her to marry him, but she didn't want to trap him. No. If Jake wanted her, he would have been there on his own.

"I'd better get Charlie," she whispered.

"Can I kick the crap out of him, at least?"

"No, not that either."

Ryan stepped back, and Sabrina could see in Ryan's eyes that her wonderful big brother was at a loss. He always knew what to do and how to act, but not this time. "I'll come by the house tomorrow. Are you guys still baking?"

"You bet. I'll put some pizzelle aside for you." Bree knew the waffle-like cookie was his favorite.

Ryan kissed her on the top of the head and then went back to the crowd of kids who were waiting for autographs. Bree on the other hand, turned toward the dressing room, and her little girl whose life was in for some big changes.

✦ ✦ ✦

JAKE SWALLOWED HARD as he slammed through the dressing room door, trying to wrap his head around what he'd just seen. Was that his daughter? Had Sabrina had a kid and not told him about it? *His kid?*

His head was swimming with thoughts and images and his heartbeat kicked up just thinking about Sabrina. Pressing the heels of his hands against his eyes, he saw her in a thousand different ways. Some of the images were from a few seconds ago; others were burned into his memory from ten years before.

"Holy shit," he said to no one in particular. The room was empty and he sat down on the bench in front of his stall. "Holy shit," he whispered again. He'd come to accept losing Sabrina because he'd left her to marry Sydney and take care the child she said was his.

A child, who, it turned out, didn't belong to him.

Sydney had lied, and he'd been forced to face the biggest mistake of his life.

And if losing Bree wasn't enough, if the universe hadn't

screwed him over with that decision, he learned today there'd been a little girl without a father he'd never known about.

Standing, he stalked the room, moving with no particular purpose and suppressing the urge to do real violence. How had this happened? How had he fucked this up so badly? With the pressure building in his chest, he roared before kicking over a small table in the center of the room that had been loaded with stick tape and water bottles, sending everything flying.

He crouched down in the middle of the floor, surrounded by the colorful tape and plastic bottles, and buried his head in his hands. "Jesus, Bree," he whispered. "Why didn't you tell me?"

"Tell me why I shouldn't give you the beating of your life?"

Jake picked up his head and saw Ryan standing at the entrance to the room, his gloves off, ready to kick Jake's ass.

Jake rose and held his arms wide. "Go ahead. I couldn't possibly feel worse than I already do."

Ryan advanced, both men still in skates, stood their ground. Jake, however, was ready to take Ryan's best shot.

"You got my sister pregnant. My baby sister! She was eighteen. What were you thinking?"

Jake shrugged and raised his hands in surrender. All the fight had left him, all he could see were Charlotte's eyes staring up at him. "I was thinking about her. I still think about her. Why didn't she tell me about the baby?"

Ryan relaxed his stance and shook his head. "She was eighteen."

"I know. I should have left her alone, but it just happened."

"That kind of stuff doesn't *just happen*," Ryan snarled. "And on top of everything, you kept her a secret. You didn't tell anyone."

"I didn't try to keep it secret." He didn't. He wanted to take her out places, but she was the one who was nervous about what her parents and her brother would do if they found out. "Bree was the one worried about us being found out. I wasn't."

"So, she was the girl you were so broken up about when Sydney told you she was pregnant? The one you didn't want to hurt?"

"The one you told me to make as miserable as possible so she'd hate me and be able to move on? Yeah."

"Oh… I…"

Jake chuckled wryly. "It worked. She must hate me good, because she didn't tell me about the little girl."

He thought about Charlie, a little peanut of a thing with fire in her eyes and wings on her feet. He wondered again, how it had happened? It had happened because he was an idiot. It happened because Jake didn't follow his heart.

"Tell me what went on."

He returned to his stall and Ryan took a seat next to him. Big and intimidating, Ryan Gervais was loyal to his family and fiercely protective of his little sister, so much so, Jake often wondered if he'd had some kind of death wish pursuing Bree like he did.

"She found out on Thanksgiving. From what my mother says, she was about two months gone when she took the test."

Jake had been out of her life for a month when she found out, which meant, when he was going back to Sydney, and breaking Sabrina's heart, she was already pregnant.

"She was miserable, but no matter how many times I asked her, she wouldn't tell me who the father was. As far as we knew, she hadn't ever had a serious boyfriend."

"It was serious for me," Jake said. "I know she was young, but I would have married her, pregnant or not."

He meant what he said; he loved Sabrina so much it hurt. It killed him to return the engagement ring he'd bought. He'd planned on giving it to her on their first Christmas together, but then the bottom dropped out of... well... it dropped out of everything.

"I wish she'd said something."

"Me too," Ryan agreed. His friend blew out a long breath. "What are you going to do?"

Jake didn't want to wait. He had to talk to her and find out when he could start getting to know his daughter. It didn't matter how Bree felt about him, he was going to be a father to his child and he had a lot of time to make up. "Does she still live in Holly Point?"

"Yeah, they live with my parents."

That settled it. He started unlacing his skates, because Jake knew what he had to do and he had a long drive ahead of him.

He remembered the day he told Sabrina he was going back to Sydney like it was yesterday. No matter how hard he'd tried to get Bree out of his head, she'd come back when he'd least expect it. He'd never been more anxious, or more miserable, in his life. Walking away from Sabrina was the hardest thing he'd ever done.

"You're going to see her, aren't you?" Ryan had been watching Jake's every move, waiting for him to say something.

Jake dried his skates with a small towel and stored them for the equipment manager. Then he got to the business of changing. "Yup. Anything I should know?"

"Watch out for my mother. She'll castrate you if you aren't careful."

Jake figured if he'd escaped a beating from Ryan, he could get around Mrs. Gervais. The one he didn't know how he was going to deal with was Sabrina. On one hand, he was so pissed he was ready to put a hole in the wall, on the other, he knew how badly he'd hurt her. What had passed between them didn't have an easy fix.

"Anything else I should know? The blonde who was with her? One of her posse?"

"Yeah, that's Jade. She's the most reasonable of the bunch. They were all with her when she found out she was pregnant. Be thankful Cass isn't out there. Or Elena or Kara. They'd be tying boulders to your ankles and tossing you off the end of the dock."

Jake had to smile. He remembered Elena with her spiky, pink hair from that summer. The kid was rebelling fifty different ways and gave Sabrina's mom a run for her money. Considering how Elena had lost her mom on 9/11, it was no wonder.

"My father is the quietest man alive, unless you mess with his family. He's not going to be happy to see you."

Based on what Ryan just told him, it wasn't just Sabrina he was going to be dealing with but her mom, her dad, and all Charlie's aunts.

And Charlie.

His daughter.

What was she going to do when she found out about him? Would she be shy, upset? There were too many things to think about, including his own family. What were his parents going to think? Jake took a deep breath as he pulled a thermal shirt over his head. They were going to be ripping pissed. His mother would blow that nice Canadian stereotype right out the window.

No, Jake was walking into a minefield. There was no way around it.

Chapter Three

THE DRIVE HOME was long and quiet. Bree knew Jade had a thousand questions and Charlie had dozed off in the back seat, but even with her asleep, she and Jade wouldn't risk talking.

Once they got back to Holly Point, she'd have to break the news to her mother and her daughter. Yeah, it was not going to be a fun night. Not at all.

Bree never thought this day would come. Jake had gone off her radar ten years ago and she never expected to see him again. She stayed tucked, safe and sound, in her little town, her dream of becoming a surgeon had been set aside to raise her baby. But even with all the challenges, she'd still managed a degree in athletic training and a clinical doctorate in physical therapy, specializing in the treatment and rehabilitation of upper extremity injuries in athletes.

She was growing herself a serious reputation, too. She treated players from the large state university about thirty minutes away and several pro teams had asked about sending their players to her for rehab. It was exciting, and helped her feel like she hadn't compromised everything.

It had been a very long day for all of them. Finally arriving home, Charlie dragged herself up the front steps, exhausted but happy from her day and Bree should have been exhausted from her shopping adventure. But the house didn't allow for negativity, and no matter what happened, Bree loved how she felt safe when she walked through the door.

The Gervais home was built more than a half a century ago when her father's family left Brooklyn for the very rural eastern part of Suffolk County, on Long Island's south shore. With an unexpected inheritance, her grandfather bought a two acre parcel of land on the water, built the house and grew his construction business. The man was an architect by training, but he loved the process of a building going up, so while he could design, Poppy made his money with his hands. The house itself had grown over the years and its grey, weathered, cedar shakes, large windows, and wraparound porch epitomized coastal living. Her mother and father had obviously been busy decorating the outside of the house while she was trolling the sales with Jade and Cass. When Bree pulled up, wreaths hung on the doors, pine garland was draped along the porch rails, and lights twinkled all over the yard. It was a wonderland and with the sudden burst of cold air coming down from the north and the prediction of snow flurries tonight, it actually felt like Christmas.

Bree had thought about buying her own house, but her parents loved having Charlie so close, and living with them kept their lives centered. It also gave Charlie more of a stable family life, with the give and take more than two people provided. Charlie had the normalcy of a family dinner every night, even if Bree had to work, because her parents were there. In the off season, Ryan made a point of coming out at least once a week.

Mom and Dad had been nothing but supportive when she

told them she was pregnant. Were they upset? Sure, but they didn't push when she wouldn't tell them who the father of her baby was. No, Enza and Edwin Gervais had simply let her deal with her predicament, given her support, and loved her the best way they could. Personally, it was all Sabrina could ask for.

But a few years ago, her mother had discovered the truth and whether or not Mom told Bree's father, she didn't know. What she did know was that her mother would bring hell fire down on Jake if she ever saw him again.

Bree and Jade went into the kitchen while her dad went up with his granddaughter to hear about her day and hang her equipment up to dry in one of the extra bathrooms. Her mother was milling around, gathering ingredients for the marathon cookie baking that was going to take place tomorrow.

"So, how was the clinic?" Her mother continued to move haphazardly around the kitchen, wiping the counter, which was already spotless and opening and closing random cabinets and drawers. When Bree finally caught Mom's eye, she could see she was fishing for information. Information she already had.

"Did Ryan call, Mom?"

When her mother's face sobered, Bree had her answer. Of course he'd called. He probably wanted permission to kill Jake, but chances were Vincenza Bruno Gervais was going to call some long lost relative with "connections" to give Jake the punishment she'd always thought he deserved.

"Your brother is worried about you. I'm worried about you. How is Charlie?"

"I think she suspects. I have to talk to her. There's no hiding it anymore."

"I wish he'd just stayed away," her mother blurted out. "We opened our home to him and he betrayed our trust."

"Well, it takes two, you know."

"You were so young and innocent, Sabrina. He should have left you alone."

There was a lot of truth in what her mother said, she *had been* young and innocent when it came to boys. There had never been anyone before Jake and only a few dates here and there since him.

Bree didn't think there would ever be anyone else again.

What her mother didn't know was that her sweet, innocent Sabrina had been the one who made the first move.

It was odd, the way her relationship with Jake developed. They had become very close friends after he'd broken things off with his fiancée, sometimes sitting at the end of the boat dock, talking for hours at a time about anything and everything. It was during one of those late-night talks, when they were both tired, but didn't seem to want to leave each other, that Sabrina leaned in and kissed him.

She didn't know why she'd done it, other than that she wanted it. Sitting close to him night after night, listening to his deep voice, feeling the warmth of his body, she couldn't think of anything she'd ever wanted more than that kiss. Considering the way Jake responded, he'd wanted it just as much as she had.

She closed her eyes and remembered that night like it was yesterday. It had been August, and already the nights were getting chilly. Bree, in a rush to see him, had gone out to the dock in a pair of yoga pants and a tank top. Jake, on the other hand, had a button-down layered over a tee shirt. When a breeze had blown off the bay, she shivered, and he'd taken off his shirt and wrapped it around her.

Bree remembered how the shirt swallowed her up. He was so big and she had been a hundred and ten pounds, soaking wet, if that. But what really got her was the scent. It was warm and musky. Clean. And it went right to her head, her heart and intensified the heat radiating through her belly.

It intensified the want, the need, and before he could stop her, Bree stretched up and let her lips brush over his. It was nothing really, the tiniest peck, but it ignited something in him and in seconds Jake had pulled her onto his lap and cradled her in his arms.

He kissed her again, and again, nuzzling her neck, coaxing her lips apart and holding her so close Bree could feel everything. His hands were large and rough, but oh so gentle, as his fingers threaded through her hair, caressed her cheeks, and touched the skin of her lower back. Never, in all her life, would Sabrina forget how she felt, how he made her feel beautiful and brave. She remembered the shuddering breath Jake had drawn when he pulled back and examined her face.

That was the beginning. It was burned in her memory. Etched onto her heart. Three and a half months later, he came out from the city to break the news to her that Sydney was pregnant and he was going to marry her. His announcement destroyed her.

It was the last time she'd seen him until today.

"Sabrina?" Her mother's hand had dropped onto her shoulder and it snapped Bree out of her trance. "You look a million miles away."

"No, I'm just lost in the years, Mom."

"Don't get swept away by him again. He's not worth it. He never was."

Jade had fixed herself a cup of coffee, and leaned against the counter, thinking and absorbing everything being said around her. As usual, she offered her cool assessment of the situation. "Aunt Enza, you can say all you want that Jake should stay away, but I saw the way he looked at her today, and as angry as I'm sure he was, he's a goner where Sabrina's concerned."

"Jade, really? You've always been so sensible. Don't start spewing romantic mumbo jumbo."

"Jade, I have to agree with my mother on this. Don't make it more than it is."

"Well, I might be *sensible*, but I'm not blind. There was no doubt about what was passing between the two of you at the rink."

Easing herself into a chair at the kitchen table, Bree dropped her head onto her arms. "There was nothing passing between us."

"Oh, come on," Jade protested. "The smolder practically melted the ice."

Bree clasped her arms behind her head. "I can't let him get to me again. It's bad enough I'm going to have to deal with him for Charlie's sake, but I can't think about anything else. Especially anything romantic."

"I don't know that you have much of a choice," Jade said as she slid onto the kitchen chair next to Bree's. "The feelings between you two are still there. I know you don't want to feel anything toward him, but you're already in the game, Sabrina, you have to let it play out."

✦ ✦ ✦

CHARLOTTE GERVAIS STOOD in front of the bathroom mirror, braiding her thick, dark hair. As she worked the different sections, Charlie wondered why she got called a boy all the time. She didn't think she looked like a boy, she looked like her mom and Mom was beautiful. But every day she looked at herself and wondered what the mean girls at school would say next.

She secured the end of the braid with a hair tie and thought about the clinic. It had been an awesome day. She won four skills competitions and won the fastest skater award. And then there was Jake Killen. *Jake Killen.*

The man she'd wanted to meet her whole life. Her father. The one she wished for every Christmas. The one she'd cried for. He was at the clinic today and based on the way he reacted, it was pretty obvious he never knew she existed.

Mommy had never told him.

But Charlie hadn't been told anything either. If she hadn't found the box in Mom's closet last year she wouldn't have been able to figure out the truth about Jake Killen being her dad when she met him today.

Grandpa was down the hall hanging up her equipment, and Charlie's mind raced. Did she have more grandparents? Uncles or aunts? Cousins?

Charlie had always been careful to keep the box hidden, scared it would be taken from her, but she now she didn't care if anyone knew she had Mom's stuff. Charlie went to her closet and pulled it out, taking the contents out of the box and laying everything on her bed one piece at a time.

When she first found the box, she had no idea what it all meant. There was hockey jersey and a t-shirt. Some pictures and a notebook that mom had written all kind of stuff. There was a photo album that said "Daddy's Little Girl," on the front and it was filled with pictures of Charlie growing up.

There was a memory book that had all the things she'd done since she was born. Mom had one in her room, too.

Then today at the rink, everything clicked into place when Charlie met Jake Killen. His pictures were in the box. His name was on the jersey. And it didn't take Charlie long to figure out that he was her dad.

But now she didn't know what was going to happen. She wondered if he would come to see her; wondered what her mother would do.

"Charlie?" There was a tap at the bedroom door. "Sweetie, are you…"

The door opened before Charlie could say anything. And while she thought she didn't care if her mother knew she had the box, she really did.

"Oh, good, you're dressed. Nona made—" Mom sucked in a breath when she saw everything on the bed.

The two of them were staring down at the contents of what Charlie called the "dad" box, but Charlie didn't look at her mother. She couldn't.

"Where did you get that?" Mom's voice cracked a little, like she might cry.

"I found it in your closet."

"I see." Finally, Charlie looked up and saw her mother blinking back tears. She wasn't crying, but she was trying hard not to. Mom sat down on the bed, next to the box, and instead of yelling, she reached out. Charlie walked into her mom's arms and put her head on her shoulder. "You should have said something to me the minute you saw this."

"I didn't know what it was then," she sniffled, wiped her eyes. "I wasn't sure until today."

"Why did you take it then?"

"I don't know. I guess I hoped it was my dad's. You have the photo album and the scrap book… I mean. I guess I knew, but I wasn't really sure. Are you mad?"

"You took something that didn't belong to you, and you knew you shouldn't. So, yeah, I'm annoyed." Mom reached out and gently tugged her hair letting Charlie know she really wasn't *in* trouble, but this wasn't going to be easy. "You should have said something to me."

Charlie nodded, but she wasn't the only one who kept something secret. Mom's was way bigger. "You should have said something, too."

The shock that spread across her mother's face made Charlie wonder if that was the moment she was going to get grounded. She'd done a lot of things wrong, including taking something that didn't belong to her, and now she was sassing her mom.

"Sorry," she muttered.

"You could tone down the attitude, but you do have a right to say that. I should have said something. I shouldn't have left things for you to find out on your own. That wasn't right."

"My father. Um... Jake. He looked really surprised."

Mom pushed her hair back. "He was surprised. You weren't the only one I should have talked to."

"Oh. Uh." She twisted her fingers. "Is he mad?"

"More than likely."

Charlie bit her lip when she felt it start to tremble. "So I won't be, like, meeting him or anything."

Mom turned to her and looked confused. "Of course you will. Why would you say that?"

"I don't know. Because he's mad about me."

"Oh, no, no, no." Mom pulled her close. "He's not mad *about* you. It anything he's angry *with* me for not telling him. It's not you. Personally, I think the two of you will hit it off."

"Really?" That surprised Charlie.

"Yes. It's going to be very awkward, but don't worry about it—you have hockey in common."

All she could do was nod. She didn't know how many Christmases she'd wished to meet her father and this year it happened. It really happened.

"Let's get some dinner in you. Nona made lasagna..." Mom poked her side. "Your favorite."

Charlie smiled. "Okay." But neither moved. "Mommy, do you think he'd go to the father-daughter dance with me?"

"I guess you should ask him." Mom didn't sound too sure about the idea. Maybe Charlie shouldn't. He probably wouldn't want to go.

"He's probably busy." Charlie didn't know if she had the nerve to do the asking. The father-daughter dance was a big deal at school for the fourth and fifth grade girls. Everyone dressed up and made a big fuss over the December holidays. Grandpa was going to take her this year, but now, she hoped maybe Jake Killen would want to.

"Like I said, I think you should ask. I'll see if Uncle Ryan can get in touch with him so you can meet."

"You don't have his phone number?"

"Not anymore. Not for a long time."

Her mom finally stood up and Charlie could see her mother wasn't telling her everything. Her mom was always so happy and funny, but now she was upset.

Feeling bad, Charlie stepped forward and wrapped her arms around her mother's waist. "I'm sorry I took the box."

Mom hugged her tight. "It's okay. Most of what's in there should be yours anyway. Or your dad's. I put those books together for him."

"I really want to meet him… you know, as my dad." Charlie was never so sure of anything in her life.

Mom nodded. "I'll see what I can do."

Chapter Four

BREE DIDN'T KNOW what to make of the exchange with Charlie, but there was some relief in facing the truth with her. The child amazed her at every turn. She was too old for her years most of the time, but at that moment, Sabrina had never appreciated her maturity more. The road they had to travel was not going to be free of bumps, and she had no doubt her girl was going to have a lot of questions, but they'd get through this. That was certain.

When she entered the kitchen, her mother was putting the food on plates, her father was filling a glass carafe with water, and Jade was grinning like she had a secret.

"Here's your phone," she said innocently. "It's been buzzing like crazy."

"What? Why?"

Her friend beamed. "Many, many text messages."

That could only mean one thing. Kara, Elena, and Cass had been told about what went down today, and based on the way Jade was smiling, she was responsible for spilling the beans.

"Give me that."

Bree keyed in her password and sure enough. Her friends, sisters really, were all over her. The wanted details and Jade wasn't giving any information. "Why didn't you just tell them what happened?" Sabrina snapped.

"Oh, no. That wouldn't have been nearly as much fun as watching you navigate this."

Jade was normally so cool, so polite, so considerate, but there were times she really enjoyed watching other people squirm. This was one of those times. She kept on typing, glancing up from time to time to smile sweetly.

Bree scrolled through the texts, which were group messages, and the reactions went from figuring out ways to hide Jake's body, to concern for Charlie, to planning some imaginary wedding. *Sweet baby Jeebus.* She finally sent a text that all of them needed to shut up.

It was all very funny, and at the same time, sad because she didn't know how this was going to affect her daughter. What she did know was, teasing aside, every one of Charlie's aunts would be there to help her through. Bree stopped scrolling when a message from a strange phone number landed in her inbox.

She tapped her thumb on the screen and froze.

Oh no. Oh no.

"It's Jake. Come outside."

"This can't be happening."

This time when Jade looked up, her face sobered immediately. "What's wrong?"

Bree showed her the text and Jade's eyebrows shot up as she considered the new development. "He doesn't play around, does he?"

"Not about this, he doesn't."

"What is it? What's going on?" Her mother asked.

"Nothing. I need some air."

"Air?" Mom blocked the door, holding up a large stainless steel ladle like a weapon. Vincenza Gervais may have been a well-respected family lawyer in her day job, but at home she was an Italian mother who would protect her family without hesitation. "Why do you need air?"

"Mom..."

"Sabrina, what's going on?" Mom motioned to her dad. "Ed, go with her..."

Grabbing the doorknob, Bree who had put on her winter coat, turned back and kissed Charlie on top of the head. Her poor baby was so confused. "I'll be back in a minute, sweetie. Stay put, okay?" She glared at her parents. "Everyone stay put."

Walking out the back door, Sabrina took a deep breath of cold, salt air. The coast was different in the winter. For obvious reasons, there wasn't the same hustle and bustle as summer, but it was more than the weather. Winter was darker—isolating—almost like a curtain was drawn around the town, hiding it from the rest of the world. Maybe that was why there were always so many lights strung up around the holidays—people craved the light, needed it, to feel less alone. God knew she did.

Turning toward the driveway, she saw a big Tahoe parked next to her Jeep, but Jake wasn't there.

Come outside, he'd messaged.

It was the same message she'd received over and over ten summers ago. The one she'd sit on her window seat and wait for. The one that, just like now, made her heart beat too fast and her breath catch in her chest.

Come outside.

Back then, when she left her room and crept through the dark house, Sabrina would meet him by a cluster of trees near the dock. Now there was only one tree left, all the others having fallen victim to one storm or another, but the remaining one wouldn't give up. To honor its fortitude, her father had set aside hours each of the past few years to completely cover the branches in white lights. It was her father's way of celebrating life. Of celebrating strength in the face of overwhelming odds. And standing next to it, in the spot where he whispered that he would always love her, was Jake. He was illuminated from all sides, almost in a cocoon of light, while the darkness from the beach was his backdrop.

He was staring off into the distance, out at the wide, dark bay, and as Sabrina approached, she didn't know what she was going to say to him. After he'd left, Bree remembered a deep ache in her chest that wouldn't go away. The feeling that she'd cried all she could, only to cry more. The discomforts of pregnancy were nothing when compared with the pain of a broken heart. The only way she got through had been to block him out. To stay focused on school, and then on Charlie. Jade, Cass, Kara, and Elena had kept her from drowning in her own sorrow. If she really thought about it, they were still doing it.

But now the ache was back, along with the longing, and a slew of questions she didn't know if she wanted answered. The truth didn't always set one free, sometimes it hurt like a bitch. "Don't let him get to you. The only person in this who matters is Charlie," she said to herself. "Stay focused. Don't cry."

She'd cried way too much for him, and while Bree could accept her responsibility in this, she wasn't going to take all the blame. He'd left her and there was no way around that part of it.

She walked toward him, wondering if she should say something or if catching him a little off guard was best. Maybe it would give her the upper hand. She thought for a moment and came to the realization she would have the upper hand for about twelve and a half seconds.

"Just breathe," she whispered.

"I'm not gonna bite," he said firmly making Bree stop short. So much for keeping him off guard.

"Maybe not, but I'm not used to being *summoned* anymore."

He stuttered, unsure of what he wanted to say, which was unusual for Jake. He possessed such a big personality and could engage anyone in a conversation. For Sabrina, who had been painfully shy around boys, he'd been a miracle. He'd made her feel alive and comfortable for the first time in her life.

"Where's the lighthouse?" He nodded toward the beach, but really, he was looking far beyond. The Holly Point Lighthouse was a town treasure. The harbor light, in one form or another, had guided boats for almost two centuries. But like so many small lighthouses, it was no longer needed. A foundation had been formed to save the lighthouse, which had fallen into disrepair over the past decade, but they hadn't raised enough money to do anything.

"The light's been dark since right after you left. Upkeep is expensive."

"Wow. Really? I remember seeing it from my bed in the apartment. I always felt like it led me here." His blue eyes shone, reflecting the twinkling lights in the tree. They locked with hers and the meaning of his words weren't lost. They were hollow, but she understood he was trying to find some common ground. Too bad it wasn't working.

But in spite of all of her conflicting emotions, his words sparked a tingling awareness because she also remembered the view from his bed. Long, beautiful nights that they'd lain together after making love, sometimes dozing in each other's arms looking out at the light in the distance. She remembered the times they'd talked tentatively about the future—a future that never happened. She'd gone to him often that summer, with no one suspecting what was going on between them.

Sabrina had given Jake everything. She'd lost her heart and she'd never been able to give it to anyone else.

In some ways, when the lighthouse went dark, Bree's light went out, too.

Silence fell between them, the only sound coming from the tiny Christmas bells her father had hung in the tree. The air gently moved around them and Bree was lulled by the music and the breeze.

"I want to know why you didn't tell me."

So much for letting her mind wander.

Jake's voice was low and steady, but he didn't sound angry and that surprised her. She expected him to be furious.

"It's pretty simple really. You left. You had a choice. You made it. Game over."

"That's pretty cold. I mean…" Jake turned and took a single step. It was all he needed to invade her personal space. "I mean, I'm her father. That game is never over."

"True enough, but I didn't want to force anything on you."

"Force anything… are you nuts?" Now he was mad. "She's my daughter. There's no forcing anything. You should have told me."

Jake's temper didn't flare often, but when he felt backed into a corner, he lashed out. This was one of those times. She got it, she did.

But he wasn't even thinking about his part in the situation. It was all fine to say Bree should have told him, but to what end?

"What did you want me to do?" She reached up and touched a branch, hearing one of the bells jingle in response.

"I would have liked you to tell me about my kid." He ran his hands through his short hair. "I mean, I know you were hurt. I hate that I hurt you, but was this some way to get back at me?"

"What? Get back at you?"

"Yeah. Do you hate me that much?"

I could never hate you. The words ran around her head, becoming a stark reminder that Bree still had feelings where he was concerned. But what he was saying, that she'd hurt Charlie to get back at him, was cruel, and she fought the tears pricking at her eyes. The last thing she could do was lose control. She'd already done that with him and look what had happened. "This had nothing to do with that. I made a decision."

"To exclude me from my daughter's life? Not your best decision."

"Oh, and running off to marry a woman who cheated on you was?" If she'd slapped him, he couldn't have looked more shocked.

"I thought I was doing the right thing. I guess you know it didn't work out?" He was pacing. It didn't take a brain surgeon to see he was agitated.

"I heard you were out of the marriage pretty fast, yes."

"Yeah. I was." He was standing at the edge of the dock and he looked back at her over his shoulder.

The bastard. He didn't get it. Bree threw up her hands, turned and started back to the house. "You know what? Call me when you want to meet Charlie. Good night."

Chapter Five

WHAT? WHERE THE hell was she going?

She couldn't walk away—there was no avoiding their situation—they were parents together, and regardless of what she thought of him, he wasn't going to be blown off. Not when he had a daughter to think about.

She'd taken maybe ten steps when he finally got his head out of his ass and went after her, catching up in just a few strides. "Wait. Stop. You can't just leave."

Jake grabbed her hand and held. Feeling her soft skin against his brought back a flood of memories, flashes of awareness, and heat. Unfortunately, while he was having a trip down memory lane, Bree was getting angry. Wrenching her arm free, she whirled on him. Her eyes were flaming. The woman glaring at him was very different from the girl he'd left all those years ago. She was ripping mad and he had to be careful. The bottom line was that she was the mother of his child and he had to maintain a relationship with her.

"What do you mean I can't leave?" she snapped. "You left, Jake. You left and you never looked back."

"It's not the same. I didn't know. If I'd *known*..."

Crap.

"*If you'd known* you would have come back? Is that what you're trying to say?"

"That's not what I mean, I mean..." He was digging himself a deeper and deeper hole. The words, *if I'd known*, said it all. Now he knew why she was upset. She had him dead to rights.

"And *that's* why I didn't tell you Jake. I didn't want to trap you. I was here. All you had to do was come back. Your marriage failed and you didn't come back for me."

"I thought you'd moved on."

"Why would you think that?"

"I don't know. I didn't expect you to wait for me."

"But did you ever try to find out? Did you call, check in, stop by and say, 'Hey that chick I married, she had some other guy's kid. Did you miss me?'"

"Come on..."

"What? WHAT?" She was walking in circles, her fists clenched, her face hard. She wasn't only furious, she was upset. Bree wasn't crying, but the tears filled her eyes. The emotion was raw, stormy, and Jake deserved everything he got.

"You don't like the fact that I waited for you to come back? Is that it?" she screamed. "I waited and waited. I knew you were single and you didn't come for me. Everything you ever said about how you felt was a lie. A big frickin' lie!"

"It was not a lie! I meant every word." He did. He could have told her he loved her that minute and meant it. She was in his soul and he'd never love anyone like he loved Sabrina.

"Yeah? I call bullshit, Jake. And that's why I didn't tell you. I'm not the kind of girl who traps a man. You didn't want me. If you had, you would have come back for me. YOU WOULD HAVE COME BACK!"

How did he respond to that? He'd stayed away, assuming

it was best if he just let her go on with her life. There was no doubt in his mind that she should have told him about Charlie, but in some way, she was trying to be as honorable as he had been. He'd gone and married Sydney in an attempt to do the right thing, and Bree hadn't told him because she didn't want him trapped. They could go around and around about it and get nowhere. Jake leaned his head back and looked to the sky for some kind of intervention.

Good God, this had to stop. "I'm sorry. I never meant to hurt you, or make you hate me…"

"I don't hate you." Her voice was soft, pained. "But I can't be around you. I just can't."

"Bree, we have to work this out." He didn't know if he was referring to Charlie with the statement, or them, or both. He had a feeling he meant both, even though he didn't think she'd ever trust him again. Why should she? He'd known the day he told her he was going back to Sydney that he'd broken her heart. His sweet, beautiful girl who always had a kind word, who brought joy to everyone she encountered, crumbled before him. She sobbed. She begged him not to go. But he got up, guilt tearing at him, and left her in the apartment at her parents' house. It was the place where they first came together and the place where he tore them apart. It killed him hearing her sobs, but he'd left anyway. He took Ryan's advice. Believing the lie that if she hated him that she'd have the best chance of moving on.

Of course, she couldn't move on with his child.

"I know I hurt you," he said again. "And I will always regret causing you pain. But we have to think about Charlie…"

"I always think about Charlie," she snapped.

He couldn't win. He was stepping on one landmine after another. "I know. Let me rephrase." *Because I want you to see that I care.* "We need to think about how I'm going to fit into

Charlie's life. We have to tell her what's happened."

They were standing near the front porch of the Gervais home. It was so perfectly turned out for the holidays it should have been in a magazine spread. Sabrina settled herself on the top front porch step, calmer now, but still visibly shaken.

There wasn't going to be any easy way to slip him into Charlie's life. He took a chance that Bree wasn't going to throw her scarf around his neck and choke him and sat next to her on the step, his thigh brushing against hers. Even through their jeans he could feel her warmth. He always loved her warmth.

They sat quietly for a few minutes. He was fidgeting with his jacket and she was picking at the pine garland wrapped around the porch rail, but not a word passed between them.

"Better?" He kept his voice steady, hoping they could find some common ground.

She nodded, but didn't speak. The only thing he heard was a sniffle here and there, and he hated that he'd brought her pain, but it didn't change the fact they had a lot to talk about. He'd screwed things up with her, but she wasn't blameless. They both had to take responsibility for what was going to happen next.

He glanced over, her profile bathed in the light from the house. Her features were, as always, soft, delicate. Her large eyes were ringed by the longest lashes he'd ever seen. Years ago, Jake had learned Sabrina's eyes gave away everything she was feeling. When she glanced up at him, he saw that was still true. She felt the same as he did... lost and helpless.

His first instinct was to take her in his arms and hold her, but he had a feeling she wouldn't welcome it. Which was too bad. They always found peace when they were wrapped around each other.

"Any thoughts about how you want to tell her?" Jake

figured he should get right to the business of dealing with their daughter.

"It's not necessary. She knows. She figured it out."

"What?" It was like he got the wind knocked out of him. "Really? Is she okay?"

"Full of questions. She's going to have a lot of questions."

The kid must have her mother's brains if she figured out who he was from their encounter. "I don't know what might have happened that would have tipped her off."

"It wasn't you. Well, it was, but it was really because of something I did."

She took a deep breath, the despair evident in the way her shoulders dropped forward.

He'd never seen her like this. "Tell me, Bree."

Bree's lip started to tremble. "I kept things. Things you'd given me and she found them. I didn't know until today."

"Oh." He wondered when the surprises would stop. "You kept…"

"Your jersey. A tee shirt. Some pictures. I don't know why."

He shouldn't be happy, but deep inside, Jake's heart steadied, because Bree keeping those personal items showed him she hadn't wanted to purge him from her life. She'd held onto items that were directly connected to him and he was going to use that as a bridge. Even if it was just a bridge to his child right now.

"I see. Tell me about her."

It was getting colder and while Jake was immune to it, simply by virtue of his upbringing, Bree pulled her coat tighter as the wind picked up off the bay.

"She's amazing. Smart as a whip, feisty." Her voice reflected the pride she had in their girl, and he already hated that he didn't know her. "She doesn't let anyone's opinion detract her from her goals." She paused and locked eyes with him. "She loves playing hockey, Jake, and she gets teased a lot for being a tomboy. It breaks my heart, but she won't give it up."

"She gets picked on?" He felt an instant connection because he'd been picked on. He knew what it felt like to be treated like there was something wrong with him. "That's such crap. I have to tell you, before I knew… before I knew she was mine, when I saw her take off her helmet and watched that braid fall out, I thought she was the coolest kid ever. She's impressive."

Bree grinned. "She loves the game. Fortunately, she didn't inherit my skating skills."

"Still can't skate?" he asked.

She shook her head, a smile teasing the corner of her mouth. "Nope. I'm pathetic."

He'd heard about Bree's complete inability to move on a frozen surface, but since he left before it really got cold, he never saw her actually try.

"Didn't I promise to teach you? The offer stands. Always." As soon as he said it he realized he'd overstepped.

The suggestion caused her to straighten her back. There was that wall. She was going to be tough. Being near her again was making him think about all the years they lost, and he didn't want to lose anymore, but he didn't know if they were too broken to fix.

"It's fine." Her voice cracked. "I doubt you'd have any more luck than anyone else. My brother tried."

"Your brother's a lousy skater, no offense, but I can run rings around him."

Her hands were clenched tight—this conversation was pointless. "Well, it doesn't matter."

There was more silence, but Jake was happy they'd made progress. At least she wasn't set to kill him.

"When can I see her?" he asked. That was the only thing he needed to establish right then. Anything else he wanted to talk about would have to wait. Charlie was the priority.

Bree thought for a second. "Can you come back tomorrow? I have to work in the morning, but I'll be home about one. We're baking."

He grinned. Nothing like jumping right in. Tomorrow. He was going to see Charlie tomorrow. What the hell would he do with a little girl?

"I can be here. Where do you work?" He knew she hadn't gone to medical school, Ryan had told him that much, but nothing else.

"I'm a physical therapist. I work at an orthopedic rehab in town."

"A physical terrorist, huh?" The comment pulled a chuckle out of her. "I'm familiar with your kind. My shoulder rehab was hell."

"I'm not surprised. Your injury is notorious for hellish rehabs." As soon as the words were out of her mouth, she stiffened.

"You know about my shoulder?"

"I keep up a little, yeah."

"You checked up on me?" This was good. This was *really* good. Knowing she might actually care was like a second miracle. But he wasn't going to push it. He couldn't. "Thank you."

She nodded politely, and that was all Jake could hope for at this point. It was a start, and considering how this whole scene could have gone down, Jake was relieved.

Looking toward the sky, Bree grinned at the light snow that had started to fall. It dusted her hair and shoulders, and the air sparkled around her. She looked like an angel.

"It's really Christmastime," she whispered.

Jake didn't take his eyes off her. He'd seen his share of snow living in the great white north, but Bree was an exquisite sight. Passionate and beautiful, he wanted to fix what went wrong between them more than anything. But there was a lot of anger on both sides, and Jake didn't know if that was possible.

+ + +

BREE BREATHED A little easier now that things had settled some. Jake would come over tomorrow, he could spend some time with Charlie, and they could start to figure out their relationship. Of course, at that point, Bree was relieved that Jake was leaving. He had his keys in his hand and Bree couldn't get him gone fast enough. She'd thought she was over him, or at best, she'd be angry enough his presence wouldn't affect her.

She was wrong on both counts.

He not only affected her, she found, even angry, their exchanges were easy and honest, and her heart ached with how much she'd missed him. Everything about Jake from his voice to his face to his body made her respond, but what Bree missed most was his innate kindness. His gentleness.

"You should have told me," he'd said. Yes, she should have.

She had to keep reminding herself that Jake Killen had broken her heart. Badly. She couldn't let him get to her, not for one second, but watching him walk to his car made her body hum. It was certainly no hardship to look at him. Bree admired the way his shoulders filled out his hoodie and the way his jeans hung on his hips, the powerful muscles of his rear and thighs shaping the fabric.

Bree didn't know Jade was standing next to her on the front porch until she let out a little whoosh of breath. "God, he's gorgeous."

Bree grinned and sighed. He sure was. "Yeah. I'm going to have to keep my wits about me when he's around."

He was just about to get into his truck when the front door flew open, and Charlie dashed out of the house, down the steps, and straight to her father.

"Wait!" she called. "You can't leave yet!"

"Oh, no," Bree whispered before she descended the stairs. She was just about to intervene when Jake turned and went down on one knee to be closer to Charlie. Staying a few feet back she watched her daughter interact with her father for the first time.

"Why are you going?" Charlie's voice cracked a little.

Jake rubbed her arm and then took her small hand in his. "I figured you were tired from your day, but I'm coming back tomorrow. I was thinking we could do something then."

"Okay. I just want to talk to you. I mean… I just…" Their little girl was overcome with so many feelings she could barely speak. "Do you promise to come back?"

Jake looked at Bree, his blue eyes revealing the love he already had for his child.

He turned his attention back to Charlie and smiled. "You bet. I wouldn't miss spending time with you for anything."

Charlie didn't hesitate and threw her arms around his neck. Jake was startled at first, not knowing what to do. But then, he did what came naturally, pulling her close and burying his face in her hair. The two of them clung to each other, and Bree, who was still a few steps back, could see keeping him from his child was the biggest mistake she'd ever made. Her heart was crying for both of them. God, she'd been selfish.

"Your hair is damp," he said. "You're going to get cold."

Charlie released him and smiled, then she reached into her pocket and pulled out the small photo album that was in the box. "Mom made this for you. It's pictures of me from when I was little."

He looked up again, surprised. "You did that?"

Sabrina shrugged, unable to do any more without completely losing it. "I hope you like it."

Jake stood and unzipped his hoodie, draping it around Charlie's small shoulders. "You hang onto this for me, okay?"

She pulled it close around her and smiled. "You won't be cold?"

"Nah. I grew up with polar bears."

Charlie's eyes went wide. "Really? Aren't they mean?"

"Only a little." He laughed and kissed the top of her head. "If it's okay with your mom, I'd like to take you to the Mariners game tomorrow night. I do kind of have to be there, and I'd love to watch the game with you."

Wow. What Jade said before was dead on—Jake wasn't playing. He had a daughter and he was all in—no hesitation, no question.

"Mommy, can I go?"

What could she say? She hadn't seen Jake in ten years, he could have changed. He could be reckless and irresponsible. But looking at the two of them, the hope in their eyes, she couldn't say no. Jake was still injured so chances were they'd be watching from the team box. He'd be with her the whole time and it was good for them to bond over something they both loved. She was almost a little jealous she wasn't going to be able to see it.

"Of course you can go."

Charlie's arms shot up in victory. "Woo hoo! Thanks, Mom!"

She danced around and ran up the steps to Jade, babbling at her the whole way.

Jake turned in Bree's direction and the smile on his face said it all. "Thanks, Bree. I would have understood if you said no. I mean, I really don't know her yet."

"She's so happy. Look at her." Charlie was still talking to Jade, then turned, ran down the steps and hugged Jake around the waist, then Bree got the same. "What time tomorrow?" Charlie asked.

"I'll talk to your mom about it. Okay?"

Charlie nodded and danced back to Jade who took her into the house. "She's going to love going to the game with you."

"I hope so. You know, you could come if you want, if you aren't sure about letting her go alone." There was the invitation she was looking for.

The three of them at a game together? The thought alternately thrilled and terrified her. She was so drawn to him, but Bree didn't know if she'd ever be able to give her heart so completely to anyone again. Her attraction to Jake demanded no less.

"Maybe you two should do this one on your own. You don't need me there."

There was no response, at least not a verbal one. His expression changed, going from disappointment to understanding. "If you change your mind, just let me know. I'll be here about 2:00, okay? The game is at five."

"Okay. Are you driving all the way back to the city tonight?"

"No, I called a friend who has a house in Bridgehampton. I'm crashing there. In fact, I think I'll be staying there for a few weeks, at least."

"Oh, that's convenient. You're sure you don't mind taking Charlie?"

"Nope, not at all. I think you're right. It will be good for us, you know?"

Bree wondered how her girl was going to handle the testosterone heavy world of pro hockey. Sure, her father lived in the house, but he and her brother kept a low profile, especially when Cass, Jade, and Kara put in an appearance. But it was time to let go a little and let Jake have a hand in her upbringing. She had no doubt he would take good care of her, it was already obvious that Miss Charlotte was going to have her daddy wrapped around her little finger, if she didn't already.

Jake held up the photo album and Bree stared at it. In the excitement about tomorrow's game, Bree forgot Charlie had given it to him. Yet there he stood holding it up and smiling.

"You made this for me?"

"I put pictures in it. Don't make it more than it is."

Flipping through, Jake passed his hand over each picture, but he went back to one of Bree holding their newborn daughter. Charlie was maybe a few hours old, and Sabrina was already so in love with her child, it hurt. She remembered the moment like it was yesterday.

"I like this one the best," he said softly. "I wish I could have seen you pregnant."

"I looked like I had a beach ball up my shirt."

He chuckled and Bree smiled, thinking that each moment of her pregnancy, right up to the day she gave birth, was a miracle. Then she went into labor—the worst thirty hours of her life, followed by the most amazing gift she'd ever received.

"I'll bet you were adorable."

"I was huge. When I finally had her, I was happy to see my feet again."

Jake flipped to different photos, looking at each on carefully, smiling at some and appearing more wistful as he examined others.

"I really do like this one best." he said once again about her and her new baby. "You look beautiful."

Man, they had to get off this topic. Bree grabbed the album and flipped the pages quickly. "There are some great pictures of Charlie from the trip we took to Disney. She was only four, but she had so much fun."

"Sabrina," He cupped her cheek and gently tilted her face toward his. His eyes were intensely blue and, once they locked on hers, Bree's insides melted into a puddle of goo. But it wasn't just his gaze that turned her to mush, it was the expression on his face which was soft, tender… it was the way he always looked at her after they'd made love, when Bree felt like the most cherished person in the world. "Thank you for this," he said as he leaned in and kissed her forehead.

Oh, jeez. Oh, God. Every nerve ending fired when his lips came in contact with her skin. The contact was everything she desired and everything she dreaded. She'd missed him, cried for him, but there was no way she could let herself give in to him again.

She stepped back, pulling her jacket around her and folding her arms safely across her chest. "I have to go in."

"I shouldn't have done that. I'm sorry. I just wanted to let you know how much I appreciate what you did"

"No." Raising her hands defensively, she took another step back. If she didn't get away from him she'd throw herself at him. "You don't have to thank me for anything. I didn't tell you about her. Don't make me a hero because I kept some photos for you."

She practically ran for the steps and the house. "I'll see you tomorrow."

"Bree—"

"Night!" As soon as she closed the door, Sabrina pressed her back against it and sank to the floor, pulling her legs close to her chest. Her head dropped to her knees with a thump, and she groaned.

"So," Jade leaned back against a table in the foyer. "That went well. He's great with Charlie."

"Oh, my God. I can't ever be alone with him again." That was a given. If he touched her, she'd do anything he asked. She shouldn't be reacting like this. Why wasn't she over him?

"Why not?" The sarcasm oozed off her words. "Things were… um… cordial."

Bree peered at her friend over the tops of her folded arms. "I hate you a little right now. You know that, right?"

Jade squatted down and moved in close. "Want to tell me about it?"

"Nothing to tell."

"You are such a liar, and you're a crappy one at that. Now tell me the truth."

Bree leaned her head back against the door. "He kissed me, on the forehead. If he'd kissed me for real, it would have been ten years ago all over again."

Jade grinned and sat next to her on the floor. "He's a panty dropper, that's for sure. God, those eyes. Are eyes allowed to be that blue?"

"It's no joke. What the hell is wrong with me?"

"Maybe nothing? He's great with Charlie and he doesn't seem angry about the situation."

"Yeah," Bree said, rubbing her temples, thinking, and then looking back at Jade. "What about that? He should be pissed off and he's not. I think I'm more pissed off at me than he is."

"He might be in shock. It could still hit him." Jade laughed, pushed herself off the floor and extended her hand helping Sabrina up. "Come on. Are you hungry? Everyone else is done already, but I'll sit with you."

Bree shook her head. Her stomach was in such knots, she couldn't eat if she wanted to. "Where is everyone?"

"Charlie's upstairs with your mom getting ready for bed. She had a big day. If you're okay, I'm going to call home and see how everyone is doing, and then go to bed myself with one of the new romances I just downloaded."

Bree wrapped her friend in a tight hug. "Thank you. For everything."

"Nothing to thank me for." Jade gave her an extra squeeze before letting go. "I know you'd do the same for me. But you have to call Cass, and Kara and Elena. They've been texting me non-stop."

"You want sympathy for that? You texted them and outed me!"

Jade pinched the bridge of her nose. "Fine. You're right, I did. I'll call."

"Tell them I'll explain everything when they're out here tomorrow. Promise."

Bree headed for the back staircase and took a deep breath before she made her way upstairs. Her mother was not going to be easy. All the anger she harbored toward Jake was based in the fierce love she felt for Bree, but what she needed from her mother was support, not wild emotions. Nope. Being angry wouldn't change anything and it wouldn't be good for Charlie.

Bree would have to remember that herself.

She'd really let Jake have it. Sabrina rarely raised her voice, but she'd lost it with Jake and he'd let her. He didn't fight back, and took a lot of the blame on himself. It wasn't fair, really, and at some point she'd have to talk to him about it because as angry and as hurt as she'd been, there was no excuse for keeping Charlie from him.

Just seeing them together, seeing how much Charlie wanted to know her father, showed Bree how big of a mistake she'd actually made. It was sobering, and the only thing she could do now was make sure they had every opportunity to get to know each other.

Stopping at the top step, she heard her parents talking in their room, so she went the opposite way, toward her own. She made short work of her clothes, pulling on a pair of old Christmas pajamas, and headed toward Charlie's room.

There was only one lamp on when Bree walked in, but it cast a quiet, peaceful glow over the space. Charlie was on her side, under the covers, fast asleep. Bree leaned in to kiss her and noticed Charlie was still wearing the hoodie Jake gave her.

She couldn't resist and laid down next to her daughter and tucked herself neatly against her back—with one arm draped over the sleeping child, and the other clutching the pillow, Bree marveled at how soundly her daughter slept, but then, considering what she'd been doing all day, it made sense. The shot to her heart came when Bree inhaled, that was when the magic took over.

Jake was there. Each time she drew in a breath, Bree realized she was in far more trouble than she'd thought. His scent was all over that jacket, sharp and clean, mixed with a combination of the salt air and snow from outside. It triggered memories she wasn't sure she was ready for.

Memories of him. Memories of them.

But those memories couldn't drive her decisions. He'd left her once and he could do it again. He'd be there for Charlie, but Bree wouldn't risk her heart on him or anyone else again. Love wasn't in the cards for her.

Kissing her beautiful girl on the cheek, Bree rose from the bed and wondered if she should suck it up and talk to her parents now, or wait until morning.

Morning won. After confronting Jake for the first time in ten years, Bree was spent, and Jade's idea of crawling into bed with a romance novel, sounded really good. But like everything else that day, this wasn't going to go as planned. No... her mother was in her room, waiting.

She and Charlie must have gathered up the contents of the box of memorabilia and put it on Bree's bed, because that was where her mother was sitting while going through pictures. Proof of the relationship her mother didn't know anything about. This was not going to be fun.

"I guess we have to talk?" Bree settled herself on the bed and pulled her legs up.

"I can't believe you snuck around behind our backs."

"I'm sorry. I don't know what else to say."

"More than anything, that's what hurts." Her mother looked up, and never in Bree's life had she felt as small as she did that moment. The disappointment was all over her mother's face. "Sabrina, I always trusted you and you never gave me reason not to. I never had delusions about anything. I figured you would have boyfriends and that you would have sex, but… I don't know. Why were you so sneaky?"

"Did you want me to tell you everything?"

Her mom shook her head. Bree felt awful because Mom's feelings were so obviously hurt. "No. not necessarily. I'd like to think I respected your privacy. But why didn't you tell us you were seeing him?"

There was the million dollar question. Why hadn't she? Yes, there was a big age different between her and Jake, but it wasn't illegal. Granted, on the experience scale there was a greater difference. Jake was a pro athlete, he'd been around, he'd even been engaged to a wealthy young woman he met in the city. Sabrina, as popular as she was in school, hadn't really dated. Hadn't shared more than a few chaste kisses with one boy during her junior year.

No, Jake was totally out of her league—then and now. Bree knew it, and her mother would have known, too. Sabrina kept him a secret because she didn't want her family and her friends telling her she was in over her head. She didn't want her parents to make him leave; she didn't want her brother freaking out and she didn't want her friends pressing her for a play-by-play every time she and Jake saw each other.

The thing her mother didn't understand was that Bree hadn't told *anyone*. And while the girls found out about Jake when Bree discovered she was pregnant, they weren't only shocked beyond words; they were also hurt and angry. Fortunately, her friends had gotten over the slight, but it made Bree think. How would she feel if Charlie kept something from her that was so important? She'd be pretty upset.

"I'm sorry I didn't tell you about him," she said as she laid her head on her mother's shoulder. "I shouldn't have been so secretive, but are you saying you would have been okay with it?"

Her mother pursed her lips and shook her head slowly. "Absolutely not. I probably would have told him to leave you the hell alone and found him a new place to live"

Bree grinned. Her mother was predictable if nothing else. "I figured you'd say something like that."

"Well, I mean come on, Bree, look at all this stuff." She waved her hand to everything on the bed.

"What about it?"

Picking up the t-shirt from the University of Wisconsin where Jake had gone to school, Sabrina held it close to her face, feeling the softness of the faded fabric, and wishing it still held his scent like the sweatshirt Charlie had worn to bed. She'd worn this shirt for weeks after he'd left just to feel close to him, to hold onto him a little longer.

It was sad, really. She was so young, and if she had gone to her mother, maybe she wouldn't have stayed with him. Maybe they would have gotten Jake out of her life. However, that would mean no Charlie, and there was no way she could ever consider her beautiful girl a mistake. Ever.

So while Jake had certainly brought her a lot of heartache, he'd also given her the greatest joy in her life. Her baby would never be a regret.

Laying the shirt across her lap, Bree reached for the pictures, and then held them out to her mother. "You looked at these already, I guess?"

Mom nodded but she still plucked some of the photos out of the batch and looked at them again as Bree let the memories seep into her. It seemed like she took a picture every time they were together. The collection spanned their short relationship in surprising detail from walks on the beach, to dinners, to a camping trip they took that August to Acadia National Park.

That trip was the biggest lie she'd ever told her parents. She certainly wasn't in Boston with a college friend. But she didn't second guess her decision. There was something new with each picture, just as something was always constant.

Both she and Jake looked happy. They looked like they were in love.

Because they were.

Thankfully, there were tissues on her nightstand, because the tears she had been fighting came with a vengeance. Sniffling, she dabbed at her eyes while her mother reached out and rubbed her back. "Why did he leave me? God. We had everything."

"You had everything but honesty. Without that, a relationship would never last."

"We were honest with each other." Sabrina remembered their talks, long and intimate. Feeling like they were inside each other's heads connected by so much more than physical attraction. Bree needed Jake like she needed her own breath.

Gazing at the picture from the Maine trip, she remembered laying out on a blanket with him and looking up at a sky, so filled with stars it appeared almost white. The Milky Way cut across the deep blue-black backdrop and Bree could feel herself changing. It was like the stars allowed her to believe she could have it all. She was no longer just a daughter, a sister, a student. or a friend. Bree felt like a woman.

She still felt that way when she thought of him, so she let herself sink into the memory.

"Are you cold?" he'd asked. "I have an extra sweatshirt if you need it."

"No, you're very warm, and I can always pull this side of the blanket up if I need it." Tilting her head, she looked up again. "I can't believe how many stars I can see out here. It's endless."

"It reminds me of home. In the summer, my dad would take us to one of the lakes to give my mum a break. We'd camp for a few days, and it always amazed me." She remembered him pointing a finger and tracing the Milky Way. "You see that? It's even brighter in northern Manitoba. Sometimes it's filled with color from the auroras and it's like looking at fire and ice. I want to take you there someday."

He kissed her lightly, pulling her so close she could feel his heart beating. "I want you to meet my parents," he whispered. "And my brother and sister."

"Really?"

"They usually come down the first month of the season."

Meeting his parents. He wanted that? "I'd like that."

He propped himself up on one arm and raised himself over her. She could see his face in the starlight, the blue glow reflecting on the angles and planes of his forehead, cheeks, and jaw. "I want to meet your parents."

"You know my parents. You're living at the house."

He brought his face closer to hers and kissed her lips. "I want to know them as your boyfriend. I don't want to be the hockey player staying in the guest apartment. Get me?"

Sabrina reached out and cupped his cheek. There was light stubble, nothing too scruffy, but he wasn't like any of the boys she'd ever dated. Jake was a man. A man who wasn't afraid to tell her what he wanted and, probably, what she needed to hear. "I understand."

"I don't know if you do." He bent in and kissed her again. "I love you, Sabrina. I love you with everything I have. But you need to tell your parents about us."

Her heart swelled and was so filled with happiness Bree thought she might drown in it. He loved her. But what he was asking her to do could cause so many problems. Her parents were wonderful people, but they were overprotective. "I'm worried about how they'll react."

"I get that. But it's time for you to be brave." He kissed her again. And again. "They love you, and the only way for me to show them that I do, too, is for you to tell them."

Bree remembered pulling him in and holding him so close she almost couldn't breathe. It was Jake who shifted his body, and kissed her with an intensity that swallowed her up. And there, under the stars, in a place that was pretty much made of magic, Jake made love to her.

When they'd returned to Holly Point, Bree promised herself she'd talk to her folks, but she hadn't ever worked up the nerve to tell them. And in the end, it was probably for the best.

"You are lost in thought, my girl." Her mother's voice, as always, brought her down to earth.

"I know I disappointed you, Mom. I know you expected more from me."

"Is that what you think?"

Bree nodded, feeling more like a little girl than she had in years.

"Oh, Sabrina. The only thing that hurt was that you didn't trust us enough to tell us about Jake. That's all. Otherwise, you've made Daddy and me nothing but proud."

That was hard to believe. Their valedictorian, pre-med daughter got knocked-up by a guy she'd dated less than three months, who then left her. Bree had to finish her schooling near home, had to change majors, and except for a year living away at college, Bree didn't have a place of her own.

She and Charlie loved living with her parents, and she worked really hard at being a mother and at building her career, but she didn't have much of a life.

"Now who's lying, Mom?"

"No, that's the truth. Now it's your turn. Tell me about Jake."

Her mother wanted the truth? *Crap*. The truth was the one thing that completely terrified Sabrina. How could she tell her mother about the man who pretty much had her heart from the minute he walked into her life? No matter what she did or how she tried, Jake owned her, and at times she cherished how much she still loved him, and at others she felt ashamed she couldn't let go.

"What do you want to know? He's taking Charlie out tomorrow."

"I know that. He'll be in Charlie's life from now on. That's a given. The question is do you want him in yours?"

Bree swallowed hard and grabbed for another tissue, blowing her nose loudly. There was no easy way to say what she had to say, mostly because she was going to have to admit the truth to herself. There was no more being tough. No more hiding.

Looking into her mother's warm, brown eyes, Bree said, "I'd like to give you an answer one way or another, but I'm so scared. I thought I was over him, but when he's around, my heart just aches, Mom. I want him in my life. I don't think that will ever change, but what if he leaves again? Forget that. What if he doesn't want me at all?"

"Then you'll go on, knowing that just like everything else

in your life, you did your best." Her mother extended her arms and Bree inched into them, sinking into the warmth like it would save her.

"Oh, Mommy. I've missed him so much. I thought I might die when he left. I don't know if I can take a chance like that and go through it again."

Her mother hugged her again, tighter this time. "I know you've been playing the toughie, Sabrina, but don't stop yourself from loving, my darling. That would be a real tragedy. Your big heart is what makes you so special."

Chapter Six

MEETING A WOMAN'S parents for the first time was usually enough to make Jake's palms sweat. He was all about the good first impression, but he didn't know if that would be possible today.

Granted, he already knew Sabrina's parents, but the last time he saw them was ten years ago, as Ryan's friend. Enza and Ed had been great to him, giving him a place to stay and making him feel like one of the family. Of course, that was before he left their daughter pregnant.

Jake could rationalize all he wanted that Bree had kept Charlie from him—that part of it wasn't his fault—and he was pissed about it, but he couldn't shake the guilt he had for leaving her in the first place. Not necessarily because of the pregnancy, but because he'd hurt her so badly when he shouldn't have. He'd believed Sydney, he'd supported Sydney, but he should have stayed with the woman who had changed the game for him.

He walked up to the front door, tugged at his shirt cuffs, and rang the bell. He felt like he was going on a first date, rather than seeing his daughter. Thinking about it though, that was kind of what it was. He and Charlie were bound by blood and hockey, but they didn't know each other. He didn't know what seeing his daughter would be all about. He wanted to know everything about her. It was going to take time; he got that, but today was a first step.

He heard a dog barking and a clatter of footsteps behind the door, which finally opened revealing a beautiful girl with a smile just for him.

Charlie stood there with a medium-sized, white dog wiggling next to her. The dog had reddish brown spots and the face of a retriever, including the big, friendly retriever smile.

"Hi!" she said, a little breathless. "Hi."

"Hey." She really did look just like Sabrina, with her long dark hair, big olive colored eyes, and a bright smile, but it was what he saw in her gaze and smile that reminded him so much of her mother. It was the intelligence, the sense there was always something cooking inside her head.

She was a little more dressed up than he expected, wearing a sweater dress in Mariner's blue with tights and little flat shoes. Her hair was pulled back into a tight ponytail, with an orange bow. She had the team colors covered, but a little differently than he expected.

"You look very nice," he said as he stepped into the foyer.

"Uncle Ryan said we might be sitting with your boss, so Nona thought I should dress up." The dog, who she'd called Holly, was sitting by her side. It was obviously a friendly pooch, but something told him the dog would rip off his arm if he made an unexpected move.

"We are going to be sitting in the owner's box, but you can wear anything you want. Are you comfortable in that?" He didn't care what she wore; just that he was getting to spend time with her.

"Uh, huh. I like it. Everyone thinks because I like sports, I don't like to dress up, but I do."

"Okay then. Is your mom here?"

"No, she had a patient come in at the last minute. She should be here soon, though."

"She's actually on her way."

Jake glanced up to respond to whoever had spoken to see he was locked in Vincenza Gervais' sights. The woman was about Bree's height, which meant maybe she was five-one on a good day, a little rounder than Bree, but she had the same dark hair and piercing hazel eyes as her daughter and granddaughter. *Please don't let me screw this up.* "Hello, Mrs. Gervais. It's nice to see you."

"Jake." She came toward him with her hand extended. "It's a pleasure to see you again."

Could he call her on that? There was no way she was happy to see him. She probably wanted to feed him to the fishes.

He decided to play along, shaking her hand and smiling, especially since Charlie was watching. "Does Bree want us to wait for her? We have a few minutes."

"You do? Wonderful. I'm sure she'd like to see you both before you go." She turned and motioned for him to follow. "Come back to the kitchen. We're doing some baking."

Bree's mom smiled warmly. Maybe things were okay. It had been a long time, after all.

"Nona doesn't like you." Charlie spoke barely above a whisper as she took his hand and they trailed after her grandmother.

There was his reality check.

"How can you tell?" If a nine-year-old could pick up the signals, he figured he was in real trouble.

"She's using her lawyer voice. That's never good."

"Her lawyer voice... great," Jake mumbled as he followed, taking stock of the place he hadn't been in ten years.

He'd always thought this was a great house. It was big, but still felt like home; not an easy feat when the place could double as a small inn. He took in the family pictures that lined the walls and stopped at a table which was filled with shots of Charlie and Bree. Even more than the photo album, this showed him all the things he'd missed, and the lump that formed in his throat was like nothing he'd experienced in his life. He picked up one of the frames, one of mother and daughter at Christmas. Both wore red dresses, and Jake wished he could have been there.

"That's my first Christmas."

She would have been six months old. "I can't get over how much you look like her."

"Poppy calls me Mini-Bree."

Jake laughed at the name. "Really? I think it fits." He placed the frame back on the table and as they got to the end of the hall, he heard a burst of female laughter from the kitchen.

Crap.

"Who's here?"

Charlie took a deep breath before she answered. "Other than Nona? Aunt Jade, Aunt Cass, Aunt Kara, and Aunt JoJo. Poppy went to the store for more butter."

He was a dead man walking, even without Bree's father there. Charlie started into the room and Jake's feet wouldn't move. She tugged on his hand and Jake swallowed. He could wait in the hall. Or the car. Yeah, he could wait in the car, couldn't he?

"Is something wrong?" she asked. Charlie's eyes were wide, and he didn't know how to tell her that her old man was afraid of a roomful of women. But she knew. Like Sabrina, Charlie could read him like a book.

"Don't be worried," she said sweetly. "I'll be right there."

If Jake didn't love this little girl just because he and Bree had made her, that moment would have sealed it. She was sweet, she was brave, and she had a heart of gold. Jake did the only thing that felt right; he went down on one knee and pulled her into a hug.

His daughter didn't hesitate. Charlie wrapped her arms around his neck and held tight. So much had happened in the past twenty-four hours, so much had been dredged up, but if he knew anything, it was that he was never going to leave them again.

"I wished for you," Charlie whispered. "Every year at Christmas."

Jake leaned back and saw the smile on his little girl's face was coupled with a few tears. Using the pad of his thumb he gently brushed them away. "Well, this Christmas, the wish came true."

Charlie nodded before she looked down. "I have something I need to ask you."

"Okay."

"At school, um, there's a father-daughter holiday dance. Usually Poppy or Uncle Ryan would take me, but I want to know if you would go with me?"

"When is it?"

There wasn't a question in his mind whether he would be there. She told him the date, and once he cleared a couple of things off the calendar, he'd be all hers. "You have yourself a date."

Charlie hugged him again and he didn't know if there was a better feeling. Once they stepped back from each other, he smiled. "You're going to protect me from the angry mob in there?"

"They aren't a mob."

He noticed she didn't say they weren't angry and he

grinned. "Let's go."

When he stepped into the kitchen, the conversation stopped dead. Mrs. Gervais smiled politely, and Jade, who he'd sort of met last night, greeted him with a nod. The other three were unknown. There was another blonde, gorgeous and very pregnant, and a pretty brunette. The older of the women shot Sabrina's mother a look that elicited a shrug, and he guessed wordless conversations were par for the course when women were friends for as long as these ladies had been. He remembered Bree telling him about her mother's sorority sisters, how they and their children were really like her extended family. The four women, who had met at university over thirty-five years ago, had almost a dozen children between them, including five girls who were very close in age. They were Sabrina's posse and the pretty, dark-haired woman who was walking toward him looked at him like he was dog food. He reminded himself, all he had to do was be polite.

She stuck out her hand. "I'm Cassandra Baines."

"Jake Killen."

"Oh, we know who *you* are," the older woman snapped.

Cassandra shot her a look. "That's my mother, Joanne, and this is Jade Engle and Kara Larsen."

Jade waved and sipped at a mug of cocoa. Jake was thinking if Bree didn't get there soon, he could sure use a sip of something, but it needed to be stronger than hot chocolate.

The tension in the room was enough to cut off his air. He felt like an ambush was coming and coming soon. Charlie jumped up on one of the stools at the kitchen island near where Cass and Jade were rolling out dough.

"Aunt Cass, why do you always wear black?" Charlie grabbed a couple of M&M's from a bowl and popped them in her mouth. Jake didn't know if Bree's friend always dressed in black, but standing in the brightly lit, cheerfully decorated kitchen, she looked very New York and a little out of place in her black sweater and pants.

"I don't always wear black," Cass said.

"Yes, you do." Charlie deadpanned. "That or grey."

Cass rolled her eyes. "Noted. I'll try to remember to wear pink or something next time."

"I have a nice Christmas sweater that would fit you," her mother said.

"I'd pay money to see you in that, Cass." Kara chuckled.

"Not a chance,"

"Please?" Jade whined. "You need to do something fun."

Jake was having a good time keeping up with the banter. It was a female version of the trash talk he shot at his teammates—without the profanity.

"Perhaps another time," Cass responded. "I am a serious academic, after all, hence why I suppose I gravitate toward black."

"You should have thought about it today," Charlie crooned. The little smirk that teased at her lips made Jake wonder what she was up to. "Black was not a good choice."

"What? Why?" Cass glanced down at her sweater and her eyes narrowed at Charlie.

"You have flour on your boobs," Charlie's giggle was infectious, but Jake could not laugh at the boob joke. He couldn't. He'd be dead if he did. So he bit his tongue and thought about the slow, painful death that would follow if he broke.

"Charlotte! That is not appropriate talk!" Okay, the kid got the full name treatment. Nona wasn't happy.

Charlie didn't seem concerned that her grandmother was horrified, raising her eyebrows and pointing. "But look! She does!"

Jade nodded. "Kind of like snow-capped mountains. Reminds me of home."

"Kara's bump has flour on it, too," Cass cried. "What about that?"

Jade chuckled. "Yes, but her bump looks cute, like a cupcake. Your's looks a little obscene."

Cass tossed a handful of flour at Jade, who then retaliated, and Charlie quickly retreated to Jake's side. All the women were talking at once and not one of them cared he was there. The pressure was off. He leaned toward his girl, who was smiling at the chaos a few feet away. "Did you do that on purpose?"

She shrugged, but the self-satisfied look that crossed her face told him all he needed to know.

"When you're sixteen," he said just loud enough so she could hear, "Whatever car you want, is yours."

Jake stepped back into the hall to avoid having his suit covered in flour. The scene in the kitchen was calming down, but Charlie was still giggling at the mayhem she'd incited. Mrs. Gervais and the woman Charlie called Aunt JoJo were yelling at the younger women and, he had to admit, they did look like they were having a great time. It was no wonder Charlie was such a sweet kid; she had a lot of good influences. There was a mischievous streak, no doubt, but she'd obviously been raised with a lot of love.

Without warning, he felt a large hand clamp down on his shoulder. He turned to see the unsmiling face of Ed Gervais glaring at him. The man was huge, a former All-American offensive lineman in college, he was a practicing pediatrician. Jake could only imagine what his small patients thought of the big man, but based on what Bree used to tell him, Dr. Ed was beloved by one and all.

He didn't look very lovable right at that moment. No, Dr. Ed, with his broad shoulders, barrel chest, and hands the size of snow shovels, was looking at Jake like he was a dirty lowlife. "Charlie, honey, go sit in the living room while I talk to Jake."

Not "your dad" or "your father" just "Jake." Nice.

Charlie was about to object, but Jake stopped her. "Do what your grandfather asked, Charlie. I'll be there in a few minutes."

She nodded and headed toward the front of the house, while Jake was steered into a room down the hall. It was Ed's office and it was as masculine as the man who took the control position behind the desk. Wood paneling, sports prints, diplomas from Ivy League universities... Jake had been playing pro sports for thirteen years and he knew when an opponent was trying to intimidate him. It was unfortunate for Bree's father that Jake didn't intimidate easily.

Ed motioned for him to sit in one of the leather chairs on the opposite side of the desk and he obliged him, crossing his legs when he sat.

"I'm going to get right to the point, Jake. I don't like that you're here. You took advantage of my daughter, you changed her life in ways you can't possibly imagine, and you hurt her. I don't trust you."

"I can understand your mistrust, but I didn't take advantage of your daughter."

"She was eighteen and you were twenty-five. How do you figure that? Then you left her to raise a child on her own."

"Dr. Gervais, Sabrina didn't tell me about Charlotte and you are well aware of that. I found out yesterday. While I'm sorry for what Sabrina went through, I would have been there for her and Charlie had I known."

"I doubt that. You left because you got some other girl pregnant. How many others have there been?"

Jake felt every muscle in his jaw tighten. Where the hell was this guy getting his information? It wouldn't be a good idea to deck Bree's dad, but Jake wouldn't be painted as some womanizing dirt bag when that wasn't the case. It may have been short, but the conversation was over. Jake stood, straightened his cuffs and gave Ed Gervais a few things to think about. "I'm not who you think I am, Dr. Gervais. I'm going to chalk up what you just said to me as a case of misinformation. You don't like me? Fine. You don't trust me? That's unfortunate. However, I'm in Charlie's life and I'm not going anywhere."

"You have a lot of nerve."

"You have no idea. We're done here. I'm taking my daughter to the game and she'll be home later."

Jake stormed out of the office, raging inside. Who did Bree's dad think he was dealing with? He wasn't some kid who was going to wet his pants and run. Jake heard footsteps racing toward him and he looked up to see Bree.

"Oh God. I'm so sorry I was late. I could have stopped whatever happened. Whatever he said…"

"You mean the lies he has in his head about me, about us?"

"Lies? What do you mean?"

He stepped close, crowding her. "I can't go into it now, but you and I will talk later. Just remember you were the one who kept her from me Sabrina. You. Tell your Mom and Dad to stand down."

She didn't say anything; she didn't move at all.

"I'm going to take Charlie. The game is at five so I should have her home around nine. Then we'll straighten this all out." He'd only taken a few steps when she snapped back.

"You can't order me to 'talk this out', Jake." He stopped and caught her defiance when he glanced over his shoulder. "There's nothing to talk about if you think so little of me."

"No, I can't. But trust me; it would be much better for us

to settle things between us than for me to call my attorney. Don't you think?"

Jake didn't wait for her to say anything else; he went to the living room where Charlie was sitting her hands folded and her head down. "Please don't fight," she whispered.

Damn. Right there, one look at his sad child and he was gut-punched. This kid had a way of tearing his heart out. Jake hadn't even known about her for twenty four hours, but she meant everything to him. "I'm sorry," he said going to her. "Mom and I still have to get used to everything that's happened. It's going to be hard sometimes."

"Charlie," he heard Bree behind him. Damn, even her voice affected him. He hated how pissed he was. All he wanted was to hold her. "We'll work it out. And we'll try not to fight, okay?"

Charlie went to her mother and the two of them, so much alike, held each other tight. All Jake could think was that those were his girls. His.

"Let's get your coat on so you can go," Bree wouldn't look at him, at all, putting all the focus on Charlie who left the room to get her coat.

"I'm sorry I snapped at you," Jake began. "I know what your dad said wasn't your fault." It was the best he was going to give as far as apologies went, even though he was certain she hadn't fed her dad lies about him, he was still pissed.

"Don't threaten me with a lawyer again. We can work everything out between us without this getting nasty."

"Okay."

"Okay? Really?"

"I was pissed and I took it out on you. I shouldn't have."

Bree sat on the sofa, looking like a slightly bigger version of Charlie, resting her elbows on her knees and her head in her hands. "God, this is such a mess. I made such a mess of everything."

Jake felt his chest tighten as he looked at her. Bree was trying to be strong, but she was hurting and he wanted nothing more than to take her mind off her troubles. Wary, he sat next to her and gently reached around her back and let his hand settle on her shoulder. It was the only thing he could think of to do. They'd always found comfort in the other's arms, and there was no reason to think, even with all the baggage, that would change.

She didn't cry. Bree was too tough to cry, but there was a little tremor when she drew a deep breath, and Jake could tell she was using all her energy to hold herself together.

"I know your family is doing Christmas baking, and I have a feeling it's kind of a big deal, based on the crowd, but if you want to come to the game, get away from here for a bit, you can. It's not like there's a limit on the number of people I can bring."

She let out a long breath, sat straight, and stretched. Bree worked hard to put on a happy face. "I'm fine. You and Charlie go and have a good time. I'll see you later."

"Are you sure? It might be fun."

Jake didn't think he said anything out of the ordinary, but something in her changed. Her expression went soft, vulnerable, and as her eyes travelled over his face and settled on his mouth, Jake's body reacted.

It could have been the adrenaline that came from being so angry that got him worked up, or the way her tongue darted out of her mouth, or her scent, which was filling him up. But Jake figured just being close to her, knowing she might need him, was enough to trigger his own want.

But damn, she had to stop looking at him like she wanted him to kiss her until they both couldn't breathe.

Bree trailed her fingers over his shoulder and down his arm, squeezing his hand before letting go. The move was harmless, innocent... and it finished him.

But he couldn't let her know.

Chapter Seven

"BREE, YOU'RE MAKING me nervous!" Kara chided. "Stop pacing."

Sabrina stopped by the window that faced the front of the property, peered out, and then turned to look at her friends lounging around her bedroom. They'd had a full day of baking, a great dinner courtesy of her mother and Aunt Joann, and now Sabrina and Kara, Cass, and Jade were camped out in her room in yoga pants and sweatshirts, eating ice cream straight from the pint. They used to do the same when they were teenagers, but now they made sure they had a good wine to accompany the ice cream.

Cass admired the ruby liquid in her glass and smiled. "Who'd have thought that you could pair Ben and Jerry's with a good Shiraz?"

Jade wrinkled her nose and shook her head before taking a sip. "Some dark chocolate, yes. Ice cream... I dunno about that."

Kara rolled over on her side and tucked a pillow against her. "I miss wine."

"Can you have wine after you have the baby?" There was

real pity in Cass's voice. She'd probably die without her favorite red blend.

"Not if I'm nursing, right, Bree?"

"Yeah. No wine."

Cass groaned. "It sounds like torture."

Bree smiled, perching herself on the window seat that had been her comfort spot for the last twenty-nine years. Her eyes focused on a distant point, and she thought about Jake looking at the same spot last night, wondering about the Holly Point Lighthouse. Bree hated that the light had gone out, that there wasn't enough money to keep that very special part of the town's history alive and bright for the future.

Nothing had felt the same since it had gone dark.

Her thoughts drowning out the conversation behind her, Bree continued to watch for Charlie, and her friends stood by, offering what support they could. Sabrina did appreciate they were there, she wouldn't expect anything less from them. The Christmas season around her house was madness, and there was always a clutch of people coming or going. Sabrina loved the activity and when Charlie was little, the season was even more magical than it was now. But Bree was a nervous wreck and as much as she loved her girlfriends, she wished they'd all just leave her alone.

"I should have gone with them," she mumbled.

"Are you insane?" Cass asked. "Why would you want to be alone in the car with him for an hour each way?"

"Not alone," Bree said. "Charlie would be there."

"Right, and do you know what would happen? You'd get all weepy, because it would feel like the family you thought you'd have with him and, honey..." Cass sat on the other end of the window seat. "I know this is going to sound mean, but you're *not* a family. You put all your faith in him, but he left and didn't come back."

Damn, that *was* harsh.

"I'm aware of that." Bree blinked hard. "Thanks." Cass's words were enough to bring every emotion she'd been tamping down right to the surface. Her trembling jaw told her she was close to losing it.

"I think you believe there might be a chance with him. And there's not."

"Right, no chance. Got it," Bree choked out.

God help her, Sabrina loved Cass. She did. But not so much at that moment. Why would Bree think there was a chance with Jake when he was ready to let her have it for what her father said to him that afternoon? No, Jake was no fan of hers.

Cass slumped down and played with the drawstring on her sweatshirt. "I didn't mean it like it came out."

"Then how did you mean it? Did you forget to put some snotty aside in there, so I'd know just how stupid you think I am?"

Jumping up like she'd been slapped, Cass reeled at the comment. "I didn't say you were stupid!"

"You didn't have to, it came through loud and clear."

"Bree, she didn't," Jade, the eternal peacemaker, stepped in.

"You all think I'm an idiot, is that it? Because why? Because you think I'm still in love with him?"

Kara rested her head on her hands. "Are you?"

"NO! No, I'm not." Bree pulled her legs up and looked away from them.

"Okay," Jade said quietly. "You're not."

"I'M NOT! Oh, my God. I'm going to wait downstairs."

"You just don't want to face it," Cass snapped. "I get how you feel. I know how it feels to have your heart broken."

Bree felt every nerve go raw. "You don't know *anything*."

The tears burned her eyes because her friends saw right through her, but she wasn't about to let go of the lie she didn't love Jake, because the truth hurt too much. "Unless you've been left like I was, terrified and pregnant, dying a little every day, you don't know anything."

"I know more than you think, and I don't want you to be hurt again."

"Well, what do you think you're doing now? *You're* hurting me."

"Bree," Jade said. "Take it easy."

Just as she was about to respond, Sabrina saw a pair of headlights out on the road turn into the driveway. "They're back."

She was out of the room like a shot, pushing her friends out of her head and wanting to hear everything that happened at the game. Bree opened the front door and saw Jake, no jacket on, reaching into the car to gather a sleeping Charlie in his arms. Just like a dad.

The muscles in his broad back strained his dress shirt, moving like a wave. Bree remembered what he felt like under her hands when she held him close and, even more, when he held her. How she felt safe and loved.

When he turned, their eyes met and everything inside her lit up just like the Christmas tree in their living room. He'd been back in her life for twenty-four hours, but her feelings for him were just as strong as the day he'd left. Maybe even stronger because of Charlie. He didn't move for a second and then came up the front steps with their sleeping daughter nestled against his chest. It was the most natural and beautiful thing she'd ever seen. He was a big man, strong and physical, but his hold on his child was gentle, and Bree felt her heart break because of all the time he'd lost with his baby.

"Are you crying?"

His words surprised her. Was she? She touched her face, feeling the wetness there, and nodded. It had been a rough day and the scene with her friends had really upset her. But all she could really focus on was her sleeping baby with her daddy and how guilty she felt.

"I'm so sorry, Jake." Running her hand over Charlie's head, her hair soft and silky to the touch, Sabrina didn't know if she could apologize enough. "I'm so sorry."

He swallowed hard, obviously feeling regrets himself, but if that was the case, he wasn't telling her. He also wasn't casting blame and that almost made her feel worse. Once they were inside, she wanted to be in his arms, to feel safe as he surrounded her. Reality hit like a bucket of cold water. *God, her friends were right.*

The attraction she felt for Jake wasn't superficial or merely physical. Bree still had serious, deep feelings for him.

"Where's her room." Jake didn't want to let go. He was going to hold his little girl until the last second.

"Upstairs. Second floor, second door on the right."

He smiled. It was a real honest to goodness smile. "Ladies first."

To the best of her knowledge, Jake had never been up to these rooms before. Maybe he'd been here with Ryan back in the day, but she didn't think so. He followed her closely, his body ridiculously near to hers. Once they were in Charlie's room, he set his girl gently on the bed. "She had a lot of fun. So did I."

Charlie was sitting up, but she was swaying so much, Bree sat next to her to keep her from toppling over. "Oh, my gosh. She's so tired," Bree chuckled. "I guess you two really must have had a good time." Leaning forward, she took off Charlie's shoes and then looked up at Jake. "Can you give me a hand?"

"Oh, sure. What do you need?"

Bree told him where to find her pajamas, and she changed her very tired girl out of her dress and tights, got her to the bathroom and then settled into bed easier than she thought. The kid was done, but she did manage to give Bree a hug and then she reached for Jake.

"Thank you, Daddy," she whispered. "I can't wait until we all go skating."

Huh?

"Me too. But I'll see you before that. I'll figure something out with your mom."

"Okay." Charlie pulled him close and Jake clutched the child like he'd never let her go.

"Good night, baby girl."

Their daughter was asleep before her head hit the pillows. All Bree could do was slump into the doorframe for support as Jake pulled the blankets over Charlie's shoulders. The two of them were melting her heart and the wash of regret she felt was palpable. He was a good man, and she'd treated him so badly. So had her family.

Stepping out of the room, Bree pressed her back into the wall and wondered what happened next. Did they work out some kind of schedule? Did she wait for a call? Did they have to get lawyers involved?

Jake pulled Charlie's door closed and then faced Sabrina. He was all sexy and sweet with his rolled up sleeves and easy manner. He stuffed his hands in his pocket and grinned at her.

"I'm so sorry about my dad today. What he said was uncalled for and I'm sorry."

"He told you?"

"I made him tell me," she said. "And I feel terrible about it."

"Forget about it. He pissed me off, but I was out of line threatening you. I don't want to upset Charlie. Or you."

"Okay, you're sure?"

"Positive. Your dad can go to hell, though."

Bree, who adored her father, had to agree because Jake didn't deserve the blame. Her dad, as good a man as he was, could get mighty nasty when he thought someone was threatening his family.

Jake moved around the upstairs hall and picked up a glass Christmas ball that was in a small dish on a table. He looked at it, ran his thumb over the pattern and then returned it to its spot. Bree on the other hand was holding her breath, waiting for him to say something—anything—about their situation.

"You should have warned me how rabid she gets at games."

Uh oh. "Why, what happened?"

"It was the third period. Team was losing, and I was sitting in the back of the seating area in the team box talking to the general manager and the owner, when all of a sudden, the three of us hear our darling daughter screaming at the refs for a penalty they called."

Bree's eyes grew wide and she clapped a hand over her mouth. "Oh, no."

Jake was smiling, thank God, because she could only imagine what Charlie said. She never actually swore, but what she did was pretty close for a nine-year-old.

"I believe I did hear her tell the ref he needed to pull his head out of his butt."

"No, she didn't."

He chuckled. "Leaned right over the rail and let loose. The fans in the section below the box started cheering for her and a guy in the box next to us gave her a high five."

"But the GM. The owner…"

"Loved her. They want her there for every game because she can say things they can't."

Bree laughed and so did he. It was a nice moment, comfortable. *Heartbreaking.*

"I'll call about seeing her sometime this week if that's okay."

"It's fine. You can see her whenever you want."

"Thanks."

There was a burst of giggles from down the hall and the corner of Jake's mouth ticked up in response. Suddenly, Sabrina felt more like the eighteen-year-old student she was when she met him than the twenty-nine-year old professional she was now. Her girlfriends were still there, still giggling.

"Having a sleepover?"

"We always do after baking days. I think during the holidays they've always slept here more than their own homes, except Jade, maybe."

"She lives upstate, right?"

Bree was shocked he remembered. "Yes. She's leaving tomorrow to go home. I don't know if I'll see her again before Christmas."

"The other two I met? Cass and Kara? You'll see them?"

"They both live in the city. Kara's going to have her baby soon."

Jake nodded and fingered the pine garland that circled the railing around the stairs. Her mother didn't just decorate part of the house, all three floors glittered with silver and gold ornaments, tiny lights, and pine, the scent of which mixed with whatever Jake was wearing and it made her think of their night in Acadia.

"I was always amazed at the bond you all had. I mean I know I never met them, except for Elena, who was around a lot the summer I was here. But you talked about them so much."

Had she? Bree wasn't aware, but they were all such an

important part of her life she supposed it was true.

"They must think I'm an asshole," he said with a wry smile.

Bree was fairly sure with her obnoxious outburst right before he'd brought Charlie home that she was the one they thought was the asshole. Boy, did she have some apologizing to do. *Change the subject, Bree. Change it.*

"I should go…" He thumbed toward the stairs. "Thanks for trusting me with her."

"Don't thank me for that." Bree looked away, completely overwhelmed by his presence. "Um, what was it she said about skating?"

"Oh, right." He snapped his fingers. "Her team is having a family skate. She asked me to go."

"That's great, you'll have fun. Ryan and my dad always go with her."

Jake nodded and cocked his head to the side. "You don't go?"

"Uh, no. I can't skate, you know that."

"I've never actually seen the train wreck that is you on skates, but you've told me. So has Ryan."

"I mean, I'll be there, but safe. On a bench. With hot cocoa at the ready." Just the thought of getting skates on made Bree's knees shake. She and the ice did not get along.

"I don't think so." Jake folded his arms and leveled a steely gaze at her. "I'm going to teach you." That wicked intense look might work intimidating some rookie player, but with her? No.

"Teach me? I don't think so."

"I think so." He reached out and tapped her nose. "Charlie said she wants you to skate with her. So I'm going to teach you how."

"Jake, I can't skate. As soon as my blades hit the ice, I'm down."

He leaned close enough for her to feel his breath on her face. "I won't let you fall."

"Jake, no. I can't." Bree started for the stairs, but he was right on her heels. She wasn't prepared for him getting hold of her hand pulling her toward him.

"If you don't try, what kind of example is that for our daughter?"

He smirked, damn him, looking too cute for his own good. Or hers. Why did he have to pull the "good example" card?

"Fine. But when I'm in the emergency room with a broken tail bone, you're going to have to explain it to her."

"I'll be there, Bree. You won't get hurt."

The words, so full of meaning, brought tears to her eyes. Hurt? All they did was hurt each other. "Jake, I…."

"You know what I mean. God, I'm sorry."

"It's okay. I've had some wine, and it's the holidays. Add all the changes to that, and I'm a lot more emotional than usual."

He brushed a tear from her cheek. "Yeah, there have been a lot of changes, especially in the last twenty-four hours, huh?"

"Yeah."

Jake followed her downstairs, the two of them lingering by the front door.

"When are you free this week? Any evenings?" he asked.

"Uh, Wednesday. Why?"

He grinned again, the gesture lighting up his eyes, and Bree's heart just stopped in her chest. Stopped. Jade was right about him.

A panty dropper, indeed.

"I need to reserve ice time. You're getting a private lesson."

"Reserve time? Um, don't go through any trouble for me."

"You want to be out there with little kids darting around

your legs?"

She didn't want to go ice skating at all. She *really* didn't want to be alone with him, but for Charlie? She'd do just about anything. "Do what you have to do. Let me know the time."

He nodded and for a second leaned forward, almost like he was going to kiss her, and Bree wanted to go the last couple inches and finish the job.

God, did she want to kiss him.

Sensing they were treading on dangerous ground, each stepped back at the same time. "Okay. I'll pick you up around eight on Wednesday."

"I can meet you wherever you want. No need to go out of your way."

"And risk you standing me up? Hell, no." He opened the front door. "I'm picking you up."

She rolled her eyes because he knew her so well, even after all these years. His leaving, smiling at her, waving goodbye as she stood in the doorway freezing—it was all a blur as she went back upstairs to her room. The second she walked in and closed the door, Bree burst into tears.

"Oh my God!" she cried. "Oh no! You were all right. I'm so sorry I was a bitch. I'm so sorry."

Cass and Jade were at her side, and Kara was making room on the bed for her. "Come here, oh, you poor thing." Kara rubbed Bree's back as she dropped her head on the pillow.

Cass and Jade knelt next to the bed, offering comfort, but there was nothing to be done. Bree was in a hell she'd never escape from... she was in love with a man who didn't love her. Sure, Jake was attracted to her, but he didn't love her. If he did, he would have come back. He wouldn't have left in the first place.

"What is wrong with me? Am I still in love with him? Am I always going to love him?"

"Yeah," Jade said patting her knee. "Yeah, you probably are."

Cass blotted her eyes with tissues, her friend's face was so kind and sweet. Bree hated how mean she'd been to Cass. If anyone understood how Bree felt, Cass did.

"You'll handle it," Cass said. "You will. You're strong."

Bree didn't think she'd ever be able to handle how she felt. Ever. And she wasn't strong. Curling up, with her friends around her, just like the day she found out she was pregnant, Sabrina cried for the man who didn't love her.

Chapter Eight

JAKE STOOD ON the front porch at Sabrina's house and he had no idea how this date was going to go. He hoped knowing he was trying to do the right thing for Charlie, and that he and Sabrina were doing okay would be enough to keep her parents off his back, but he had a feeling he was going to have a hard time with Ed Gervais no matter what.

Sure enough *The Big Guy* was the one who answered the door.

"Hello, Dr. Gervais."

"Jake."

The man was holding an iPad, and eyeing him up and down. It was uncomfortable until Charlie came bouncing in the room with Holly following. His girl jumped into his arms and rewarded him with a strong hug and the dog sat at his feet, tail wagging. Her grandfather, however, was pretty pissed off about the open affection Jake received from his daughter. Jake, on the other hand, didn't care what Bree's dad thought. The only person who mattered at that moment was Charlie.

Jake set her on the floor tugged her finger. "How was school today?"

"Okay, I guess."

"Those girls still bugging you?" Charlie had told him about the girls in fifth grade, just a year older than her, who teased her about pretty much everything.

"Kinda. They said I was lying about you coming to the dance. Marissa said everyone knows I don't have a dad."

Jake rubbed his thumb over her knuckles. "I guess they'll be surprised to meet me then."

"Charlotte?" Her grandfather squatted down. "Who's teasing you? Marissa Lake?"

Charlie nodded and Bree's dad reached out and pulled her into a hug. "You don't let anyone make you feel bad. You know the truth, and that's all that's important."

"I know. But I overheard the class moms talking about Mommy, too."

That changed the game. Dr. Gervais looked at Jake over Charlie's head and instead of his angry look, he'd softened and appeared more concerned. "Your mother loves you, my dear girl. Don't you listen to a word."

"Even if the word is bad?"

Jake felt all his muscles tighten. His urge to protect not only Charlie, but Sabrina was strong, and while he should have been surprised to feel that way, he wasn't. It felt right.

"Why don't you go tell your mom Jake is here."

She nodded, and without another word, ran upstairs with Holly in tow, leaving Jake and Bree's dad alone again.

"I hate that this kind of nastiness is touching Charlie." So much for feeling intimidated. He and Dr. Gervais were feeling the same thing—concern for family.

"Has it been going on for a long time?" Jake asked.

Dr. Gervais rubbed his hand on the back of his neck. "People forget this is a small town and I know everyone. The place is a blessing and a curse. I grew up here. Marissa's mother, Amanda, was a mean girl growing up and she hasn't let age change her ways. She's a year or two younger than Ryan. Had a crush on him that didn't work out and she's been spewing venom in our direction ever since."

"So now her kid is taking it out on Charlie?"

"Kids make mistakes, Jake. They're kids. Bullying or teasing is never right, but it happens. Our job is to teach them so, as they grow up, it's not part of who they are. Unfortunately, some parents don't learn, so their kids will keep the cycle going. If I remember, Marissa's grandmother wasn't very nice either."

"I'd like to give that mother a piece of my mind."

"She's very involved in the mothers' group at school. You might see her at that dance."

Jake nodded, hoping he'd get to tell Amanda Lake exactly what he thought. The soft thumps behind him made Jake look up. Coming toward him was Bree. She was wearing a big chunky sweater, a scarf, and was carrying a skate bag. Her dark hair was pushed back off her face with a headband and his heart tripped just like it always did when he looked at her. She was more beautiful now than she was when they were first together—inside and out. While Jake loved the person she was, he was in awe of who she'd become.

He drew a breath as she grabbed her jacket off the hook on the wall, not letting her father's presence affect her in any way.

"So, are we going to do this? I had wine with my dinner to keep me from chickening out."

He put his head down and chuckled before looking up again and locking eyes with her. "That's great. Do you think wine will keep your feet under you?"

She walked right up to him and lightly poked him in the chest. Her eyes were bright and her lips were pink and kissable.

"No, that's your job. You should say thank you to the lovely Chardonnay that kept me from running off to the city to see Cass."

"Fair enough. Let's get going. I reserved the rink starting in an hour."

"Awesome."

+ + +

THE HOUSE SMELLED like Christmas. Nona was baking special Christmas cookies and the smell of warm vanilla and cinnamon was making Charlie hungry. Wandering into the kitchen, Charlie found her grandmother looking through a recipe box. Everyone said Christmas was Nona's time of year. Poppy told her once he believed Nona was one of Santa's helpers which was why she loved the holiday so much.

Charlie didn't know about the whole Santa's helper thing, but she did know that the whole world felt more special at Christmastime. Hopping up on one of the kitchen stools, Charlie watched her grandmother look through stacks of cards.

"Another cookie recipe?"

Nona smiled. "Not exactly. I'm going to make Struffoli. It's little balls of dough that are fried and then covered with honey and sprinkles."

"Hmmm. Have we ever had them?"

"I haven't ever tackled them on my own, but my mother made them every Christmas."

She loved hearing about Nona's big Italian family, and she especially liked when Nona's two brothers, Sam and Joey, came to visit. Uncle Joey always had peppermint candies in his shirt pocket, and the first thing she did when they walked in the house was give both of them big hugs and go through Uncle Joe's pocket. The best part though, was when Uncle

Joey would tell stories about the family and traditions, like the cookie baking, which started with Nona's grandmother.

There had been a lot of changes since Friday, and she had so many questions to ask, but she didn't know what to say first. Instead, she watched the lights on the tree in the family room and wondered if what she wanted to know about even mattered. Reaching for the cookie tin decorated with the Santa Claus, she took one of the pretty pizzelle and shook off a little of the powdered sugar.

"Something on your mind, topolina?" Nona always called her that. It meant 'little mouse' in Italian.

"Do you think your wish box works?" The wish box was another family tradition Nona said started with her great-grandma back in Italy. The weeks before Christmas were magical. Nona talked about the energy and light that surrounded the holidays, and Charlie understood—she'd always known, even as a little kid, that something was different around Christmas—but she didn't know if everyone did.

The box was just a fun thing for most of the family, but Charlie took it seriously, waiting for Nona to take it from the shelf in the hall closet and remove it from the heavy red velvet that kept it protected from year to year. After dinner on Thanksgiving night, when the house was filled with people, Nona walked around with slips of paper and had everyone write down what they wished for that year. The wishes were then put in the box. Supposedly there was magic when someone made a wish from the heart.

Every year since she could write, Charlie thought and thought, before her wish went in the box, but it was always the same. She wished for her father.

Her grandmother wasn't answering, so it made her wonder. Maybe it was just a game. "So, do you think it works?"

"If I didn't believe it worked, I wouldn't bring it out every year. Wishes are powerful things." Pulling a faded recipe from the stack and placing it to the side, Nona sat back and turned toward her. "Why do you ask? Did you put something in the wish box?"

"Just wishes." That was the truth. She'd never put anything in Nona's box that didn't belong there.

"Do you want to tell me what you wished for?"

Weren't wishes supposed to be secret? Charlie's heart squeezed tight. Maybe, they were, but telling Nona felt like the right thing to do.

"I wished for my father," she confided.

Nona's eyes filled up. "Oh, my girl. That must have been hard for you. Wondering if you would ever know him."

"I wanted to believe he'd be here someday. I'm glad it finally happened." Charlie had never been so happy, but she thought about people who she knew weren't so happy. "I hope maybe will Mommy stop crying now."

"She cries?"

Uh oh. Maybe she shouldn't have said anything. But...

"Sometimes. At night." She broke off a piece of the cookie before she continued. "Do you think it's about daddy? I think it is."

Nona hesitated and then nodded. "Probably. They were very close. Your mother wasn't herself for a long time, but when you were born, she was happy again."

Charlie wanted to help her mom be happy all the time. Daddy, too. She could see when they looked at each other they were sad.

"Nona, can I make another Christmas wish and put it in the box?" Charlie knew whatever was going on was private between her mom and dad, but a wish couldn't hurt, could it?

"Honey, you can put in as many wishes as you like. Let me get it for you."

Nona went into the dining room and came back with the large, carved box. Charlie loved the box because it meant special things were always possible. She ran her hand over the lid which had a picture of the Christmas star carved in the middle, and all Charlie hoped was that something special would happen for her parents. Nona brought her some paper and a pencil and Charlie thought about what she wanted to write. It was pretty simple.

I want Mom and Dad to be happy THIS Christmas.

Nona smiled when she looked at the paper, then she kissed it for luck before putting it in the wish box. "A little impatient, miss?"

Maybe she was impatient, but some things needed to happen now.

"I guess, but people shouldn't have to wait to be happy, Nona."

✦ ✦ ✦

THE LOCAL RINK he reserved was almost deserted as Jake walked with Bree toward the ice. There were a few maintenance guys hanging around and the skate shop was closing for the night, but they had the place to themselves.

The rink felt like home to him just like the hundreds of small arenas he played in as a kid. Christmas wreaths were positioned on the walls all around the ice and Christmas carols were playing quietly over the speakers. When he trained with Ryan the summer he stayed in Holly Point, Jake found the facility more than adequate. But in the ten years he'd been gone, it had been fully renovated.

"Wow. It's different from the last time I was here." The cinderblock wall on the far end of the building had been replaced by a wall of windows that faced the harbor and the dark lighthouse. "It's really a shame the lighthouse isn't lit anymore."

"It's funding. There's a foundation, my dad is on the board, but they need another big influx of cash to make a go of it. It's not just the renovation, which it needs, but the upkeep. I miss the light. I grew up with it shining in my window."

He recalled how the lighthouse cast a soft flickering glow across the town, making it seem like it was from another time and place. He would never forget how the light shone in the apartment window and trickled over Sabrina's skin as she slept in his bed.

He remembered all too well, and based on the look in her eyes, Bree remembered, too. Which was dangerous. He needed to change the subject.

"Are you ready to skate?"

"No. I'm terrified."

"Relax," he said. "It's ice skating, not sky diving. I won't let you fall."

She was holding onto him with a death grip and he could feel how wobbly she was on the skates. It would pass. After getting her legs under her, she would adapt and get a feel for the movement. Skating wasn't hard, but for some people learning seemed like more effort than it was worth.

"I can't do this," she whispered. "Ryan tried and it was a disaster. The last time I actually tried skating, I hurt myself."

"I won't let that happen. Promise." He looked down at her and tried to calm her with a smile, but it wasn't working. He'd never seen someone so afraid of ice skating.

They arrived at the entrance to the ice and Bree froze. "Jake," her voice shook. "Can't we do something else?"

"Do you want to be able to do the family skate with Charlie's team?"

"I guess."

He turned her toward him and bent at the knees so he could look into her beautiful green eyes. "It would mean a lot to her. You know it."

Sabrina nodded. He wondered what happened that made her so afraid. "Let's go. One step at a time." He turned and backed onto the ice, reaching out for her. Bree's hands slipped into his and with her eyes looking down at her feet she took a shaky step forward. "Look at me, honey. Don't focus on your feet, look at me."

"But I might trip."

"You'll definitely trip if you look down all the time. Look at me, Bree."

When she did, Jake felt that familiar trip in his chest and when she stepped on the ice, he was unprepared for her sudden stumble. Still, he managed to catch her before she touched down.

"See," she said. "I can't do this."

"You may just need some extra coaching. Keep your feet still and let me do the work. Just so you can get a feel for the ice under you."

Jake set her feet and then positioned himself behind her, wrapping one arm around her waist, his hand settled on her hip, and he held her free hand with his own. "Don't move your feet. Just let me move you along."

He could feel the tension in her body, hear her rapid breathing. When he finally pushed off and started around the rink, he felt her wobble a bit, but then she relaxed and leaned into him. It was an amazing feeling, holding her like this, and it was as close as she'd let him get other than a kiss on the forehead. Their breakup had crushed her, he knew that, and now, holding her, he wanted nothing more than to fix her broken heart. To be the man, the father, he always thought he could be. Jake wanted to be whoever Sabrina needed him to be, and more.

"Okay," he said after getting halfway around the rink. "How's that? Better?"

She glanced back at him and nodded. "Now, with your right foot, give a little push."

"Really?" She sucked in a nervous breath. "What if I can't?"

"You can. Have faith."

"I want to, but I'm afraid." Her voice was barely there and Jake knew her fear wasn't only about the skating. It was about the past, and it was also about the future; about what they could mean to each other if they went back to what they used to be.

"I know you are, but there's nothing to be afraid of. It's just me." They were at center ice and Jake couldn't help himself. He stopped, turned her in his arms and gazed down into that beautiful face. One tear ran down her cheek. And Jake's thumb brushed it away as he cradled her face in his hands. Sabrina wrapped her arms around his waist.

All it took was seeing the look in her eyes, the tracks of her tears, and the emotions hit him like a slap shot to the chest. They'd agreed to try and be friends. *Friends?* No, they were more than that. Why didn't he see it sooner? Why hadn't he seen it coming? "Don't be afraid."

Please don't be afraid of me.

"I'm trying. But in case you haven't noticed, I'm kind of a hot mess."

He smiled and nodded. "I noticed. Why?"

"Everything. I've made such a mess of everything."

"I think there's more than enough blame to go around, but it won't do any good now."

Bree rested her head on his chest and Jake felt the familiar ache in his muscles that let him know his body wanted her.

That hadn't changed. He didn't think it ever would. More and more, he thought about being with her again. The feelings he had for her, buried for so long, were still there. Now that they had Charlie, he had to find a way for her to see this could work between them. It had to work between them, because the loss he felt when they first broke up, when he'd left her, was bubbling back to the surface.

Holding her tight, so she wouldn't fall, Jake leaned in and kissed her. His lips brushed over the corner of her mouth and the little intake of breath, the whoosh of air when she exhaled was like music. She still responded to him, and that was like a gift from the heavens. "Sabrina..." he rested his cheek against her hair and held her close, sinking into the familiar feel of her body, the rhythm of her heart. *Damn.* One kiss. One kiss and he was done for.

She trembled beneath his hands and he figured she'd had enough skating for now. It didn't look like she'd learn tonight, but if she let him back in her life; he'd take on the job of teaching her for the rest of his.

"Hang on to my neck," he said.

"Why?"

"Trust me," he said softly. "Please."

Bree did as he asked and slid her arms around his neck, once he felt her holding tight he scooped her up in his arms. He figured if he skated between the goal line and the blue line, he'd keep his speed down and make her feel comfortable with the motion. All he wanted was for her to feel like she might be able to trust him again.

"How was the tree lighting last night," he asked. She'd gone to see the big tree in Rockefeller Center. "You went with Cassandra, right?"

"Cass. Yes."

She shifted and rested her head on his shoulder as he

skated slowly and Jake prayed he didn't say the wrong thing. Holding her like this brought back his best memories. "You had a good time?"

"I did. Mostly."

He examined her face wondering what she meant. "Problem?"

Bree scrunched up her nose and waggled her head. It was not quite a yes, not quite a no. "Long story, and… I don't know. I tried to call her earlier, it's about a guy."

Jake let it go because he didn't know Cass, and her issues weren't his business, but also because he didn't want Bree to think about her own guy problems.

"I love Christmas music," she said dreamily about the song that was playing over the loud speaker.

Inside his sweatshirt pocket, he felt his phone buzz and Bree shifted because it vibrated right against her hip. Normally, he wouldn't answer, but she let go of his neck and rooted through his pocket, retrieving his phone.

"What are you doing?"

"My phone is in my bag in the car. What if it's about Charlie? There could be an emergency."

"Bree, she's with your parents. And your father's *a doctor*."

"Still. I'll only answer it if it's about her, okay?"

"Okay."

Bree looked at his phone and Jake knew there was a problem without her uttering a word. He felt her whole body tense and he wondered what had happened to change what was shaping up to be a very good night.

"You should take me home," she said, her voice as tense as her body.

"Why?" She wasn't looking at him. She was staring at his phone. "I mean I know this isn't much of a skating lesson, but it's not bad, is it?"

Something was definitely wrong though, and he could only interpret her silence as a bad sign of things to come. He did what she asked getting her off the ice. As soon as her feet hit the floor, she handed him his cell and even though she was wobbly, Bree straightened and made her way to the benches.

He stood there, stunned, wondering what made her bolt. What was he going to have to do to get her to trust him? Jake didn't go right after her because he honestly didn't know what to do.

Looking down at his phone he pressed to button to wake it up, and proceeded to swear under his breath when he saw the notification.

Missed call: Sydney.

How could his luck possibly be this bad?

✦ ✦ ✦

JAKE FOUND SABRINA, small and huddled against the cold on a bench outside building. She was obviously upset and Jake felt responsible. He knew he couldn't help Sydney's call or bad timing, but Bree didn't need to feel like she was second best. She never was and she never would be.

Walking up behind her, he removed his jacket and draped it over her shoulders. He'd hoped to see a flash in her eyes, something. Even if they fought, the air would be cleared, but instead she was resigned, defeated.

"Are you all right?" he asked.

"I guess." Bree folded her arms close to her body.

"I should explain?"

Examining her profile in the soft glow cast by the tiny lights strung in the nearby trees, she took his breath away. But he kept a bit of distance between them, ever cautious of overstepping his bounds. It seemed just as they started get close again, something would happen to push them apart.

"Don't let it bother you, Jake. I'm oversensitive about her."

"I think you have a right to be. She changed everything for us."

She ruined us.

"You still see her?"

"Once in a while. I was there for almost two years and her son is a good kid. We hang out sometimes."

"I didn't know."

She wouldn't know. He saw Destin, Sydney's son, twice a year. He saw Sydney even less, but his ex lived in New York, and now that he was back, the chance of seeing more of her existed. Considering everyone's past history, he could understand why Bree was upset.

"Tell me what you're thinking." He touched her arm gently and she shivered, Jake could almost hear her thinking. "Bree, don't make this harder than it has to be. We could always tell each other anything. Why don't we start there?"

Sabrina shook her head. "It's not the same anymore. Everything is so complicated."

Jake grabbed her hands to keep her from twisting off her fingers. She was hurting and it killed him to see her like this. "Let me help," he whispered.

He could see her trepidation. She was so smart, so pretty, so unbearably sweet. Everything about her was soft, feminine. Jake's hand came up and he caressed her cheek. Her skin was like velvet, and when she pressed her face into his palm, Jake's heartbeat kicked up the way it always did when she responded to his touch.

As soon as his lips touched her temple, and the cold air around them warmed because of the contact, Jake felt like he'd come home. "I've missed you," he said against her hair.

"I missed you, too. So much."

The feelings he had for her, the burn that consumed him all those years ago, shot through his body. Being close, touching her, was all it took to remind Jake that the feelings he'd thought were long gone were still there. "Sydney is not in my life. Not in any way you need to worry about."

As soon as the words left Jake's mouth, he realized he sounded like he was soothing a brokenhearted lover and maybe he was. Maybe he wanted to soothe her now, since he did nothing to buffer the hurt ten years ago.

He brushed his lips over her cheek and down the side of her face, remembering everything he loved about being close to her. Sabrina fit him, and no one had ever been in tune with him, body and soul, the way she was.

Even with the time that had passed, she was still was the only woman who made him want like this.

Finally, when his lips touched hers, his world lit up like a Christmas tree and Jake felt like a man who had been delivered.

"I don't want to lose any more time." He was weak from her, her smell was intoxicating, a cross between peppermint and chocolate, and he was trying to rein in his desire, but failing miserably. With her, he lost all sense of reason. He thought of evenings they spent together doing nothing but kissing. Kissing her was an addiction. Memories of how she felt and how she tasted merged with the reality he held in his arms. Her face hovered near his neck. Her eyelashes brushed against his skin.

"You're so beautiful, Sabrina."

"Jake."

Hearing her say his name again was like forgiveness. She was dissolving in a pool of memories and emotions right before his eyes. Feeling the subtle changes in her body, he grazed her face with his thumb, while his other hand tangled in her hair. Her body shuddered with each touch and his head tilted slightly as he noticed.

"You still tremble when I touch you," he said.

Her response was nothing more than a hoarse whisper. "Yes."

Then she looked up. Their eyes held and ever so slowly he bent toward her. Teasing a little, making the most of the moment, their lips finally touched. Then he sealed his mouth over hers and took her in a kiss that was soft at first, but deepened until it seemed their bodies were melting together. Finally, after all this time, Jake was back where he was supposed to be.

✦ ✦ ✦

BREE INHALED SHARPLY and her mind began to cloud. Her resistance gave way and she responded to his caress in the only way that seemed natural. His mouth glided over hers while his hands moved from her face and drifted over her shoulders and down her sides, finally settling on the small of her back. She pressed against him; her hands rested on his chest and then, without a second thought, she let her arms wind around his neck.

Surrendering, feeling his heartbeat against hers, feeling the strength in his arms, was like a dream. Like she was eighteen again. Sabrina knew she should get up and walk away. He'd hurt her once and there was a good chance Jake could break her heart again, but no matter how much she tried to will herself to step away from him, she couldn't. Foolish or not, she'd been wishing for him since the day he left, and while she should have had more strength, more pride, where Jake was concerned there was no holding back.

"If only you'd said something about the baby. You

wouldn't have had to deal with it alone."

Sabrina looked into his eyes. How could she explain it to him? How did she explain, on one hand, she couldn't imagine being without him, and on the other how she never wanted to see him again? Bree wasn't sure herself.

"You'd left me. I didn't know what to say or do. I was trying to get past thinking about you with her. I could handle just about everything except that."

He didn't say anything, for which she was glad. There were no words that could comfort, no way to escape that part of their past. But for the first time in ten years, Sabrina's heart softened, just a little, and she wondered what it would be like to let him in her life again.

But giving into love—trusting her heart to someone—wasn't something Bree could handle. Maybe not ever.

Chapter Nine

WATCHING THE HOUSE grow larger as Jake drove down the long driveway Sabrina didn't know if she was relieved to be home or sad she had to leave him. The night had been nothing if not a reminder as to why she had to be so careful of her heart around him.

The kiss was proof that she hadn't gotten over him, and probably never would. She felt safe and protected, but Bree knew there was nothing safe about him. No, Jake would be able to walk in and out of her life if that was what he chose to do. Bree had been warned by more than one person that every woman had a guy like this. One who could own her and destroy her at the same time.

More than anything, she wanted to believe they could be a family, that there was a chance for them to be happy beyond their physical attraction to each other.

"You're quiet." His voice was soothing, deep and steady. So many things about him had faded from her memory over the years, but she always heard him. Jake's words, his voice, lingered in her head. She would never forget the way he said 'I love you' or 'I need you' or how her name sounded when he whispered it in her ear.

"I guess I was thinking. You and Charlie have a lot of catching up to do."

"Yeah, but I think she's pretty easy to get to know. Kind of an open book." He glanced over when he pulled in front of the house. "Like you."

"Open book? Me?"

He grinned, reaching out to stroke her cheek. "Yeah. You put it all out there. You always did. It's one of the things I loved most about you."

Bree felt her heart break.

"Jake," she said in a broken whisper. Should she tell him how much those words stung? Thinking about how he loved her—and then left her—hurt like nothing else. "Please don't talk like that."

"Why?" Jake ran the pad of his thumb across her lips and Bree prayed hard to force herself not to sigh audibly.

"This is a bad idea."

"What's a bad idea?"

"Us. It's been too long. I know you think we should try, and part of me wants to, but I don't know if I can."

"I understand why you'd want to keep me at arm's length."

He took her hand loosely in his, and the rightness of him, of his touch, wasn't lost on her. "Don't. You were always so brave, Sabrina. Braver than I ever was. You aren't alone anymore. I'm right here."

And although she wanted to say yes, she was terrified of what he represented. He had the power to turn her life upside down, cause changes that would affect her and Charlie forever. As much as she cared for Jake, as much as part of her loved having him back in her life, the thought of giving herself up to him again frightened her. But then Jake smiled, grasped her hand more firmly, and nothing else seemed to matter.

"It's just not fair, you know?" Bree looked at their clasped hands and took a deep breath. "I should be smarter. Be able to call the shots, but with you, I don't know…"

Silence settled between them, because at that point, what was left to say? Her own fear was the thing that would keep them apart, and as a result she'd never really be happy. She'd realized long ago she'd never be able to feel with anyone else what she felt with Jake. But, she didn't trust him. Talk about a Catch-22.

"Can I come in and say goodnight to Charlie?" Her first instinct was to say no and run. But it was a reasonable request, and other than wanting to put some distance between herself and the man who pushed her libido into overdrive, there was no good reason to send him home.

Charlie was probably asleep, but again that wasn't really a reason. He wanted to see his daughter, and that was enough for Sabrina to agree. "Come on. I'll take you upstairs."

Walking up the front steps, Jake looked around at the porch, which was draped with pine garland that was tied up with red bows. "Your parents go all out for the holidays."

"They do. It's their favorite time of year." She slid her key into the lock and kept talking. Conversation was her friend. If they were talking about some benign subject their relationship wouldn't come up. "They kicked the holidays into high gear when Charlie was born. Things went over the top. Toys everywhere, my dad playing Santa—you should have seen it."

Turning to him once she'd unlocked and opened the door, Jake's expression stopped her cold. It only took a split second for Bree to realize how insensitive she'd been. "Jake, I'm sorry. That was awful of me. I know that… I shouldn't have said…" She reached out and touched his arm, almost recoiling at the contact. The warmth, the spark went right through her.

"It's okay. I hate that I missed it, but it wasn't just your fault, was it?"

"Still. I feel horrible."

He took her hand and Sabrina didn't resist. They were both hurting, and even though she didn't want to acknowledge it, his being there helped. She felt better, calmer, knowing Charlie had two parents who loved her, even if they couldn't be together.

"Is everyone in bed already?" He looked around the foyer and except for a lamp on the table and the lights from outside, the place was dark.

"The house turns in early. Don't you remember? How do you think I was able to sneak out so easily?"

He chuckled warmly and Bree noticed he wasn't letting go of her hand, even when she gave a little tug. Barely able to put down her bag and keys, Jake pulled her toward the stairs.

He didn't have to ask where they were going, remembering where Charlie's room was, they stopped at the door and gazed at their little girl. "I can't get over how much she looks like you," he whispered.

Stepping into the room, they stood by the bed admiring their baby.

Baby. Charlie wasn't a baby anymore. She was nine, almost ten, and full of questions. Soon, Bree would be able to answer her honestly. Reaching out, she stroked a lock of hair away from her girl's face. Charlie did look like her, possessing the same eyes and hair, but her competitiveness, her gracefulness came from her father. Her daughter might not have resembled her father, but she was very much like him, and a constant reminder.

Sabrina's mind drifted back to the day Jake walked into her life. She had just turned seventeen, was a senior in high school, and Cass had come out for the weekend. They bounced down the stairs on a Friday night, ready to head out with friends, when her brother Ryan walked inside the house with his new buddy from the team. They had an off night and decided to take her mom up on the offer of dinner.

Bree froze on the bottom step when she locked eyes with Jake Killen for the first time. He was big and movie-star gorgeous, but it was his easy smile, and the spark in his eyes, that finished it for Sabrina.

The only other time Sabrina felt that same rush of emotion was the day when their newborn baby was placed in her arms.

When they'd met, she was just his friend's kid sister, and Jake was already involved with Sydney, the rich, sophisticated New York City girl he'd met within minutes of having moved into his apartment. From that point on, he and Sydney were pretty much inseparable, and eventually Jake slipped a diamond ring on the pretty redhead's finger.

Sabrina never thought she had a chance with Jake, but she was pretty sure Sydney Talbot wasn't the right woman for him, either.

But circumstances threw Bree and Jake together.

Then they became friends.

And then he broke it off with Sydney. Bree never knew why. Not that she asked, all she cared about was that Jake was free. He was free and it appeared, by some miracle, he wanted her. It spun out of control from there, and Sabrina's life hadn't been the same since.

Sabrina turned to leave but then heard the rustling of the sheets.

"Mommy? Daddy?"

She rarely heard that name anymore. It was the sleep that made Charlie say it. She sat up and rubbed her eyes with clenched fists, squinting at the light from the hallway.

"Hi, sweetie," she said. Sitting on the edge of the bed, she patted her leg under the covers. "Did you have fun with Poppy tonight?"

Jake went around to the other side of the bed, sitting opposite Bree and their daughter's face washed with happiness. This is what she'd missed.

"Yeah." She smiled. "We watched a movie and ate a whole tin of cookies."

"A whole tin? Nona must be livid." she said. "I'm surprised you fell asleep. I'm sure you're loaded with sugar."

Jake chuckled. "Didn't save any for me?"

Charlie shrugged in a way that basically told Jake he was out of luck.

"Nona said Poppy is corrupting me."

"He is, but that's his job. It's my job to be mean and heartless."

Charlie grinned at Sabrina's stock phrase.

"Did you have fun skating?" she asked.

How did she answer that? She had fun part of the evening, but skating wasn't what she was doing. "I'm still pretty hopeless on skates."

Charlie looked at Jake. "Bad?"

Jake nodded. "Awful. It's a good thing she has, ah, other talents."

Sabrina nailed him with a look. *Other talents*. It wasn't what he said, but how he said it. How he looked at her when he did. He was a dirty tease. That was what *he* was.

"Poppy and me…"

"Excuse me?" she said quietly.

Charlie looked at her sheepishly. "Poppy and *I* are going to the hockey game Friday night."

She smiled after she made the correction. "Great. More sugar?"

"Yup," she said on a yawn. "It's his job."

Sabrina held her daughter's shoulders and eased her onto

the pillows, cupping her cheek as she yawned again.

"Well, you'd better get some sleep. You have school tomorrow."

"Okay, night, Mom. Night, Daddy," she said.

Charlie's soft skin melted into Bree's palm as their daughter curled on her side, and Sabrina kissed her on the forehead. Jake leaned in and did the same.

"Night, baby," Bree whispered.

Her baby. Jake's baby.

✦ ✦ ✦

TAKING CHARLIE TO the hockey game the other day was probably one of the best things he'd done in his life. He loved having her there, and showing her off. It was a statement. But sitting with Bree while their little girl drifted off to sleep, got him right in the heart. That was what he was missing. Not the big, grand events. Jake realized he was missing the little things. The kisses goodnight, the movies, the barbecues. He missed reading her stories. Looking at Bree as she made her way toward the stairs, he also realized he needed her as well. She was the woman who could make everything in his world make sense.

They walked down the steps silently, Bree's arms folded, her position guarded. "She likes seeing you," Bree said.

He liked seeing Charlie, too, but right then he was focused on Sabrina, on the way her breasts filled out the soft white sweater she was wearing and the way her hips swayed when she moved. She was beautiful in so many ways and he had to figure out a way to show her how much she still meant to him. He got that she was skittish. It didn't matter. It was time for action.

In one movement, Jake grabbed Bree's hand and tugged

her close, not giving her a second to object. Realizing he had to make this count, he spun her and pressed her back into the wall before he brought his mouth down on hers and stole the breath right out of her.

Sabrina's resistance, if there was any, gave way to complete surrender. Jake didn't hold back, but neither did she. Twining his fingers with hers, he slid her arm up the wall and pinned it over her head.

There was nothing gentle between them this time, nothing soft and romantic, this kiss was desperate—it was hot, deep—and he was sure she could feel his hard-on right through his jeans. Bree would know, in no uncertain terms, he wanted her, and he only hoped moving on her like this didn't backfire. When she reached around and pressed him closer, Jake relaxed into the kiss, because the need was on both sides and he couldn't have been more relieved. He reminded himself they were taking small steps back to each other, but feeling the friction of her lips against his, the sweet invasion of her tongue in his mouth, was testing his restraint, pure and simple.

When Sabrina's hand slid just slightly into his jeans, she sent him a clear message she didn't want the kiss to end any more than he did. He ran his free hand down the length of her body, sliding it around her back and up under her sweater. Bree moaned at the contact and just about set Jake off. She was beautiful, responsive, and if he pushed it, she would be his again.

She would always be his.

Releasing her arm, it dropped gently on his shoulder and Bree's eyes fluttered open. She examined his face and for a moment he thought maybe they'd made a little progress, that she wouldn't fight what was growing between them.

"I should probably go," he said smiling down at her. "Before your father comes down and kicks my ass."

She chuckled nervously and looked away. *Uh oh,* he thought.

"I'll, ahh, I'll call you. Okay?" Her body tensed like a drawn bow.

"Bree?" What the hell? She was trembling, scared. He didn't know what was going on, but he didn't want her to start figuring out ways to put the brakes on a relationship before they'd even had a chance to talk about it. "It's going to be okay. We're going to be okay."

"Right," she said. "Okay."

Jake held her hands and forced her chin up, focusing his gaze on her eyes. "Sabrina, don't shut me out. We're finally fixing what went wrong—"

"You should go, Jake."

"Bree—"

"Really, you should. I'll call you. Goodnight."

She practically shoved him out the door, closing it firmly behind him.

Jake uttered an oath under his breath and resisted the urge to hit something. He could still taste her on his lips, still feel her pressed against him like she might die if she couldn't be close. It made no sense that in a matter of a minute everything changed between them.

But it had. And he didn't understand any of it.

✦ ✦ ✦

BREE CHANGED INTO a pair of sweats, went to the den, and turned on the TV, hoping for something to distract her. The old sofa almost gave her a hug as she sat down. Warm and familiar, it smelled of her mom's perfume and her dad's soap. It was home, the one place that made her feel safe and secure. God knew it was the only place she might be safe from herself.

That was depressing. Reaching out, she picked up the tray of brownies she'd brought from the kitchen. Holly lay at her feet, hoping for a crumb to drop, but Bree was going to make sure not a single bite went to waste. The house was decked out in all the Christmas finery. Gifts were hidden in closets and drawers. There was a dusting of snow outside. Bree should have been counting her blessings, but she was miserable, because plain as day, Jake being back in her life showed her what was had been missing for so long. Jake was the missing piece. She never stopped loving him—she never would—but they couldn't be together.

Digging into the dark chocolate in her lap, Bree tried to push him out of her head, knowing it was impossible.

"Sabrina? Still up?" Two hours had passed and her father, dressed in a pair of pajama pants and a t-shirt, his dark hair mussed, found her still on the couch, nursing a cup of herbal tea.

"I can't sleep"

"How was skating?" he asked and settled himself next to her on the sofa.

"Okay, I guess." She cuddled into him as he brought his arm around her, but she couldn't look at him, couldn't let him see her face.

How she loved her father. His practice in town was thriving, but he was indulging in a new found passion for writing, and had decided to take on a new pediatrician in his practice. He loved history and was researching his French and Scottish ancestors, hoping to spin what he learned into an epic historical novel. He was the kindest man she knew, the most generous of souls, while still being fiercely protective. She loved him more than words could explain even when she was furious with him for meddling.

He was also Charlie's partner in crime.

"I hear you're poisoning my daughter with sweets," she stated with mock seriousness.

"You betcha, poisoned you and your brother, too," he said. "So, did you have a good time?"

He didn't miss a beat. His question was so direct, so to the point, it threw her a little. She could never lie to him, he'd see right through her. So, she decided to be equally straightforward.

"I can't skate worth a damn, and being alone with Jake again was... confusing."

"He didn't do anything, did he?"

"No. Nothing." She sipped her tea. "It was a nice time." Why was she lying? God, this was absurd. She should at least be able admit her feelings.

"A nice time?" One dark eyebrow shot up past the rim of his glasses.

Bree smiled, because that was *so* believable, but sobered when her dad set his face in a know-it-all father look. He knew she wasn't being honest with him or with herself, for that matter, but he wasn't going to call her on it. He would just wait.

It was no use.

"Fine, I'm a lost cause where he's concerned," she admitted.

"I figured. What are you going to do? If you need me to take care of him, let me know." He stretched and took the last piece of brownie from the tray she'd obliterated. "I'm a doctor. There will be no evidence."

"That's not funny, Daddy."

"It wasn't supposed to be."

"Great. I think Charlie might have a problem with that."

"I don't want him near either of my girls." He paused, thinking. "Unless that's what *you* want."

Forcing the tears down, Bree allowed herself to admit what she wanted when her father pulled her close. "I want him, Daddy. I always have."

"Then you're going to have to screw up your courage and go after what you want."

She looked up at her father and then stretched up her hand to feel his forehead. "Are you sick? You want me to get back together with him? You hate Jake."

"I don't hate him. I don't *trust* him, but the bottom line is, I want you happy, Bree. That's all. But you have to take responsibility for that happiness."

"This sucks. Why does it have to be so hard?"

"What? Being with someone? I'm married to your mother. Don't ask me."

"Mama loves you, Daddy. She does."

"Oh, I know that, but she makes me work for it, and that's okay."

"I have to work for it? Is that what you're saying?"

"How is this different than any other advice I've given you?" He rubbed a hand over his chin, contemplating his next question, but before he had a chance to speak, Bree snapped.

"Great. I'm almost thirty years old and I'm getting a life lesson."

"What makes you think life lessons stop at some arbitrary age? You never stop learning, and in your case, you seem to have forgotten something—you have to work for what makes you happy."

She turned her face and met her dad's eyes. "I'm so scared. Tonight I... I just... it was nice between us. I want to believe everything could be that good all the time, but I don't know if it can be."

"Nice?"

She hesitated, but then couldn't hold back and the words

shot out of her mouth. "I mean I didn't expect it…"

Seeing where this was going, he held up his hand before she could elaborate. "Obviously *something* happened. Quite frankly, I don't want to know, but I'm going to tell you this again: you have all the control here."

"Control? How do you figure that?" she shot back. "You don't understand how hard this is for me."

"No kidding it's hard. But we've been through this a hundred times. You were feeling the same kind of fear when you first found out you were pregnant. You can't let what's happened in the past stop you from having a future."

Bree slipped her arms around her dad's waist and curled against him, looking for some kind of protection. But she wasn't going to find what she was looking for. Her father loved her—unconditionally—but that love wasn't going to protect her heart. He was right, she either had to resign herself to the fact that she and Jake wouldn't be together, or she had to embrace the possibility of a life with him. If she went with the first option, she'd be miserable simply because she didn't try. If she took a risk and tried to work things out with him, she could get the biggest and best payoff of her life.

In response, her dad rubbed his hand up and down her back in the same gentle motion she remembered from her childhood when he'd tried to soothe her after a bad dream.

"It'll be all right, baby," her father crooned.

"I'm not a baby anymore, Daddy."

His hand stopped for a moment and then resumed its gentle motion. "Sabrina, you will always be my baby."

Chapter Ten

NEW EXPERIENCES WERE becoming the norm, and Jake had no idea what was expected as he escorted Charlie into the elementary school father-daughter holiday dance. This was an entirely new scene for him and it was times like these that the anger he felt for being kept out of Charlie's life, bubbled to the surface.

Sure, Bree had been great the past few weeks about letting him spend time with his daughter, but he should have spent the last nine years with her. The anger, however, was short lived because when it came to Bree, he couldn't stay mad.

Not that he'd even had the chance to have a fight with her because she'd been avoiding him since their explosive kiss a couple of weeks ago. That night he thought they'd turned a corner, and started to make their way back to each other, but except for the contact they had because of Charlie, there'd been no more kisses. Jake was lucky if he got a two sentence conversation and it killed him because he wanted so much more.

He'd missed her over the past ten years, but getting to know her again, as a grown woman, and a mother, brought his feelings to a whole new level.

He'd stopped in at her physical therapy practice one morning, hoping to get her to agree to go get coffee with him so they could talk, but instead, he watched her work with an elderly patient.

The woman, who was struggling with arthritis in her knees, was getting discouraged because her progress was slow, but Sabrina wouldn't let her quit. Her technique was a combination of firmness and compassion. She understood people intuitively which served her well in her professional life. Those traits were also what made her a wonderful mother. There was no doubt Bree's patient had total confidence in her and, as a result, got through the session feeling like she'd accomplished something.

While he'd watched Sabrina work, he realized he was going to have to do a lot more than pay her lip service. In many ways, she possessed the sweetness she had when she was younger, but now she was so much more, and he was going to have to show her not only how much he needed her, but how much he wanted to make a life with her.

Looking down at Charlie, who was dressed in a beautiful, dark red velvet dress, he warmed at the site of his child beside him. Once again, images of Bree holding her as an infant flashed through his mind and Jake marveled at the life they'd created. His daughter's hand was wrapped in his and she wore a smile that made him feel ten feet tall.

The entrance of the gym had been transformed into the gateway to the North Pole with large candy canes flanking the doorway. Once he walked inside, he felt like he was no longer in Holly Point. The room sparkled. Snowflakes hung from the ceiling, and twinkle lights and gold and silver ornaments decorated the Christmas trees encircling the room. Tables had red and green table cloths, with poinsettias at the center. Even Jake, who hadn't felt much like celebrating anything for the past ten years, smiled. He squeezed Charlie's hand and let her lead him to her friends and their fathers.

Introductions were easy, and he settled into easy conversation about sports and family.

He expected to feel a little awkward because everything was so new, but it also affirmed for Jake that having a family was on the top of his Christmas list. If things went like he wanted them to, he might actually get his wish.

Music started and the little girls grabbed their dads' hands and pulled them to the center of the gym to dance to *Jingle Bell Rock*. Jake figured his life was pretty much perfect.

✦ ✦ ✦

AN HOUR LATER, he watched Charlie by the refreshment table with a group of girls from her class. They were smiling and giggling—everything *seemed* fine. Several women from the mothers' group were behind the table, helping with refreshments, and Jake noticed that one of them, a redhead with a very tight sweater and a snarl on her face, was eyeing him.

"Who are the women behind the table," he asked. A teacher from the high school, Dan Russo, turned to answer. Dan coached the high school hockey team along with his job teaching biology, so he and Jake hit it right off. His daughter, Lara, was in Charlie's class.

Dan leaned back in his chair and rested an ankle on the opposite knee. "The mothers' group committee. It seems the same people are always volunteering. The brunette at the end is my wife, Kristan. The blonde on the other end is Jane. She's a doll, never has a bad thing to say about anyone." He looked around the room and pointed to a big man who could have played Santa if they'd given him a red suit. "She's married to the village mayor, Ray Hamilton. The redhead is Amanda Lake.

And the reason she's giving you the stink eye is because she and Sabrina's brother Ryan had something going and it didn't work out."

"Seriously, man? Her daughter has been giving Charlie a hard time."

"It's no wonder. Marissa is a handful." Tilting his can of soda toward the table for a little emphasis. "Talk about timing. Something's going on."

Jake glanced over and sure enough he saw Charlie with her head dropped and her little shoulders shaking. Marissa Lake and her mother were saying something that had her so upset she bolted from the gym.

Jake didn't waste a second and went after her. He thought for a moment about doubling back and ripping into Amanda, but Charlie had to be his first concern. He found his daughter sitting on a step near the cafeteria. All he had to do was reach out, and she lunged at him, holding on with all she had. Breaths were coming in little gasps and when he felt her wet cheeks against his neck, Jake could barely contain his rage.

"Shhh. Shhh. It's okay. I'm here. Whatever happened, I'm here for you."

"They're so mean, Daddy. Why are some people mean?"

"I don't know. What did she say to you?"

"That you weren't my real father. And… and she called Mommy a bad name, I think."

What was wrong with some people? It was the holidays, this was a child. Why would any adult say something about a kid's mother? "You stick with me. Killens don't back down from bullies. Got it?"

She pressed her lips together tight and nodded, but tears flooded her eyes, breaking Jake's heart. "I'll try."

Jake could see his little spitfire was hurting. It was interesting that when Charlie was on the ice, nothing fazed her. If she had to play against a boy who was bigger than she was, she dealt with it. But he was coming to a quick realization that mean ten-year-old girls were something else altogether.

Kneeling down on one knee so he could be closer to her, he could see she just wasn't up for a confrontation.

Pure instinct took over and Jake pulled her close, holding tight so Charlie knew she could count on him. "Are you going to tell me what they said?"

Charlie shrugged. "Why did Marissa's mom say that? That you weren't my dad?"

"I have no idea. Adults can be dumb sometimes." He said dumb, but he wanted to say something a lot stronger. In fact, if he could get her alone, he would have gotten right into Amanda Lake's face and told her exactly what he thought of her and her kid. "It's up to you. Are we staying or going?"

"I want to go home."

Jake wished Charlie had opted to stay, but he could see how upset she was, so he wouldn't push it. He hated feeling like the bad guys won, but he wasn't prepared to make Charlie feel worse. No, he'd shelter her now, and deal with the bitch and her daughter another time.

"Let's go then."

"Okay," she sniffled. "I'm sorry."

What? "Why are you sorry? You didn't do anything."

"Well, not sorry so much. I'm… I'm scared."

Jake sat next to her on the step and pulled her on his lap. "What's going on, sweetheart?"

Charlie rubbed the back of her hand across her eyes and looked up. "I don't want you to leave."

"Wait, what? Why would you think I'm leaving?"

A big, fat tear trailed over her cheek. "That's what Marissa's mother said. Marissa said you weren't really my dad because you'd never been here before. Her mom got mad at her for saying that but then she told me I shouldn't get too attached because you'd leave us again." Charlie sniffled and went on. "She said the truth was hard to hear sometimes, but it was better if I knew now."

The only thing Jake saw was red. Pure red. If he wasn't so worried about Charlie, he'd go and rip Amanda Lake's head off. Who made a kid feel like that? Who played on a ten-year-old's insecurity? He was at a loss what to do about Sabrina, but holding their little girl against him, he had a thought. Maybe he should ask the person who knew Sabrina best what exactly he should do.

"I need your help with something," he whispered in her ear. "But first you have to promise to keep a secret."

Charlie nodded. "Okay. What's the secret?"

"I'm not going anywhere."

"You're not?"

Jake smiled at her wide-eyed hope. "I love Mom, honey. A lot. And I want to marry her."

Charlie's eyes sparkled and it took a second, but a smile bloomed across her face. "You do? That's awesome!"

"Yes, so if anyone ever insults you or tries to scare you again, tell them to stuff..." he stopped himself. "You tell them they don't know what they're talking about."

She nodded and kept her eyes locked on him.

"I need your help. I have to figure out some way to show Mom what she means to me." It was truth time. He just hoped Charlie was mature enough to hear what he had to say. "Charlie, I did leave Mommy. It was before you were born, probably before she knew she was even carrying you."

"Why would you leave her?"

"It's complicated. I thought there was someone who needed me more and that leaving was the right thing to do. Your mom was young and I thought she'd forget about me and move on."

"She has the box of stuff you gave her. The jersey and the t-shirt. Some sunglasses. There was some jewelry, too. And the pictures. It's all back in her room now. Except the jersey and the sunglasses. I got to keep those."

Talk about a Christmas gift. Charlie just gave him hope.

"She still cries for you, I think."

"Why do you say that?"

Charlie shrugged. "Before you came back it only happened once in a while. I'd wake up and hear her. Since Thanksgiving, I don't know, she's been different. I hear her at night."

Jake could relate. He wasn't crying, but he thought of her all the time. He hadn't had a good night's sleep since he'd seen her again.

He set Charlie back on her feet and took her tiny hand back in his. "I need to show your mom how important she is to me. It's easy to say words but I want to show her."

They walked out of the school into the dark night and it took a second for his eyes to adjust to the lack of light. He came from a fairly small Canadian town and it seemed Holly Point was the darkest place on earth. Fortunately, there was a moon out tonight, but without that, he'd be tripping over his own feet. It was too bad the lighthouse wasn't still operational. He didn't think it would do a heck of a lot of good, since the school was a good distance away from the coast, but it couldn't hurt.

"Mom doesn't like things," Charlie said while climbing into the truck. "I mean she does, but that's not important to her. People are important."

That much about Bree hadn't changed and Jake was glad.

✦ ✦ ✦

SABRINA'S HEART BROKE as she listened to Charlie tell her about the dance. Jake had texted her that he was so pissed he might need bail money, but he wasn't angry as much as helpless as they both listened to Charlie's story. "I hated listening to what Marissa's mom said. Why did she call you a slu—"

Jake cut her off. "Don't repeat it, Charlie. It's bad enough what they said to you and about your mother. Don't keep feeding that monster." He leaned in and kissed her goodnight. "Just remember, you have two parents who love you. I may have been a little late to the party, but you have nothing to worry about."

Bree's heart warmed, listening to Jake talk to their daughter. He was such a good man, kind and considerate, as well as a wonderful father. She'd missed seeing him over the past couple of weeks, and she had no one to blame but herself.

Stupidly, Bree thought keeping Jake at arms' length would help her get grip on her feelings. She couldn't have been more wrong—the longing grew worse by the day. He'd been back in her life less than a month, and already Bree didn't want to think about life without him.

Charlie asked him to read with her and after the night they'd had, there was no way he would say no. Jake sat against the headboard, and with Charlie tucked safely in the crook of his arm, he opened her copy of *Harry Potter and Chamber of Secrets* and launched right into a section featuring Moaning Myrtle, British accent and all.

Bree slipped out of the room and made it to hers before allowing herself to entertain thoughts that were going to send her right to hell. She wanted him.

She wanted him bad.

And Bree was considering seducing him.

Her parents had made their annual trip into the city with

Aunt Joanne and Uncle Roger. They were out for the night, leaving her in the house with her daughter and her daughter's big, sweet, gorgeous father. The love of Sabrina's life.

Sabrina took out her phone and shot off a quick group text to the girls. She didn't know who was going to answer—hell, she didn't know why she was sending it—but she needed help.

"Parents are in the city. Jake's here. I'm thinking I might do something stupid."

"You think?" Kara was the first one to respond. *"Just jump the guy, would you?"*

After that it was a floodgate of texts, all the girls had an opinion, but it was Cass who finally broke the cycle and called. "Are you okay?"

"I'm not sure." Bree opened a drawer in her dresser and stared at a long, red satin chemise adorned with delicate matching lace. She didn't know why she'd bought it the other day, but it looked so pretty and sexy, and red was a Christmas color, wasn't it?

"This could be a huge mistake, Cass."

"It could. But if you don't go for it, that could be a mistake, too."

"I know. Why am I such a chicken?" Reaching for the chemise, her hand grazed the fabric, and Bree thought about how it would feel to wear it for Jake.

"You have good reason to be. But I think deep down you know it's not going to end like it did last time."

That was certainly what she hoped. The future hadn't proved easy to predict. "Okay. I'll call you tomorrow." Remembering Cass had her own drama going on, she didn't end the call. "How's it going, by the way?"

Cass giggled. "It's going."

Bree heard a deep voice in the background. "You should

go."

"I'll call you tomorrow. Good luck."

The call ended and left Bree with a decision.

Pulling the chemise from her drawer, Bree went into her bathroom, slipping out of all her clothes and letting the silky fabric slide over her body.

She spritzed on a little perfume, fluffed her hair, and took a deep breath. God, she was nervous. In all this time, there hadn't been anyone else and the idea of making love with him was new all over again. But that was exactly what she wanted.

Cass was right. Looking back at the texts, all the girls had said pretty much the same thing. Hiding from her feelings, playing it safe, hadn't worked out for her. Now she had a second chance with the only man she'd ever love. If she wasn't sure of that before, she was now.

Was it a risk? Yes. But staring at herself in the bathroom mirror, Bree didn't want the reflection that stared back at her for the rest of her life to be one full of regret.

She heard Jake's footsteps in the hallway and then on the stairs. He was looking for her. It was now or never, and Bree didn't want it to be never.

It was the longest walk of her life. The house was so big and, as she walked past the photos, she was reminded of how she felt when she would take this same route all those years ago to meet him. It had been thrilling, terrifying, and being with him was something she would never regret.

Sabrina promised herself, no matter what happened, she wouldn't regret it now either.

Instinctively, she knew where to find him, and once she got to the bottom of the big staircase, the flared bottom of her gown teasing her feet, she turned into the living room and lost her breath.

He was beautiful.

Standing by the Christmas tree, which provided the only light in the area, he'd shed his jacket, his sleeves were rolled up and his broad shoulders filled out the blue dress shirt he'd worn to the dance. But it was his face, his kind face that got her. His right hand reached out and touched an ornament on the tree, then another, and finally he touched the bell she'd bought for Charlie's first Christmas. It filled the room with the most beautiful sound—clear and light.

Jake bent his head and looked out the side window and must have noticed it had started to snow and it was coming down pretty hard.

"It must have started right after you got here," Bree said.

She was glad she'd finally found her voice, but didn't know if she'd be able to speak again. Everything in her stomach started to flutter when she thought about the step she was about to take.

Jake turned and his lips parted, like he was going to respond, but nothing came out. His eyes widened and he walked to her, leaving the slightest space between them. The heat coming off his body warmed her and Bree reached out and laid her hand flat on his chest. Jake immediately covered it with his.

He still hadn't said anything, but his eyes were glazed over with emotion and Bree had never been so happy in her life.

"You're a dream come true, but what about..."

"My parents are in the city for the night."

He grinned and nodded toward the window. "It's a good thing they aren't driving in this."

She nodded and leaned into his hand when it caressed her cheek. "You shouldn't either."

Everything seemed to be going in slow motion. It felt like an eternity, but his lips finally touched hers and the world spun out of control.

The room seemed to lift up, the tiny white lights casting a

glow around them that was more magic than real. His mouth soft against hers, the pressure increased with every sip, until his tongue slipped past her lips and Bree collapsed against him.

His fingers threaded through her hair, holding her head firmly so he could take her mouth in the most exquisite dance. Bree felt his hardness against her belly and she let her hand travel from his waist to his broad back, leaning into him, remembering how he felt before and realizing she wasn't the only one who'd changed.

Her therapist's hands noticed the ridges of muscle on his flank and back. The way he moved and everything flexed and relaxed. When his arms slipped around her, and he lifted her, it was effortless.

Bree looped her arms around his neck and left a trail of kisses along his jaw as he carried her back up the stairs.

"I love how this gown feels on you, but I can't wait to get it off," he growled.

Burying her face in his neck, Bree's heart pounded in her chest. Everything about this was right. He was hers, he'd always been hers, and nothing had been right since they'd been apart.

He walked through her bedroom door and pushed it closed with his foot. He stood in the center of her room, the place where she waited to hear from him, where she watched from her window, and Jake brought it all home and kissed her. He kissed her like he did when they first came together. He kissed her to make up for all the years they'd been apart and, finally, Jake kissed her for the future they were destined to have.

Bree inhaled his breath, felt the fire in him warm her skin, and her desire flared in a way it never had before.

He set her on the floor and ran his hands over her shoulders, pushing the straps down her arms and the gown followed, slipping off her body and pooling at her feet. Jake rested his forehead against hers and caressed her face with such tenderness Sabrina thought she might cry.

Slowly undoing the buttons of his shirt, Bree ran her hands over his bare chest, feeling his need in every one of his muscles before she relieved him of his clothes. Jake's fingers grazed over her body, his touch feather light. He wasn't rough or aggressive, but gentle, probing, perfect.

"I've missed you," he whispered. "I've never forgotten how your skin felt or how sweet you smelled. It's the same."

Getting even closer, Bree pressed her lips to his chest and her hands dropped down and stroked his erection, making him gasp with pleasure. "You've been in my dreams every night for ten years, Jake. You were my only lover."

Gazing into her eyes, he seemed to understand what she'd told him. Backing her up slowly, he eased her down onto the bed. Kneeling in front of her, Jake nudged her knees apart and settled himself between her legs. Leveraging himself over her, he kissed her lips, her neck, her breasts, and left a warm trail of kisses on her belly before pressing his mouth to her center. His gentle ministrations were raw and deep and meant to take her over the edge.

Which is exactly what happened.

Sabrina fisted her hands in the bedclothes, riding the sensations as Jake gripped her hips and didn't let her scoot away. He didn't stop when she begged, and she dissolved when the scruff of his beard grazed the inside of her thigh and his mouth nipped and teased her core.

There were no words.

He chuckled, warm and sexy, as he watched her come apart. "How did you like that?"

Bree was barely conscious, so she couldn't really answer. She only had a vague sense of him gently moving her and tucking her under the covers.

Her body was heavy, boneless, and yet she responded instantly when he climbed in next to her and kissed her yet again.

The gentleness was gone replaced by heat and passion. His mouth went deep, capturing her with no question as to what he wanted. Dipping his head, he teased her breasts and Bree suddenly felt self-conscious. The last time they'd been together, her body had been perfect and now she bore the wear and tear of having a child. But when he touched her again, running his hands up and down her sides, Bree stopped thinking altogether.

"I want to be inside you," he whispered against her ear.

Stroking his face, she nodded and he didn't hesitate, protecting himself before easing past her entrance. Sabrina, tensed at the invasion, but remembered it was Jake, and once the initial burn cooled, he'd be gentle and loving. Entering slowly, Bree remembered how much she loved the feel of him as he filled her. Each bit of progress brought her closer and closer to the magic his body promised. Finally, burying himself deep, she could feel the tightness, but then, as with everything else, he became familiar and her body opened and accepted him like it always had.

Their movements were in perfect sync, his thrusts firing every nerve ending until she peaked again, and the orgasm rushed over her like a flood. Jake followed and she held his damp body close as he surged into her, crying out.

"I love you," she whispered against his shoulder. "I've never stopped loving you."

He held her close and Bree wanted being with him to be her reality every night for the rest of her life. But when he didn't return her words, the doubt wiggled in her head and Sabrina prayed he wouldn't break her heart again.

✦ ✦ ✦

THE SNOW LEFT six inches on the ground before it stopped at dawn. Bree awoke when the bed became chilled and she saw Jake at the window, buttoning his shirt and tucking it into his pants.

"I wish you didn't have to go."

They'd talked about his first road trip since his injury. On one hand, Bree was happy he was strong enough to skate with his team again, even if it was just to practice, but on the other, she'd miss him. There was no getting around how much she'd miss him.

Jake turned and smiled when he heard her. "God, you look gorgeous."

"I'm probably a mess."

"A beautiful mess. You look like you had lots of great sex."

She smiled because she'd had plenty of great sex. Bree was sure she'd be aware of it for a good part of the day. "Why so early? I thought the team charter wasn't until later. Are we getting more bad weather?"

He leaned in and kissed her, nibbling her lips and touching her in the way only he could. "No, thank God. Getting into the city sucks when it snows. It would take me forever, and I…" He hesitated, and his expression grew serious. "I have someplace I have to be."

This was not going at all like Bree expected. It was a week before Christmas and she thought they'd have some time together. Jake obviously had other plans; plans she didn't know about. The city? Why was he going… her heartbeat kicked up a notch when she thought about what, or more likely who, he had to see in New York.

"You have someplace to be?" Her thoughts went right to

his ex, who lived on the Upper East Side.

Jake sat on the edge of the bed. "I didn't want to upset you, so I didn't tell you. Destin, Sydney's son, goes to a private school in Manhattan. I promised him I'd go to his Christmas concert before I fly out with the team."

Bree felt a little crack form in her heart. "Oh, I see."

"Sabrina, don't." Reaching out, Jake cupped her cheek and dropped a sweet kiss on her lips. "There's nothing going on, but I'm the only father he's ever known."

God, she was a horrible person. They'd talked about his relationship with Sydney, and how by the time Jake found out the toddler wasn't his, the two of them had bonded. Destin was just a child and it wasn't his fault his biological father deserted him, but Sabrina couldn't help feeling he and his mother represented a threat to her future. It was his mother, after all, who had lied to Jake all those years ago. "His father never turned up?"

"No. He was a loser Sydney went to high school with, and when she got pregnant, he left."

And that's when she went after you. She took you away from me and our baby.

He kissed her again. And again. "You have nothing to worry about."

Sure she did. He was leaving Sabrina's bed to go to another woman and her child. It felt like history was repeating itself.

Nodding, she willed herself to play it cool because she'd put everything out there for him the night before. She'd not only given him her body again, she'd opened her heart, telling him she loved him.

He'd said nothing.

Sabrina rose and went to the bathroom, not realizing she'd put on the Wisconsin t-shirt he'd given her ten years ago until he said something. "It still looks better on you than it ever did on me." His smile was bright, happy, but suddenly Bree felt her heart seized with fear.

She returned to the bed, sitting cross-legged, numb, and Jake leaned in, kissing the top of her head like nothing was wrong. "I'll call later and say goodbye to Charlie. You behave. And don't worry," he said before dropping a kiss on her lips one last time.

Jake strode out of the room. He was always leaving and it was likely Bree was going to know how that felt over and over again. She could handle his work, that wasn't the problem, but Jake was torn between two families, and Sabrina didn't know how she felt about playing second fiddle to his ex-wife and her son.

She heard her phone buzz and glanced down to see she had fifteen text messages. Two were from her mother telling her they would get home when they could and the rest were from Cass, Jade, Kara, and Elena. Of course they wanted to know everything.

Looking at the puddle of red satin that was in the middle of her floor, Bree opened a group text, feeling more foolish than ever.

"So, how was it?" Elena was the only one who hadn't beat around the bush.

"Everything is fine," she wrote back. *"Nothing has changed."*

"Seriously?" Elena shot right back. *"Awesome!"*

"I guess." Bree responded.

✦ ✦ ✦

IN THE WEEKS since he'd seen her again, Jake's entire world had turned upside down. His priorities had shifted, but for once, instead of feeling off balance, he felt at ease. He was exactly where he should have been all along, in love with Bree.

All the time apart, the years without each other and he still found his way back to her. When they were younger, their love was huge, explosive, and all consuming. This love was settled, wiser and incredibly intense. It had become part of him, making him feel whole.

There were probably reasons why they shouldn't be together. But all the reasons in the world couldn't stop what he felt.

He and Charlie had hatched a plan on the ride home from the dance that would show Bree how much she meant to him. He'd have to do a lot of the leg work from wherever he was with the team, but if he could get a little inside help, he could make this Christmas something really special.

Jake thought only of her eyes and her smile. How she laughed and cried. How she seemed to need him again. What he could do to make her happy.

When he had kissed her goodbye earlier that morning, Jake realized he didn't want to be a part-time person in her life; he didn't want to be a part-time father. Jake made a promise—he'd be there this time. She wouldn't have to do it all alone anymore.

Chapter Eleven

JAKE HAD NEVER been so nervous in his life. But then again, the stakes had never been this high. Timing, as they said, was everything, and in his case that was no lie. A week ago he'd put a plan in motion that would show Sabrina how much he loved her and that having a family with her was all he really wanted.

If she had any doubts at all about how he felt, and he knew she did, by the time it was officially Christmas, those doubts would be gone.

He hadn't wanted anything more in his life. Now he just had to convince her.

St. James-by-the-Sea was an old, well established church that had served the families of Holly Point for over a hundred years. The stone church had survived nor'easters, hurricanes, and blizzards and Jake remembered Bree telling him that every year Christmas Eve Mass was something truly special. The service started at ten o'clock and just like the rest of Holly Point, the church sparkled.

Light shone through the stained glass windows and, standing at the bottom of the steps, Jake heard the choir singing *Silent Night*. He looked up at the heavens completely stunned by the number of stars overhead and said a quiet prayer that Sabrina would put aside her fears and worries and allow herself to have faith. Faith in him and faith in the love they shared.

The Christmas carol ended with a flourish and within a few minutes people started filing out of the church. Young and old, families big and small passed by nodding or wishing him a Merry Christmas. This was the kind of place his daughter should be raised, someplace warm and loving, and surrounded by her family.

Now he just had to convince Bree the family should include him.

The first one out of church was Bree's mom, who was holding Charlie's hand. As soon as his girl saw him she dashed over, throwing her arms around him.

"Oh, my gosh! You're here!" Looking up and motioning him to come closer, she whispered conspiratorially. "Are you gonna ask her?"

"Shhhh," he said. "You don't know who's listening."

Just as Jake answered, Bree stepped out of church with her arm linked through her father's. Dr. Gervais spotted him first, and he couldn't help but scowl a little. Jake understood. It would take time, but Bree's father had given his approval when he helped Jake put his plan into motion. Eventually, her dad would understand that his daughter and granddaughter were the center of Jake's world.

Bree stopped when she saw Jake at the bottom of the staircase. Her hair was pulled back on each side, showing off her wide green eyes. Those eyes of hers told Jake everything he needed to know. She was his. Right then she may have been worrying about whether he would stick, but Bree was his and all he had to do was not screw this up.

She stood in front of him and looked up. Her cheeks pink from the cold, her hair lifting off her shoulders because of the light winter wind coming off the bay. If he'd timed this right, Bree was going to get the surprise of her life.

"You're here. I didn't think I'd see you."

His hand came up, fingers grazing her face and Bree's eyes brightened. But she was a little distant and cold toward him and Jake guessed his week away had made her question if she really wanted to be with him. If he was worth the risk. Suddenly it dawned on Jake there was a real possibility he'd already messed it up.

"I'm sorry I didn't get here earlier."

"It's okay. Based on what you said, I thought you'd be in Canada, or the city, or something. I wasn't really expecting you."

He narrowed his eyes when she mentioned the city. She was worried about Sydney and Destin, but he hadn't known how much until that minute. "Did you think I wouldn't see my best girls on Christmas Eve?"

Bree looked down, her hair falling forward to hide her face. Yeah, she was upset. He hadn't counted on that. But Jake supposed he deserved it. It had been tough to communicate last week when he was away simply because they had trouble catching up with each other; but he'd also been a little worried he'd spill the beans and tell her how he felt before his plan was in place.

After everything that had passed between them, Jake understood Sabrina was so scared about what might happen, she wouldn't let herself believe in the future they could have together. He would spend the rest of his life making up for causing her to feel that way.

Charlie watched intently as she stood with her grandparents and Uncle Ryan. Just as Jake was about to surprise Sabrina with the ring he'd bought for her, a collective gasp went up from the crowd.

A flash of light illuminated the church and the grounds. And then another. And another. Bree spun around, bringing her hands to her mouth in surprise.

"Oh, my God. The lighthouse." Walking to the bulkhead at the edge of the bay, Bree gazed across the harbor at the Holly Point Light which was not only operational, the entire building was strung with Christmas lights. As the beacon at the top lit the harbor and the town, the festive colored lights let everyone know this was a very special Christmas.

Jake followed Bree and stood close.

"I can't believe it's back," she sobbed. "The light's back."

"I want your light to be back," he said. "That's all I want."

"What?" Sabrina turned and Jake figured it was now or never. He took her hands and pulled her close.

"Jake what are you doing?"

"Bree, I've loved you since the first minute I laid eyes on you. I know I've messed up a thousand different ways, but I can't imagine going through a day without you, so in front of..." Jake looked around and figured there wasn't a better audience for this. The whole town was there—the people who mattered most to her. "In front of all the people who care about you, I have something to ask you."

There was an immediate cheer as Jake got down on one knee and kept hold of her hands.

Her eyes closed and tears spilled onto her cheeks. He'd surprised her. Score one for him.

"Sabrina, Christmas is magical, but it pales next to what I feel for you. I love you. I have always loved you. So, I'm asking you, please, will you find it in your heart to forgive me and marry me?"

He breathed a sigh of relief when she didn't even think about it. Bree nodded her head in response, because when she moved her lips nothing came out. Jake stood and looked toward Ryan, who tossed him a small velvet box. He opened it and showed her the ring.

"Will you wear this?" That morning, just as he arrived home, Bree's mother dropped Charlie off with him, and he and his daughter went on the most important shopping trip of his life.

Jake wanted to give her a traditional diamond ring, but the style was the problem. He figured Charlie would know exactly what her mother would like. Based on Bree's reaction, they'd succeeded. Sabrina was so stunned she muttered a barely audible "Yes."

Neither of them heard the townspeople clapping, didn't see her parents, and friends crying with her. Their daughter ran up and hugged them as Jake slipped the ring on Bree's finger.

Sabrina's arms reached around his neck and he pulled her close.

"I didn't think..." she whispered. "I didn't think you wanted this." They'd had such a tough month, marriage hadn't been something they'd even talked about, but for Jake, the minute he saw her again, there was never a question.

"Are you kidding? I'm yours," he whispered into her temple. "I've always been yours."

He brushed away the tears on her face with the pad of his thumb. "But I asked you here, in front of your family and friends, in a place I knew was special to you because I wanted to see your light go back on, too. Now I have."

She stared in his eyes, and suddenly awareness flashed. "The lighthouse? Was that you?"

He smiled. "I found a couple of corporate donors who made it possible to get the light functioning and provide for upkeep and restoration."

"Oh, Jake. You did that?"

"I did it because it's always been special to you, but it also means a lot to the town. And Holly Point…" He surveyed the scene, taking in the place he was planning on calling home. "They took care of you when I wasn't there. I owe them."

There were so many things he wanted to say, but the most important things would be said in the years to come. The fights and celebrations and holidays to come would all provide a chance for words and wishes, and Jake and Bree would celebrate each milestone, each festivity with all the love in their hearts.

The holidays were a magical time, but sometimes the magic and blessings felt extra special just like they did this Christmas.

The End

A Light in the Window

A New York Christmas Story

Jolyse Barnett

Acknowledgements

I'm so grateful to the entire Tule Team and specifically Jane Porter for her insights regarding my initial concept and to Lilian Darcy for her expertise throughout revisions and edits. You made this project a joy!

To my Christmas in New York Series collaborators, Patty Blount, Jennifer Gracen, and Jeannie Moon, you are talented and amazing women. I'd do it all again in a heartbeat.

To Alison Butler, my colleague and good friend, thank you for helping spark the inspiration behind the book with our common love of Christmas and American history. Those brainstorming sessions were instrumental in giving my story life.

To all my family and friends who have believed in me and supported my dream, thank you. You know who you are.

Chapter One

JADE ENGEL STRODE the short distance from her gate in the Burlington International Airport to the car rental counter, spinner suitcase by her side. Why bother with checked luggage when the bulk of her winter clothes were still in her bedroom closet and drawers at home?

Home.

Although she had lived in Florida these past eight years, she still thought of Starling, New York, as her town.

She handed her car reservation to the tall woman in beige behind the counter, and waited briefly as the agent answered a phone call, while "Jingle Bells" piped through the PA. She smiled to herself. Her father had always sung that tune on the ride home from her grandparents' house on snow-covered country roads. She and her brothers, their bellies full of Grandma's chicken and dumplings and their bodies tired from playing outside on their red plastic toboggans, would snuggle in the backseat, their eyes drooping and arms wrapped around boxes of knitted gifts.

The agent keyed in Jade's reservation number. "You're returning the vehicle here in a month?"

"Yes." Jade bit her lip. Had she made the right decision, quitting her job and the city of Tampa? Her girlfriends considered her change of direction a brave choice. She saw no alternative. It was more that her choices had failed her.

"If you're headed to the Adirondacks, you may want to check the weather conditions," the agent advised. She explained the charges, swiped the credit card, and handed her a receipt with directions to the rental lot.

Jade tucked the credit card in her wallet. "Thanks for the warning." She turned and began her trek. After living out of her suitcase the past three days at her friend Sabrina's on Long Island, she had been eager to complete her flight, drive the two-hour trip home and settle in before dark. Now, she'd have to take it slow, and Mom would have to keep her dinner warm for later.

In the parking garage the wind howled between the cement pilings, while snowplows rumbled past on nearby Route Two. She fastened the top button on her toasty leather coat and pulled on her matching hat and gloves, but still her teeth began to chatter.

Ten minutes later, the rented Kia crawled along South Williston Road headed west with the rest of the traffic. She hadn't even made it to I-89 yet. Visibility was poor and becoming worse, the roads were slick with snow and sleet. She gripped the steering wheel with both hands against the buffeting wind and leaned forward, muscles tense. If only she could see the apron, she could pull over to use her cell phone's GPS and locate a hotel, but the fresh snowfall covered the road's markings. She rubbed her eyes and turned the wipers on high.

A light to her left caught her attention. University Mall and a cluster of hotels lay ahead. She turned onto Dorset Road and made a quick right into a parking lot crammed with vehicles, but then the Kia lost traction. *Yikes. Black ice.* She steered into the turn, hands clammy and heart almost beating out of her chest, until she regained control. *Phew. That was close.* She concentrated on breathing at a normal rate, inching around the back of the hotel to a lone open space. Turning off the ignition, she slumped against the steering wheel.

There'd better be room at the inn.

Luckily, there was a vacancy. She was safe for the night. After calling her parents with her change of plans, she texted her best friends Bree, Elena, Kara, and Cassandra that she'd arrived then took a much-needed cat nap in her room's pillow-top bed before freshening up for dinner.

But when she came out of the elevator and turned the corner toward the lobby, she stifled a groan. A line of hungry guests spilled from the Green Mountain Bar and Grill entrance. She had no choice but to be patient about the grumbling in her stomach and step behind the last person in line, a tall businessman occupied by his phone. Taking his cue, she pulled out hers to check her new messages.

Of course, there were texts from the girls about how much fun they all had Black Friday shopping at Long Island's East End outlets. She took another few steps forward as the line moved. *What would I do without my four girls?*

Their mothers had been sorority sisters in college and best friends afterwards. It only made sense that Jade and the gang had been raised like sisters, which was nice considering Jade was the only girl in her immediate family. The families had gotten together for holidays, taken getaways to the Poconos and Catskills, and once in awhile enjoyed vacations like Disney and Caribbean cruises. Now that the girls were adults, they struggled to carry on the traditions in addition to busy careers and growing responsibilities. Still, they had social media and texting. In that way they were inseparable.

"Excuse me, Miss."

Jade glanced at the couple behind her then ahead to the gap between her and the rest of the line. "Oh, sorry." She moved forward, almost there. She clicked off her phone, and turned to people-watching, to take her mind off the hunger-inducing aromas of burgers and steak.

The businessman in front of her wore a well-cut black suit with white dress shirt and had thick dark hair and an athletic build. She looked up. He had to be at least six three. *Nice.* His phone chirped and he answered—his voice a deep, sensual rumble. Was he talking to his wife or a girlfriend? He turned and she glimpsed his profile. Sexy scruff graced his rugged face, not pretty like the Floridian men she used to date, but salt of the earth handsome.

The man turned toward her and caught her staring. He smiled, emerald green eyes focused on her as he finished his conversation with, "We'll talk after I get home." Wow, those eyes. It had been almost two years since she'd felt that flutter of warmth deep in her belly. He tucked his phone in a trouser pocket, his eyes still glued on hers. "Hey. Imagine seeing you here of all places."

She snorted and shifted her weight, hands on hips. *Pretty lame, fella. Got a better line?*

"Been a long time, hasn't it?" he said. "Wow!"

She gave him a sidelong glance. "Excuse me?"

"Since you've been north."

Okay, I'll play along. "Yes it has."

He hooked a thumb toward the restaurant. "Want to join me? My buddy had to leave a day early. His kid was sick."

Do you have a wife and kid waiting at home while you play these games? She turned to him, her stance wide and chin out. "No thanks. I'm good."

The stranger continued, "No? I could use the company.

It's been a long week on the road." His smile, at such close quarters, was lethal.

She caught her breath and stepped back. Did he think it was her first time on the slopes? She knew how this game worked, and she was done playing. She crossed her arms and pursed her lips. "You don't even know my name."

His eyes widened, the grin disappeared, and his hands dropped. "Jade Emily Engel. Of course I know it." He enunciated each syllable.

Her jaw fell open as she frantically searched her memory. He knew her middle name, too? The only time she ever heard it, herself, was when her mother gave a reprimand. Surely she'd never seen this man before in her life. "How do you know me?" The squeak that passed from her lips sounded nothing like her usual matter-of-fact self. She needed to pull herself together.

"Huh. You don't remember me." The man stepped back, arms crossed.

Her face flushed with heat, the tips of her ears burning. "I'm sorry." She looked at him closely, past the fine cut of his suit, from the tapered waist to the broad chest and chiseled jaw. She searched until she met his gaze again. Those eyes did seem familiar, but from where? Suddenly, childhood memories flooded back...and she saw a boy digging in the dirt next to her with tousled black hair and bright green eyes. She clapped a hand over her mouth. "Oh, my." She blew his name out in a rush, a name she hadn't uttered, much less allowed herself to think in over a decade. "Benji?"

"People call me Ben now." One hand moved to his pocket and the other gestured toward her, palm out, a smile tugging at his lips. "What did you think? That I was hitting on you?"

Jade pulled her arms in close, a death grip on her purse. "I, of course not. I—"

The hostess appeared, tapping the menus in her hand, saving her from digging an even deeper hole for herself. "Sir, your table is ready." She glanced between them. "Table for two?"

Benji signaled for the woman to wait a moment and turned back to her. "C'mon, now will you join me? For old times' sake," he said, as if their shared history was filled with sunshine and roses. What alternate universe did he recall?

"Uh, okay." She tilted her head at him. The crowded, noisy restaurant and upbeat Christmas music fell away as she followed him to a small table, trying to wrap her brain around the differences between the man in front of her and the little kid who used to be her neighbor.

He held out her chair.

"Thanks." She sat and folded the linen napkin on her lap and glanced across the table at him. He'd known all along that it was her and was just being friendly. "Wow. You look so different. I mean, I can't believe how tall you are. You certainly grew into those big feet of yours."

Did I really just say that? Oh God, just let me sink through the floor.

He took off his suit jacket and placed it on the chair back. He sat, rolling up the sleeves of his dress shirt, revealing lean, muscular forearms dusted with dark hair.

Yeah. He's all man. Perspiration trickled between her breasts under her lightweight sweater. He caught her gaze and she looked away, swallowing and plucking at her scoop-neck collar.

He smiled at her and picked up the drink menu.

She slowly buttered a roll from the wicker basket between them then cleared her throat. "So, what's it been? Ten years?"

He set down the menu. "Something like that."

She stared at his large, capable hands. *He's not wearing a ring.* She tamped down the flare of hope. Some married guys didn't wear wedding bands. Yeah, she knew of one in particular. She tore off a piece of roll and chewed it with a bit more gusto than necessary.

Men.

The server approached their table and introduced herself before filling their water glasses. "Anything to drink?"

Benji looked at her. "Red or white?"

Jade leaned back and shrugged. It wasn't his fault she'd had such horrible luck when it came to relationships. "Either's fine."

He ordered a bottle of Riesling and handed the drink menu to the server before she left. Turning back to her, he asked, "Celebrate with me?"

She swallowed the last bit of warm, buttery roll. "What, the weather?"

He rolled his eyes. "My next project has been approved for an educational grant. I own an indie film company. My assistant and I've been hoofing it all over the northeast the past six months to win this one. We learned the good news this afternoon."

"That was who you were talking to on the phone out there?"

He nodded. "And my mom. She was concerned about me traveling in the storm."

She fiddled with her fork. "I guess the anxiety comes with the job description."

He cocked his head at her. "Excuse me?"

"You know, parenting."

He lifted a shoulder. "I wouldn't know."

"No wife either?"

"Nope." The word rolled off his tongue with a decisive pop.

Well, now she knew. "Me neither." It felt like another

gaffe. "No *husband* I mean." She curled her hands around her middle and stared at her plate. *Okay, time to change the subject.* She risked a glance at her dinner mate. He didn't appear to have picked up on the significance of her comment. She released her pent-up breath and leaned forward on her elbows, chin in hand. "So, tell me about your new project."

He swallowed his roll. "I produce educational films—hence the grant—for school children. My next production will be a virtual field trip filmed in Lake George. I'm pumped about it, actually." He eyed her closely. "Last I heard, you were in marketing. Right?"

"Um."

Their server reappeared, bottle in hand.

Jade watched the server pour the wine, and forced her mind to go blank. No crying with strangers or former best friends allowed.

When they were alone again, Ben asked, "So, marketing?"

She looked around at the packed dining room. *What should I say? Do I tell him I spent eight years, eighty hours a week, dedicating my life to a firm that didn't appreciate me?* She clenched her hands in her lap. No, she didn't need to rain on Benji's parade by talking about her own nonexistent career. "Not a lot to discuss, there. Hey, but what's going on with this weather? And it's busy!"

He gazed at her over his glass. "Ski season. Everyone's eager to get out in the white stuff and play. I have a feeling some flights may have been cancelled too."

She nodded. "For sure. I consider it a minor miracle I found a room."

"Perhaps it was." He appeared to mull that one over. "Your dad picking you up?"

She shook her head. "Rental."

"What kind?" He took a sip of his wine.

"Compact."

"Four-wheel or all-wheel?"

She squinted over her glass. "Is this some kind of interrogation?"

He raised his eyebrows.

"Okay. Front wheel." Her rental car hadn't been the wisest selection, considering the conditions, but with no job she hadn't wanted to spring for a larger vehicle. She might have to, now, if the company would let her swap.

His tone was matter-of-fact. "Ride home with me. I'm heading out as soon as the weather clears."

She scrunched her nose. He appeared harmless, he was Benji after all. "I need a car to get around while I'm in Starling. I like to be independent."

"We look after each other back home, remember? Besides, most places you'll want to go will be within walking or snowmobiling distance."

Flying through the woods on snowy trails with her brother, Jeremy, and Benji when they were kids flashed through her mind. She hesitated. "I don't know." True, though, she hadn't planned on the extra expense of a hotel room tonight and the car rental had already put too much of a dent in her savings.

"What's to know?" He asked, misinterpreting her hesitation. "I'm not a serial killer. Hell, you've known me since we were in kindergarten together."

"It's not that. I'd just prefer to drive myself."

He shrugged. "If you don't want to take me up on my offer, I suppose you won't get to meet my Sadie." Ha! Girlfriend! She knew it. He held out his phone. "Isn't she pretty?"

Jade hesitated before reaching out to accept the device. She peered at the screen and stifled a gasp. She couldn't help but laugh at the shiny-coated Golden Retriever with long tongue falling adorably to one side. "Oh my, you weren't exaggerating. She's beautiful." Her finger bumped the screen. "Oops." A picture of Ben in front of a massive, modern log cabin appeared. "Wow. Nice digs." She handed the phone back.

"Thanks. I had it built last year," he said modestly. "Moved in a few months ago." He set the phone on the table.

Benji seemed to have it all—and probably a sophisticated girlfriend lurking in the background.

I don't even have a goldfish.

Jade shook her head. Riding home with him would be far too risky for her mental health.

"Well, let me know if you change your mind." Holding his drink, he said, "To chance meetings."

A jolt zipped through her body, as she lifted her glass and took a healthy sip.

Their server arrived to take their order.

Jade picked up her dinner menu, sneaking another look at the man across from her. Benji was the neighbor boy she befriended because her brothers couldn't be bothered with girls and all the girls in her town wanted to play Polly Pocket or dress up their American Girl Dolls instead of exploring outdoors. Yeah, Benji and she had some great memories. Too bad they were overshadowed by later, awful ones.

She would do well to remember that.

Chapter Two

BEN HAD THOUGHT the day couldn't get any better—and then out of nowhere—the girl who had fractured his fragile pre-teen heart had reentered his life, as beautiful and unattainable as ever, and was sitting across from him eating dinner.

Jade.

He almost hadn't recognized her when he first saw her in the lobby. Where she once had angles she now had incredible curves, and her dirty blond ponytail had transformed into sun-streaked, pin-straight tresses.

He twisted his napkin under the table. He had to stop thinking about her physical assets. What lay beneath a person's skin was far more important. His ex-girlfriend claimed he didn't know his own heart, but she was wrong. He knew what he wanted, and Sofia was peeved it wasn't her. Thank God he'd finally seen the light.

"So, tell me about your videos." Jade dipped two more fries into ketchup and bit them in half, her tawny eyes fixed on his. She didn't peck at her food like Sofia. He liked that. But then, he knew that about her already. He rubbed his chin.

Maybe the reason he'd hooked up with a woman like Sofia—high-maintenance and ultra-feminine—was because she was as much of an opposite to Jade Engel as he'd been able to find.

He swallowed and shifted in his chair. The timing may have been off when he and Jade were teens, their hormones at odds with their brains and good sense, but now they were adults. He gazed at her and realized she was still waiting for his response. "You won't be surprised – American History."

"Wow, that's right. Remember how many trips I took with your family?" She smiled a real smile for the first time this evening, one that reached her eyes. "I was practically your adopted sister. We went to Fort Ti, Crown Point, Lake George, and—" She sat up straight and slapped her hand on the table. "Hey, did you ever make it to Colonial Williamsburg?"

"I did."

"Did you love it? I always wanted to go but never got the chance."

"You should go. When we got there, it was like we'd time traveled and landed in the late 1700s. The guy who impersonated John Adams was the best."

"Your favorite president, right?"

"Yes." *She remembers*. A strange bubble rolled around in his chest, a lightness he hadn't felt since he was a kid. "He was incredible. He had the dialect, the stories, the mannerisms." He took a sip of wine. "There was a tour and a bunch of hands-on activities. Inspirational." He stopped; tempted to tell her how she had inspired him, also. But he couldn't. She had been cruel, in the end, and he refused to allow anyone that kind of control over him again.

She was still there, eyes glued on him, chin in hands.

Those eyes captured his imagination and his head swam with ideas. He wanted to get close and personal with this girl from his past. "It's too bad you couldn't go with me."

"When was it?"

He rubbed the scruff on his chin. "Summer before I started high school."

She sat back in her chair and pulled her hands onto her lap. "I see." She swallowed. "That was after…" Her voice trailed off and she looked at her hands.

Was that anger or sadness he glimpsed in her eyes before she looked away? He sucked in a breath at her pinched expression, the same look she'd worn that horrible day, the last time he'd spoken to her—until today.

Ben entered the cafeteria of their K-12 school with racing heart and sweaty palms. He was going to surprise Jade with the most amazing gift, and by next weekend they would be girlfriend and boyfriend. He arrived at their usual table, the one they had claimed as a pair since fourth grade. She wasn't there. He scanned the room twice. On the third sweep, he realized she was the girl in the off-the-shoulder shirt and painted-on jeans with her back to him. She was sitting at the popular table. That was why he'd had trouble finding her. She blended in with all the other girls in their class.

He walked up to her and said hi and she whipped around, her face covered in clownish make-up like the other girls, as well as that pinched look she wore when her mother yelled at her to clean her room. "Why are you wearing all that?" he blurted out.

She hissed at him under her breath. "MYOB." She turned away and whispered to Amy Wilder next to her.

Slow to get the message, he thrust the envelope between the two girls toward her like an olive branch. "I got Medieval Times tickets for next weekend." His voice cracked on the last word.

All the girls laughed—including Jade.

With burning ears, he stepped back in confusion. "But you love Arthurian Legend. That's all you talked about this summer. I mowed lawns and saved money to—"

Jade exploded from her seat, a sneer twisting her face. "*Amy was right. You're such a geek.*" Her voice rose. "*Do you really think I'd waste my weekend by spending it with you?*"

He stood, frozen, as forty pairs of eighth-grade eyes turned to witness his social demise.

Jade looked around, hesitated, then stomped all over their eight-year friendship with her words. "*Do you really think I would want to eat with my fingers like a heathen while grown-ups dressed in stupid, old-fashioned costumes ride around on stinky horses in a fake battle? Really?*" She glanced at the tickets. "*Did you forget we have our eighth-grade dance next week? A bunch of us girls are going to the mall in Plattsburgh this weekend to shop for dresses.*"

"*W-we can go to the dance instead, if that's what you want.*"

She looked him up and down like he was a worm she was about to dissect in Science. "*Danny Fitzgerald asked me. I'm going with him.*" And then she finished him off, ripping the tickets and throwing them up in the air, laughing with the rest of the room as they fluttered like discarded confetti onto the cafeteria floor.

Fifteen years on, Ben didn't remember anything after that. He shook his head and focused on the woman sitting across from him.

Her pinched look had disappeared, replaced by a frown. "I bet you're the heartbreaker now." Her voice was soft.

He swallowed the last of his wine to ease the bitter taste in his mouth. The past was the past. He wasn't the pimply, greasy-haired geek mooning after the pretty girl any more than he was the commitment-phobic man Sofia accused him of being. Maybe Jade and he could start over. They had both made their mistakes. Let it go. "You still living in Florida?"

"I'm home till January third."

He had a month. If he wanted it.

Her next words interrupted his train of thought. "I can't wait to see my grandmother. Her stroke was such a shock to the whole family. It made me realize how little time I've spent with her over the past few years."

The spunky lady had been at church a couple of weeks ago, living in Starling with the Engels since rehab for her stroke. "She looks like she's on the mend."

Jade fiddled with the stem of her glass. "Yes, Mom was with me on Long Island for Thanksgiving and she said Grandma's speaking and starting to walk with a cane." She gave him a tremulous smile. "No keeping an Engel down."

Ben had almost forgotten Jade's sweet, ethereal side, the one she had mercilessly covered to fit in with the other girls.

Or had she? At that moment, she glanced up from her plate and quickly averted her gaze, her back suddenly stiff and her face tight, as if she wanted to distance herself. He remembered that expression. "Where is that server?" she said, sharp and almost jittery. "I hate when people can't do their job right. This steak is practically mooing. I can't eat it." She waved the harried woman down. "Excuse me. Can we get some service here? I'm sorry but this meat is inedible."

Her tone dredged up another torrent of memories. The day she'd broken his heart had been only the first of many times she'd belittled him in front of their schoolmates. And he'd just taken it. Why? In the hope she'd some day go back to being his sweet friend from childhood? Did people ever go back?

He took another gulp of wine. He suddenly didn't feel much like celebrating.

✦ ✦ ✦

JADE WOKE THE next morning with an unsettled feeling in the pit of her stomach. She glanced at the clock on the nightstand

and groaned.

Damn.

She'd overslept.

She rolled out of bed and promptly tripped over her Pilates mat left on the floor after her middle-of-the-night routine. One of the doctors she'd seen for her stress-related insomnia had suggested it, but so far it had done more for her figure than her sleep.

Meanwhile, she had less than thirty minutes in which to get dressed, return the rental car to the airport, and meet Ben in the parking lot. Grabbing clothes out of her open suitcase on the floor, she tossed them onto the bed.

Why did I agree to share a ride with him?

She began yanking on her clothing as she considered. Maybe it was about giving herself a chance at correcting the bad impression she knew she'd made. He'd given her that smoking hot stare and she'd been so flustered about this very new, very different Benji Stephens, she'd turned on Ms. Bitch to that poor server. Apparently it was the only defense strategy she had, where this man was concerned.

Ben Stephens didn't seem like the kind of guy bothered by all that much. He marched to his own drum, was true to his own heart. But she had been mean to him in the past and rude yesterday evening. He had a right to be upset, but she didn't want this to be where it ended.

So she'd said yes.

At nine on the dot, grimly proud of her efficiency, she reached the parking lot outside the hotel, her errands finished and the cabby paid. The howling wind and sleet from the night before had been replaced by thundering snowplows sanding the main road. She looked across the parking lot from where the taxi had dropped her.

Ben stood next to an SUV, windows cleared of snow and

engine running. He saluted in greeting.

She waved in response and stepped across the icy pavement to the vehicle, pulling her carry-on behind her, handbag slung over a shoulder.

Quiet, Ben placed her luggage in the back seat.

Jade moved around the vehicle to the open hatch. A Golden Retriever greeted her, tail wagging. "So you're the beautiful Sadie," she crooned to the silky dog, holding out a palm for the inquisitive canine to sniff.

She turned to Ben, tempted to apologize for her moodiness last night and for the past that stood between them. She had worked so hard to put those years and memories to rest. That was one of the reasons she hadn't returned home in so long. She'd needed distance from the town, her old friends, and her old self. Seeing the hurt in Benji's eyes last night triggered that self-loathing she'd lived with as a teenager when it came to how she'd treated him. She hadn't been nice, but he hadn't given her much of a choice either. He should realize she reacted that way to survive. Or was it unfair to expect him to perceive that much?

She looked up and her gaze glued to his mouth, her mind pulled in a different direction. What did he taste like? Was he a slow kisser or one who dove right in? Heat spread through her stomach and thighs and she leaned toward him, considering all the possibilities. It had been way too long since she'd been with a prospective "panty dropper" as her friends would have said. All she could think about was getting closer to him. What would it feel like to snuggle against that muscular chest, touch those beautiful lips with hers? She blinked.

Wait a minute. What am I thinking? This is Benji.

She looked anywhere but at him. "I really appreciate this." *Damn.* Why did she sound so out of breath?

He grunted and rearranged the dog's blanket.

She patted the dog's head, getting a sloppy kiss on her cheek in return.

At least Sadie likes me.

"Let's get moving," Ben said, and they both climbed in.

As the vehicle picked up speed, Jade leaned her cheek against the chilly window and watched the ice-covered bushes lining the road rush past her window. Ben turned on the stereo, tuned to a local station playing Christmas songs. She recognized Michael Buble's version of "Santa Claus is Coming to Town." She sat upright, relaxing her shoulders, but soon her head began to nod. She fought the feeling.

"Trouble sleeping last night?"

"No, it was fine."

"Mm-hmm."

She didn't care if he believed her. She wasn't losing sleep because of a boy she'd done wrong back in middle school. That was just plain crazy. She'd struggled with this damned insomnia for years. She snuggled further into her coat and stared at the road ahead.

He merged onto the interstate heading south toward the ferry to cross Lake Champlain.

Memories of family travels between New York and Vermont popped into her head. "Going via Charlotte?"

"Yup." He eyed her closely. "You can put the seat back if you want."

"I'm fine." She bristled, unsure how to react to kindness from him. She might not deserve his hatred, but she didn't deserve his consideration either. It would be better if they both remained neutral—like Switzerland.

He turned up the heater and changed the radio from music to news before settling back into the drive.

Her phone vibrated against her hip. Elena, one of her closest friends from downstate, had sent her a private message.

The poor girl felt trapped in New York City until her sister, Kara gave birth.

Jade punched in a few words: *Aww, honey, you can do this.* She hesitated, hating the inadequacy of her sentence then started over. *One day at a time, right?* She grimaced and deleted that too. Why couldn't she erase her younger friend's trauma and fears as easily as she did the trite words? Sadly, there was little Jade or any of the girls could do for Elena. They had all been devastated by the events of 9-11, when Elena and Kara had lost their mom, but the young woman's spirit had been crushed, her vibrant personality all but drained out of her. Their mothers assured them all they needed to do was give her time and unconditional love, but so far it didn't seem enough. There was nothing worse in this life than watching someone she loved suffer when she was helpless to ease the pain and loss.

She wiped away a tear and glanced at Ben. A momentary pang of grief engulfed her, and what-ifs swirled through her head. No, it was too late. She'd burned all bridges related to him long ago. Some things couldn't be fixed, no matter how much time passed or how many apologies were given.

His eyes were on the road ahead, oblivious to the tug-of-war in her head. It was just as well.

Jade returned to her texting: *Focus on your work with Kara's charity foundation. That baby will be born and you'll be back in the sunshine before you know it.* She hit SEND as her phone vibrated again, signaling another text.

This one was a reminder message from State College. They needed a final decision regarding her acceptance by January second, the same date as USC. California's graduate program was the smart, prestigious choice. The colleges were each giving her a month to make a decision; she would use it. She didn't want to mess up the career path again.

She tucked her phone back into her coat pocket before leaning back to rest her eyes. She was so tired. When would she ever catch up on all that lost sleep?

A bump in the road jarred Jade's eyes open. She rubbed a hand across her face and blinked. "Where are we?"

"Ferry."

She rolled her neck. "I slept?"

"Yeah."

She looked out the front window and focused on the view instead of the driver. Their vehicle was first in line. What a perfect first day of December, the shimmering water navy blue with frosty whitecaps that rocked the vessel gently as it crossed Lake Champlain. To the west, about an hour southwest of the valley villages that lined the shore, the Adirondack Mountains sheltered her childhood community of Starling. Part of her soul lived in that rugged terrain. She took a deep breath to ease the tightness in her chest.

She was going home.

Ben held out a thermos. "Coffee?"

She shook her head. Two cups a day was her limit and she'd met it at the hotel waiting for the taxi to arrive. More than that and she was jittery.

"Sub?" He held out a portion of the huge sandwich.

"Sure," she said, her stomach grumbling as usual. She reached out to take a hunk. Their fingers brushed in the exchange and she pulled back, spilling some of the sandwich's contents on her lap. "I'm such a klutz."

"Here, let me." He leaned over and began picking pieces of shredded lettuce off her new leather coat.

She shooed him away, heat rising up her neck onto her cheeks. "Got it. Thanks."

He leaned back and looked out the driver's side window. He was humming that Santa Claus song.

Her brain played fill in the blank with the lyrics. *You better watch out. You better not cry. You better not pout. I'm telling you why.* She finished cleaning the mess. No mayo or mustard had made contact with her clothes. Good. She examined her hand where his fingers had touched hers. It looked the same. Impossible. Wow, and she had thought his gaze was potent. She bit what was left of the ham, turkey and American cheese, and leaned back against the headrest.

She had no sooner closed her eyes than an image of Ben handing her an envelope in Starling Central's cafeteria popped into her brain. She pushed the memory away. She had been mean to him, but that was in the past, just as the reason behind her cruelty couldn't hurt her any more either. Yet she'd never had the chance to apologize.

Correction, she'd never tried to find it.

She opened her eyes and turned to him. "Hey."

He glanced her way.

"I'm sorry," she said, her throat painful and tight. "Not just for last night, but for everything. For eighth grade. For… not finding a better way."

He was quiet for a long moment before looking at her. "Don't stress it. We were kids, both of us. We both got things wrong." He took a swig of his coffee. "Let it go, Jade. I have."

She swallowed the lump in her throat as she gazed out the window. How she wished it was that simple, like releasing a leaf on a current of wind. Maybe the reason she had come home was more than to help with Grandma Bertie or celebrate Advent and Christmas with family. Maybe her subconscious had been telling her for a while that it would be impossible for her to truly move forward in her life until she took a long, hard look at her past, and she was only just beginning to listen.

Chapter Three

BEN PASSED HIS parents' ranch house with its sprawling lawn and turned into the Engels' driveway, the homes in this part of Starling set further back from the road than the ones near Main Street. Where northern Vermont was covered in ice, his part of the Adirondacks had received a healthy layer of fresh snow. It made sense the Engels and his parents, like most residents here, decorated their homes with Christmas lights and wreaths over the Thanksgiving weekend. Winter came early in this part of the world.

He parked behind the Engels' Subaru sedan and shifted into park, his SUV in line with the shoveled stone path leading to the front porch of the yellow four-bedroom contemporary cape. How many hours had he and Jade spent as little kids sitting on that split rail fence on the perimeter of their properties—blowing bubbles, sharing knock-knock jokes, or plotting their next adventure? Sure, he'd been friends with her brothers, Jack and Jeremy, too, but they'd been more into Star Wars and video games, and he couldn't have cared less about those things. He and Jade were the ones who'd really connected, in their shared love of being outdoors in all kinds of weather.

His gaze fell on his passenger, the afternoon winter sun reflecting off the snow onto her face, her guard down in sleep. His breath caught. How could the mere sight of her affect him so much?

Hell.

He swallowed the thickness at the back of his throat. She had apologized, after all this time, and he honestly didn't know if she'd needed to. He hadn't given those memories much attention in years. In the end, he'd dismissed the painful end to their friendship as just the differences between girls and boys when they hit puberty. What surprised him was the pain in her voice, and that he now felt so compelled to make her feel better about her actions. Today was the first time he'd ever considered there might be more to the story. What had caused Jade to turn on him so suddenly?

She opened her eyes and turned to him, stretching. "Wow. I can't believe I slept again." She threw him a sheepish look and pulled her designer handbag onto her shoulder. "Thanks for the ride." Her chocolate eyes filled with gratitude and something else.

He ignored the immediate response in his gut. Jade Engel was oh so tempting, and that could only spell trouble right now. "Sure thing."

"You want to come in?"

He shook his head and gestured to the back where Sadie sat on her haunches, coiled with unleashed energy. "Got to get her home and let her run."

She reached for the passenger door handle. "Oh, okay then." She glanced up at him through chestnut lashes, smiling shyly. "Guess I'll see you around."

He opened his door, ignoring the urge to pull her toward him. "I'll get your stuff in back." He made quick work of retrieving her luggage and met her on the sidewalk, handing her the suitcase. She was careful to avoid contact, which probably sent more of a message than if she'd touched him.

Sadie whimpered, sending a message of her own.

"Coming, girl." He jogged around the SUV and hopped in the driver's seat, with a feeling deep in his bones that this Christmas was going to contain a gift and a miracle or two.

✦ ✦ ✦

JADE REACHED OUT to open the brick red door to her parents' house but stopped short, turning around as Ben Stephens' SUV pulled back into the street. She dropped her hand. He was the first man in eighteen months to make her rethink giving up on love. That wasn't good. She should know better after what happened that last time. She shivered and wrapped her arms around herself as she pressed her forehead against the cold, hard door, thinking back...

Alex sank next to her on his pristine white bed that matched the rest of his house, or at least the rooms she had glimpsed upon entering it for the first time tonight. He nodded at the bottle on the nightstand next to them. "More Cristal?"

She shook her head and smiled. They had dated for months and he was as close to a perfect man as she had ever known.

I'm ready, she thought. He's the one I want.

The roughness of his jeans brushed against her thighs as he turned to her, one hand snaking under the short skirt he'd bought her.

She leaned into the man she trusted and welcomed his kiss.

"I like you in this," he breathed against the nape of her neck. "You should wear a skirt like this every day."

She swallowed. He was so damned sexy in his black silk button-down and pressed jeans. Her heart swelled and she opened her mouth to share those three little words on the tip of her tongue, three little words she'd never shared with any man before him.

But he broke eye contact, pulling her close, their chests pressed against each other, and his mouth seeking hers, hot and insistent. "You have such gorgeous legs," he said between kisses. "Don't hide them." His fingers reached her panties.

She gasped; nerve endings on sensory overload between the champagne and caresses.

As Alex lifted the silk tank top he'd gifted her over her head, she let go of coherent thought, her eyes closing in anticipation. "I love you," she vowed.

A woman's shriek tore into the bedroom. "I knew it!"

Alex jumped to his feet, tossed the discarded blouse in Jade's direction, and threw his hands up in the air. "Are you crazy?" He pointed at the polished, irate blond. "If you thought I was doing something, why would you bring our child into it?" he spat. "You're sick."

The woman shoved him backward, knocking him into the nightstand, the bottle crashing to the floor, champagne soaking into the white carpet. "I'm sick?" She glared at Jade. "You're the one with the whore on the bed."

"I am not—" Jade stopped and looked down. She was half-dressed, her hair a mess, her pale skin heated from Alex's touches…that woman's husband. She looked at the little girl standing there, frozen and wide-eyed, the one with Alex's eyes. Jade's heart stopped and she clutched her stomach.

He was married. Had a family. Didn't love her. Just wanted a piece on the side.

Hands trembling, unable to look at the piece of slime apologizing to her for getting them caught, she bolted with what was left of her dignity.

Jade hadn't dated since.

Now, she pushed the memory aside and opened the door to call, in a voice that still shook way more than she wanted,

"Mom? It's me. I'm home."

Her mother called from the back of the house. "In the kitchen."

Dropping her backpack and purse on the bench beside the door, Jade parked the suitcase in front of it and followed the mouth-watering scents of cinnamon and pumpkin. She took deep, steadying breaths. *Everything will be fine.* She smiled at the family photos lining the wall as she ambled into the airy kitchen. "Hey, Mom."

Gabriella Engel turned from her work at the counter, hands dusted with flour. People in town had always said Jade was the spitting image of her statuesque mother and she considered it a compliment. As far as Jade was concerned, the laugh lines around her mother's eyes and the pounds she'd slowly added over the years only accentuated the woman's blond beauty. "Hi, darling. I'm so thankful you're home. I was so worried." She looked behind Jade. "He didn't come in with you, did he?" she asked in a rush. She meant Ben.

"No. Why?"

Gigi wiped her hands on a kitchen towel. "I've been a wreck, thinking about that boy bringing you home. Your father would have picked you up if we'd known you didn't want to drive by yourself."

Jade took a step back. What had Ben Stephens done to garner that much dislike from her mother? "What's so wrong with Benji? You've known him forever."

Her mother's expression turned stubborn and closed. "He's changed. I'm sorry. He's a bad influence on people who should be his friends. Like Jeremy."

"What? How?"

"Enabling your brother's drinking. Encouraging it. Making it worse."

"I can't believe that!"

"That boy is a bad seed." The stubborn expression grew stronger, while Mom's hands shook. "We could have lost your brother."

Jade took a step toward her mother. "But we didn't. And I can't believe it was Ben's fault. In any case, Jeremy is sober, and as for me, nothing bad happened on the ride home."

Gigi locked eyes with her. "Promise me you'll have nothing more to do with him."

"Mom, I'm a big girl. I can take care of myself."

"You're right. I – I get a little carried away. Let's not waste our precious time together talking about it." She leaned forward and brushed Jade's hair back like when she was five. "Come here." She pulled her close. "I've missed you so much. It's not the same when we visit somewhere else. I like having you here."

Jade leaned into her mother's soft, welcoming embrace and breathed in her sweet scent. "Me too. Glad to be home." After a long moment, she stepped back and took a seat at the large farm table. She needed a little distance to share what she needed to tell.

"You must be hungry." Her mother opened the fridge. "Want something to eat? There's plenty of beef stew left over from yesterday."

Jade dismissed her offer with a wave. "I'm good." *Thanks to half of Ben's sub.*

But her mother grabbed a large bowl anyway, spooning a healthy serving of the comfort food into a saucepan and setting it on the stove to heat. "Have I told you lately how proud we are of all you've accomplished?" She checked on the pies in the oven before joining Jade at the table. "You've put that marketing degree to good use. Didn't make the same mistake I did." She snorted. "What good's an art history degree in upstate New York?

No, I didn't make the mistake you did. I make different ones. Jade scrunched her nose. How was she going to tell her parents she'd quit the job they considered the perfect profession for their only girl? "Mom?"

The oven timer buzzed and Gigi popped out of her seat. "Your stew needs stirring or else it will stick."

Jade joined her at the stove and began to stir. How could she tell her mother about her self-doubt? Her loneliness in a city of more than four million people? Her belief that this wasn't how life should be at a few months shy of thirty? She listened to the ticking of the kitchen's wall clock. "Where is everyone? The house is so quiet."

Her mother turned from the cooling pies on the counter. "It's a school day, so the little ones are there. Jack and your sister-in-law are at work, of course, and your father took Grandma Bertie for her weekly hair appointment." She caught Jade's expression and shrugged. "I guess he figured it was better than staying here and washing dishes." She glanced at the clock. "Oh dear, I'm cutting it close. Your grandmother insisted on dressing up for her outing and she's too proud to have her son help, so I stepped in." She placed three more pies into the oven and reset the timer. "We're having a bake sale today to help pay for the new altar at church. Wait till you see it, it's beautiful." She pulled a small bowl out of a cabinet and handed it to Jade.

"What about Jeremy?" Jade filled her bowl with stew, grabbed a spoon from the silverware drawer, and returned to the table. Her younger brother had been unemployed since a serious motorcycle accident that had left him with chronic pain and deep depression.

That was why the drinking had started, surely, not because of Ben's influence.

Her mother leaned back against the counter and crossed

her arms. "He's still living over at Del Harvey's old place on the north side of Starling Lake all alone. I don't know how he manages to pay the rent. Don't expect to see him in town much this month while you're home. I practically have to beg him within an inch of my life to get him here for Sunday dinner once in a blue moon." She sighed. "But he's sober now. Knock on wood," she said, rapping the oak cabinet next to her, "he doesn't start again. He needs more in his life…"

Jade listened to her mother vent. Gigi didn't often get a chance to share her worries. She was always the strong matriarch, holding the family together, guiding everyone's life with a firm hand. She'd suffered her share of losses in life, starting with the early death of her parents, being raised by her stern grandparents, then suffering a late-term miscarriage between Jade's and Jeremy's arrivals. Then on September 11, her close friend, Marie, had been killed when the Twin Towers came down.

Jade's mother had a strong faith, and, in spite of it all, looked at the bright side of life. She liked to think she'd inherited her mother's optimism in addition to her looks. Returning home without a job and without solid plans wasn't a tragedy compared to those her mother had endured, but a minor hiccup in her career plans, an opportunity for new adventure.

If only she could find the words to tell her mother about the plan. In the meantime, "Jeremy's a fighter. He'll pull through this." Jade's throat squeezed.

"We didn't get a chance to talk much last week while we were at Enza's in Holly Point. What's new? How's work?"

Jade bit her lip. She wanted to tell her mother, she really did. But how could she add to the burdens the poor woman already shouldered, worrying about her mother-in-law's health and her youngest child's struggles? Thank goodness Jack and

Hannah were doing well at the factory, both having worked their way up to supervisor positions after more than a decade of dedication. Their five-year-old twins were precious, too. She couldn't wait to spend time with them this month and get reacquainted.

She rose to bring her empty bowl and spoon to the sink. "I promise to tell you everything, but how about I help you clean up first and we'll talk while we take these pies over to the church hall?"

"Oh my, yes. We've loads to do." Her mother scurried over to the sink and filled it with warm water and dish liquid.

As Jade dried dishes, she mulled over all her mother had shared. They had always been close, perhaps because she was the only girl sandwiched between the two boys in the family, but her mother's stubborn opinion about Benji made it crystal clear that she couldn't inquire about the man's romantic status. It wasn't relevant, anyhow. She was only going to be home for a short time. If Gigi didn't want her near him, she'd stay away. It would make everyone's life more pleasant.

Chapter Four

BEN ARRIVED AT his log cabin on the edge of Starling's town limits, about fifteen minutes from his parents' house. After letting Sadie run off her energy in the pine trees surrounding the south side of his fifty-acre property, he brought her inside. He loved his house, situated as it was on Starling Lake and sheltered on the other three sides by mountains. He'd like to say he'd earned all the money that had gone into the building of his dream home, but as an only child of parents who were themselves only children, he'd inherited a healthy sum of money in his early twenties after his fathers' parents died.

The inheritance hadn't been good for him, back then. He'd lost too many people he cared about, he'd been bitter and full of questions. What was the point of anything, except partying hard?

It had taken a few years and a brush with death, but he managed to turn his life around and finish college a year late. He'd invested a third of his grandparents' hard-earned money into his fledgling business, another third into stocks and mutual funds, and the final portion into the property, and he was secure now, and sure of himself.

Okay, not in everything.

He walked into the gourmet kitchen of stainless steel appliances and ran his hand along polished granite counters. He'd fooled himself into thinking that if he included all the modern touches in this dream house Sofia had desired, she would fall in love with Starling and stop complaining about living in the middle of nowhere.

Hadn't happened.

His landline phone rang in the living room, pulling Ben back to the present.

He grabbed a beer out of the fridge and walked into the next room to pick up the receiver. "Hey." He sat at one end of his leather couch the same hue as his ale and flipped the cap off the bottle.

"I have a question for you." His friend Jeremy's voice sounded a little too cheerful, and the usual preamble was absent. "Millie at the post office tells me you drove my sister home."

Ben remained silent, suddenly wary about what was coming next.

"No response?" Jeremy prompted.

"I'm waiting for the question."

"Okay, then. What the hell is going on? You leave for Vermont with one woman and come back three days later with someone new? And she's my sister?"

"All I did was offer her a ride home. I just wanted to save her the trouble of a rental."

"I don't get it. What happened with Sofia?"

Ben leaned back, beer still waiting. "That's over. We broke up last week. She didn't come with me to Vermont." They'd had their blow-up argument the night before he left. She must have packed and left shortly after he had the following morning. If he were honest, the relationship had been over much longer than that. What healthy couple in their twenties had sex only once every few months? He'd blamed it on their busy schedules, but now he realized they hadn't been compatible in many ways.

"What about Jade?" Jeremy said, still sounding antsy about it. "She's not the rebound type."

Ben pinched the bridge of his nose and exhaled. "Which is fine. Because nothing happened. Your sister and I go back a long way—as friends—and people know that." He left off the part about how he'd felt he connected with her today and how he planned to pursue the spark between them. Jade's family would have to back off and let her make her own decisions.

His friend cursed under his breath. "I don't want her hurt, Ben."

Ben stood and walked over to his wall of windows overlooking Starling Lake. "Jeremy, you know me well enough to realize nothing is going to happen between Jade and me unless *she* wants it to happen."

His friend expelled a long sigh. "Yeah, okay, makes sense."

"Good, because it's the truth. And you know my motto, "If you're not with me—"

"You're against me. Yeah, yeah. I know. It's a moot point, anyway, I guess. Jade hasn't shown any interest in you since she decided to act like a girl."

"True," Ben agreed lightly. Jeremy's comment would sting if he didn't know better. Jade may not have thought twice about him as a teen but she sure as hell had noticed him last evening and again this morning. "If you're done talking nonsense, I'd like to talk business." Finally, he felt able to pause for a long pull on his beer. "I told Craig to call you." Craig was his first-in-command at Stephens Productions. "We'll take a few trips to Lake George this month before we start shooting first full week in January."

The other end of the line was quiet.

Good. Craig and the other half-dozen employees were one hundred percent on board with their mission. If Jeremy wanted to be part of the team, he needed to toe the line and not go off half-cocked about personal issues. "I'll have Craig call you with the details once I firm up the schedule."

Jeremy agreed and thanked him again for giving him the opportunity.

Ben ended the call, took another swallow of beer, and leaned back on the couch.

Sadie jumped on the couch and licked his face.

Tension drained out of his shoulders. "You hungry, girl?" He ruffled her fur and she nuzzled his shoulder before they raced each other into the kitchen. Ben pulled out the bag of food and poured the remaining kibbles into her bowl. "Guess we'll drive to Clyde's tonight, huh?"

After calling Craig with an overview of the month's assignments and watching the sports highlights, Ben grabbed Sadie's leash and headed out to the car with her.

He had opened the passenger door for Sadie when he noticed an article of clothing sandwiched between the seat and console. "Hold on, girl." He leaned into the vehicle and retrieved Jade's glove, turning the soft fabric over in his hand. Her scent filled his nostrils. He laughed, thinking back to when they were kids. He'd once asked why her mittens were connected to each other by a long string and she'd responded her mother didn't want her to lose any more pairs. In many ways, he'd liked her far better when she'd been a tomboy, unconcerned about hair and nail and clothes. He stuffed the item into a coat pocket, moved so Sadie could jump onto the seat, and closed the door behind her.

Another errand to add to the list. For some reason, he

wasn't as annoyed about the second one as he'd been by the first. In fact, he was rather looking forward to it.

✦ ✦ ✦

JADE PARKED HER mother's silver Subaru on Main Street under a banner advertising Starling's upcoming Twelfth Annual Winter Festival on the twenty-eighth. She plucked the grocery list from its spot inside the cup holder and exited the car, stepping onto the sidewalk in front of Clyde's Country Store.

A tiny bell attached to the door signaled her arrival. The woman behind the counter didn't look up from her magazine. "Welcome to Clyde's. Let me know if you need anything."

Jade peered at the lady. "Laura?"

Recognition crossed her old high school classmate's freckled face. "Oh my goodness." She hopped off her stool behind the small wood counter. "Jade. I can't believe it. I thought you were kidding when you said on Facebook that you were coming home December. You once told me you'd never set foot in this town again."

Jade gave her a squeeze. "Well, I'm here. It's great to see you." Laura was one of few girls from Starling Central she had kept in touch with after moving to Florida. "You look terrific."

Her friend puffed out her chest. "Lost eighty-five pounds in two years."

"I saw those Before and After pictures. Amazing."

"I learned what three kids and an addiction to reality TV can do to a girl's figure." Laura laughed. "Anyway, I'll let you get cracking with that list."

Jade nodded, accepting the plastic shopping basket Laura handed her. Her friend had married right out of high school, one of those happy real-life romances, like Jade's older brother,

Jack and his wife. It was good to know that true love was alive and well—at least in the Adirondacks.

The bell announced another customer's arrival and the two women turned to look.

Laura whistled under her breath. "Oh my, that man makes it worth working the closing shift."

Jade locked eyes with Ben Stephens before tearing her attention away, only to be drawn back by those rippling muscles beneath his fitted long-sleeved tee shirt.

He closed the distance between them. "I've got something for you."

Laura's eyes grew wide, glancing between the two of them.

He pulled Jade's missing glove out of his pocket. "You left this behind."

Jade took the item, warm from where it had nestled close to his—*Don't go there. This is Benji.* "Thanks."

"Is there something I missed here?" Laura's voice broke the magic floating in the air.

"Benji," she said, emphasizing the nickname, "gave me a ride home from the airport."

His emerald eyes darkened. "Well, I've got shopping to do. Excuse me, ladies." He leaned between them, close enough that he grazed Jade's chest with a shoulder as he reached for a basket from the stack.

Laura waited until he walked to the back of the store before grabbing Jade's arm. "Dish."

Reeling from his accidental touch, she searched for the right words. "It's Benji, for Pete's sake. We haven't had anything in common since I started wearing a training bra. There's nothing to dish. It would be weird."

"I'll tell you what's weird. The air sizzled with chemical attraction just now. Any fool can see you connect."

"No..."

"C'mon, get in the Christmas spirit. You know, love thy neighbor." Laura giggled under her breath.

"Ha ha, very funny."

Laura leaned close, glanced toward the back of the store then whispered. "Sparks like that are rare. Trust me." She moved behind the counter with a knowing expression.

Jade began shopping, her mind warring with her body on the subject of her hunky ex-neighbor. Yes, Ben was attractive. Yes, there were some major fireworks between them, but that wasn't a basis for a lasting relationship. No, they would be friends at most and nothing more.

She plopped the last item into her shopping basket and came up to the cash register just as Ben set a large bag of dog food and assorted items on the counter.

He glanced at her car through the storefront window. "I see you have transport."

She nodded. "My mom's. Where's Sadie?"

"In the truck. We're headed out for a walk along Main Street as soon as I'm finished here. It's a pretty time of year with the snow and decorated storefronts."

"That's nice." She set her basket on the counter. "Thanks for my glove."

"You're welcome." He nodded to Laura. "Say hi to Kenny for me."

No sooner had the door shut than Laura whirled on her. "He was asking you to join him. Why didn't you say yes?"

She played dumb. "Huh?"

"You treated him like he was barely there."

Heat rushed onto Jade's chest. "I did not." She handed Laura her credit card.

Laura swiped the card and handed it back with a receipt. "Didn't you?"

She shook her head and picked up her grocery bag. "You

must be imagining things."

Her friend shrugged and walked her to the door. They talked about old friends and recent news, before Laura said, "I have next Tuesday off and Kenny's taking the kids ice skating after school. Do you want to get together then?"

Jade wasn't sure of anything right now but she didn't want to be viewed as the town Grinch. "Sounds fun."

They said their goodbyes and Jade headed back into the chilly night. Ben's vehicle was still parked behind hers. He crossed the street toward her, Sadie loping beside him.

She placed the groceries in the trunk and opened the driver's side door.

"Hey."

She froze, his deep voice sending a shiver of awareness through her. "Hey."

He stepped onto the sidewalk next to her. "Want to stop by the Main Street Café, have a cup? They make a mean mocha latte." He nodded toward the brick building down the block with white twinkling lights and big red bows.

"Sorry, can't." She pointed to the car. "Mom needs it back soon."

"I could follow you, drop Sadie off at the parents, and bring you back."

She shook her head. "I think Jack may be bringing the kids over tonight and I don't want to miss them." That was a bald-faced lie, but he didn't need to know that.

Ben moved away from the car, Sadie quiet beside him. "Well, have fun with the twins. Maybe another time."

She ducked her head and slipped into the car, avoiding his gaze. Ben had been her best friend from the day after his family moved next door when they were about to enter kindergarten until the second week of eighth grade. She had hurt him enough, and hurt herself just as much, turning her back on who she really was. Now, finally, she was trying to get her life back on track, with plans for graduate school that would take her far away again. Mom was worried enough about her quitting her job and starting this new plan, not to mention the fact that Ben Stephens wasn't her flavor of the month, right now.

How could Jade possibly respond to him when they had no future?

Chapter Five

BEN WATCHED THE Subaru disappear around the corner of Main Street.

She'd turned him down. She trembled when she accepted her glove from him, held his gaze for longer than was deemed merely polite, yet she'd turned him down. He hadn't had too many experiences since hitting adulthood where a woman interested in him refused his advances, and this one really bothered him.

She'd called the shots on their relationship in the eighth grade, and left him bewildered and ashamed. This time, he wasn't going to let that happen. She would be in Starling for a month. He had shot award-winning films in less time. He had thirty days to find out exactly what Jade Engel was really about, and what he really felt about her after all this time, and he was going to do it or die trying.

✦ ✦ ✦

THE FOLLOWING MORNING, Jade stepped into her parents' sunny kitchen, where a plethora of delicious aromas filled the air. Her mother was making a batch of peanut brittle at the counter while her father and grandmother ate breakfast at the table. She made the rounds, hugging and kissing them each before she slipped onto the chair next to her grandmother snuggled in a daisy-yellow housecoat.

Her grandmother pushed her round wire-rimmed glasses onto her nose. "Morning, my girl." Her plump face beamed and short white curls bobbed as her scooped scrambled eggs using a spoon in her good hand.

"Sleep well?" Her mother cocked her head.

She nodded and poured a glass of orange juice from the carton. No need to worry the family about her insomnia. She'd get back on track with sleep once she settled into her new routine and life.

"Your father is taking Grandma to the Senior Center after PT then he's off to work. Would you mind bringing her home when she's done? Also, I offered to make the angel costumes for the Children's Nativity Pageant. Pastor Dan called and said they have the materials ready for pick up. Could you stop at the church hall on your way to the Senior Center?"

Jade smiled. These were the kind of activities she needed to take her mind off her murky future and lackluster personal life. "Sure. Anything else?"

Her father handed her the bowl of scrambled eggs. "Eat. From the looks of you, you can't afford to lose any more weight."

She rolled her eyes. "No need to worry about me. I love to eat." She spooned two healthy scoops of eggs onto her plate then reached for the platter of bacon. "I've missed Mom's cooking."

An hour later, Jade pulled into the church hall parking lot at the far end of Main Street. An older, heavyset woman with short black hair shaped in a stylish bob appeared at the entrance of the white building next to the gray stone church, her arms filled with packages.

Ben's mom.

Jade exited the car and called to her. "Hi, Mrs. Stephens. Need a hand?"

"I'm fine." She came puffing up the walkway. "Ben told me you were home. Good to see you." She deposited her cargo onto the back seat of her Volvo before turning back for a quick hug and kiss. "Hate to run, but I'm late for my dentist appointment." She climbed into her car. "See you all at my house the twelfth."

Jade waved goodbye and headed down the cement path to the church hall. She was met by a handful of ladies she'd known since childhood along with Pastor Dan, new to the congregation since she'd moved away. He was a pleasant man about her age, married like all of the ladies' sons. Jade was an Old Maid by Starling standards, single at twenty-nine.

The ladies motioned for her to join them at the large table laid out with fabric in neat piles of blue, beige, brown, and white. Alice took charge as usual. "Your mother's making the three angel costumes." She pointed to the first packet on the right. "There's the pattern. Read the list of materials on the sheet stapled to it and take what you need."

"Thanks." Jade measured and cut the correct number of yards of white satin for the robes and tulle for the wings then gathered two spools of wide silver ribbon, a spool of wire, and two large plastic bags of downy white feathers.

She couldn't help but overhear as Alice spoke to the group. "I don't know what we're going to do. Millie was supposed to be in charge of the project, but she has her hands full with work and family."

One of the women replied, "What we need are some young people to take over the job."

Jade glanced up from her task. This could be another activity that would help pass the days. "Can I help?"

The five church ladies gazed at her with hope.

Alice shook her head, her gray mane bobbing. "Oh, dear, I'm sure you're busy helping your mother. She has her hand in everything. I imagine you'll be running errands from now until New Year's."

Jade pulled up a chair and joined the group. "I'm the same as Mom. I like to be busy. What does the project involve?"

Alice patted her hand. "Well, let us tell you…"

Jade listened as the five ladies explained the project. By the end of the conversation, she had signed on as lead volunteer. She would visit shut-ins and other people in need, decorating their homes for the season and delivering holiday meals and goodies provided by the Starling Women's Guild.

She thanked the women and drove next to Starling Senior Center to join Grandma Bertie. She stepped out of her car and walked through the center's automatic doors. A group of elderly gentlemen sat in a circle in the large, airy foyer with a roaring fireplace as its centerpiece, laughing and playing with a Golden Retriever that looked like Sadie.

At the sound of footsteps, Jade turned. She caught her breath. The dog *was* Sadie.

Ben smiled at her, coffee in hand. "Following me?"

"I believe I was at the Country Store before you."

"True that."

She smiled. "Is Sadie a therapy dog?"

He nodded. "One of her many talents."

"I thought you had a business to run. How do you have the freedom to lounge around while people pet your dog in the middle of a work week?"

"There are many perks to running your own business. One is that you make your own hours." He smiled and greeted a resident rolling past in a wheelchair.

She looked around for her grandmother, but didn't spot her.

"Looking for Bertie?"

She nodded.

"I saw her in the Media Room with a couple of her girlfriends." He pointed to a closed door of an adjacent activity room.

"Oh, thanks." She glanced around, looking for a quiet place to sit.

"Coffee while you wait?" He handed her a to-go cup and indicated the coffee urn behind her.

She poured a steaming cup and sighed. *Ah, hazelnut.* Thank goodness for caffeine.

"How are your mom and dad?"

The question reminded her of her mother's concern about Ben. She added two creams and stirred. "Fine. Are you and Jeremy still friends?"

He tilted his head at her. "I recently hired him. Does that answer your question?"

She stirred in the sugar. "There are people with the impression you encouraged his drinking. Any truth in that?"

Ben flinched before crossing his arms. He leaned back against the wall. "I'm not perfect, and yes, I did drink with him—before and after the accident. Is that the reason he started having trouble? I guess you'd have to ask Jeremy."

"I've been gently warned to stay away from you," she said.

He turned toward her, his face mere inches from hers, his voice soft. "And do you want to?"

She ignored his fresh mountain scent, addictive like the coffee in her hand. "I want the loved ones in my life to be happy," she answered.

I want myself back. But how does that happen?

If it involved keeping Ben Stephens out of her life, she didn't know.

His voice was direct, without a trace of hurt. "I'll take that as my cue to leave then, because I apparently don't fit in that category." He whistled softly to Sadie then turned back to her, pinning her with those brilliant green eyes. "One day you'll want to follow your own path instead of the one set before you by others. You know, like you used to do before you entered middle school."

"I had to grow up, think about the future. I couldn't party my days away the second half of my teens and first half of my twenties like some people I know. My family couldn't afford for me to do that."

"I'm not talking about being responsible, Jade. I'm talking about following your passion." He bit out the words. "You're not happy. Anyone with half a brain can see that." He ran both hands through his hair. "What are you searching for?"

Her jaw dropped open. If she had the answer to that question, she'd be sleeping at night. She wouldn't be hesitating about which grad school program to choose, and she certainly wouldn't be standing here wanting him to kiss her but sending him away because her mother didn't trust him and she didn't understand or trust herself.

"Think about it," he said quietly. Sadie joined him and he bent to reattach her leash. "I miss the girl I used to know, the one who followed the beat of her own drum, without a care for what everyone else expected of her." He frowned. "I wonder if I'll ever see her again." With that, he turned and left.

Chapter Six

JADE ENTERED HER bedroom and closed the door behind her, a mixed bag of emotions after one day in Starling. She sank onto her bed as her cell phone chimed.

Bree had texted. *Have you told your parents?* She texted back. *They took the news well, aside from Mom's concern about my choosing a profession that pays poorly and is thankless.* Her phone chimed again. *Sounds like Aunt Gigi. You okay? I'm concerned about you. How's your grandma?* She swore Bree had a sixth sense when it came to reading people. It was utterly useless keeping secrets from her. She typed: *Remember Benji, my next door neighbor? Well, he's all grown up. Took me awhile to recognize him. Oh my. But he's a real PITA.* Bree shot back. *Panty dropper potential?* Jade snorted before typing one last message. *Not going there. Not worth it. See "pain in the butt" reference above.* Bree typed back. *Why not? Maybe he's your Christmas gift.*

Jade sighed and set her phone on the nightstand so she could begin her nighttime routine. Bree suggested hooking up as if she did it herself, but Jade knew better. In fact, her friend was the most conservative of the five girls, in spite of her status as a single mother.

Jade moved to her bathroom to wash her face. Bree would have been an incredible physician if she hadn't gotten pregnant at nineteen and needed to turn all her efforts into raising a child. Everyone loved Charlie, the girl was a blessing in their lives, but Bree's life had been forever changed because she'd lost her head over a guy. So had Cass's and Kara's, for that matter.

Her face clean, Jade threw on a tee and yoga pants. She tiptoed downstairs past Grandma Bertie dozing in her favorite chair in the living room, and turned on the kitchen light before opening the fridge for some milk.

Her father appeared in the doorway. "Any trouble on the roads with that dusting of snow?"

She shook her head and poured two glasses of milk. Her father liked to eat as much as her. "How was work?" She set their drinks on the kitchen table.

"Good." He sank onto a chair and folded his beefy hands under his sizeable chin. "Speaking of work, are you sure about this change you've made?"

She picked up the platter of peanut brittle and set it on the table between them as she sat beside him. "I'm sure about leaving marketing."

His voice echoed in the quiet kitchen. "Your mother was pretty upset yesterday. We worry you're making a big mistake." He leaned forward. "But it's not too late to fix it. You could call your old boss, apologize, and ask for your job back. No shame in that."

She pasted on a smile. "Thanks, Dad." She handed him a chunk of peanut brittle. "I'll take that into consideration."

He took a bite. "Your mother also thinks there may be something going on in, ah, your personal life."

Ah, so her mother was behind this late night chat. Her back went rigid. "I'll be fine, Daddy. Things are different than when you were my age. Lots of twenty-nine-year-olds are still single." Like all her best friends. Their lives were cautionary tales about why a woman needed to take her time when choosing her soul mate. She washed the candy down with a swig of cold milk.

All four of her friends were intelligent and beautiful and sophisticated. Three were unlucky when it came to love. Cass was successful, but loneliness oozed out of her pores, and all because of that wandering Irish musician she'd fallen for years ago. The girl had even gotten a tat, for God's sake. That was serious stuff. Kara's boyfriend had seemed like he was in the relationship for the long haul. Jade had become hopeful there may be good guys in her generation, but as soon as he learned he was to about to become a father, the jerk had split, leaving the girls to pick up the pieces of their friend's heart. So what if he sent child support payments like clockwork? He wasn't there for Kara like he should be. What was he going to do, show up in a decade and throw her into a tailspin like what was happening now with Bree and Jake? No, thank you.

Loving and losing was too much to bear.

Besides, look what had happened when she'd let down her guard and fallen for Alex. Finished with her brittle, she stood and kissed the top of her father's bald head. He was better off not knowing the sordid details. "Love you."

"Love you, too. Sleep well." Her father patted her shoulder.

Sleep well? Yeah, that had been working so well for her lately.

✦ ✦ ✦

THE FOLLOWING MORNING, Jade arrived at the first home on her list for the Starling Lights Project. A green SUV was parked in the driveway. "What the—" She double-checked the list of addresses Alice had given her with the boxes of supplies. Yup. She had the correct address. She exited the car and began the short walk up the dirt driveway, frowning at the man on the ladder partly responsible for her enduring yet another poor night of sleep.

"Morning." Ben's deep, cheery voice floated down to her. He stopped stapling a string of Christmas lights along the front roof line to glance down at her. "What's doing?"

She shaded her eyes with a hand and peered up at him, his broad shoulders flanked by brilliant morning sun. "That's what I was going to ask."

"I told you to stop following me around." He smiled.

"I'm serious." Her neck was starting to hurt from staring up at him. "This is my job. Alice assigned me as lead volunteer for the Starling Lights Project. You're not supposed to be here."

"Actually, I am. Alice stopped me in town last evening and begged me to train the new lead volunteer with the work. She didn't give me the details, but that gleam in her eyes makes perfect sense now." He laughed and returned to his task, as if small town match-making rolled off him like water from a duck's back.

She fumed. "That was nice of her but I'm quite capable of hanging decorations and connecting strings of lights without instruction."

He descended a few rungs. "Can you give me a hand?" He pointed to the package of staples on the driveway next to the ladder.

She stepped between two snow-covered bushes and handed him a strip of staples. "I was tricked."

"Appears we both were."

"You don't seem too bothered about it," she observed.

He shrugged. "Why should I? It's a beautiful day. Have you been away so long you forgot how everyone in Starling is in cahoots with everyone else's business?"

His words from their last conversation popped into her head. "I thought you don't worry about what people think." She was being bratty but she couldn't help it. Her mother would be worried about her working with Ben and the rest of the town would speculate about their relationship. And she'd already heard the rumors about his ex.

He finished attaching the last of the lights to the house and inserted the prongs to the other set's plug around the corner before stepping down. "Look, you can stand there, go home, or stay and work. I don't care which you choose. I can handle this myself."

She dug in her heels. "I was really excited and I wanted to do this." She stuffed her fingers back into her gloves.

"Then stay. It's completely up to you. This will be my only full day, anyway. I have business the rest of the week." He walked ahead of her to the house's front door.

Inside the cozy home that smelled faintly of mint and cinnamon, an elderly woman sat in a wingback chair next to a china cabinet filled with beautiful collectible teacup and saucer sets. "You all done?" The elderly woman leaned forward to pet Sadie.

Ben spoke a few decibels louder than normal. "Outside's finished, Mrs. Reichert. "Remember Jade Engel?"

The old woman joked, "I'm lucky to remember my own name." She pointed to the seven-foot silver tree in the corner of the room. "You young ones going to help me decorate too? Always was my husband's favorite part of the holiday." Her voice caught.

The woman's words tugged at Jade's heart. So what if a nosy body in Starling was trying to push her and Ben together.

She sat on a chair next to the lady. "I'd love to."

She opened boxes of ornaments and listened to Mrs. Reichert's stories about each one as Ben wound the lights around the artificial tree. Once the lights were set, the two of them arranged the ornaments onto the tree under the older woman's direction.

"All we need is the angel," Jade said. She looked around at the array of empty boxes. "It's got to be here somewhere."

Mrs. Reichert sighed. "Oh dear, it must be in the attic."

"I'll get it. Be right back." Ben zipped up the stairs.

Mrs. Reichert patted Jade's shoulder. "I like your young man. So respectful."

"We're not a couple." *No matter how much my girly parts tingle when he's around.*

"Oh, beg your pardon. My mistake."

Jade turned to stack the empty boxes for their return to the attic. "Would you like me to make you something to eat before we finish up here?"

"A cup of tea would be nice. The homecare lady will come by later to fix me lunch."

Jade nodded and scurried into the woman's functional galley kitchen, putting a kettle on to boil and locating three mugs and the teabags before she returned to the living room to find Ben teetering on the stepstool, positioning the angel just right.

"There." He stepped down and grinned at Mrs. Reichert.

The old woman clapped her hands in delight. "Beautiful." She wiped at the corner of an eye with an embroidered handkerchief.

He sat on a chair facing the lady. "All the lights, indoors and out, are on a timer so you don't have to worry about that, and remember, SLP will reimburse a portion of your electric bill for the month." He handed her a sheet of paper. "This is the number to call if you have any questions or need anything. Okay?"

The woman smiled up at him. "Stay for tea?"

He caught Jade's eyes and held her gaze. "I wouldn't miss it."

The kettle whistled and Jade jumped. She sped back into the kitchen, poured their tea, and carried the tray with the three mugs to the living room, reciting her mantra about figuring out what she truly wanted before she dove into another relationship.

Thirty minutes later, they said their goodbyes to the sweet lady at 24 Graham Street and headed out the door.

Ben turned to her. "Want to share a ride? Saves gas."

"I can't leave the car here."

He glanced at the sheet. "There are only three more jobs on the list today. I'll have you back before dark."

"Okay." She risked a smile. "But only for the gas." She waited for Sadie to jump into the SUV between them before she perched on her corner of the passenger seat.

"Going green is good," Ben said lightly.

Chapter Seven

THEY MADE QUICK work at the next two houses, placing lights in the windows on the one-story homes and attaching an Adirondack pine bough wreath to each of their front doors. By the time they arrived at the final house of the day, Jade was famished. She had drunk tea at Mrs. Reichert's, eaten a slice of pie at the second house and chocolate fudge at the last, but she craved protein and veggies. Tomorrow she'd pack a lunch.

They pulled up next to an ornate wrought iron fence surrounding a distinguished cream, purple, and gray Victorian house set in the center of a huge corner lot at the intersection of Kirk Street and Dunn Avenue, two of Starling's most exclusive streets.

Jade counted three windows on two of the third-floor turret room's four sides. "Wow."

"It's the oldest house in Starling and dates back to 1840." Ben turned off the ignition and exited the car.

"Pre-Civil War Era." She accepted the box Ben handed her. "I've always admired this house but never been inside. Other kids told me the owner was a mean hermit."

"Mr. V is okay." Ben opened the gate to one of three cleared cement walks that led to the impeccable home. "Wait until you see the inside." He whistled to Sadie, who romped ahead of them, tail wagging, snuffling the snow.

Jade stepped onto the expansive covered porch and lifted the brass knocker on the purple door. After several knocks, a man standing behind a walker opened the door with a grunt.

She and Ben introduced themselves while Sadie licked the man's fingers.

Mr. Van Salzberg waved them in with one hand. "They called to tell me you were on your way." He shuffled back to a lounger in front of a TV and eased into a sitting position with a sigh.

Jade wanted to sit and chat with the man but their errand came first. Sadie loped over to the man and rested her head on the arm of the lounger, gazing at him with adoring eyes, but Mr. V acted like he didn't notice her. Did he live here all alone in this huge house? No family or friends? She glanced at the TV tray in front of his recliner. Did he always eat alone, with only the TV for company?

"Let's start at the top floor." Ben's gruff voice pulled her out of her thoughts.

They arrived at their destination and Jade peered inside the box she carried. "Do we have enough for all these windows?"

He peered into his box too. "If not, I have more in the back of my truck."

She set the box next to his and pulled out the first electric candle to hand over to Ben. She had managed to avoid contact with him all day, but her luck ended at that moment. The candle hit the hardwood floor with a smash and a curse split the air. "Sorry."

"I've got it," Ben said.

They crouched simultaneously to retrieve the dropped

item and brushed knees. Jade fell back hard onto the glossy wood floor. "Ouch."

Ben held out his hand. "You okay?"

She rubbed her bottom and scrambled to her feet by herself. "I'm fine."

He reached into the box for a new candle then stopped. "Remember that time we were climbing that big old willow tree at the edge of Robinson's property and that branch broke?"

"I still have a scar between my ribs from where I landed on that sharp rock." She shuddered. "I couldn't breathe, and...you half-carried, half-dragged me to their house to get help."

"You were turning blue."

"All I remember was thinking I couldn't take a breath. Next thing I knew I was lying on a blue velvet couch and I thought I'd died. But then I saw you sitting across from me, those big green eyes staring at me. You looked so scared." She picked up the remnants of the broken candle and placed it in the tote bag slung over her shoulder. "I was lucky."

"Yeah, kids do dangerous things." He chuckled. "We kept our guardian angels plenty busy."

She laughed. "Still, we had some great adventures." Her voice trailed off. Why had she thrown away their friendship? They had been inseparable. He had been the one person who accepted her as she was and encouraged her to follow her dreams. He didn't care that she hated the color pink, and loved to climb trees and play in the dirt—unlike most girls in Starling. Her throat tightened and she searched his face for a hint of her former best friend, unspoken yearnings growing inside her.

He cursed and pulled her close, wrapping his strong arms around her.

"Ben?" Her protest sounded more like a plea, everything else slipping away but the desire to be close to him. She reached up and pulled his head toward hers.

She wanted him. He wanted her.

And they both knew it.

His lips were hot and wet on hers, seeking she-didn't-know-what and bringing her along for the mysterious ride. It was too overwhelming, too confusing, too risky.

I have to stop...

"No." She unthreaded her fingers from his thick hair and pushed against his shoulders.

He lifted his mouth from hers, a question in his eyes.

She dropped her head against his chest and listened to his racing heartbeat. It matched hers. *We can't do this.* Her mother had warned her away for a reason. He wasn't married like Alex, but he surely had secrets that could destroy her just as easily. She looked up. "I'm sorry."

He nodded, wiping his mouth with the back of one hand before reaching out and tipping up her chin so he could look in her eyes. His words were soft but filled with intent. "I want you. That's not going to change. Let me know when you've figured things out."

She leaned back against the turret room's floral wallpaper, slid down wall to sit on the gleaming wood floor, a boneless, miserable pile. She rested her head in her hands, her legs splayed in front of her. "I'm too tired to think."

He crouched next to her and placed a hand on her knee.

The heat from his palm seared her, spreading warmth from her knee to her inner thighs and beyond. Part of her didn't want the delicious sensations to end, but logic warned that giving into this could only cause them hurt—and they had both hurt enough.

"What's going on, Jade?" he said softly.

She dropped her hands. "I knew coming home would cause memories to resurface. I guess I just underestimated how many. I'd hoped it would bring my life clarity, but—" she twisted her hands in her lap, "I'm more confused and conflicted than when I arrived."

He sat back on his heels. "Yeah, the past has a way of haunting us when we least expect it." He turned and sat next to her, his back against the wall. "What's haunting you?"

She took a deep breath, now picking at her sweater's hem. "Remember how we used to tell each other everything?"

"Uh huh." He sat next to her. "Until we didn't."

She crossed her arms. "I treated you like you were my worst enemy and you'd done nothing wrong. I buckled under pressure. One of the popular girls singled me out, targeted me because I was different."

He leaned close. "Your differences are what I've missed the most," he whispered. "It was when you followed the crowd that we lost each other."

She gritted her teeth. "Being different is social suicide in junior high."

He sighed. "Was it really that bad, Jade, so bad that you resorted to targeting your best friend?"

A tear rolled down her cheek. "I'm so sorry. I wish I could undo it. But I can't." She squeezed her hands together until the tips of her fingers turned white. Talking about this didn't change what she had done, or fill the hole in her heart created by her own hand, but he deserved the explanation anyhow. "I hated that our friendship put me on the school bully's radar. That's why I was so cruel to you. It's not an excuse, but it's the reason. I wanted to end the name-calling, the jokes with me as the punch line." She sighed. "Looking back, I suspect I still would have been targeted. Your friendship with me wasn't the cause, but a side-effect of my condition."

"Condition? I don't understand. What could have been so bad that you turned on me?" He reached over and wiped her tears with the flat of his palm. "Tell me. What happened?"

She took a ragged breath and swiped a hand across her runny nose. "I—I can't talk about it." Another shudder racked her body and she squeezed her eyes shut in a feeble attempt to block the painful images, but they flooded in, consuming her.

Before she knew it, she was spilling her guts to him, telling him all that she had held in for almost eighteen years. "It was the first day of eighth grade. I had just covered my hands with that slimy pink goo Starling Central called soap. I was about to turn on the water when the door to the bathroom opened and four of our classmates spilled in, chattering about boys and clothes…"

"Well, look who's here," Amy Wilder remarked to her cronies.

Jade looked in the mirror at the girls approaching from her left. They crowded in behind her, their trendy clothes and clunky shoes, pin-straight locks, and Sunflower perfume mocking her plain white button-down, jeans, and Converse sneakers. Jade had never been particularly close with this crew, or any of the girls in her class for that matter. She was what her teachers called a flitter, friendly with everyone but close to no one. Except for Benji. He was her buddy.

Amy pulled out her LipSmackers and threw a sideways glance at Jade. "The boys' room is down the hall."

"The boys' room?"

The other three girls giggled.

Jade's mouth fell open. "What's so funny?"

Amy leaned over the sink to reapply color to her already pink, shiny lips. She stopped. "Don't look at me. I don't want to turn you on."

What was going on? Jade's stomach dropped like she was in a roller coaster that had just begun its rapid descent from an impossibly steep incline.

Nicolette chimed in. "It will be so uncomfortable changing in gym if you are." She shuddered.

"*Well, are you?" Brittney's shrill voice bounced off the tile walls.*

Jade turned around and looked from one girl to the next, pink goo dripping unheeded to the floor. What were they asking her? She felt slow. She was *slow.*

"I see I need to spell this out for you." Amy clucked with displeasure. "You're gay, Jade, and you don't even know it. You're a lesbian."

The last word echoed in the small space and into Jade's brain. Comprehension dawned. She clutched the sink with gooey hands and fought to keep down her breakfast, that coaster inside her stomach racing around a sharp corner and out of control, off the tracks.

She stared at herself in the streaked mirror. Her hair was short, her face nude, and her eyebrows thick and untamed. She looked down. Her nails were bitten short and had never been polished. She didn't wear jewelry and her only scent the citrus deodorant her mother made her wear because she refused to use perfume.

She thought about her friends from downstate. They didn't dress and act like her, either. Maybe they accepted her only because they had to. Their mothers were best friends. Or maybe they just hadn't noticed the truth about her yet – a truth she'd never even considered. Would they turn against her too?

She felt stupid for taking so long to understand what the girls were even talking about, stupid for having no idea if they were right. They said it as if there was no question.

More girls entered the bathroom, banging open stall doors in the mad pee-dash and checking their make-up in the large wall mirror. A few joined the semi-circle around the sinks, some curious, others like they simply enjoyed being part of a hyena pack, waiting for the kill.

"Well, are *you gay?"*

Amy's voice slipped down Jade's back like ice water, a cold wake-up call. She covered her ears with her hands, pink goo now in her tangle of hair, and gave the worst possible answer. Worse than either yes or no. "I-I don't know."

The girls squealed and clutched each other, looking to their fearless leader for guidance.

"You. Don't. Know." Amy crossed her arms like Mrs. Warren in English class about to impart a kernel of knowledge significant to the test. "So work it out. Normal girls dress like us, not you. Normal girls aren't friends with boys. We date them, if they're cute, but that doesn't include geeks like Benji Stephens." She tucked her lip balm back into her purse and snapped it closed. "You get the picture? Do you still not know?" She gave Jade a last deadly look-over before she turned to leave with the other girls. "See ya."

Jade waited until they had all sashayed out in their pastel tops and short skirts. The third period bell rang, and on numb legs she managed to get herself to class.

Now, she stared at the pattern of flowers on the wall opposite where she sat. "All I could think was that I wanted to be like all the other girls. I wanted to know I was fine, normal, sure about things." She heaved a long sigh, dreading the part she was going to share next. "I turned on the water, and as I cleaned the pink off my hand and out of my hair, I made up my mind. I would change. I would learn to be like the rest of them, and the first thing I needed to do was cut you out of my life."

"And you did."

"And I did."

He stood, cleared his throat, walked around, looking everywhere but at her. "We should get moving if we want to finish before nightfall."

"Yeah." She brushed off her jeans, her limbs as weak as they'd been in eighth grade. Did she have the energy to stand?

Would Ben look at her differently now? Was he wondering, as she had, whether what the girls had said was true? She didn't have an issue with other people's sexual orientation, but maybe he did. Maybe he would despise her for having so little knowledge of herself, and so little faith in who she might turn out to be.

But no. When his eyes met hers, they crinkled back at her with...friendship.

Her heart swelled. She had missed him so much. So much. Maybe sharing her private pain had been worth it. Maybe it wasn't too late to make amends. Start something. Find something.

Smiling, she reached out, his hand enveloping hers. "Okay, let's do this."

Chapter Eight

JADE PEERED INTO Mr. Van Salzberg's living room. Sadie was asleep near the old man's feet while a game show blared from the big screen TV in the Victorian mansion.

She and Ben had worked side-by-side, placing an electric candle in each of the home's windows, connecting them with extension cords and setting up the timers. The simple, repetitive task did little to alleviate the sizzle in the air between them. An accidental hand brush here, a heated glance there, they'd worked their way from floor to opulent floor and room to beautiful room. By the time they reached the ground floor where they stood now, Jade's nerves were shot.

One more touch or glance and she'd break into a thousand pieces.

He'd been holding back, she was certain of that. What if he kissed her again and let it all go? She shivered, rubbing her sweater-clad arms.

"Why don't you sit in front of the fireplace while I take care of these last few windows?" He didn't wait for a response, taking the box with the remaining materials toward the back of the house.

Jade strode into the living room. "We're about finished with the lights. Are you sure you don't want us to get a tree for you?"

The man turned watery eyes toward her. "No children. No wife. No need for a tree."

She sat on the couch next to his recliner. "Do you have plans for Christmas, any friends coming to visit?"

The man ignored her question, turning his attention back to the TV.

"Mister Van Salzberg, would you like me to get you anything to eat or drink?"

"I could use a Scotch."

"Anything to eat?"

"Pizza's in the fridge."

"Do you want it heated up?" She resisted the urge to wring her hands as a helpless feeling washed over her.

"I like it cold." Her voice was flat.

She strode to the kitchen, holding back tears.

Ben leaned over the sink, placing a candle in the window above it when she entered. "There. All done."

She walked to the refrigerator, turning her face away from him so he wouldn't sense her fragility.

"Hungry?" he asked.

"Getting Mr. V. a snack." She located the leftover pizza on the bottom shelf. "Where would someone keep Scotch in a house like this?"

"I'm that horrible a co-worker?" Ben joked.

She rolled her eyes. "It's for Mr. V."

"I'll get it." He disappeared into another room, somewhere off the kitchen, returning with a bottle to join her at the counter. He gave her a long, thoughtful look. "Do you know the history of candles in windows, the idea behind the Starling Lights Project?"

She dropped her shoulders. "It's about sharing the Christmas spirit, right?"

He threw her a sidelong glance and opened the Scotch.

She handed him a tumbler with ice cubes. "Something to do with the Star of Bethlehem?"

He gave a brief nod. "Close. In Ireland, people placed lit candles in windows to signal secret religious gatherings. In other European nations, especially ones like your home country of Germany," he nudged her with his elbow, "a lit candle in a window symbolized the hearth, the center of family life." He poured the drink.

She scrunched her nose. "Why do you think this tradition so important to the community?"

Ben lifted a shoulder. "The Adirondacks can be a harsh environment. Only the bravest of souls traveled to the New World and the hardiest of them eventually ventured to settle here. I imagine it was comfort to carry on those traditions from their homelands." He chuckled. "We're still isolated here to a certain extent, with all major roads, train lines, and airports an hour or more away. So we depend on each other, and hold fast to our ways." He stopped. "I'm sorry. I didn't mean to ramble. Did any of that make sense?"

"Yeah, oddly enough, it did." She smiled.

He nodded at the plate in her hand. "Ready?"

The thin man dozed in his recliner, his face lined and unhappy even in sleep. Ben turned off the TV and set the drink on the table beside the lounger. Jade set the plate near the Scotch and reached for an afghan on the couch to cover the gentleman.

Ben shook his head.

She stopped and mouthed, "Why not?"

He pointed at the ashtray with the smoldering cigar on the table. He leaned toward the sleeping man. "Mr. Van Salzberg?"

he whispered.

Sadie woke. At the dog's movement, the man opened his eyes.

Ben pointed to the table. "Here's your snack, Mr. V. I left the papers with SLP's phone number if you need anything else. Okay?" At the man's nod, he walked toward the foyer where Jade's and his coats were hung. "Nice seeing you."

Mr. Van Salzberg blinked at Jade. "You're leaving too?"

She leaned forward and patted the man's frail arm. It trembled beneath her hand. "It was wonderful meeting you today. I promise to come back." She gave his arm a gentle squeeze.

A glimmer of a smile graced the man's face. He nodded. "See you tomorrow then." He closed his eyes again.

She and Ben bundled into their coats and left the house, quietly locking the door behind them. He threw a quizzical look over his shoulder as they walked down the long path to his vehicle.

"What?" Jade asked, as she pulled on her hat and shoved her gloves into her coat pockets.

He didn't break stride. "So…I see you like older guys, much older."

"Really?" She ran to sock him with a playful punch, but he was too quick for her, catching her fist in his hand. They squared off in the middle of Mr. Van Salzberg's path. She watched, mesmerized, as Ben brought her hand up to his mouth and planted a kiss on her bare knuckles. There was a teasing glint in his eyes. "You're eager to strike up a friendship with grumpy Mr. V. but you refuse to have a coffee with a charming guy like me?"

"Stop already," she laughed, tugging against his grip.

Ben released her hand and stuffed his bare ones into jeans pockets. "Seriously, Jade." He began walking backwards on the path in front of her. "Why the effort?"

She glanced back at the huge house. "He needs a friend." She strode forward.

He turned as she started past him. "Yes, and you used to be mine. We can have it back. The truth is out between us. It can't hurt us anymore."

Her breath hitched at his words and she glanced over her shoulder. "I'm only here for a few weeks."

He lifted a shoulder. "I'll take it."

She pulled on her gloves against the growing chill, and gestured for him to join her. Sure, they both felt the attraction but they were adults. They could control themselves. Why risk losing out on the potential of a lasting friendship because of a short-term thrill?

Together, they walked the rest of the way to his SUV. Ben started the engine, readied the car for the short trip, and soon they were on their way. She relaxed, sinking into the heated leather seat, listening to the whirring tires until they arrived at the street where her mother's car was parked.

Blue shadows nestled in the snow, the sky overcast, and dusk falling. She picked up her purse and patted Sadie's soft head draped over the front seat between Ben and her. "Thanks." She threw her SLP partner a smile.

Ben shifted into park. "I'll be away on business the next couple days, but I should be home Friday the latest." He turned to her. "I'd like to see you."

Bree's text about Ben being her Christmas gift came back to her. No one could ever have too many friends, and mending her relationship with the boy next door seemed as good a place to start as any. "I'd like that. Friends?"

"It's a start." He leaned forward and gave her a kiss, hotter than the one he'd snuck in Mr. Van Salzberg's house, causing her fingers to wrap around his broad shoulders and her toes to curl inside her toasty Uggs.

He pulled away with a stifled groan. "Enjoy the rest of your week."

"You too," she breathed. She struggled with her seatbelt, managed to unbuckle it after three tries, open the car door, and stumble to her mother's vehicle. *Whoa. Friends?* Who was she fooling?

+ + +

TWO DAYS LATER Ben stood in his living room, staring out his floor-to-ceiling windows that formed his home's east wall as the sun set on Starling Lake's serene waters. He'd expected the view, along with the pine scent of his freshly cut Christmas tree to take the edge off his restlessness, but they hadn't done the trick. He turned and stared at the paltry number of ornament boxes stacked next to the couch.

This was his first Christmas in the new house. The tree deserved to be decorated with respect, not look like one Charlie Brown had bought. "Time for another trip into town, girl." He scratched behind Sadie's ears. "We've got some shopping to do."

But then his phone trilled out its Christmas ring tone and when he picked it up he heard his mother's voice. "How was Lake George?"

He jingled the leash as he paced in the foyer. "Fine."

"I won't keep you, just calling to remind you about the party next Friday."

He chuckled. "Have I ever missed your holiday dinner party?"

"Well, there's always a first." She hesitated. "I heard from Alice at church that you volunteered for SLP."

"Yes." He scratched his head. Where was this conversation

headed?

"Would that be before or after Jade Engel signed up?"

Aha. Real reason for the call. "You tell me. Alice was the one doing the arranging."

"You didn't have to agree to it."

"Now that wouldn't have been Christmassy of me, now would it?"

She sighed. "Benjamin. You just ended things with Sofia. Do you think dating my friend's daughter so soon is wise?"

"Wise? I thought being with Sofia was wise, but look how that turned out. Let's not over-analyze it." He pulled on his leather jacket.

"Gigi is very protective of her kids."

He snorted. "Are you saying you're not? Say hi to Dad for me. See you next Friday if not before. Right now I've got things going on."

"I hope you know what you're doing."

The familiar sing-song of his mother's parting words used to annoy him as a kid but slid right off at twenty-eight. Yeah, he knew what he was doing. He grew more sure of it by the minute. He stuffed the phone into his jeans pocket and whistled for Sadie. "C'mon, girl, let's get some fresh air."

Chapter Nine

JADE STROLLED DOWN Main Street, watching snowflakes shimmer in the glow of the streetlights beneath an ink-black sky while shoppers flitted in and out of the many shops open late for the weekend. Volunteering and helping care for Grandma Bertie kept her busy from dawn to dusk, but the nights continued to stretch out long and sleepless.

I should have known going cold-turkey with sex would have consequences. She had foolishly given into her curiosity about Ben, and now she was paying for it.

He hadn't called.

She stopped at a storefront window of enchanting nutcrackers. They cheered her, grounded her once again in the reason she was home: To renew, recharge, and refocus.

I'm not here to get involved with my ex-neighbor for the month.

On the move again, she hummed to the beat of "The Little Drummer Boy", swaying her shopping bags back and forth in the frosty air. She smiled when she saw the man on the corner in red velvet and a fluffy white beard ringing a shiny gold bell. She pulled out her wallet and deposited a few bills into the red metal bucket next to him. "Have a wonderful Christmas." The bells' chimes and the man's thanks added to her feeling of goodwill. She tipped her head back once more and gazed at the heavens.

And then she was falling, knocked sideways, her humming cut off by a frightened squeal. *Sadie?* Her shopping bags flew out of her hands, her legs tangling in the leash as the large dog double-backed. And who was at the other end cursing a blue stream that could peel paint?

Ben.

The guy she determined to avoid yet continued to bump into—and quite literally tonight.

Strong arms reached out, catching her before she smacked her head on the sidewalk. *Thank God.*

"Sadie. Bad girl," he said. His eyes were filled with concern and something else, something that made her heart skip a beat. Maybe three. *Burr-rum-pum-pum-pum.* A girl could get lost in those evergreen depths.

"You all right?" He brushed hair out of her eyes. "You've got a weird look on your face."

She blinked. "I'm fine."

He rose.

Her world swayed as he brought her vertical with him. She looked around. "My bags."

Ben loosened his grip around her waist but didn't let go. "I'll replace anything that's wrecked." He frowned at the dog now lying next to them on the sidewalk littered with Christmas presents then shrugged. "Guess she's excited to see you." He moved his hands to her shoulders and squeezed gently. "I don't blame her."

"If you missed me so much, why didn't you call?" Jade pulled out of his embrace and crouched beside Sadie. "It's okay, sweetie." She gave the repentant creature a reassuring pat. "I wasn't paying attention either." She looked up at Ben, now holding her retrieved packages.

"I guess you didn't receive my messages."

"Uh, no." *Mom. Shit.* "How about I give you my cell number?" she asked without thinking. *Double shit.* She rose, wiping her hands on her jeans.

"I'd like that." He handed her the bags and picked up the leash handle. "Hungry? We were on our way to Main Street Café."

Burr-rum-pum-pum-pum. Me and my drum. What could be more pertinent to the season than milk and cookies? She couldn't say no. "Well, I did hear that their chocolate macadamia bars are absolute heaven."

Ben patted Sadie and laughed. "Then what are we waiting for?"

The three of them walked to the little café at the next corner.

Jade stepped inside behind Ben and Sadie, her mouth watering from the blended aromas of coffee, cinnamon, and nutmeg. She pulled off her mittens—she'd misplaced one of her gloves again—and unfastened her coat as she peeked around Ben to view the dining room on their right.

Uh oh. Almost every holiday-plaid-covered table in the room was occupied. What had she been thinking? There was sure to be a friend or two of her parents seated at one of them. She groaned, wishing for the first time in her life that she wasn't a younger replica of her mother.

Ben turned and grinned at her. "Looks like we're in luck." He pointed to a table being cleared. It was a cozy, romantic spot, nestled in a corner between a window overlooking the street and the fireplace on the adjoining wall.

"Uh."

Ben eyed her, his grin fading. "What's wrong?"

His question gave her an idea. It was naughty not nice, but

she was desperate. She couldn't take the risk. "It's—it's just that, well, suddenly I'm not feeling well." She pressed her palm to her head. "Maybe I'm a little more shaken up by that fall than I realized."

"Why didn't you tell me?" He muttered something under his breath. "I knew something wasn't right." He fastened his coat and shuttled her out the café's front door, back into the night air. He peered at her. "Are you nauseous or dizzy?"

"No, it's just a little headache. I'm sure I'll be fine. I just want to go home."

His voice was take-charge. "Here's what we'll do. The Starling Clinic is closed but we can contact the doctor on call and give him your symptoms. Worst-case scenario I'll drive you to Lake Placid. They have an overnight ER, or at least they did last I checked." He took out his phone and held it up as if checking the number of bars. "Are you sure you're not dizzy?"

She put her hand on his arm. "Please don't call anyone. I'm fine."

"If you were fine, we'd be enjoying hot cocoa and gourmet cookies beside a crackling fire instead of standing here on the cold sidewalk." He sighed. "But we're not. So let's go." He reached out a hand.

She lifted her shopping bags. She couldn't let him think their relationship was headed anywhere. She could understand why he'd gotten the wrong idea. She'd been as into those two kisses as he had been. She turned and began the long walk back toward her mother's car. She paused mid-stride and winced, a sharp pain in the middle of her forehead.

Serves me right for fibbing.

Ben was by her side in an instant. "This is nonsense. I'm taking you to the ER in Lake Placid."

She started walking again, faster now. She had to reach the car. She couldn't let him near her or she would be consumed by curiosity once more. "No, really, I'm fine."

"You keep saying it but you don't look it. You're so pale."

She arrived at the Subaru. *Thank goodness.* "I appreciate your concern, but I'm feeling better already, must be the fresh air." She took the keys from her purse.

Ben's tone was adamant. "If you insist on driving, I'm following you. If you feel ill or dizzy at any point, pull over. I'll be there to take care of you."

"You're not going to budge on this, are you?"

He shook his head. "Nope."

"All right."

He settled her in with the shopping bags before issuing his final orders. "Wait here. Oh, and give me your cell number like we talked about. I'll call and check on you later."

She gave him a feeble smile and nodded, giving her number to him so he could add her to his contacts. All the while, she watched the streets for signs of nosy townspeople.

"I'm going to call you now so you'll have my number. Cell service is pretty reliable between my parents' and my house, so we should be fine."

He followed her home, waited until she was safely at her parents' door before driving away.

Gigi met her at the door. "Was that Ben Stephens' truck I saw?" her mother accused. She looked at Jade's bags. "Did he go shopping with you?"

She closed the door. "I'm not in the mood to answer twenty questions tonight. I have a headache." She'd just lied to a man she liked, all because of her mother's opinion of him and her past mistakes. Both, which had nothing to do with him in particular. She walked to the coat closet. "His parents live next door."

Gigi followed. "He wasn't out front before you arrived, and he called here twice today, leaving messages for you." A hand flew to her throat. "Tell me you two didn't go out." Her voice rose. "Please tell me you aren't seeing him."

Jade set her shopping bags on the floor. "Of course I'm seeing him. We both volunteer with SLP." She took off her coat and hung it into the closet, tossing her mittens in as an afterthought.

Her mother picked the mittens off the floor and handed them to her. "Why would you do that?"

"It's not a big deal." Jade tucked her mittens into her coat pockets. "We worked together one day. She gave her mother a quick hug. "I'm sorry for not telling you. I didn't want you to worry. But you need to trust my judgement." She closed the closet door and pressed a palm to her forehead. "*And* relay my messages."

As expected, the request fell on deaf ears. Her mother paced, pointing at her with an accusing finger. "Jade Emily, I've warned you about that man already. He may mean well but I don't trust his judgement. Look at Jeremy."

Jade headed toward the downstairs bathroom off the kitchen. "Ben followed me home tonight because I'd fallen and wasn't feeling well." She stepped back. "In my opinion, those are the actions of a kind man, not one with no judgement."

Her mother followed her, her tone turned anxious. "You're hurt? What happened?"

Jade entered the bathroom and opened the medicine cabinet. "I was shopping on Main Street when Sadie accidentally—" She stopped. She was about to prove her mother's point, but Ben hadn't been the only one at fault. She hadn't been watching where she was walking. She grabbed the bottle of pain reliever and popped off the lid.

A vein pulsed at Gigi's temple. "If his dog was to blame for your fall, of course he followed you home. He knew if anything happened to you we'd sue his ass." She handed Jade a paper cup off the shelf. "I don't blame the dog. He should have left her home. Look what happened to you."

"Yeah, look what happened to me," Jade responded, sarcasm dripping off her words. She popped two pills in her mouth, and washed them down with a swig of cold water. "I'm fine. I have a headache, but it's totally unrelated to the fall. I didn't even hit the ground. He caught me, for goodness sake." She lowered her voice and exhaled, walking her mother to the bottom of the stairs. "Please let's stop the melodrama. I'm not sixteen, and I don't agree that Ben Stephens followed me home because he was afraid of me suing." She took a deep breath. "In fact, I believe he likes me."

"Jade Emily, he has a girlfriend."

She shook her head. "Not anymore."

"Well, that's news." Gigi paused. "What are you going to do about it?"

Jade turned to walk up the stairs. "Nothing. I'm leaving, remember?"

Now there was a smile in her mother's voice. "Yes, you always were smarter than Jeremy when it came to the big picture."

In her pink-walled bedroom, Jade walked to her dresser and gazed at the stranger in her mirror. *He likes me. She hates him. He wants me. She loves me. He wants to take care of me. Can I trust him?* She moved to her bed and sat on the edge in the dark quiet. Nothing but the ticking of the clock on her nightstand and the muffled sound of her grandmother's TV in the next room. It was going to be another toss-and-turn night.

The least she could do after making a total mess of the evening was to call Ben and let him know she was feeling better.

✦ ✦ ✦

BEN UNLOADED THE contents of his shopping bags onto his kitchen island. He stacked the new ornament boxes on the others in the living room and placed the cookbook for Mom and electronic gadget for Dad on a shelf in the hall closet then returned to the kitchen to examine his one impulse buy. According to the label, the jar's contents should smell like evergreens and freshly fallen snow. *Yeah, right.* He opened the jar's lid and sniffed. *Okay, well maybe.* It definitely smelled like pine mixed with spearmint.

He set the jar on the windowsill above the farmer's sink. His ancestors had performed the very same ritual, lighting candles during the holiday season to welcome loved ones to their hearth and home. His candle in the window would have an additional purpose—to welcome weary travelers.

Or more to the point, one weary traveler in particular.

He held up the lighter and paused, looking at Sadie. "What do you think, girl? Should I do it?"

She barked and thumped her tail.

He nodded. "I agree. Can't hurt." As a scholar of history, Ben was cognizant of the passage of time. Life was short. He knew what he wanted and he was ready to move forward.

Jade, on the other hand, needed more time. That was painfully obvious after tonight's debacle. He'd gone over the fall in his head again and again. She hadn't hit her head. She wasn't feeling well for a different reason. The lilt in her voice on the phone a few minutes ago proved his suspicion.

She had been afraid of what other people would think.

Or worse, she's afraid of me.

He leaned forward and clicked the lighter. Flame licked out to touch the waxy wick. It sputtered and died. He clicked the lighter again. This time the flame caught and held. He stood back and watched the yellow glow reflect off the windowpane into the darkness beyond. She might not stay, but if he played this right, she might gather her courage and give their relationship a chance to grow.

+ + +

JADE NAVIGATED THE icy cement walkway to the church parking lot, her parents and Grandma Bertie having walked ahead after Sunday service while she finished the Nativity Pageant practice in the church hall with thirteen rowdy children.

"See you on Wednesday. Thanks for help with my lines." Kendra, one of the seven-year-olds in Jade's group, skipped past, holding her mother's hand.

Jade waved to the mom and smiled at the little firecracker. "Your mom has my number if you need more help."

The little girl giggled and looked past Jade's shoulder. "Okay."

Jade turned to find Ben standing behind her. "You're in charge of the Children's Pageant too?" His gaze roamed over her.

She unfastened the top of her coat. What was it about his voice that made her libido kick into overdrive every time he uttered a sound? They stood outside a church, of all places. "Hannah and I are co-directors. It's fun working with the kids, plus it gives me a chance to be with Maggie and Mitch." She kicked a chunk of ice at the edge of the walkway with the toe of her boot.

"I'm happy you're feeling better."

She stared at the snow.

"Would you be up to going skiing this afternoon?"

She stilled. "Aren't the mountains crawling with tourists on weekends?"

"Not for cross-country." He smiled. "The trails I'm thinking of are beautiful, and we'll have them all to ourselves."

She glanced toward the parking lot. "Where's that?"

He explained and then added, "Bring the twins if you'd like."

"Thanks for offering, but Mitch has hockey practice and Maggie dance."

"Tuesday, then?"

She stuffed her cold hands into warm coat pockets. Ben made her feel alive and happy, took her mind off an uncertain future. Ah, what the heck? It was the holiday season and she deserved a little fun. They both did. "Actually, I'll go with you today. I've been feeling cooped up and skiing sounds like a great activity to shake off cabin fever."

He grinned and glanced at his phone. "Pick you up at two?"

"How about I meet you at your place? I have other errands in the evening." She began to walk to the car.

His voice followed her. "Don't be late."

Chapter Ten

BEN PLANTED HIS ski poles in the snow and propelled forward, using the last bit of his energy to move forward on the level trail cutting through the woods that encompassed a bulk of his property. He arrived, out of breath, at the edge of the trees, and stopped at the top of the large hill in view of his house. The sun shone there, causing the pines to cast long shadows. They had been out for at least two hours.

He bent down, his head resting against his knees and fingertips brushing his skis. After a few moments, he stood and twisted around to watch Jade coming around the last bend. She was breathtakingly beautiful in her element, cheeks and nose tinged red from the cold, her mouth determined, exhaling white puffs of breath. She glided next to him, caramel eyes flashing at him, damp curly tendrils of blond framing her flushed face beneath her wool hat. "That was incredible," she panted. "Did you see that deer peeking at us through the trees? And the red fox that crossed the trail?" She crouched down, resting her butt on the back of her skis. "I can't even count how many rabbits I saw." She grinned up at him.

"So I guess you never want to do this again?" he teased.

She scrunched her nose. "Oh my goodness, I could get used to this kind of exercise. I almost forget I was working so hard to keep up." She used her poles to push herself back to a standing position. She wobbled. "Oh, wow, a little dizzy."

He reached out and wrapped his arms, poles and all, around her, steadying her. "You okay?"

She peeked up at him. "Yeah, everything went gray for a second. I must have stood too quickly." She moved to back away.

"Just relax here for a second." He repositioned himself so they faced each other, her skis between his.

She glanced up with a drowsy smile. "That's nice."

Her body was sweet and soft against him as he rested against her silky hair. "That was quite a workout for a beginner." He squeezed her and she snuggled closer. "You did great."

Next thing he knew he was picking her up, bringing her face even with his and kissing those lips he couldn't get out of his mind. *So much for waiting.* She was mint and heat and plunging desire, her tongue tangling languidly with his. He couldn't get enough.

I have to stop. She needs time. This isn't skiing. I need to let her set the pace.

He lifted his head, slowly sliding her down until her skis touched the snow again. "Feel better?"

She nodded. "Thanks, doc." She smiled and backed up then glanced at the long slope ahead.

"It's all downhill from here," he joked.

"Good. Then I should have enough energy left to make it the rest of the way." She pushed off, looking back at him as he swung around to face downhill once more. "Race you," she called.

They tore down the hill at a strong clip, and he only caught her near the end. They both slowed to a stop and unfastened their skis. He leaned both sets against the side of the log cabin then led the way around the house to the front porch.

She glanced at his house then at the Subaru she'd parked in his driveway. "Well…" her voice trailed off, the air thick between them.

He stuffed his hands in his pockets and sat on the porch's top step. He gazed out at the mountains above them. "My grandparents always called the Adirondacks God's Country. I didn't understand what that meant until recently."

She ambled toward him and hesitated before she sat next to him. "I've taken Starling's beauty for granted too. Thanks for inviting me along today. I definitely want to do it again."

"You're welcome."

Minutes passed and they sat there in companionable silence, watching the sun and clouds move across the open sky, listening to the wind whispering through the pines, and feeling the nip of winter on their faces.

Jade broke the silence. "I was just thinking. Every other guy I've known expected me to entertain them or expected to be entertaining me. With you, I can just…be."

Ben's heart stopped for a long moment. In one simple statement, she'd nailed the defining difference between herself and Sofia, and it rocked him. "I hear you." He nodded toward the house. "Want to come in?"

She shook her head and glanced toward her car again. "I promised to deliver the meals for the SLP recipients tonight."

"Seen Mr. V lately?"

"Every day."

"Really?"

She turned to him, her gaze steady. "He's a nice man, and I feel bad for him. He's all alone."

He didn't want their day to end. "Want company on your

errands?"

She waved a hand in dismissal. "You don't have to. I know you have a business to run."

"I can't move forward with the project for another day or two at least, waiting on information from the city of Lake George. So I'm free."

"Well, only if I drive." She looked at the window where Sadie peeked out. "And only if she joins us."

The dog barked in agreement.

He laughed. "Deal. Mind if I grab a shower first?"

She stood. "No problem, I was planning to catch one at my parents' before I go back into town."

"We could save time." He stood next to her. "You could take one here." He let the unspoken invitation sink in.

She broke eye contact and shook her head slowly. "That's okay. I'll wait here, play with Sadie."

When will you be ready to play with me?

He swallowed his disappointment, but saw the flush creeping up her neck. She was imagining them together in his shower, he knew it. Good. "Be right back." Ignoring the tightness in his crotch that had become his constant companion, Ben zipped into the house.

He could be patient. She was worth it.

✦   ✦   ✦

THE FOLLOWING FRIDAY evening, Jade stood in her bra and panties in front of her mirror, make-up and hair products lined up on her dresser, hair straightener plugged in and heating.

She looked at her bare face then at the items designed to cover and accentuate. Ben's words came back to her.

What was she hiding from? What was she searching for?

She scanned the items and plucked the tinted sunscreen/moisturizer, a tube of lip gloss, and face wash off the dresser onto her bed next to the red holiday dress her mother had encouraged her to wear. Then she grabbed the wastebasket next to her desk and with her free arm, swept everything—the mascara, eyeliners, eye shadows, rouges, concealers, foundations, lip liners, lipsticks, and perfumes—except for the straightener into the garbage.

A weight the size of Mt. Marcy lifted from her shoulders, Jade walked back to her bed, picked up the three items she'd saved, and returned them to the dresser. She opened the tinted sunscreen and applied it to her face, followed by a dab of gloss to her lips. She smacked her lips together and smiled at her image. There. *That's me.*

She walked past the dress on the bed and opened her closet. After a few minutes, she settled on wearing her favorite black cable-knit sweater, black leggings and knee-high black leather boots. Cass would approve. For a pop of color she wore little green metallic ball earrings and a twinkling light holiday necklace the twins had given her as an early Christmas present.

She looked at her reflection on her bedroom wall mirror and smiled. *I'm in the holiday spirit all right.*

Her mother called up the stairs. "Jade?"

"Yeah."

"Maddie Stephens called. They had to switch the party to Benji's house, supposedly because their refrigerator went on the blink."

"Supposedly?"

"Well..." Her mother sounded a little ashamed of her negative attitude. "I guess it can happen. You almost ready?"

She looked at her long wavy hair in the mirror then unplugged the hair straightener. She smiled and twirled twice, just for the sheer joy of it. "I'm ready."

Thirty minutes later, Jade's father parked the family car on the side of the road nearest Ben's modern log cabin behind a long line of cars. There had to be at least a dozen cars.

Jade stepped out of the Subaru and helped her grandmother navigate the uneven ground until they reached the long, sloping driveway that led to the humongous house perched at the edge of the lake. The last time she'd been here she'd been too afraid to step inside. She'd had trouble keeping her hands off him even in the open. "I can see why everyone calls it a mansion. How many bedrooms is it?"

Gigi glanced over her shoulder and stared at Jade's hair. "You mean you haven't counted them for yourself, yet?"

Her mother's flippant tone set Jade's already taut nerves on edge.

She looked at her father for help.

He refused to get involved, lifting a shoulder in defeat before jogging ahead to open the door for them.

Her mother pulled her only daughter to one end of the porch as her father assisted Grandma Bertie up the steps. "I'm sorry, but what can I say? I have dreams for my children, and they don't include this town, or this kind of man."

Jade hardened her heart. It had been easier at eighteen to let other people make her choices. Not anymore. It didn't matter how many people tried to tell her what to do, she would decide for herself whom to date.

Her mother leaned close. "I understand you two have a history and you were friends, but you're not children anymore. Men and women cannot be just friends."

Jade's head snapped up, her mother's words reminding her of Amy Wilder's hurtful taunts all those years ago. "Why is that, Mom?"

"They just can't. Chemistry takes over."

"But can't they be both?"

"Both what?"

"Friends *and* lovers."

Gigi looked stubborn and doubtful.

"Gigi, Jade," her father called from the door. "Are you two joining the party or going to stand out here on the porch all night?"

"Well, like it or not, Mom, I'm friends with him. We've had a wonderful week, and it's been strictly platonic." She gave her a quick hug. "Don't worry. I'm leaving in a few weeks."

✦ ✦ ✦

BEN PATTED SADIE'S back in reassurance as she wagged her tail and uttered a short bark at the ringing doorbell. More guests. He rose from his chair next to the fireplace and addressed the men gathered in his spacious den. "Anyone ready for a refill?"

Two put in their requests while the others shook their heads, sipping their drinks and socializing. Most of the men here tonight worked at the local factory while others, like his father, were small business owners or worked for one. They all had known each other pretty much their whole lives and all shared a passion for pro football.

A familiar voice from the living room caught his attention. He was eager to see Jade. She had become the best part of his days. Every day this past week, they had skied or sledded, or skated after she finished her volunteering and errands. Had he given her enough time? Did she trust him yet? He sure as hell hoped so. His restraint was wearing thin. He hadn't worked this hard for a girl's attention since...he was twelve.

Same girl.

That said it all.

His father held out his hands. "Want me to take this tray

in?"

"Thanks, Dad. Two are for Jerry and Aaron."

"Gotcha." His father and Dennis ambled into the next room, the two lamenting their football team's abominable stats.

Ben's mother appeared next to him with two bags of chips in her arms. "Oh, there you are." She gave him a hearty peck on the cheek. "How's Sadie with all the commotion?"

"Great." He pointed to the dog under the tree, her head resting on her front paws. "I think all the tail wagging and sniffing tires her out."

He had no idea if his mother said anything else or if he answered, because at that moment the woman he'd been looking forward to seeing all day entered the living room from the foyer. His fingers itched to run through those long blond curls and caress that silky pale skin. And that mouth. He couldn't resist it. It had been far too long since their last kiss.

Nine days long.

Jade's caramel eyes caught his and she stumbled slightly, her Christmas red lips forming an "O" as she corrected her gait.

Ben's gaze dropped to the baby she cradled in her arms. Warmth and something else, something indefinable, filled him—hot and sweet and protective.

She slipped onto a chair next to the sectional, her face flushed pink and her attention focused on the cooing bundle. Jack and Hannah's twins left their card game with their grandma to run over and play with the baby on her lap while peppering their aunt with questions. Conversation and laughter filled the air while his mother flitted from table to table like a hummingbird in a summer garden, refilling chip bowls and cookie trays.

Ben swept his hand through his hair, entranced by the sight of Jade with an infant. Sofia had often been surrounded by children and babies, but he'd never pictured her carrying his child—like he did now with his former neighbor. His mind flashed back to his middle school days when he couldn't string four words together when near Jade. He knew what he wanted to say to her now, what he wanted to do with her, and he wasn't afraid to say it.

Was she ready yet?

He gazed at her face and read all the signs. Those parted lips, her flushed cheeks, and the longing in her eyes when she turned to look at him above the baby's head.

Having tired of the baby, Maggie and Mitch returned to their card game with Mrs. Engel.

Ben took that opening to move in, sitting on the edge of the sectional closest to her. "Whose baby?"

"Mine." Laura stood in front of them, eyeing him curiously before she turned to her old friend. "She's good with you. Ever think about having one or two of your own?"

Jade laughed off her friend's question, her blush deepening.

Mrs. Engel chimed in from her spot on the floor. "No need to worry about Jade. She's got her new life all planned out. Don't you, darling?"

Ben's blood heated at Gigi's pointed comment and he leaned closer to his friend.

Jade had flinched at her mother's remark but didn't respond. "Thanks for letting me hold her." She handed the cooing baby to Laura. "She's beautiful."

"No." Laura smiled. "Thank you. My arms needed the rest. You don't realize how heavy a fourteen-pound baby is until you carry one around all day. Don't wait too long before you start. Children require lots of energy."

Jade rose from her seat. "Wow. Did you check out the spread over there?" She rubbed her flat stomach. "Those coconut snowball cookies and chocolate cheesecake are calling my name."

"Be careful," Laura warned. "I didn't gain my weight until after the kids."

Gigi moved to her daughter, speaking softly but loud enough for Ben to overhear. "Laura's right, sweetie. If you're not going to have a high-paying job, you'll want to focus on family." She shook her head. "And we both know that's not going to happen if you let yourself go." She tilted her head at her daughter and petted her arm. "That's why you're wearing these long sweaters and stretchy leggings instead of that beautiful dress lying on your bed at home. Isn't it?"

Ben had heard enough. "Any of you ladies in the mood for a drink? Wine, egg nog, Winter Wonder?"

Mrs. Engel glared at him.

"I'll try the Winter Wonder," Jade said, glancing briefly at her mother before turning back to him. She lifted her chin. "Want any help?"

"Definitely." He led the way to the kitchen, the two of them leaving Gigi to grumble in their wake. She located the tumblers under his direction as he opened the fridge. "I think you look terrific tonight."

"Thanks. Not everyone shares your opinion, apparently."

He pulled out the pitcher of his mixer concoction, measuring it along with the shots of white alcohol into the glasses. "I mean it." He looked at her. "How was your day, before your mother went complete bonkers?"

"She's not usually like this. She's just worried about me. It doesn't come out in the prettiest of ways."

"You don't need to defend that kind of behavior, Jade. I've known your mother practically my whole life. She seems to be a really good person, but even good people can be wrong. What she just pulled in there was tactless and rude, and not just to you." He handed her a glass.

"Thanks." She took a sip. "Yum." She wiped her lips. "No one heard but you and Laura."

He set the rest of the drinks on a tray. "No, and neither one of us cares about that nonsense."

"So, let's drop it, okay?" She took another sip.

He nodded. He'd drop it for now, but Mrs. Engel had better curb her tongue around him in the future or he would give her a piece of his mind. "How was your day? I missed you."

She stood there, leaning in, looking back at him. "Grandma taught me how to play Mexican Train."

He breathed in her fresh, clean scent. "That's cool, the game with dominoes, right?"

She nodded. "You have a beautiful home."

"Thanks." He held her gaze. She had chosen to skip the make-up and let her hair go wavy tonight. He reached out to touch a silky lock. "I take back what I said. You don't look terrific tonight, you look fantastic. I love the natural you."

Her smile reached her eyes. "It must be all the fresh mountain air I've been getting. It's inspiring."

"It could be the beginning. If you stayed, we could play outside year-round, like the old days."

She took a deep breath. "I-I know. I've been thinking the same thing."

Something she said gave him an idea. "Wait here," Ben ordered before picking up the tray and leaving her in the kitchen so he could track down his mother. He located his mother in the dining room and handed off the drinks. "Jade and I are going upstairs for a few minutes. If you need anything, feel free to yell." He didn't wait for approval. He didn't need it. And the sooner Jade learned to be her own person, the better the chance of the future he was starting to picture for them becoming reality.

He turned the corner between the dining room and kitchen and stopped.

Jade sipped her drink, staring at the candle in the window like he often did, but instead of a relaxed pose like the rest of his holiday guests, her arms wrapped protectively around her middle.

He frowned, his frustration with her mother threatening to return. But then he had an idea that would make her smile. He walked the rest of the way into the room. "Ready?"

She turned. "For what?"

He put a finger over her lips. "Shh. Do you hear what I hear?"

She tilted her head at him and pulled his finger away with her hand. "That's the name of a Christmas song."

He smiled at her confusion. "No, silly. Listen."

"All I hear is a rowdy party." She looked at her empty drink and hiccupped. "I suspect the Winter Wonder consumption has something to do with it."

"Perhaps. We'll cut them off soon, no fears. Do you get it though? Everyone is having fun, celebrating, letting loose." He grinned and took her hand, pulling her through the dining room to the foyer at the front of the house, out of view of their guests. "Now it's our turn."

"What are you doing?"

"I want to give you the nickel tour. You haven't been inside before. This is the perfect opportunity."

She glanced into the living room where her mother was locked in a huddle with her father, still looking unhappy, and her back went rigid. "Why do some people want to live our lives for us, tell us what to do all the time?"

He said softly, "I'm not telling you to do anything. What do *you* want, Jade?"

Emotions flitted across her face. "Right now, I want you to give me that tour."

Chapter Eleven

JADE FOLLOWED BEN up the spiral oak staircase to the second floor. She had to be careful. He didn't need to know she would follow him just about anywhere right now.

At the top of the stairs, he turned right and showed her the four bedrooms with en suite bathrooms. All beautiful, charming Adirondack-style rooms with all the modern touches. He led the way past the stairway to the left and stopped at a closed door. "Forgive the mess. I wasn't planning on guests tonight."

The deep rumble of his voice sent heat racing between her legs. She shifted her weight. "I don't need to see it." But she did. Then her mind could put a real place in her fantasies about the man she had become reacquainted with the past few weeks, the one she was considering having a holiday fling with—whether her mother approved or not.

"There's something I want to show you, something really special that got me to where I am today." He winked. "And then we can talk—in private." He held out his hand.

They had held hands on many occasions, as kids and then a few times as adults over the past two weeks. But if she reached out for him now, it wouldn't be for help but for comfort. Should she take it? Cass and Bree would egg her on, tell her to go for it, while Kara and Elena would tell her not to. Two against two. No answer there. *Wait a minute. What do I want? I keep saying I'm going to make my own decisions from now on, yet I keep depending on others. I started by quitting my job, but what about my personal life?*

"Jade?"

She looked at him, drawn into those emerald depths. She reached out and took his hand, grasping firmly. His eyes darkened further, almost black, as he closed his fingers over hers.

I want to give us a chance.

She took a step toward him. "What do you have to show me?" Her voice was breathless, like she'd power-shopped with the girls and had no energy left to expel the air from her body.

He swallowed—the muscles working in his throat. He tugged on her hand and stepped into the master suite with her. He pulled her into the bedroom, past his king size bed over to a tall oak dresser. He let go of her hand and opened the top drawer, a mess of silk boxer briefs in neon colors and tube socks. He pulled out a box and moved to the bed. "Sit."

She did as he asked, perching on the far edge. "What is it?" She inched closer.

He set the box between them and opened the lid.

"Oh." She leaned forward to peer at the Indian arrowhead nestled on a bedding of white cotton. Long-forgotten memories pushed their way to the front of her brain. "Wow. I can't believe you still have this."

He grinned. "Remember when we found it?"

"Of course. When you and I were digging around Starling Lake. What were we? Seven? Eight?" She reached out and stopped. "Is it okay if I touch it?"

He nodded.

She turned the arrowhead over, and examined the other side. "Do you know which native group this came from?"

He leaned back next to her. "Can't tell for sure. My area of expertise is the Revolutionary War, at least five centuries more recent than this baby."

She handed it back to him.

"I treasure this," he told her. "Thanks for letting me keep it."

She shrugged. "You wanted it."

"You're the one who insisted on digging in that spot. I just went along for fun." He sat up, bringing her with him. "I want you to know you were the one who inspired me to follow my dreams." He set the arrowhead back into the box and closed the lid. "You seemed so much more suited for anthropology or archeology. Why marketing?"

"It was always my mother's dream for me, not mine." She glanced toward the hallway. "I didn't trust my own judgement, after what happened with those brutal girls at school. I'm trying to change that, make my own decisions. Mom's a little bent because of it, but she'll work through it. She'll have to. I'm not going back."

"What happened?"

"I resigned six weeks ago. I'd used my vacation days to be at the hospital with Grandma, and when I returned to the firm, the twenty-two-year-old I'd been training had been given one of my major accounts. Purely because I'd taken days I was entitled to, for family. On top of that, I was passed over for the promotion I'd been working toward for the past two years."

"That sucks."

"Yeah, but I'm over it." Surprisingly, she was. "I mean, who wants to work for a company that thinks it owns you, body and soul?" Images of playing in the snow and sun with

Ben popped into her head, making her smile. Maybe there was hope for her yet.

He touched her cheek with the pads of two fingers. "I'm sorry you had to go through that. What next?"

She looked in his beautiful eyes. "I want to be a social worker, maybe specialize in geriatrics."

"You'd be great at that, and there's definitely a need. You're good with your grandmother and Mr. V. and all the folks at the Senior Center." He moved off the bed to return the box to its drawer before turning back and leaning against the dresser.

She caught sight of the collage of photos on the wall behind him…school pictures, candid shots. There was one of him hugging a petite woman with long black hair and charcoal eyes. "Is that your ex-girlfriend?" He never talked about her.

He glanced at the collage. "Forgot that was there." He pinched the bridge of his nose. "Did you hear the gossip?"

She hesitated. "I heard you had a long-time girlfriend, but I don't know the details." She generally steered away from the town grapevine. "Why?"

He told her.

She stood and began to pace. "Wow. I figured it was recent, but I had no idea." She did the math. He had kissed her less than a week after he ended a five-year relationship. She stopped and looked out the window into the black night.

He walked up behind her. "Does that change how you feel about us?"

She turned around, her hands in the air. "What do you think?" She glanced at his bed, the one she had pictured Ben and her on. Now it was replaced by an image of him with the tiny, black-haired woman. "My mom has a point. You didn't even let the sheets cool." She frowned at him. "Are you one of those guys who can't be alone?"

His said steadily, "My relationship with Sofia was over long before we ended it. We were one of those couples great at dating but couldn't live together. I had convinced myself that we were right for each other because she was in the education field, but that's where our interests ended. We wanted different paths in life."

She looked at him through wet lashes. "I'm leaving in a few weeks." She gestured between the two of them. "We're on different paths too."

"Back to Tampa?"

"California."

"Whoa. California?" He scrubbed his scruff before reaching up and wiping her tears away. "How about we cross that bridge when we come to it?" He sank onto the bed, pulling her with him. "We're both adults, we're great friends, and we both—don't you dare deny it—are crazy hot for each other. So, what do you say we give our relationship a shot, enjoy ourselves while we can, and see where it goes from there?"

She stared at his white button-down shirt inches away. He had a point. This very second her fingers itched to pull that dress shirt out of his trousers so she could run her hands along his bare skin...up his rib cage and over his pecs. She swallowed. *Focus.* "Only problem is I'd be your rebound girl."

He tipped her chin up. "We don't know that. You inspired me when I was eight and you're still inspiring me."

She closed her eyes, tired of denying her desires, eager for his lips to touch her and quench her thirst for him.

His voice rasped. "I want you so badly." He pulled her to him, taking her down onto the downy softness of his satin comforter.

Thundering footsteps in the hallway had them bolting off the bed. She glanced out the door and turned to look at Ben. "Maggie and Mitch."

He stuffed his hands into the pockets of his black trousers and moved to look out the window.

The twins burst into the room, their voices in chorus. "Aunt Jade. We can't find Sadie and we want to play with her. Have you seen her?"

Jade held up her hands. "Not here."

"Help us find her." Maggie tugged at the hem of her aunt's sweater.

Jade stroked her niece's copper hair. "Give us a moment. I'll be right there."

Ben leaned forward to address the two munchkins. "Why don't you check in the kitchen? It's her dinnertime."

Mitch hopped around the room. "Thanks, Ben."

The twins bolted out of the room and down the stairs as quickly as they'd come.

Jade sank back onto the bed and punched the comforter. "How much you want to bet my mother was behind that little interruption?"

"Shh. Don't worry about anyone else." Ben joined her, playfully pinning her on her back, his fingers threaded with hers above her head. "Now, where was I?"

She forced herself to stay rigid, Maggie and Mitch's brief visit a wake-up call. No need to start something they couldn't finish. "Nothing's going to happen tonight and you know it."

His tone was teasing. "No? You sure?" He leaned forward, letting her feel his interest.

She shook her head and did her best to ignore the sweet torture. "We're old friends getting reacquainted."

He leaned to the side on one elbow and laughed. "Old? Speak for yourself."

She took advantage of his movement and rolled him onto his back. "That's right. I'm pushing thirty while you have another year before the gauntlet strikes you down," she joked, triumphant until she looked down and saw that her low-cut sweater gaped open.

He gazed at her cleavage inches from his face. "You'll be one smoking hot thirty-year-old."

Why couldn't they send the guests home right now? "Let me go? Before there's real smoke in the room?"

He released her hands and she scrambled off the bed, smoothing her hair and rearranging her clothes. She was checking her appearance in the mirror above his dresser when he asked the same question she'd been contemplating for months.

"Is it true women your age want to settle down, get married, have two point five kids?"

She locked eyes with him, serious. "Don't know about women in general. As for me, I haven't figured it all out yet." She glanced out the door and then smiled. "I'd better get back. Thanks for the tour."

She skipped down the stairs, humming a few bars from Eartha Kitt's soulful "Santa Baby." She was eager for their next adventure…indoors.

Merry Christmas, indeed!

Chapter Twelve

BEN PARKED HIS Ski-Doo at the brow of the secluded hill. He turned to look down the incline through the deepening shadows in the snow, blue and gray tinges within the white. The buzz of a second snowmobile joined his as Jade tore up the hillside on the packed trail.

He stood, straddling the machine to enjoy the strength and grace that was Jade, his heart racing and his head filled with wonder. Her blond hair flew out behind her in a shimmering mass. Yellow-tinted snow goggles, black hat and black scarf dwarfed her small face and covered all but a speck of her cute nose.

His crotch responded. She made him feel like a horny teenager again and last night at his parents' annual holiday party, his patience had paid off. She finally had opened up to him about her recent life. The announcement about California had taken him by surprise, and she was justifiably peeved about Sofia, but they could work through those issues.

Jade pulled up next to him with a grin and stopped, her machine tossing fresh snow over him with a whoosh. Their idling engines mixed with her laughter and his shout of surprise.

She lifted her goggles and peered at him, an impish glint in her eyes. "Sorry."

"Right." He brushed off the snow then wagged a gloved finger in her direction. "I'll get you when you least expect it."

"Counting on it." She snapped her goggles back into place, revved her snowmobile's engine, and nodded toward the lights in the distance before she wound her way around boulders along the slope.

Encouraged by her playfulness, Ben revved his engine and raced after her.

The Adirondacks were part of Jade. He didn't have to worry about her being frightened by a wild animal or falling through thin ice on Starling Lake or any of the million other concerns he'd always had with Sofia. Jade knew what signs of danger to look for in the North Country, as easily as she breathed its fresh air. How could she not see she belonged here?

With me.

He parked his snowmobile off the trail next to hers and followed the prints of her snow boots to find her sitting on a large, flat boulder, camera in hand. She looked up and smiled. "I've hiked up this way during summertime, but never in the snow." She lifted her camera and snapped a few photos of the landscape below. "It's postcard perfect."

He moved next to her, soaking in the quiet solitude of the snowy hillside. There was usually the hum of traffic below, the buzz of a random plane overhead, and chattering or chirping forest animals scampering and flitting about in the Adirondack pines.

But here, in this moment, it was silent.

All he could hear was the thumping of his heart, the blood rushing through his ears. He was going to kiss her. And this time, they both knew would be a prelude to a night of intimacy. There were no other obligations pulling them apart, no prying eyes or big ears, interfering mothers, or little kids. It was just the two of them. At last. He was through with being patient. The timing was right. "You're beautiful."

Her eyes opened wide and her voice was hushed. "Even without makeup and wavy, wild-woman hair? Don't say that."

He stepped closer. "Especially."

"I hate skirts and dresses, too."

"Then don't wear them." He pulled her into his embrace and breathed in her skin's scent, clean and light, the scent that filled his waking and sleeping moments. Her scent called to him, blended with the evergreen and fresh snow—the same scent as the candle he had lit every evening for the past nine days.

She melted against him.

He nuzzled against her ear and whispered his intent. "I want to make love to you."

She put her hand, feather light, on his chest. Rather than pushing him away as he half-expected after all her mixed signals, her hand rested there, warm and relaxed. She looked up at him, her eyes a dark chocolate. "What about our friendship?"

"We'll always be friends first."

She snuggled closer.

That was all his body needed to know. He tipped her chin with the leather tip of his gloved finger and dipped his mouth to meet hers. At first contact, she tasted sweet, like a tray full of his favorite holiday cookies, all warm vanilla and sugar. Then he pulled her closer, wrapping his arms around her small frame, and deepened the kiss. His knees nearly buckled. She tasted of more heady spices, cinnamon and nutmeg, her sigh and hands wrapped around his head pulling him even closer telling him she wanted this to happen every bit as much as he did. He leaned against her in a full body hug, letting her know exactly how ready he was.

✦   ✦   ✦

THEIR KISS WENT on forever, and just when Jade thought she'd die if he didn't touch her further, he backed away, the crisp night air rushing between them.

"Look," he breathed.

She pulled back slowly and turned in the direction Ben gazed. Night had fallen over their hometown. And it was beautiful.

Ben checked his watch. "We'd better get going." He kissed the top of her head. "The Snowmobile Club has their evening run tonight. Let's get down the hill ahead of the group. Practically half the town will be zipping through here in about thirty minutes."

Sure enough, as soon as he finished speaking, faint buzzing of snowmobiles sounded from down below. "Oh," she said.

He pointed to her camera. "Take your shots and then we'll head out."

Her hands trembled as she slipped them out of her gloves to take the pictures, her body still decompressing from the sensations his lips and tongue wrought. Sex would be good between them. She tingled with excitement and anticipation. What else could they experience together? Whatever it was, now that she had made her decision she wanted all the time in the world to do it. Would three weeks be enough for their attraction to run its course?

It has to be.

Ignoring the heaviness in the pit of her stomach, she swallowed and focused on the scene below. She snapped a dozen or so shots then turned to him. "Take a selfie with me?"

"Sure." He moved close and they smiled for the camera, the picturesque scene laid out behind them.

"Ready?" Ben grabbed her hand and helped her over the ridge, back to their sleds. The look in his eyes told her all she needed to know.

Oh, I'm ready all right. She put her camera in her pocket and slid her goggles on as she straddled the machine. She glanced at him for directions, and he signaled he'd take the lead.

She followed at a safe distance, their headlamps cutting a swath of brilliant light through the darkness ahead. They would have a fun Christmas together. He said she wasn't his rebound relationship but she knew better. That was okay. She was in transition too. They would heal their past and go their separate ways, and she would have to find someone else for her forever.

In spite of her decision, that constant yearning she equated to her ticking biological clock grew inside her as they zigzagged down the rest of the hill toward his house. Did she want to keep searching for the mythical man or did she want flesh-and-blood Ben?

✦ ✦ ✦

BEN BOUNDED UP his side steps two at a time, prepared to rip open the door to his home and continue from where they'd left off when a movement in the corner of the porch caught his attention.

"Hey." Jade sat in one of his two Adirondack chairs, a plaid woolen blanket wrapped around her shoulders. Her knees bounced inside her bibbed snow pants.

Was she nervous? She had repeatedly told him how she didn't want anyone in town to get the wrong idea about them. They hadn't encountered any snowmobilers on the mountain and inky darkness and evergreens shrouded his house from prying eyes on the main road. But could anyone really have secrets in a town the size of Starling? Or was she excited like him? He stuffed his hands into his front jeans pockets to hide the growing bulge in his crotch, and leaned against the porch column closest to her chair. "Why didn't you go in?"

"I wanted to wait for you." She held out the key, her dark eyes solemn.

Or was she trying to stay warm?

"Are you cold? Your knees are bouncing like crazy."

"A little. My blood isn't used to sub-zero temperatures anymore."

"It's not that cold. It's at least twenty."

"Well, it feels colder."

"Let's go inside and warm up then, unless you've had a change of heart?" He waited.

She stared at gloved hands clasped in her lap. "This is really friends with bennies? You don't expect more? We're not going to hate each other afterward?"

He bent over the chair and leaned forward, his hands gripping the furniture's arms. "Yes. No. No." He held her gaze. "What's going on?"

She stuck out her chin. "I just want you to know, even though we're going to do this, I'm still leaving. I can come home more often in future, but I'm not going to settle in Starling. It's not in the plan."

He touched a finger to her lips. "I can handle reality, I think. I'm a big boy."

Her knees stopped bouncing and her eyes fell to the fly of his jeans. "I see that." She smiled up at him.

Her eyes sparkling up at him almost undid him. He nodded toward the door. "Want a drink by the fire?" He'd planned to move inside right away, but then her lips fell apart and her lashes fluttered onto her pale cheeks and all he could do was slide his tongue across her chilled mouth and inside toward her heavenly warmth. Ahh, she tasted so sweet.

She slid her hands along the sleeves of his ski jacket to his shoulders and gripping the collar, pulled him closer. She moaned as their kiss deepened.

He pulled away and sucked in a ragged breath. If they didn't stop, he was going to take her right here, in this uncomfortable chair on his freezing cold side porch. "C'mon." He grabbed her hands in his and pulled her to a standing position.

Jade leaned against him. "I just want to warn you. I may have forgotten how to do this."

He rubbed his hands along her arms. "I'm happy to take a refresher course with you if you still want to stay?"

She nodded.

He walked with her to the door and turned the key in the lock. Inside, they removed their coats and boots before he led the way through his dimly lit house. It smelled of pot roast cooking in the crock pot and pine from his Christmas tree.

Sadie greeted them with a sniff and lick, her nails clicking on the kitchen and living room floors before she returned to her spot next under the tree.

He clicked on the lights to his tree then turned to face her between the large leather couch and crackling fire. "Well, here we are."

She tugged at his shirt. "These layers have to go." She smiled and stepped back. "Don't you think?" She shrugged out of her top and tossed it on a nearby chair. Her dark eyes flashed at him, daring him to play along.

Game on.

He stared at her pink satin bra and pale skin reflected in the soft glow of the fire as he doffed his flannel button-down.

She shimmied out of her bibbed snow pants, wobbling as one foot tangled in the elastic cuff liner.

"Whoa." He reached out and caught her before she face-planted on the hardwood floor.

"You're always catching me." She giggled. "I can't blame your Winter Wonder this time."

"Oh, so you did have another after our talk. I thought so. Did you like it?" He stepped out of his flannel-lined jeans and added them to the pile.

"Sweet yet packed a punch." She stared at his lower half a long moment before slipping out of her baby blue yoga pants, which left her standing in a wisp of pink satin triangle. It matched her bra. Not that he cared. He was far more interested in the secret parts of her they covered.

He stepped toward her, his gaze sweeping her from head to toe. He was eager to begin his exploration.

"Wait." She put a small hand on his chest. She plucked at his long sleeved tee shirt. "It's your turn."

His gaze swept her from head to toe. Impatient, he removed the offending garment that separated them.

She smiled at his chest and neon green boxer briefs. She whispered, "Now we're ready."

"Come here." His voice sounded gruff to his ears.

She stepped into his arms.

They body hugged for a long moment, skin touching skin, a gradual getting to know each other. He cupped her ass. She stepped up on her tip toes, muscles flexing under his hands. It felt good.

"Ben?"

"Hmm?" He sank to the couch with her, the butter-soft leather rough compared to the silkiness of her skin. He nuzzled his face into her neck, inhaling her scent. She was all the intoxicant he desired. "I'm here." *I've always been right here.* He kissed the woman he'd lit a candle for every day the past nine days. Finally, nothing was going to interrupt them. He felt complete and they had yet to consummate the relationship.

"Ben?" she whispered.

He pulled back and looked into her eyes. "Everything all right?"

"I should have thought of this before, you know, when we were talking about how long it had been." She bit her lip. "I'm not using any protection. Do you have some?"

He signaled for her to give him a moment, jogged into the bathroom off the kitchen and returned with it in hand.

"A whole box?" She gave a nervous laugh.

He sank back onto the couch next to her and growled against her neck. "Anything's possible with you." He caressed her collarbone. "Who knows? Maybe it will be a Christmas miracle." He moved his attention to her soft, pert breasts. Joking aside, he couldn't get enough of her. He needed to be closer, be inside her, part of her. But he wanted this to be a night she never forgot. He moved back. "Why don't you lie back against the pillows?"

She complied, her legs on either side of his body.

He gently slid his hands up her long limb, leaning forward and moving down toward that triangle of satin…to her most private, sweet most heady scented place. He moved aside the fabric.

At first she lay quietly but as he licked and kissed and suckled her heat, her hands found his head, urging him closer, arching against him, her soft moans interspersed with the crackling of the fire glowing on her pale, perfect skin. He lifted his head for a moment to catch his breath and the rapture on her face, her beauty etched into his memory. She was perfect, all woman. She was his for the night.

"Please don't stop."

Her words tugged at his heart, even though he knew this was no more than a physical release for her. "No, baby, going to just slide down a bit more. There you are. So beautiful. I knew you would be." He reached up and caressed her breasts. Unable to get enough of her he moved his hands to her entrance—she was so hot and tight. He inserted a finger, then two, and soon she was squirming again, arching against his hands, her body begging for completion.

"Yes, oh, yes." He was harder than he ever thought possible, straining against the fabric of his underwear, yearning to make contact with her liquid heat. He had held himself back, but now that she was ready, more than ready, he let go. He bent his head one more time and, along with his fingers, brought her to the peak and beyond. She shuddered against him, crying out, and then pulled him up and over her. "I want you. Inside. Please."

The need in her voice was palpable. This was all he'd ever dreamed of, having Jade in his bed, begging him to take her, to make her his, but somehow it meant more to him. This wasn't a personal triumph as he'd expected. It was a shared victory. They had found each other. He kissed her eyelids, her cheeks, her hairline, her lips—his heart swelling with something indefinable. He'd never felt this way with Sofia, or any woman before that. Having sex with Jade was a completely different experience.

"I'm right here." He leaned back, grabbed the box of condoms. A few moments later, he leaned back over her, nudging against her wetness. Gazing into her eyes, seeing his passion reflected in hers, gave him the signal she was ready for him to drive them both home.

So he did.

Chapter Thirteen

JADE ADMIRED FREDERIC Van Salzberg's newly decorated Christmas tree. Her month in Starling was turning out to be far more than she could ever have imagined—between the fulfilling volunteer jobs, getting reacquainted with family and...Ben. A thrill raced through her at the memory of their intimacy two nights ago. She turned to the old man sitting on the couch whom she now viewed as a kindly uncle. "I promised this would bring you joy."

Frederic shook his head and patted the seat cushion beside him.

Her heart sank. "You don't like it? I can change the lights; use the large colored bulbs instead of the twinkling white."

"No, no, it's not that. The tree is fine. Thank you."

She moved across the room and sat next to him. "Then why are you so sad?" Had he received bad news after last week's doctor appointment she had driven him to? Her stomach clenched. "Tell me your blood tests didn't show—" She couldn't get the words past dry lips.

He shook his head again. "Tip top shape." He reached out a wrinkled hand. "This isn't about me, my dear girl. I'm fine, or at least as fine as an old coot like me can be."

"Then, what's—" She stopped. She had never asked the question, the elephant in the room between them. Why was Frederic alone? Was he finally comfortable enough to tell her? Jade folded her hands and waited. His next words would be important. She felt it deep in her bones.

"My dear girl, you've given me so much the past weeks. I've been thinking for the past number of days how to repay you for your kindness."

"I don't want anything," she said in earnest.

He smiled and nodded. "Thought that's what you'd say. But this gift is one I hope you'll accept. It's the gift of hindsight, Jade."

"The ability to see your past clearly?"

"My dear, I have no wife, no children, no close friends. Fifty years ago, I was a go-getter, focused on the prize instead of the journey, always thinking what I had wasn't good enough, and I should wait for something better. It never came. It doesn't. The journey is the prize. The best is what you make yourself, not what you wait for."

Jade's thoughts about searching for the perfect job and perfect mate popped into her head. He'd seen so much, this elderly man.

"Success comes in many forms," he said. "I missed my chance." He set his jaw and pinned her with his gaze. "But you don't have to."

Jade stood, wringing her hands and fighting the urge to pace the marble floors. "What are you saying? I'm in transition right now."

She pushed away the memory of snuggling in bed in those wee morning hours with Ben. Satisfied. Complete. Nothing that incredible could last.

Frederic was talking to her. "Just don't make the same

mistake I did, always waiting and not recognizing that what I wanted had been in front of me the whole time. That's my gift, Jade. It's odd. It has no wrapping paper or card. But I hope you like it."

"I do. Thank you." She leaned over and gave him a hug. He accepted it but didn't return it.

Baby steps. For both of them.

✦ ✦ ✦

BEN PARKED HIS SUV in the street next to his parents' house and glanced at the Engels' driveway. The Subaru was absent. He swallowed his disappointment and opened the driver side door. His night with Jade had been unlike any other in his twenty-eight years. It was more than three intense rounds of sex followed by a late-night feast of pot roast and veggies naked in his kitchen. He smiled to himself and walked around the vehicle to open the passenger door.

Sadie jumped out.

His night with Jade was more than a shared shower and falling asleep with her in his arms, more than waking next to her and wanting to do it all over again, satisfied to cuddle next to her in bed afterwards and watch a movie.

He glanced down at Sadie loping beside him, and told her, "I'll do casual…for now." They had until the end of the year.

After visiting with his parents and receiving a reminder from his mother to call when he reached Lake George tomorrow, he and Sadie began the short trek back to the SUV.

The silver Subaru turned into the driveway next door.

He grinned. Perfect timing. "Good afternoon." He waved to the three females exiting the vehicle then jumped the split rail fence before jogging through packed snow to the driveway. "Let me help." He took the groceries from Mrs. Engel and peered over the two bags at her mother-in-law and daughter.

Mrs. Engel closed the car trunk and gave him a brief nod. "Hello there, Sadie." She patted the happy dog and headed toward the house.

He turned to greet the other two women.

His heart squeezed when he got a good look at Jade. Was it possible for a woman to grow more beautiful by the day? She gnawed her bottom lip with her pearl white teeth when he kissed her on the cheek.

He dropped his gaze to the tiny woman next to her. "You're looking well, Bertie."

The older woman's sharp eyes sparkled. She eyed him up and down before her gaze lingered on his shoulders. "Do I get a kiss, too, beefcake?"

"Behave yourself." Jade scolded her grandmother with a smile. "That's sexist, treating our neighbor like a juicy piece of meat." She hooked her arm through Bertie's and winked at him behind the woman's back.

He smiled. "I don't mind." He leaned down and kissed the older woman's powdered cheek.

Inside the Engel house, he watched Jade settle her grandmother into her favorite knitting chair then accompanied her into the kitchen where her mother had replaced her outerwear with an apron. There were an array of ingredients next to a mixing bowl and measuring cups as Mrs. Engel rifled through an old recipe box, ignoring his presence. "Could you find the flour in one of the bags for me?" she requested of her daughter.

Eyeing the sugar and cinnamon, Ben's mouth watered. "Kaastengel?"

"I prefer the holiday Dutch straws made with chocolate, but Mom promised to make those with the leftover dough later this week." She handed her mother the flour. "Want shortening too?"

Mrs. Engel nodded. "These seem more like Christmas to me, but I can appreciate the girls' requests."

Jade slapped her forehead. "That reminds me, I have to call Cass, apparently there's more drama involving Bree." She turned to Ben. "Sorry. You remember my friends from downstate, the ones I've known forever."

He accepted a star-shaped sugar cookie from Jade. "Sure. There's another, too, right?"

"Two actually, Kara and Elena." Jade turned to her mother. "I'll help make a double batch of the Dutch chocolate straws later this week, okay? I want them to be super-fresh for our trip downstate—whenever that will be. This December's turning out to be a crazy month for all of us."

Mrs. Engel laughed. "From what I saw at Thanksgiving, Elena could probably use a batch all for herself."

"She's a shameless chocoholic, but who can blame her for eating all those chocolate chip cookies? Your baking is stellar, Mom."

Jade's mother hugged her. "Thanks, sweetie." She turned to Ben and her smile faded. "Jeremy told me you two are working together." Her eyes flashed a warning.

He held her gaze. Gigi had a right to protect her children, but there had to come a time when she accepted her son's responsibility for his alcoholism and allow Jade to cut the purse strings. If he was going to remain in her children's lives, they needed to mend their fences sooner rather than later. He told her firmly, "He's a hard worker and a talented writer. We're lucky to have him."

"He said you two are going to Lake George this week," Mrs. Engel volleyed back.

Jade's head snapped up.

He glanced at her. "That's correct."

Jade lifted her chin and addressed her mother. "I hear The Sagamore serves the best lobster roll."

He stifled a grin. She was beginning to show that backbone with her mother that she displayed to him. How about that? "We're booked at The Sagamore. You could join us, get some of your Christmas shopping done in town. You free tomorrow and Wednesday?"

Gigi's eyes went wide and she shook her head in her daughter's directions. "Oh, I don't know about that." She turned to him. "I really need her here, you know, with her grandmother and all."

"I haven't seen Jeremy yet," Jade shot back, "and this would be the perfect opportunity. We could catch up on the car ride."

Mrs. Engel stopped stirring her dough. "What about pageant practice on Wednesday?"

Ben bit the sugar cookie in half, waiting for Jade's counterattack.

She sighed and dropped her shoulders. "You're right, Mom. I completely forgot."

He piped in. "How about this? We'll go down tomorrow, you have the day to yourself and we meet for dinner, then we can drive you back Wednesday for your pageant practice."

Jade's eyes lit. "I suppose…" She tapped her chin and appeared to consider her options. "Okay, I'll go."

He resisted the urge to lift and twirl her around, settling instead on clapping once to get Sadie's attention. "Walk us to the door and I'll give you the details." He turned to Mrs. Engel, her face beet red, stirring her dough with a vengeance. Part of him felt guilty for upsetting her but being with Jade was more important to him than Gigi's opinion of him at this particular juncture. "Thanks for the sugar cookie." He smiled at the two women as he popped the other half into his mouth.

Jade grabbed his shirt sleeve and pulled him out of the kitchen through the living room to the foyer. She waited until Sadie ran into the front yard and the door was closed behind them before speaking. "You enjoyed that."

He ran his hands up and down her arms. "Because it was overdue."

She played with his hair. "I can't believe you invited me on an overnight trip, in front of my mother, and lived to tell the tale." She snickered. "She must be getting soft on you."

"Yeah, right." He pulled her to him for a quick, scorching kiss. When he came up for air, he hugged her. "I'm proud of you."

The hum of a car around the corner had him stepping back out of her personal space. *Damn.* He wanted to kiss her again, make her remember how good it was between them. He locked eyes with her.

She backed against the door, her eyes dark and filled with want.

Yeah, she remembered. He smiled and gave her all the details for tomorrow. He enjoyed his work, but bringing Jade along would take his passion for work to a whole new level.

Chapter Fourteen

JADE STEPPED OFF a wood-paneled elevator into The Sagamore Resort's chandeliered lobby. The space overflowed with poinsettias and comfortable chairs. She moved to the east side of the room for a few moments to enjoy a woman in a red evening gown playing Beethoven on a grand piano before she strode across the glossy parquet floor to the left hallway. Walking up carpeted steps to the restaurant entrance, she checked the time on her phone. Six fifteen. Ben and Jeremy should be there.

She smoothed her fitted blue velvet v-neck blouse and black slacks while she scanned the stylish dining room packed with guests. The clatter of silverware on china and animated conversations was offset by the classical music filtering in from the lobby.

A black-suited hostess approached her. "May I help you?"

Jade nodded to the far wall where Jeremy waved to her. "Oh, I've located my party. Thanks." Ben's back was to her, and she ached to run her fingers through that thick black mane of his. How long could they keep their relationship secret when part of her wanted to shout it to the world?

Her brother stood. "Hey, sis." He greeted her with a kiss on the cheek.

"Hi." She slid onto the chair next to him. "Did you boys have a productive day?" Aside from a few new wrinkles around Jeremy's eyes left as a reminder of his recent struggles, he looked the same as before the accident.

"We did," he responded.

She smiled. "That's great. I did too." Like hers, Jeremy's scars were internal. It was only after she had talked with him for a few hours on the car ride here that she learned he was no longer the idealistic young man she'd left behind eight years ago. She looked across the table and met Ben's eyes. Yeah, he missed her too. Her knees started to bounce and her mind wandered, thinking about the night ahead.

Jeremy hadn't yet noticed the electric pull between herself and Ben. He leaned around the table and gave her a rare hug. "I'm glad you came along for the ride, sis. Did you finish your shopping?"

She nodded. She'd spent hours searching through the little touristy shops along Route 9N in Lake George Village, finally finding an outdoor wall thermometer for Ben's house—complete with a picture of a Golden Retriever. That way, his guests would always know the correct temperature.

"Great. Want to do mine next?" her brother joked. "That way I can stay on my lazy ass and just let Christmas flow right over me."

Jeremy was grinning, but something about the statement irked her, reminding her of her mother's accusations about Ben, and the whole family's fears that Jeremy might again fall down in his resolve. She took a sip of water and shook her head. "Christmas shopping is personal. Get into the spirit. You've already lost two years, Jeremy, and that scared Mom and Dad so much. Please don't waste any more." She registered Ben's steady gaze and her brother's sudden stillness. "I'm sorry. I know you were joking, but it's something I needed to say."

Jeremy's voice was flat. "Noted."

"I'm sorry," she said again.

"It's okay. If you needed to say it, maybe I needed to hear it. I'll do my own shopping. You're right. My whole life is a slippery slope."

"You've done great. You're doing great."

Jeremy signaled the waiter, signaling to Jade at the same time that they'd both said enough. "Ready to order?"

She nodded, gazing at Ben across the table. He'd stayed quiet and watchful through the moments of tension, only relaxing when he saw that things were going to be okay. He cared about both of them. It was so clear, and it touched her so deeply. She opened her mouth to speak but everything she wanted to say was far too revealing, too personal.

I love you.

Ben's mouth turned up slightly as he relaxed. "Jade, do you mind if Jeremy and I talk shop so he and I don't have to meet after dinner?"

"Sure. Talk away."

"Thanks." He turned his attention to her brother, in business mode. "We haven't talked about casting. What do you think about…"

She enjoyed listening to Ben as he explained the logistics of interviewing potential cast members with Jeremy over appetizers and salad then moved onto filming location details during the entrée. Ben's mind was quick yet her brother seemed to follow along easily, taking notes on his electronic tablet at intervals.

Jade picked at her salmon Florentine, determined to focus on the positive. Jeremy was finally starting to sound like the boy she once knew, happy to be alive and looking forward to an adventure. Sure, there was that underlying sadness he covered with jokes and smirks designed to keep people at a safe emotional distance, but at least he'd connected with Ben enough to work at Stephens Productions. It was great hearing them talk about the upcoming project together. Maybe this was her Christmas miracle instead of her happily-ever-after with Ben, as she had begun to hope for ever since their night together.

If so, it was enough.

Dessert arrived and the three were enjoying their coffees when the center table caught the dining room's attention once again. One of the diners was celebrating her birthday and the wait staff invited patrons to sing Happy Birthday. Everyone joined in the celebration, clapping when the young woman blew out the candle on her cake.

Jade took a final bite of her Crème Brulée and set her spoon down. *I'm not old, but I'll be blowing out thirty candles on my cake in a few months.* Who was she fooling? She had assumed she was losing sleep when her subconscious realized she wasn't going anywhere in her career. She had made the right move by leaving marketing behind and forging a new path with more education. But she hadn't started sleeping full nights again until after she had slept with Ben.

Love was the answer to my problem.

Yeah, but the timing wasn't right. She was ready for a serious relationship. If she were honest with herself, she was ready for marriage…and more… with Ben. But how could he be in the same place? He'd so recently broken up with a woman he'd dated for years. He said it was because they were on different paths, but perhaps the reality was that he wasn't ready to share his home and his life with someone. There was no way Ben could be serious about her after such a short time, and after their rocky history.

He cares for me, he desires me, but he couldn't possibly love me.

The check arrived. Soon, they would say good night and return to their respective rooms. She wouldn't seek him out, but if he came to her room, she wouldn't turn him away. They would have one more memorable night together, and then she'd have to call a halt, for her own emotional protection.

Her bittersweet Christmas gift.

✦ ✦ ✦

A SOFT RAP came on Jade's hotel door about an hour after the three of them had parted ways. She turned off the TV, the only light left in the room cast by the vanilla-scented candles on the dresser and nightstands. She swished to the door in the new silk and lace nightgown she'd bought in town today in anticipation of their romantic evening.

Heart pitter-pattering, she peered through the peephole. Ben's ebony hair was damp, as if he'd showered in a rush, and he wore a black golf shirt and slacks. He was beautiful, and he was hers for the night. She opened the door, her throat tight. "Hey," she breathed.

Without a word, he swept into the room, closing the door with a foot as he folded her into his arms and took her mouth with his.

She threaded her hands through his hair and held his head close, savoring his lips and tongue as they ravaged her mouth. *I love you, I love you, I love you.*

He leaned back and growled, "This is all I could think about all day." He took her mouth again.

By the time they came up for air again she was dizzy with wanting, surprised to find herself with her back against the wall, arms above her head and hands entwined with his, her beautiful white silk nightgown in a heap on the floor.

Ben took a ragged breath and leaned his forehead against hers. "I can't get enough of you. Why did we wait so long?"

Her mind a slave to her body, she could only moan in response as he slid his hands down the sensitive skin on the inside of her arms and cupped her shoulders, bending his head toward one breast. He was like a man coming home after days on the road, his suckling and kneading a mixture of desire and reverence and desperation. Her heart squeezed painfully. How could she ever let him go?

She could be herself with Ben. He knew all her secrets, and he accepted her without reservations. He didn't care whether she wore makeup or had a career or ate like a bird. Lifting one leg, she curled it around him and rubbed his muscled thigh.

He hooked a hand under her knee and lifted.

She slid up and around him, both legs wrapping firmly around his waist. She let instinct guide her, rocking up and down, teasing his hardness beneath his trousers as she kissed him—letting him know without words all she would never say.

We've got to get closer.

He must have read her thoughts, because he swung her around and set her on the king size bed while he stripped quickly, stooping to pick his trousers off the floor and retrieve packets out of a pocket before scooting next to her. He lay on his back next to her and reached out a hand.

She wound her fingers with his and concentrated on breathing.

He rolled toward her, leaning up on one elbow to look down at her. "I kind of like this arrangement. How about you?"

She let her eyes trail the long, beautiful length of him. "Mmm." Her heart cracked just a little at his words.

He straddled her body in one fluid motion, still holding

her hand as he peered down at her, a smile on his face. "In fact, I could get used to it, having you in my arms like this."

Her breath caught. Had their night together changed the game for him too?

He leaned down to kiss her. "I'll miss you, but we'll have so much fun when you come home."

A quiet tear rolled down her cheek. There would be no more nights like this for them. She didn't dare keep it open ended. She knew she had to cut it off clean.

He brushed back her hair from her face. "Hey, what's wrong?"

"Nothing." She smiled. "Just happy."

For now.

She pulled him close as she pushed away the sadness.

Chapter Fifteen

"THERE'S NO ROOM at the inn."

Jade gave Kendra two thumbs-up from her spot in her front pew. Midnight service on Christmas was her favorite, between the soft glow of the individually handheld candles, the altar decorated with brilliant red poinsettias, and holy incense—all lent to the festive, sacred vibe in her community church.

"But if you want, there's a shed where I keep the animals. That will be warm and dry for the night."

Jade signaled for the change of scenery.

"They're doing a great job," Hannah whispered next to her. "But I'm worried about Mitch. Does he look green to you?"

Jade eyed her nephew, one of the three angels walking up the aisle to stand behind the makeshift manger on the altar. "Did he get into the cookies again?"

"I told him only two," Hannah groaned.

Jade gave her a sidelong glance as they stood with the rest of the congregation for two verses of "O Holy Night."

Her sister-in-law looked behind her. "I don't see Jack. Do

you?"

She looked back and spotted Ben, three rows back on the end. She whirled around to the front and shook her head.

Hannah was biting a nail. "What are we going to do? I think he's going to hurl."

"Pray?" Jade joked, still shaken from the sight of the man who had stolen her heart.

"I'm going to take him downstairs. See you in a bit." Hannah blew out her candle and set her hymnal on the pew bench behind her.

Jade nodded and snuck another peek at the tall, black-haired man singing with the rest of the congregation, his rich baritone one more piece of what she adored about him.

She turned back to face the altar and signaled the appearance of the wise men.

She and Ben hadn't been together since returning from Lake George a week ago, between his work and her volunteering and trip downstate to see her friend with her mother. She had told herself it was just as well. She peeked over her shoulder and this time he caught her eyes. If looks could melt, she was a puddle.

The service ended and people spilled out of the church with smiles and yawns. She congratulated the children on their performance and wished their families a Merry Christmas. She looked around for her green wool coat and then remembered she had left it in the church hall. She turned to look for her parents and Grandma Bertie, but they were nowhere to be seen. Must be in the car.

She sped to the church hall, retrieved her coat, and was walking to the exit when a shadow crossed it. She stopped short.

"Want a lift home?" Ben stood in the doorway, looking better than a man had the right.

"Grandma didn't make it through the service, did she?"

"Nope. Jack asked if I'd mind bringing you home. I don't." He smiled.

She walked with him to the parking lot, empty except for his SUV. "People must have been eager to get their little ones home in bed before Santa's visit," she said to fill the silence.

They stopped at his vehicle and he opened the passenger door for her.

She slipped onto the chilly leather seat and rubbed her new pair of gloves together.

"So what's up? I got your texts about the excitement downstate with your friends. Everything okay?" He closed her door and jogged around to his side.

She chattered away, catching him up on all the details of her girl friends' dramas, omitting the part about how much she missed him and had a change of heart.

"It's like a living soap opera, isn't it?"

"You'd love them," she said without thinking.

"I bet I would."

His gaze had her thinking impossible thoughts. "Where's Sadie?"

"She better be sleeping on her bed instead of eating the presents under the tree."

"Well, here's a present she has permission to chew to her heart's delight." She pulled out the mega rawhide bone she'd purchased for her favorite pooch. She sniffed and swallowed hard. *I'll miss that cuddle bug.*

He started the car and turned on the heater. "We could deliver it to her personally. She's at the house."

She fought the temptation. It would only make leaving all the more difficult. "You'd like that, wouldn't you? You're on Santa's naughty list, for sure."

"Fine with me, as long as my gift is you."

"We'd better not." She set the present on the seat between them. "It's late, and I'm worried about Grandma Bertie. She's had some setbacks recently."

"But it's Christmas." He tossed the gift onto the backseat and pulled her close for a kiss.

She savored the touch of his lips against hers. But she couldn't let herself lose sight of the hard truth. She loved him but he didn't feel so strongly. He wanted a temporary gift, she wanted forever. She pulled away. "Yes, Merry Christmas."

He cocked his head.

She pushed a silver-wrapped box onto his lap. "I got something for you, too."

He smiled. "Can I open it now?" At her nod, he ripped off the silver wrapping and opened the lid. He chuckled.

"Now you'll always know exactly how cold it is on your porch."

He leaned forward and gave her another slow, mind-numbing kiss before pulling away. "Thank you. It's perfect." He reached inside his jacket and pulled out an envelope. "And this is for you. I really hope you like it."

She stopped breathing for a long moment, not having considered what Ben might give her. "You really didn't have to."

"I wanted to. C'mon. Open it."

She tore open the envelope and pulled out a folded paper—a travel brochure. A smaller envelope slipped out as well, falling onto her lap. "What's this?" She stared at the round trip plane ticket. "Oh." He'd put thought into her gift too.

He wants to see me again.

"You said you never got to Williamsburg." He pushed back a lock of her hair that had fallen to cover her eye. "Say yes. I'd love for you to join me on your Spring Break."

Every fiber of her being wanted to say yes, to accept his

generous gift. It would guarantee they'd see each other, be in each other's arms again—for an entire blessed week—a few months from now. But she couldn't. It would only curtail the agony. "Ben, I really appreciate all the thought you put into this gift. I do." She swallowed, struggling to stay strong. She carefully placed all the papers back into the envelope. "But I'm sorry. I can't accept it."

"I thought you said you'd love to get together, do stuff." Anger laced his words. He turned away, but not before she saw the hurt in his beautiful eyes.

God, this was harder than she'd anticipated. But they'd both move on sooner if she made a clean break. "I—I've changed my mind about our arrangement."

"I see." He shifted the truck into gear and shot onto Main Street.

She stared out the window until the festive storefronts gave way to clapboard houses and snow-covered fields. Turning the envelope over in her hand, she leaned forward and placed it inside the glove box.

Was it her imagination or did he flinch when she clicked the glove box closed?

Eventually, he pulled into her parents' driveway. He shifted into park, fingers rapping on the steering wheel. "Well, at least you didn't make confetti out of it this time."

Eighth grade, again.

"So that's it?" he said. "We're over?"

"No strings, we said."

He turned and met her eyes, a confused expression on his face. "And for you that means pulling the plug with no warning."

She forced herself to breathe. He had a right to be angry. She was cutting him off, cold turkey, like she had the sleeping pills. And it sucked—for both of them. "It's not what I want any more."

"Why not?"

How could she tell him she wanted more, that she couldn't bear the thought of being his sometimes girlfriend until he eventually found the one he could love and marry and make babies with? She sucked in a breath. That would break her heart. And if she told him she wanted more, he'd have even more right to be angry, since she was changing the rules after they'd already played the game for weeks. No, it was better to say nothing. "I'm leaving. I don't know what's going to happen after I get to university…" She heard her voice trail off.

"That's it, then." He nodded toward her house, signaling the conversation was over. "Merry Christmas."

She leaned over, tears in her eyes, and brushed her lips against his. "Merry Christmas, Ben. I'll miss you." All the energy drained out of her, she stumbled out of his SUV and into her parents' dark house, up the stairs to her bedroom before she burst into tears.

She stared out the window in the darkness. His SUV sat in her driveway for a long time. Finally, it rolled away down the street into the night.

"Goodbye Ben," she whispered through a tear-choked throat.

✦ ✦ ✦

JADE WALKED INTO her parents' living room on Christmas evening and sank onto the sofa next to her mother. "Grandma's settled."

"Thanks, Sweetie." Her mother relaxed next to her in the soft glow of the Christmas tree lights, sipping her decaf.

Cheers broke out in the den on the other side of the house and excited stomping shook the floorboards.

Her father stirred from his post-dinner snooze. "What is all that racket?"

"The kids are playing their new game system in the den with Jack and Hannah," Gigi explained.

Jeremy laughed. "Maggie and Mitch must be winning."

"Those kids could wake the dead," Dennis grumbled and shifted in his recliner.

Quiet descended on the four of them.

Jade fiddled with the sleeve of her sweater. She had always enjoyed Christmas, but today, she was eager for it to end. She struggled to continue the charade that her world hadn't crumbled after last evening's Midnight Service.

"Are you sure you're all right?" her mother asked her for the hundredth time since breakfast.

She nodded and swallowed hard, a lump the size of a snowball forming in her throat every time she pictured Ben's reaction to the rejection of his gift. She had managed to hurt him again, in spite of her best intentions. She sighed.

"She's lying," Jeremy observed.

Jade shot him a look. "Dinner was fabulous, Mom. I forgot how much I love your cloved ham and mashed potatoes with pineapple gravy."

"Not that you ate any of it," her father added.

Jeremy rose from his chair. "So, what's up with you and Ben?"

I'm ready. He isn't. End of story. She ignored her brother's pestering and stared at the Christmas tree until it swam in her vision, a kaleidoscope of primary colors.

Gigi spit out her coffee. "Ben? Excuse me?" She glanced between her two children.

"My guess," Jeremy drawled, "is that they argued. That would account for all her moping around today, on the most wonderful time of the year." He sang the last part and stepped between Jade and the tree. "That about right, sis?"

Jade glared at her brother before pasting a smile on for her parents.

They weren't buying it.

Shit.

"What's this about?" Gigi's eyes lit with concern.

Jade pressed her lips together, her stomach churning.

"Is there something going on between you and Ben?"

She shook her head, tears threatening at the back of her eyes. "No, Mom," she whispered past the growing lump, "you'll be very pleased to know there isn't." She folded her hands together to keep from flying apart.

Her mother set her mug on the coffee table, the clang of ceramic on glass ominous, like the clanging of a bell before a prisoner's execution. "But there was?"

"Yes."

"Well, dear, you can't say I didn't warn you."

Her mother's words struck her like a whooshing guillotine. She wrapped her arms around herself and sank further into the sofa.

Jeremy's voice came through a wind tunnel. "Ben's a good guy. He's helped me out a lot the past few years."

Gigi shot off the sofa, trembling with anger. "How can you defend that man? He enabled your drinking." She pointed at Jade still frozen on the sofa. "He broke up with a girl, set his sights on my daughter just a few days later and broke her heart – your sister."

Jeremy wove a hand through his dark blond hair. "I didn't need anyone to enable my drinking. No one poured the stuff down my throat or twisted my arm." His voice shook with emotion. "My old boss didn't want me back. No one else in town thought I deserved a second chance, except for Ben. He was the only one. I have a job today because of him, and I'm proud to call him my best friend."

Jade leaned forward to watch the drama unfold. She glanced at her father, his face mottled with red.

"He encouraged you to go out and party with him," Gigi retorted.

"Other way around, Mom."

"He threw around his money. You were in a fragile condition after the accident. He may have meant well, but he put you in harm's way," Gigi finished her well-rehearsed litany.

Jeremy moved to gently grasp her by the shoulders. "Mom, listen to me. Ben has never been one to throw money around. That was all Sofia. She liked his money more than he does. She's the one who would call for rounds and have it put on Ben's tab." He sighed. "Besides, Ben wasn't with me when I snuck drinks at work, or drank myself into a stupor each night at home." He shook her gently, his voice brooking no argument. "He had nothing to do with it. I'm the one who caused my problems. Me, and no one else."

Squeals of excitement from the den split the tension-filled silence.

After a long moment, Gigi reached up and placed her hands on her youngest child's face. "I wish I had known how much you were hurting. Maybe that's what this is about. I should be beating myself up, not hiding behind anger against someone else." She glanced at her husband, their eyes both wet and faces lined with regret. She shook her head. "We had no idea. It took us too long. I'm so sorry." Tears tumbled onto her cheeks.

Jeremy's voice was soft. "Don't cry, Mama." He hugged her close, rocking her like she was the child. "Ben didn't do anything wrong and neither did you or Dad. In fact, you all saved my life." He glanced at his father. "You put together that intervention." He gazed at his mother. "You gave me all the love and support I could want." He leaned back enough to poke a finger at his chest. "This has always been my problem. Always remember that."

Jade's father rose to wrap beefy arms around his youngest child and wife.

Jade's heart swelled and she burst into tears. Jeremy looked at her over their mother's head. "Come here, you."

She unfolded from her cocoon to join them, savoring this moment of acceptance and love.

"Hey, what's going on in here?" Jack asked. Soon, he and his family joined the group hug, making the unit complete.

Almost.

Grandma Bertie was sleeping upstairs...and Ben was next door at his family's house.

As they slowly parted amid tears and smiles and hugs, Jade wandered into the den and gazed out the window through the dark to the lights next door. They drew her in, welcomed her. She ignored the tears still flowing onto her cheeks and trailing down her neck.

I wish I could go to him. I can't. It's over.

She turned away from the window and wandered back to the living room.

Her father was talking to her brothers. "So what *did* happen between Ben and Jade?"

Jade stilled and stepped back into the hallway, peeking around the corner.

Jack shrugged and turned to his younger brother with a quizzical look.

"They were crazy for each other." Jeremy leaned forward. "You should have seen them at The Sagamore. I never saw Ben look at Sofia the way he did Jade that night over dinner."

"But what about her?" Jack asked. "Jade has always been a flitter. Do you think she loves him? Would she turn down the opportunity to attend USC for him? Ben's business is on the East Coast. He couldn't just pick up and move to California."

"I don't think we need to worry about it. It's far too soon after his break-up with Sofia for him to get serious with anyone. Even someone as wonderful as your sister," Dad observed.

Jade turned, pressing herself back against the foyer wall, her eyes squeezed shut. Even her father could see their relationship was doomed. She pulled out her phone and sent a mass media message to her four girlfriends: *Merry Christmas! Anyone want company tomorrow? I'm headed your way. oxo*

✦ ✦ ✦

BEN'S DOORBELL RANG. Thank the Lord, three excruciating days had passed but she had finally come to her senses. He grabbed the envelope he'd set on the mantle early Christmas morning before running to whip open his front door. "Hey."

"Hey back." Jeremy stepped across the threshold. "I broke my phone so I couldn't call you first." He patted the binder under one arm. "I have the scripts Craig sent." At Ben's blank look he added, "You mentioned going over them prior to shooting next week. I figured now was as good a time as any." He looked at the envelope in Ben's hand. "Or not?"

Ben shook his head. "No, it's fine." He led the way to the kitchen. "Can I get you something? I still have Christmas leftovers. My mom wouldn't let me leave her house without enough food for an army."

They grabbed refreshments then moved into the dining room and sat together at the table, soon immersed in the details of the script. Sadie eventually rose from her spot under the table and left the room, her nails clicking on the tile as she trotted into the living room. The clicking stopped, replaced by a short whine.

"She must want out." Ben stood and stretched.

"Whoa." His friend looked at the clock and stretched his arms high over his head. "I had no idea I'd been here this long." He stood and grabbed his coat off the back of the couch. "I promised Mom I'd be there later for dinner and I have other errands yet to run."

"Did you end up going there on Christmas?" Ben asked.

"Got there late. It was hard at first, I won't lie. But it was nice." He stuck his arms through his coat, and asked, as if an afterthought. "Have you talked to Jade?"

Ben shifted. "Why?"

"Well, I may be a recovering alcoholic, but I'm not blind. The way she was acting the other night, I'm guessing my suspicion is correct. She played with the kids, participated in conversations, but she was off. You know what I mean?"

Ben sat back down and wiped a hand across his face. "Look, I really care about her. I actually thought we could have a future together, but I figured we'd work it slow, and then she just cut off."

Sadie uttered a short bark.

"Just a minute." He strode to the sliding door and let the dog out. "Was I wrong? Hell, I would have given her a ring if I'd thought in a million years she'd accept it."

"What did you give her?"

He glanced at the envelope on the table. "Plane tickets for a getaway, and she turned them down. Did you talk to her?"

"She wouldn't. That's how I knew you were the one responsible." Jeremy fastened his coat. "Maybe...you gave her the wrong gift."

Ben walked his friend to the front door. "This doesn't make sense. I put a lot of thought into it. She's always wanted to go there. I thought it signaled... all the right stuff."

"Maybe she was looking for something more."

Ben shook his head in disbelief.

"She's turning thirty soon. The writing's on the wall, as they say."

"Slow was wrong. Despite what she said." His heart skipped a beat before jump-starting again. He spit out an expletive. "You think she wants a commitment?"

"Why not?"

"Because she's Jade."

"Yeah, and you're Ben, the guy who ended a five-year relationship a week before you ran into each other."

Ben grabbed his coat and followed his friend outside.

Jeremy glanced over his shoulder. "Where are you going?"

"I have to talk with her."

Jeremy jumped in his truck. "Too late."

He grabbed the door before Jeremy shut it behind him. "What do you mean?"

"She left day after Christmas. Sorry, buddy, she's in the city, seeing her friends before she starts school in January." Jeremy yanked the door shut and started the engine before powering down his window.

Ben's mind swirled and he started back toward the house, leaving a string of curses in his wake.

"What are you doing now?" Jeremy called.

"Taking Sadie to my parents. I've got to go see Jade, wherever she is."

He stepped onto the porch, the porch where they'd made that stupid agreement about friends with benefits. He should never have accepted those conditions. He'd felt far more for Jade than friendship or a casual hook-up. He yelled across the yard to his friend and gave him a wave. "There will be an update on this, trust me. And thanks. I owe you."

"You don't owe me anything, Ben. Go get her." Jeremy backed out of the yard onto the main road heading back into town.

Chapter Sixteen

JADE SAT IN the Westchester County airport waiting for her return flight to Plattsburgh, her trusty carry-on at her side and knees bouncing non-stop. She had been lucky the airline agreed to change her itinerary without charging extra. Then again, it seemed like everyone around her was in a jolly mood, including the ticket agent at the counter. The Christmas spirit must have staying power, since New Year's was around the corner. She'd take it, and bring it home with her, if she could.

Being with the girls had centered her. They'd listened to her story, Bree offering advice, Kara offering wine to go with Elena's offer of chocolate and Cass's serious offer to slap Ben Stephens silly.

Now, she smiled. They were true friends and she had been wrong to cut them off, keep them at an emotional distance. Coming to New York for a few days had been the right choice, and now it was her choice to go home. In the few days she had been away, she'd missed Starling, her family, the community's Christmas spirit and…Ben.

✦ ✦ ✦

"IS JADE HERE?" Ben asked the petite brunette.

The young woman came onto the porch of the beautiful old house, closing the door behind her very deliberately. "Is she expecting you?"

"No, but...you're Sabrina, right?"

She nodded, giving him a thorough once-over. He'd made a visit to Jade's parents and bared his heart to them. Something had happened over Christmas. Mrs Engel's attitude was softer, warmer. She'd given him the addresses he'd asked for, and she knew exactly why he wanted them, and what he planned. Whether he would receive the same cooperation from Jade's friends now seemed doubtful. He set his jaw.

"Wow." Sabrina said coolly. She glanced at her phone. "Yeah, so you hit rush hour, although it had to be lighter than usual with the holidays."

"I apologize for arriving at the dinner hour," he answered steadily.

I-87 had been a nightmare as far as Albany, with winter weather advisories in effect. It had opened up until he hit Manhattan. There, the pedestrian traffic clogged the intersections, making most a two-light wait minimum. Not to mention the three-hour crawl on the Long Island Expressway to Holly Point. But he had made it. That was all that mattered.

He looked past the pretty woman with long brown hair and peered in the window next to the door. A girl made in the same image as her mother peeked through the panes at him, a slice of folded pizza in her hand.

Two seconds later, the door opened again.

"Who are you?" the girl in tee shirt, jeans, and sneakers asked as she bit the end off the slice.

The scent of spicy tomato sauce tickled his nose and his stomach growled in earnest. He hadn't eaten since breakfast, stopping only once in the Diamond District to pick up his purchase from a cousin who worked there. His ears perked up. Were there women talking and laughing inside? Yes, there were. She had to be there. He bounced from foot to foot. "Hi, my name's—"

Sabrina's tone was matter-of-fact. "Charlie, this is Ben. He's the reason Aunt Jade is so sad."

The child called Charlie stuck her tongue at him and trounced away with her delicious pizza and bad attitude.

Bree closed the door again and smiled without humor. "Normally I wouldn't stand for such rude behavior from my offspring, but in this case, I think I'll let it pass."

He tried again. "I really would like to talk to Jade. If you could let her know I'm here."

She folded her arms and stuck out a well-shaped hip.

He sighed. How many people would he have to spill his heart to before he had the chance to spill it to Jade herself? From the look on the woman's face, he wasn't done yet. "Bree…"

"My friends call me Bree. You can call me Sabrina."

His fingers tightened into fists. "Sabrina then. Look, I'm in love with her, and I want to tell her that in person before she goes to California."

She wasn't impressed.

"I plan to join her there if she'll let me."

Still no dice.

He pulled out the black velvet ring box. "This is for her—if she'll have me."

That got a reaction. Jade's friend clucked her tongue and frowned in mock disappointment. "Yeah, well, I hate to tell you but you made the trek for nothing. She's over at Cass's place." She opened the door and moved to slip inside.

"Wait." He pulled the paper Mrs. Engel had given him out of his pocket. He read the address for one of two Manhattan addresses. "Is that it?"

She nodded, smiling like a Cheshire cat as she closed the door in his face.

Two hours later, another front door, another questionable welcome.

The chilly wind whipped through the alleys on either side of the three-story brick building, carrying yesterday's newspapers and assorted trash on its currents. He pressed the button for Apartment Six and waited. No response. He pressed again.

"Hey. Who's bugging me this late? Don't you know I'm on deadline? If I don't get this article done, I will hunt you down."

He took a step back then leaned forward to press the intercom. "Sorry. This is Ben. I'm here to see Jade."

"Ben? Okay. We've been expecting you."

She buzzed him in.

Finally. His heart threatened to leap through his chest. He was going to see her, feel her lips, touch her skin, inhale her scent, and tell her all the things he should have said on Christmas. He jogged into the building, punched the UP button and paced in front of the tiny elevator. Too impatient to wait a second more, he ran up the three flights instead. He scanned the doors, searching. Last door on the right, jackpot. He took a deep breath, ran his hands through his hair then rapped once.

The door flung open.

Where Ben expected to see the woman he loved, there stood a cynical stranger. She hooked a manicured finger in his direction. "I'm Cass. Come in." She welcomed him as if inviting him into her evil lair.

He stepped over the threshold into the tiny apartment. "Nice to meet you. But where is she?" There appeared to be two bedrooms about the size of his master suite's walk-in closet but those doors were open and no one was inside. He leaned to peek into the third and final door, the bathroom. No one was in there either. He turned back to the woman circling him like prey. "You said we. If you weren't referring to Jade, who did you mean?"

"Whom."

He blinked. "Excuse me?"

"It's 'whom' not 'who.'"

And after the hours of driving and lack of sleep, and now what appeared was going to be another dead-end interrogation, his temper got the best of him. "I'm here to see Jade. I need to talk to her. Now if you don't mind, can you tell me where she is or when she'll be back?" He put up a finger when she opened her mouth to respond. "And please, don't answer me with a question or correct my grammar."

"Jade didn't tell me you had a temper."

"I think it's justified, right now."

"Only you don't know whom you're messing with."

"I just want to see her, okay?"

"After you offer her nothing better than a romp in the hay?"

"She was the one who wanted friends with benefits, not me."

"And you were the one who just ended a five-year-long relationship less than a week before you ran into her. Can you blame her for trying to protect her own heart a little? She had no choice, faced with someone not capable of commitment."

He whipped out the black velvet box for the second time that evening. "Does this look like I'm incapable of commitment?"

She stared, her brown eyes wide, and told him the truth. Jade had flown back to Plattsburgh this afternoon.

Chapter Seventeen

BEN WOKE FROM a dead sleep and felt Sadie's big body beside him. After the drive last night, he'd crashed fully dressed on his couch, and now there was bright sun streaming through the windows. He blinked and sat up.

Jade.

He sprang up and grabbed his phone off the end table, while Sadie circled around his legs. It was ten already, and after what her friends had put him through yesterday, he couldn't wait another moment. Hadn't he proved himself enough? He needed to find out from Jade herself, not her parents, not her brothers, not the over-protective sisterhood of her friends. He ignored the hollow hunger in his stomach and texted her. *Where are you? Want to see you. Tell me where we can meet.*

Then he paced. Fed Sadie in the kitchen. Dived into a change of clothes. His phone chimed finally. *I'm at the Winter Carnival with Hannah and the twins. You here?* He texted. *Not yet. Meet me at the ice castle. Twenty minutes?* She texted one more time. *Okay.*

Yes. This was it—do or die.

Nineteen minutes later, he stood on the stage set up within

the ice castle, bundled up but still freezing his ass off.

"You sure she's coming?" asked Alice, the lady in charge of the town's annual winter event.

He glanced at the time on his phone. "She said she would. I'm early."

"Just remember, we need to set up for the live entertainment. I pushed them back ten minutes so you could do this." She patted his shoulder. "I hope it works out for you."

"Me, too." He waved as she stepped down to street level. "Thanks again, Alice."

"Good luck." She turned and soon disappeared into the crowd clogging Main Street.

In the twenty-four hours that he'd been away, the community of Starling had transformed Main Street into a winter wonderland, complete with seasonal murals painted on storefront windows, winter-themed carnival games, and dozens of ice sculptures, the largest of which – in the shape of a stage – he stood on at the end of the street, waiting for his moment of truth.

"Ben?"

Ten feet away, with a blue snow cone in her hand and a twin on either side, stood the woman he loved.

He grinned, and his heart started to thump in his chest. What if everything he'd said to the people who cared about her didn't make a bit of difference? What if all of them were wrong? "Come here," he called, with more authority than he felt, right now. She owned him, if only she knew it. Did she know it? Did she want it?

She turned to her sister-in-law, handed off her snow cone, wiped the blue off her lips and ruffled the twins' hair before winding her way toward him through the people gathering in front of the ice stage. She stopped at the bottom of the ice-cut stairs. "What are you doing up there?" Her face was flushed pink and beautiful as ever.

He gestured for her to join him. "Come up."

She looked out at the crowd. "Are you crazy?"

"Probably. I have something important to ask you, and rather than depending on the grapevine, I figured we'd give them the details straight from the horse's mouth, so to speak."

She shook her head and crossed her arms.

"C'mon."

"Not happening."

This wasn't how he'd envisioned his afternoon going.

Alice interrupted their stand-off. "Ben, five minutes."

He nodded.

"What's that about?" Jade rubbed at her lips.

"Everything, I hope." He lifted the mic out of the stand near him, and turned to her.

But she held out her mitten-clad hand, not to climb up to him, but to push him away. "Ben, I don't need the grand gesture. I already know how you drove all over Long Island and New York City looking for me. I heard what a hard time the girls gave you. They didn't need to do that."

"No?" he said softly.

"No. So come to me. I want to talk with you—just the two of us."

He set the mic back in its holder, walked across the gleaming, frozen stage, and took the chiseled steps two at a time. He could do this her way. He'd do it any way she wanted. "Where to, Milady?"

She giggled. "Funny you should say that. I have the perfect hideaway in mind." She led him under the stage through a long ice hallway behind it to a huge ice room.

Ben looked around. "Cool." He'd forgotten about this part of the castle, which would be used for local media photos of the Winter Royal Court after tonight's parade. He looked up at the ceiling made out of white cloth draped over white wood beams. High ice walls had slits for windows, allowing the sunshine in without giving away privacy—in spite of the crowds outside its walls.

They stepped into the space and moved together across a snow floor toward two oversized ice chairs outfitted with purple fleece cushions. He smiled. "You're right. It is perfect."

Then he bowed.

She grinned and curtsied, allowing him to escort her to one of the chairs. She sat and looked for him to take the seat beside her.

He shook his head and sank to one knee.

She stared at him, eyes shining.

He glanced at her hands. "May I?"

She nodded.

He slid off her mittens and tucked them in his suit pocket. "There. Now we're ready." He took a deep breath, saying the words that lived in his heart. "Jade Emily Engel, I love you with my whole heart and soul. You are my fellow explorer, my best friend, and love of my life. I will follow you to the ends of the earth, as long as we can be together. I want to make a life with you. With *you*. The real you. The person I've always known, not the person you tried to become, only to hurt yourself so much. Will you marry me?" He pulled the ring from his trouser pocket.

She looked down at him and at the ring, her voice shaking. "You would leave Starling and everything you love behind to be with me?"

He nodded.

"I thought I was your rebound girl."

He shook his head. "Like I told your parents, ending my relationship with Sofia right before bumping into you was meant to be. It was our second chance."

Her jaw dropped. "You talked to my parents?"

"I asked them for their blessing, and your mom's the one who gave me the girls' addresses so I could find you." He leaned toward her. "I had to tell you I love you, I couldn't wait another day. I want to spend the rest of our lives together."

She clapped a hand over her mouth, tears running down her face. "I thought you weren't ready. I thought you couldn't be, so soon."

"Soon?" he whispered. "How long have we known each other?"

She laughed and held her finger out for the ring. "Yes, Benjamin Stephens, I'll marry you. I love you, too. You're right, I think part of me dreamed it from the first day we sat together on that split rail fence."

He slipped the diamond solitaire onto her chilly finger then stood, pulling her into a strong hug. He'd never have to let her go again. "Cold?" he teased.

She nuzzled against him. "Yes. You can warm me up, and I'll warm you right back." She looked at the cold, wet ice surrounding them. "But not here, although I will always cherish that you asked me to marry you here. On a throne."

He grinned. "I agree it establishes the parameters of our relationship quite well. Your majesty. Whose wish is my command, et cetera, et cetera." He handed her mittens back with a flourish. "By the way, your tongue is blue and tastes incredible."

She accepted the mittens with grace and promptly swatted him on the sleeve for his remark. "In that case, I wish to live with you in that beautiful big house of yours with Sadie. I wish to earn my Social Work Degree at State College then find a job close to Starling. And most of all, I wish to travel with you, make love with you in all four seasons, and be best friends forever."

"Well, what are we waiting for then?" He led the way back through the ice castle and into the crowd. Tonight, after they made passionate love, they'd snuggle together, and they could light a candle in the window together, every winter's night for the rest of their lives.

The End

All I Want for Christmas

A New York Christmas Story

Jennifer Gracen

Acknowledgements

I love the vibrant Tule Publishing family. What a wonderful group! Thanks for welcoming me into it. Thank you, Jane Porter, for giving me the opportunity to write this story. Thank you, Lilian Darcy, for being an editor and brainstormer extraordinaire. And thanks to you both for your enthusiasm and your kindness.

Thank you to Maitiú Ó Raġallaiġ and Donna Lutz for your willingness to answer all my questions. If anything's amiss with Sean's Irishness or Cassandra's academic world, that falls squarely on my shoulders. You two were so cheerfully helpful; your assistance was invaluable.

Dedication

This one's for my three closest writing sisters: Jeannie Moon, Patty Blount, and Jolyse Barnett. Writing the *Christmas in New York* stories together was challenging, exciting, and mostly, just plain fun. It was such a pleasure to take this ride with you, and I hope one day we get to do something like it again. I love you. #Fab4

Chapter One

STANDING ON THE crowded, bustling sidewalk of Seventh Avenue, Cassandra Baines sipped her peppermint hot cocoa as she waited for her best friend. She'd placed herself at the center of the top step so when Bree came up the escalator, out of Penn Station, she'd be right there and easy to spot.

The familiar smells and sounds of Manhattan barraged her from all sides as she stood in the midst of frenetic activity. So many people—hustling into Penn to make their trains, coming out of Penn eager to roam the city, or just trying to get through the crowds to wherever they were headed. Cars and taxis bulleted down the street, horns blaring, the exhaust fumes mixing with the smoky smell of pretzels and chestnuts in the cold air. A group of teenage girls hustled by, all of them talking simultaneously.

Cassandra wasn't fazed by the chaos. She was a lifelong New Yorker, born and raised on Long Island, less than ninety minutes away from Manhattan. She'd spent her undergrad years at NYU and done her graduate program at Columbia, and now she had a tiny apartment in Chelsea and taught English Lit at NYU. Noise didn't register and crowded sidewalks didn't make her claustrophobic. The only thing ruffling her at the moment was wondering where Sabrina was. She should have been here by now.

A cold gust of wind blew, lifting the ends of Cassandra's shoulder length hair. She shivered, glad she'd chosen to wear her fuzzy wool hat, thickest scarf, and heavier wool coat. The temperature hadn't gotten above forty degrees that day, and sure felt like it was dropping into the low thirties now. She took another sip of the hot chocolate to keep warm.

"Cass!"

She turned in the direction of the familiar voice, and there was Bree, coming up the escalator. In a few seconds, they were hugging and chatting and all was bright again.

Going to see the lighting of the tree at Rockefeller Center had been an annual tradition since the girls were babies. Four women had been sorority sisters in college, became the closest of friends, and bonded for life. After graduation, they'd made a point of getting together several times a year, which had been fairly easy, since all four of them lived in New York. So when those four women had their own daughters—Cassandra, Sabrina, Jade, Kara, and Elena—the next generation of girls were practically raised as sisters. They'd become an expanded loving network that shared in each other's lives as one big family.

Some of Cassandra's best childhood memories were of huge Thanksgivings with everyone at Aunt Enza's house, out east on Long Island. A few days later, they'd all meet up in the city for the tree lighting. The four moms especially loved holidays and loved creating celebratory traditions . . . but things had changed after Aunt Marie had died in the Towers on September 11th. A black hole ripped all of their lives open. Kara and Elena no longer had a mother, the other moms had lost their sister, and the sorrow was a tangible thing none of them had been able to shake off for a long time. Having one another to lean on had gotten them all through those dark days.

And the years passed, and the girls all got older, and some of the traditions had changed slightly. Elena, the youngest, had refused to set foot in New York City after her mother died and she moved away with her father—and really, no one could blame her. Jade had moved to Tampa a few years ago. Even though they had all made it to Aunt Enza's for Thanksgiving this year, not all of them were going to the tree lighting ceremony. In fact, for various reasons, Cassandra and Bree were the only ones making the pilgrimage.

And they planned to make the most of it.

Bree had dropped her young daughter off at her mom's for the night so she could make it into the city. Now, she and Cass made their way to Rockefeller Center, heads down against the cold gusts of wind. They walked up 33rd Street so they could look at the holiday displays in the picture windows of Macy's. After that, they walked up another few blocks and made the left onto Fifth Avenue. It wasn't a short walk from Penn Station to Rockefeller Center, but they loved to do it every year, even in the cold.

They passed all the big department stores that decorated their window displays for the holidays. The scent of sugared nuts and pretzels and smoke floated on the frigid air. Cassandra looked around and smiled happily. There was a different energy in the city at this time of year; it was like the holiday season itself had sprinkled magic and light all around, and everyone just seemed to be . . . brighter. Happier. Excited. The vibe was a tangible thing, and Cassandra loved it. Every year, it revitalized her and filled her with joy.

Two hours later, after the tree lighting ceremony, they pushed their way back through the crowds. They were even

ALL I WANT FOR CHRISTMAS

colder now, but they linked arms and chatted as they walked. Cassandra spoke of how busy her schedule was with final exams looming next week. Bree talked about how her daughter, Charlie, was kicking ass on the local hockey team—the only girl, she skated circles around all the boys, a natural talent. Cassandra marveled at that. Her nine-year-old goddaughter was a spitfire, all right, much like her mother. And Cassandra adored them both. A rush of affection shot through her and she smacked a kiss on the back of Bree's gloved hand.

"What was that for?" Bree asked, looking at Cassandra strangely.

"I just love you. I'm so glad you're here."

"Aww. I love you too. Wouldn't have missed it, Cass." Bree gripped Cassandra's arm tighter. "We have to keep these traditions alive, even if everyone else had to crap out this year."

"I wish Jade could have stayed a few more days and come out with us tonight," Cassandra said. "She hasn't come to the tree lighting in what, three or four years now?"

"Aunt Gigi's mother-in-law had a stroke," Bree reminded her. "They had to get back home."

"Yeah, I know," Cassandra said softly. "I didn't mean that to sound bratty." She hesitated, wondering if she should speak her next thought aloud, then realized of course she could: it was Bree, her best friend in the world, her sister. "Can I ask you something? I feel like Jade's . . . mad at me. Or something. She was distant at your mom's house." She shrugged and offered, "Maybe I'm being paranoid."

"You're not," Bree said, fielding a bump from a passerby, which in turn sent her bumping her into Cass. They both snorted at it. "Look, I'm sorry you felt that. But you know she's having a hard time right now. I think she's a little . . . jealous, actually."

Cassandra's eyes flew wide. "Of *me*?"

"Yeah."

"Seriously?" Cassandra couldn't wrap her head around that. "*Why?*"

"Because you're doing so well," Bree said, as if it were obvious. "You're making your career happen, just as you planned. Now, you're one of the youngest assistant professors at NYU. You're on the right track, and you're successful. Jade's in between jobs and not sure what comes next. I think she's just a little jealous. In the 'she has it going on and I don't right now' kind of way."

Cassandra blinked, walking in silence with Bree as she processed that. Finally, she just sighed and said, "God, I hope you're wrong. I feel terrible."

"Don't. That's on Jade, not on you," Bree countered. "And when she gets her act together, she'll be able to be happy for you again." She pulled Cassandra around a crushed cup of soda on the sidewalk. "Don't worry about it. Jade loves you. It's not really about you. She's just . . . well, at a low point."

"I wish she'd talk to me about it," Cassandra lamented. "I'm here for her."

"She's not really talking to anyone. Besides, I'm only speculating."

"Your instincts are usually right on the money."

"True," Bree said with a grin. "But still. No worrying tonight! We're going to have some fun."

"Fun, huh?" The wind gusted and Cassandra shivered as they continued their walk up Fifth Avenue. "Fun. Yes. I think I remember fun."

"Really? 'Cause I don't think you do." Bree slanted her a sideways look. "Charlie's sleeping over my mom's. I can hang out for a while. We're going to go to a bar, get a little drunk, and have a good time."

"We are?" Cassandra asked. "Okay. Any ideas where?"

"No, but I'm freezing. Like, I can't feel my face anymore freezing," Bree sputtered. "How about we just duck into the next place that looks decent?"

"Fine by me."

They made it another block, heads down against the cold, harsh wind, before Bree said, "Here. This one. Looks nice, looks *warm*. Okay with you?"

Cassandra peered at the storefront. O'Reilly's Tavern. A huge wreath with red bows and gold sleigh bells hung on the door, and lively classic rock could be heard rumbling through the large glass windows. "I guess . . . "

"Good, because I need to be inside. Now. Come on." With a firm hold on Cassandra's arm, Bree dragged her through the heavy wooden door.

Inside, it was warm and welcoming. The music was louder now, but it set Cassandra's limbs moving instinctively. It was a decent size for a midtown bar: long and narrow room, high ceilings. White walls with framed pictures and all things Irish, hardwood floors, a few tables and chairs along the walls. The main lights were dimmed, so the endless strings of white Christmas lights cast an ambient glow. It definitely felt cozy. Cassandra quickly counted eight barstools lined up in front of a sturdy, polished mahogany bar, with enough people talking and drinking to fill the place almost to capacity.

The bluesy classic rock song ended and morphed into the Eagles' version of *Please Come Home for Christmas*, which Cassandra had always liked.

Still, something inside her wanted to leave. Almost like a whisper of intuition . . .

"It's a little crowded," she said, loudly enough to be heard over the noise. "Maybe we should go someplace else."

"No, this is great," Bree said with a smile. "I like it here. Cozy but fun. It's not a dive, but not fancy. Perfect." She pulled off her hat and unbuttoned her heavy coat.

Sighing, Cassandra pulled off her hat and her black leather gloves and shoved them into the pockets of her forest-green wool coat. Bree was already subtly shoving her way through people to get to a visible spot at the bar. Cassandra unbuttoned her coat and followed her friend. There were two bartenders working—one at the far end, and one close enough to be in earshot of Bree, his back turned as he fixed a drink.

Just as Cassandra got through to stand at Bree's side, the taller bartender turned around. Her heart stopped in her chest, then dropped to her stomach. It was *Sean*. Sean McKinnon, whom she hadn't seen or been in contact with in over seven years, standing mere inches away. The man she once thought she'd marry . . . before he left her and broke her heart. Left *her* broken.

She could barely breathe. It was like the air in the room had dried up and vanished.

Drink in his hand, he froze where he stood. His deep blue eyes went wide and locked on her. Shock openly washed over his handsome face as it paled.

Bree was the one who spoke; the only one apparently capable of speech. "Oh. My. God."

Cassandra's heart took off with a gallop and her blood roared in her ears. She didn't know what to say or what to do. Sean McKinnon was standing in front of her. They were separated only by the bar. It was unfathomable. Her mind went blank.

He broke the gaze first, setting the drink in his hand down for the man to Cassandra's left. He placed both hands on the bar, as if to brace himself, and looked from her to Bree and back to her again before saying, "It's really you."

"I thought you lived in Los Angeles," she choked out.

"I moved back two years ago," he said. The familiar

smooth tone of his voice, the cadence, the lyrical way his Irish brogue made his words sound like music, all pierced her heart.

They stared at each other in open astonishment before he said, "God, Cassie, I can't believe this. I mean . . . what are the odds? New York's a big city." He gave a wistful grin. "It's good to see you."

Something bubbled inside her chest and her throat closed up. Oh, how she'd loved him. And oh, how he'd hurt her in the end. A torrent of emotions whooshed through her in crashing waves: anger, shock, indignation . . . and longing, tinged with plain old lust. He was so gorgeous. Maybe more so. Sexier than ever, that jerk.

"You look wonderful," he said quietly. The corner of his mouth curved up in the lopsided grin that used to make her melt. It made her knees weak now, too. "Ya cut your hair. And it's so straight."

Unconsciously, her hand flew up to touch her hair. Back in college, when they'd been a couple, her wavy hair had flowed almost to her waist. Now, as an almost-thirty-year-old English professor, she'd made sure she looked the part: she'd had her waves straightened chemically, and cut it to rest on her shoulders. "Yeah. I cut it. A while ago. You did too."

He grinned again. "Aye, no more pony tails." His hair was still shaggy, but only reached his jawline now and no longer went past his shoulders. It was a little darker as well. Back then, she'd thought of his hair as being dirty blond, but now it was more like a golden brown. She remembered how his hair would lighten in the summer, the strands bleaching to a shimmering gold. A flash of running her fingers through it as he kissed her went through her mind . . . she felt her stomach do a slow flip and looked away, hoping her cheeks weren't flaming like her insides suddenly were.

His blue, blue eyes flickered to Bree. "Still friends, eh?

That's nice. Hello, Bree."

"Hi." She glanced at Cassandra, then back to him. "Wow. Um . . . so. You work here?"

"I work here, and I own half the place." His gaze stayed glued to his ex-girlfriend's face.

"You don't play guitar anymore?" Cassandra said in surprise.

"Oh, I play gigs. I even play here once or twice a week. But I needed something more solid, as well. Remember my best friend, Jimmy O'Reilly?"

"Of course I do." Cassandra recalled the blond instantly. He and Sean had been like brothers growing up together back in Ireland. Jimmy had moved to New York first, at nineteen, with Sean following less than a year later. They'd even shared an apartment together down in the Village. Jimmy was laughter and good times, whereas Sean was intense and thoughtful. She'd spent a good amount of time with Sean's best friend. "How is he?"

"He's good. When I came back to New York two years ago, we partnered. This bar—he owns half, I own half. We're in it together." He couldn't take his eyes from Cassandra, even when the guy on Bree's right asked for a beer. It was like he was in a trance. It unnerved her.

She swallowed hard and said, "Well then, we should let you should go back to work."

"Will you stay a while?" he blurted. "I . . . it'd be nice to talk to you." His marine blue eyes captured hers and held. "It's been a long time. I'd love to catch up. Please, Cassie."

She and Bree exchanged a quick glance. "Up to you," Bree murmured.

What am I, crazy? I should walk away right now, Cassandra thought. *The same way he walked away from me when I begged him not to.* But the look in his eyes was so earnest, so raw and open . . .

he was obviously glad to see her and didn't want her to leave. His twinkling blues were practically pleading with her.

And who was she kidding? She wanted to talk to him, to sit and stare at him, try to wrap her head around this incredible chance meeting. How many times had she wondered where he'd ended up, what he was doing? How many times had she wondered what he looked like now? She wanted to sit and memorize every feature.

Taking a deep breath, she nodded. "I guess. I mean, we'll be here for a little while."

"Fantastic," he breathed, grinning brightly. "Ehm . . . so, what are you two drinking? It's on me."

"You don't have to do that," Bree said.

"Sure he can," Cassandra said, the slightest edge to her tone. "It's the least he can do."

Sean met her eyes, and the grin faded. "It is."

"Sam Adams for me, then," Bree said. "Thanks."

"And you, love?" Sean asked Cassandra.

She gasped softly, taken off guard by his casual use of his old endearment for her. *Cassielove*, he'd call her, making it one word. Or just *Love* . . . all the time. Always.

He realized it immediately and paled a bit. "Sorry, Cassie. It just slipped out . . . "

"It's okay," she said quietly. Remembering, she added, "I'll have the black stuff."

The sexy grin returned and his eyes sparkled. "Ah, that's a good girl." He turned away to get their drinks.

Bree grasped Cassandra's arm. "Holy crap. Are you okay?"

"No," Cassandra said. Aftershock was setting in. Waves of disbelief made her insides wobble and her legs tremble. "I'm in shock. I can't think straight."

"We can leave right now," Bree said. "Oh God, you're shaking."

Cassandra hadn't realized she was until Bree said so. A deeper tremor rocked her body.

Bree squeezed her friend's arms and rubbed them, meant to soothe. "You want to take off, we're outta here. Seriously, Cass. Whatever you want to do, we do it."

"I don't know what I want. I... I just can't believe it," Cassandra breathed. She stared back at her friend. "I mean, like he said, what are the odds? New York is *how* big? This is insane." She glanced at Sean, halfway down the bar at the tap, pulling a pint of Guinness. Sean McKinnon, right there in front of her, mere feet away. Unbelievable.

"Well, it is the season for holiday miracles, isn't it?" Bree said dryly. She peered closer at her best friend. "Cass? You sure you want to stay?"

She let out a hard puff of air and said, "Yes. I want to hear what he could possibly have to say to me. I do." Her lips twisted as she added, "He looks good, doesn't he? Gotta admit it."

"Oh yeah. He certainly is aging well," Bree said. "In fact, he's hotter than he was seven years ago, the rat."

"I know. He totally is. It's not fair. Damn him." Cassandra swallowed hard and craned her neck, looking for a place to sit down. "I don't think there are any empty chairs . . . "

"Well, we're going to find at least one," Bree said with determination. "Not just because you're shaking, but because we're not going to hang out here at the bar, looking like we're hanging all over him. No freaking way."

Cassandra just nodded. Her head was spinning. He'd been happy to see her. He lived in New York? He co-owned a bar? It was overwhelming. Her brain was in overload, and her stomach was in knots. "I'm glad you're here," she whispered into Bree's ear.

"Me too. When you two saw each other, I thought you

were both going to fall over. I know I almost did." Bree squeezed her arm again.

Cassandra scowled as she admitted, "My pride and ego are yelling at me. Saying screw him, just leave right now and never look back. Like he did to me . . ."

Bree stayed quiet, watching her friend.

Cassandra heaved out a heavy sigh. "He hurt me so badly, Bree. Just looking at him brings it back." She licked her suddenly dry lips. "From how good we were, to how he devastated me when he left . . . ugh," she shuddered.

Bree put an arm around her shoulders. "Anyone who would've walked away from something like what you two had . . . I said it then, and I'll say it again now: he was an all-out dumbass."

Cassandra snorted out a laugh. "Yup. And I'm giving him a chance to talk to me anyway. So maybe I'm a dumbass too."

"Nope. You're human. It's curiosity, plain and simple." Bree squeezed her, a hug of support. "Look, whatever happens here, I've got your back."

"You always have. And I'm so grateful for that."

Chapter Two

SEAN GLANCED OVER at Cassie and Bree for the hundredth time. After he'd given them their drinks, they'd moved further into the bar and found one open chair. He'd watched as a young guy offered them another chair and helped both women off with their coats, making Sean's insides tense. But the girls had apparently brushed him off, because for the past twenty minutes, they'd been sitting closely, huddled together and talking.

He had some idea of what—*who*—they were chatting about.

His head was still reeling. Of all the bars in all of New York, she'd walked into his? Unbelievable. An insane coincidence. Fate, perhaps? Who the hell knew.

Looking at her was like being in some weird dream—she was hauntingly familiar, and it didn't seem real that she was there. He couldn't believe she'd agreed to stay and talk with him. She was gracious, even with the flare of anger he'd seen spark in her beautiful brown eyes.

Those eyes . . . they had drawn him in from the moment he'd met her. Deep, coffee-colored, brimming with warmth and intelligence, they had captivated him in an instant. Then, when she was his girlfriend, he used to stare into them endlessly, feeling like he could sink into her soul through that warm, dark gateway . . .

As he gazed at her now, memories that hadn't surfaced for years came swarming back.

Kissing her, running his fingers through her shiny, waist-length hair . . . endless hours of exploring her enticing body, making love with her night after night . . . laughing together when they'd sit and talk in the bar after a gig . . . how her gorgeous eyes would widen, just a drop, when she first saw him, and he felt slammed with a wave of her open love for him . . .

He remembered the day they met, a day very much like this one. He could recall it easily, almost every detail.

It had been particularly cold for the first day of December. A few months shy of twenty-three, he'd lived in Manhattan for about three years then. Itching to get out of his overcrowded house—being the fourth of eight children, he never had any space to himself—and get out of his dead-end small town, he'd left Ireland to come to America. Jimmy, his best friend, was loving life in New York City since he'd moved the year before, and kept encouraging Sean to give it a try.

Sean had thought about it for a few months before deciding to take the leap. He'd have to find a job, of course. Something physical, something that didn't demand a lot of reading or sitting still. But New York City had plenty of jobs like that, and it was a fantastic place to play his guitar, sing, and find steady gigs. That was what his true passion was, what he really wanted to do, and he couldn't do that in County Kildare.

He'd moved in with Jimmy, down in the Village. He'd found a job in a Midtown corporate mailroom, lifting the heavy stuff, and worked there a five days a week. And, after a scant few weeks, he'd found places to play and sing. He sang cover songs, and he sang the handful of songs he'd written. He sang solo acoustic gigs, and after a while, he hooked up with a cover band. The shows were all in cramped little bars and clubs, sometimes with only a handful of people to listen, but he didn't care. He just wanted to play. It kept him going.

Jimmy worked as a bartender at a small but popular place down near Washington Square Park, and Sean spent time there when he wasn't working, be it knocking back beers or playing an acoustic set one night a week. And there was no shortage of girls. There were lots of them. As Jimmy had predicted they would, they flocked to him. They swooned over his Irish accent, his charming manner, his long, dark blond hair that went to his shoulders, his singing and playing guitar... for him, life in America was pretty sweet.

On that first day of December, he'd got out of a taxi, pulling his guitar and large amplifier out of the trunk. The amp was so heavy and clunky, and it was so cold, he'd had to take a cab, it was too far to walk. Denny, the drummer of the band he'd been playing some regular gigs with of late, had invited him over for dinner before they headed to that night's show together. Denny had a new girlfriend, a sweet Italian girl named Gina who loved to cook and lived over in NYU territory, close to that night's gig. As much as he loved pizza, if he ate any more of it, Sean thought he might turn into one. Eager for a decent homemade meal, he had accepted the invite.

He was so focused on dragging his heavy amp up the stone stairs of Gina's apartment building that he didn't see the girl standing at the top, holding the front door open, until he almost slammed into her. He looked up into the face of one of the prettiest girls he'd ever seen. Dark wavy hair, super long, framed a pale face with bee stung lips and eyes that twinkled at him. They were such a warm brown, he wanted to just fall into them. And he kind of did. For the first time in a very long time, he found himself tongue tied in front of a gorgeous girl.

She smiled at him, and it was like bathing in light. "Come on in," she said. "I've been watching you wrestle with that, I wanted to help."

"That's really nice of ya," he said, his brain clicking back into gear. "Thanks so much." He angled himself past her to get into the foyer, dragging the old amp with him and stealing glances at her. She was average height, but most of her body was hidden under that long, brick red wool coat. Her hair went down to the middle of her back, and he had a flash of wanting to thread his fingers through the thick, shiny mane.

She went inside with him and buzzed open the main door.

"Are ya going upstairs too?" he asked.

"No, actually, I was just leaving," she said. "I live here." Her voice was sweet, but had that edge—she was smart, he could tell. Really smart. He heard it in her voice and saw it in her eyes; it emanated from her as much as her kindness. She was ... respectable. A nice girl. Bloody beautiful. And all of it appealed to him. He was immediately captivated.

Wanting to hear her talk more, he continued on. "You live here, eh? I have a friend here, they invited me for dinner." He couldn't take his eyes off her. Something in him felt an actual physical pull to her ... it didn't make sense, but he felt it all the same. He didn't want her to walk away yet. So he flashed a broad smile and went for it. "Any chance you'd like to join us?"

She blinked at him, wide eyed. "Um ... thank you, but no, I can't. I'm on my way to dinner with a friend of my own. But thanks."

They stood and stared at each other for a few seconds. The air around them seemed to crackle with electricity. He extended a hand. "Name's Sean. Sean McKinnon. It's nice to meet you . . . ?"

"Cassandra Baines." She smiled again and shook his hand. Her hand was warm; he felt the warmth even through his glove. That was one of the things that drew him in: her warmth. She was softly radiant with it.

"Lovely to meet ya. That's a beautiful name." He stared a few more seconds, then realized he was staring too much and broke the gaze. He looked around. "Ehm . . . could ya tell me where the elevator is?"

"Right there." She pointed down the hall, but then appeared to change her mind and walked to it instead, pushing the button on the wall. She turned to look at him as he followed, rolling the bulky amp along the hallway floor. When their eyes met again, they held. A faint blush rose in her cheeks and she shyly bit down on her bottom lip.

His heart skipped a beat. Christ, she was beautiful. Absolutely adorable. "Do ya like music?"

"What?" She blinked. "Music? Yeah, of course."

"Good." He gestured to the guitar still slung over his shoulder. "I play. Obviously. I sing too." He grinned, hoping he didn't sound like an idiot. "I have a gig later tonight. Over at John-O's, down on 12th and 1st. We're playing from ten to midnight. Why don't ya come down? Maybe you'd like it."

Her eyes widened. "Um . . . I don't know . . . "

"C'mon, it'll be fun! I'd, ehm . . . I'd really like to see you there. Think on it?"

The elevator door opened and she raised her arm to hold it open for him. He moved past her, thanking her as he got his amp, his guitar, and himself into the compartment. But when she lowered her arm, his hand flew up to hold the door open, and his eyes held hers as he asked in a cheerful tone, "So, Cassie? Will I see you tonight?" *Please say yes*, he thought, willing her silently to accept.

A shy but delighted smile crept across her face. "I'll think on it."

"I'll buy you a drink," he promised.

"You can't," she said with regret. "I'm only twenty. Won't be twenty-one until April."

"Ah. Well, you can still get in, though. I'll buy ya a soda," he teased. "But come to the gig."

"I'll think on it," she said again, more firmly this time.

Don't push, lad. "Okay. Hope you show up." He looked at her, taking her in, hoping to God she would. "Thanks again for the help. Very kind of ya. Appreciate it."

"You're welcome. Nice to meet you, Sean."

"The pleasure was mine." He hit the button for the fifth floor. "Right. Well, Happy Christmas, if I don't see ya."

As the door slid closed, she said quickly in response, "Merry Christmas."

Later that night, he was about half an hour into the gig and had given up hope that she'd come . . . and just as his mood started to dip from that disappointment, she walked into the small club. His heart skyrocketed as he watched her come in with two other girls—safety in numbers, he supposed. They found a table on the side, he smiled brightly at her, and the girls stayed for the rest of the gig. After he was done playing, he went straight over to her and sat down . . . her friends moved across the bar to another table to give them some space, and he and Cassie started to talk. The connection was instant. He might have fallen in love with her right then. He'd always thought so. They'd talked for hours, until the club closed . . .

And that was it. They'd been inseparable from then on, for a year and a half. His life had changed irrevocably on that night.

Now he looked at her, sitting across the room, and a million flashes of memory flooded him. It made his chest hurt and his blood race. He'd loved her more than any other girl, ever.

He'd shut down after their breakup, by choice. Made himself busy, too busy to even have time for a girlfriend. Decided he was better off, didn't need the trappings of a relationship... and didn't want the responsibility of holding someone's heart in his hands again.

He knew how deeply he'd hurt Cassie when he'd ended them, and didn't ever want another woman to look at him that way again. The looks of desperation, then the pain, then the anger on her face, as her love for him turned to fiery hate right before his eyes in a few gutwrenching weeks... it was sickening. It was his own bloody fault, he'd done it, and he knew that. Didn't make it easier to take. He'd had to leave. Couldn't stand the thought of running into her around Manhattan. So he'd moved to Los Angeles. Gotten as far away from her as he could.

Now, he looked at her for the hundredth time and felt his chest tighten. He could steal glances from his position behind the bar, and he did, as often as he could. Cassie was even more beautiful now than she'd been back then, if that was possible. Yet she was different now, in many discernible ways. It wasn't just her haircut, it was the way she carried herself: more assured, refined, mature. And the way she looked at him was wary, guarded. She used to look up at him like he held the world in the palm of his hand, along with her heart... not now, that was for sure. She was a polished, professional woman.

He was dying to talk to her. Not that he knew what the hell to say. But sweet Jaysus, she was in *his* bar, of all the bars in New York City. Was it a Christmas miracle? He laughed at himself for thinking it. But one never knew...

Only problem was, the bar was packed. He hadn't stopped

serving drinks for a minute since people had poured in after the tree lighting, just as Jimmy had predicted.

Finally, he caught his younger sister's eye as she came out of the kitchen. She was waitressing and serving, but he insistently waved her over. Anna approached him with a smile.

"Hey, Seanie," she said, her choppy blonde hair peeking out from beneath a Santa hat. "You like the hat? I thought it'd be cute."

"I need a favor," he blurted.

"Ha!" Anna rolled her eyes. "What's the story?"

"Remember the girl I told ya about, from a few years back? Cassie, from NYU?"

"The one ya dumped and then mooned about for who knows how long?"

Sean winced, cringing. "Aye. That girl."

Anna chuckled. "So, what about her?"

He leaned in so she could hear him better. "She's here, Annie. In the bar. She's sitting *right over there*. I want to go talk to her, but it's so bloody busy in here—"

"Go! Of course, Sean, go! I'll tend bar. Take as long as ya need." She impulsively hugged him and added, "Ya softie." She was already walking to the end of the bar so she could get behind the counter.

"God bless you, Anna," he said to her back. He quickly filled two new glasses with Guinness, grabbed another bottle of Sam Adams, and put them on a small round tray to carry to where Cassie and Bree sat talking. He sent another quick prayer up to the heavens, dropped a kiss on Anna's cheek as he passed her, and started threading his way through the noisy bar.

Chapter Three

"He's sure taking his sweet time coming over here, isn't he," Cassandra remarked.

"Cass. Give him a break," Bree said. "It's packed in here. He's working. He's busy."

Cassandra slanted a look her way. "You're making excuses for him."

"What? No. They're facts." Sabrina Gervais narrowed her eyes at her lifelong best friend. "I'll make no excuses for him, ever. Not after what he did to you."

"I know." Cassandra drank the last of her Guinness. The song over the sound system changed again, now to the Ronettes' bouncy version of *Sleigh Ride*. The cheeriness of the old classic didn't undo the knot in her chest, however.

Bree drained her bottle of beer before saying, "Cass. I'm the one whose shoulder you cried on for months after he left. It hurt my heart, seeing you like that. You were devastated. *Beyond* devastated."

Cassandra shuddered as she recalled those days. "Yup."

"There were times I didn't think you'd ever get over him. So yeah, I'm a little protective of you where he's concerned, and wary too." Bree shrugged and arched a thin brow. "I don't apologize for that."

"Good. Don't." Cassandra leaned in and gave her best friend a quick hug. "Love you."

She couldn't say it aloud, but Bree had been right. Just seeing Sean confirmed her gnawing fear—she still felt something when she looked at him. But the anger was there, too, and she had every right to it. He'd tossed their relationship aside like day-old trash, without a reasonable explanation. No matter how she'd cried, or tried to talk to him, or even begged... once he'd made up his mind that they were over, that had been it. Nothing she'd said or done had swayed him.

After the breakup, her heart had throbbed for weeks before the paralyzing sadness morphed into red hot anger. How dared he treat her that way? He didn't deserve her love; he didn't deserve *her*. Her fury, her scorn, had gotten her through the nights when sorrow threatened to overtake her. It took a long time, over a year, but she slowly got over Sean McKinnon. And pushed him out of her mind, and moved on with her life.

Or so she'd thought.

What bothered her now was, if she was one hundred percent over him, she wouldn't feel anything at all. The opposite of love wasn't hate, but indifference, and she sure as hell didn't feel indifferent when she glanced over at him. Tall and lean, ruggedly handsome, oozing sex appeal from behind the bar, doling out drinks and patter with charm and ease, he was as alluring to her as he'd ever been. *Damn*.

She hoped it didn't show. She wanted him to think her indifferent. It was better that way. She certainly wished she was ... she threw her shoulders back and stiffened her spine, reaching deep inside for her most cool and collected expression. It didn't work. "God, I loved him, Bree," she said.

"I know, honey," Sabrina murmured, squeezing her forearm.

Cassandra glanced over at him again. He was talking to one of the waitresses, a short, pretty blonde wearing a Santa hat. She wondered fleetingly if they were dating. Why not? He was gorgeous, sexy, charming—he probably had women throwing themselves at him all the time. Why did that make her insides wince with jealousy? It was none of her business what he did, or *who* he did.

"Oliver Pottson asked me to go with him to the faculty holiday party," she told Bree, trying to change the subject.

"Oh. Ew." Bree wrinkled her nose. "Like, as a date? Or just as a companion?"

"I think as a date, and ew is right," Cassandra said. "He kind of skeeves me. He looks at me like I'm... a meal or something." She shuddered.

"What'd you say?"

"I turned him down as politely as possible, of course. I mean, hello, he's the head of my department."

"That can get sticky," Bree cautioned. "Be careful."

"I'm trying! But he's relentless."

"That's harassment," Bree spat.

"Not yet, but it's borderline." Cassandra sighed. "Who would I even go to? He's the head of the English department. I just try to stay cordial, polite, and non-encouraging."

"Sounds like he doesn't need much encouraging," Bree grumbled.

"I know. Yuck." Cassandra turned to steal another peek at Sean. He was filling a glass with ale, focused on his task. "Oliver is the exact opposite of Sean."

Bree barked out a sarcastic laugh. "No kidding! But that's who you've dated ever since. Men who were..."

"Suitable," Cassandra mumbled. "No musicians, no

charming Irishmen, no one who radiates sex appeal and makes me want to rip their clothes off."

"Yawn," Bree said dryly.

"Yup," Cassandra admitted "Sean and I were so connected... it was all consuming. And after it was over, I felt so hollow and gray when that passion and feeling were gone..." Her eyes fell away, a bit embarrassed at having admitted something so intensely personal.

"Been there," Bree reminded her softly.

"Yeah. I know. You get it." She cleared her throat and looked around the crowded bar, taking it all in.

It was loud, the energy frenetic. Not her scene anymore. Even though she was only twenty-nine and lived in the biggest, most lively city in the world, she didn't go to bars and get drunk. She hadn't hung out in places like this since her college days...

Long nights out with Sean. They'd been inseparable for the year and a half they were a couple, the end of her undergrad years at NYU. Several nights a week, when she was done with her studies, she'd sit in the back of bars and clubs all over Manhattan, while he played gigs. He'd play guitar and sing, and she'd sit at the back, nurse a Sex on the Beach, and watch her gorgeous, talented, charismatic boyfriend. After he was done playing, they'd have a few drinks, get something to eat, then go back to one of their apartments and make love until sunrise...

Long repressed memories bubbled up and inundated her with emotion. She didn't want to remember how good they'd been together. She didn't want to feel wistful or nostalgic. She shot a hard glance Sean's way. "I shouldn't be here. We should leave."

"So let's leave," Bree said without a pause.

"He wrecked me," Cassandra blurted in a sudden burst of

anger. "I shouldn't even have spoken to him, much less stayed in his bar. I told him I'd wait? What was I thinking?"

"That you're curious to hear what he has to say?" Bree suggested.

Cassandra huffed out an exasperated sigh. "Yeah. Yes. That. And I shouldn't be. I shouldn't care."

Bree set her empty bottle on the floor beneath her chair. "So listen. When he does get over here to talk to you, you want me to stay, or you want me to get scarce?"

Cassandra bit down on her lip. "I don't know. I . . ." She shrugged.

"We'll play it by ear, then. I can read you well enough that I'll know what to do." Bree turned her head to look again. "Well, he's finally coming. With another round of drinks. Good tactic. Charmer."

Cassandra rolled her shoulders. Her eyes were already glued to Sean, watching as he balanced the tray, while making his way towards them through the crowded bar. He moved languidly, with prowess and masculine grace, dressed simply in a black long-sleeved T-shirt and worn jeans that hung low on his narrow hips. She swallowed a sigh. God, he was sexier than ever. Heat rushed through her body just from looking at him, making parts of her ache in a way they hadn't in a long time. Her eyes greedily roamed over him. Still lean and broad-shouldered, a day's worth of gold stubble covering his jaw, his thick honey brown hair begging to be played with and pushed out of his eyes . . .

And those eyes. Oh, how she'd always loved his eyes. That deep, dark blue, so intense and sharp. They would lock on her like heat-seeking missiles, searching, as if trying to see deeper into her soul. Or he'd just hold her captive with long, adoring looks that made her melt inside.

Kind of like he was right now. He was focused on her as

he stood before them.

"So sorry I couldn't get over here sooner," he said, handing Cassandra a fresh pint, then giving Bree her beer. "It's really busy tonight. I finally got my sister to do me a favor and cover for a while."

"That was nice of her," Bree said.

"Your sister?" Cassandra was surprised. "One of your sisters is in New York now? Which one?"

"Anna," he said. "The youngest." He pointed to the blonde in the Santa hat, and a lance of embarrassment for her jealousy carved Cassandra's pride. "She moved here at the end of the summer, and she works here for cash. She's twenty-five now. Taking courses at FIT. She wants to be some kind of designer."

With no free chairs around, Sean crouched down to their eye level. He was so close, Cassandra could see the blonde ends of his long lashes and smell his faint scent, musky and masculine. It made her head swim.

"It's good to see ya, Cassie," he said softly. His eyes bore into hers. "I'm... stunned. I mean, of all the bars in the city... it's a helluva coincidence, eh? And I'm so glad. Honestly, I didn't think I'd ever see ya again. It's really nice... and startling, really."

She couldn't speak. Suddenly overcome with emotion, with feelings she couldn't even label washing over her, she sat there frozen, staring back at him. He still evoked such powerful stirrings in her heart. He still had that way of looking at her like she was the most important person in the world. His very presence affected her, still, as strongly as it ever had.

This was bad. This was... dangerous.

Because she couldn't think straight. And ever since she'd gotten over the initial heartbreak, she'd worked hard to think straight. To be smarter about her choices. To not be seduced by passion, or intense emotion. That he had such an effect on her now, out of nowhere, made her both scared and angry. She wanted to shove him and send him sprawling onto his ass... but also to throw her arms around his neck and breathe him in.

She was a mess inside. She just prayed it didn't show.

"Are you okay?" he asked gently.

"No," she whispered. "I'm... I think I'm just in shock. I didn't think I'd ever see you again either."

"I know," he whispered back. "I just can't believe it." The bright blues swept over her face. "I can't stop staring at ya, I'm sorry. It's so bloody good to see you. I, ehm... well..."

Bree bolted to her feet. "Here, sit down," she instructed Sean. "Take my chair. Sit."

He cleared his throat and rose as well. "No, no, you sit."

"Sean. You two need to talk. I'm in the way." Bree looked at her friend. "Hey."

Cassandra blinked, the spell broken, and looked up at her. "Yeah?"

"You're okay."

It wasn't a question, it was a reminder. Cassandra nodded.

"Why don't the three of us go back to the office?" Sean suggested, holding his glass of Guinness in one hand while he gestured towards the back with the other. "We'd be able to hear each other better, have some privacy. There's enough space for all of us to sit—"

"No," Bree said. "You two go and talk. I'm gonna head home."

"This was our night together," Cassandra objected.

"Yes, and it was great," Bree said. "But I'm going to finish this beer, then take a cab to Penn and go home. It's fine. You two go ahead." She fixed Sean with a hard look. "I know where to find you now, though. Remember that."

Sean looked down at the petite brunette's determined

expression. If she was five-foot-two, that was a generous assessment. But he saw the set of her jaw, the fire in her olive green eyes, and said somberly, "I have no doubt."

"Good." Bree leaned down to hug her friend and whispered in her ear, "You got this. Don't give him an inch without making him beg for it."

Cassandra hugged back and said into her hair, "I'll call you in the morning."

"No, you'll text me tonight as soon as you're done," Bree corrected her. "I don't care what time it is. Text me." She straightened and grabbed her coat from the back of the chair with her free hand, then gestured to Sean with the hand that held her beer. "Okay. I'm going. Thanks for the drinks."

He nodded silently.

Bree shot one last glance at Cassandra, then walked away.

Sean sat in the vacated chair and sighed. "She hates me," he said.

"Yup," Cassandra said. "But do you blame her?"

"No." Sean's eyes flickered away to Bree's retreating back in the crowd. The song over the speakers changed to Bryan Adams' version of *Run Rudolph Run*, and he turned back to Cassandra. "Actually, I'm surprised you agreed to stay and talk. I thought you hated me too."

"I did. For a long time," she said.

He stared at her, jolted by her bluntness. "I'm sure you did."

"I'm past that now," she informed him coolly.

"Good to know," he murmured. Something inside him rolled, a wave of regret, that made him slightly nauseous. He'd made her hate him. He scrubbed a hand over his jaw, the bristles reminding him he hadn't shaved in three days.

She'd hated him.

At the time, when he'd broken up with her, that was what

he'd wanted. He'd thought it better that she hate him than pine for him, that hating him would help her move on. But hearing he'd succeeded... it hurt. It made his stomach churn. "I'm truly sorry for that."

"For what?" she asked, a trace of annoyance in her voice. "For making me hate you?"

"Yes."

She shrugged, her gaze flickering away.

His face felt hot. He lifted his pint and took several long gulps. She wasn't going to make this easy on him. But hey, he was the one who'd asked her to stay.

She sipped her pint of Guinness and licked the foam from her lips, an innocent gesture that made his breath catch. What she used to do to him with that tongue. Those lips. That luscious mouth... his blood rushed through his body, and suddenly his jeans felt too tight. Jaysus, had he no shame? He cleared his throat.

"Do you want to talk out here?" he asked, loudly enough to be heard over the rollicking Christmas tune. "Or do you want to go back to the office, as I suggested? There's a couch, and a chair. Whatever ya want, Cassie."

She took another sip of her Guinness before remarking, "No one calls me that."

His brows creased. "Calls ya what? Cassie?"

She nodded. "I wouldn't let anyone. I was called Cassie as a kid, all the time, but I made everyone stop when I hit my teens. I thought 'Cassie' was childish. Then I met you... you always called me that, from day one."

"I did." The corners of his mouth lifted.

"Well, I never let anyone else call me it after we broke up. Because it reminded me of you." She held her glass of Guinness with both hands, on her knee, her posture rigid.

"So hearing me call ya that brings back memories?" he

asked, looking into her eyes.

She gazed at his face. His beautiful face, so familiar and yet strange at the same time. A few laugh lines were etched at the corners of his eyes now, only adding to his sex appeal, which was already off the charts. The small silver hoop in his ear glinted in the light. Through the sea of dark gold stubble that covered his strong jaw, his lips were sensual, alluring . . . he had been the most amazing kisser. She bet he was even better at it now. Heat flowed through her at the thought. "Maybe," she murmured.

"Maybe, eh?" His voice dipped as he asked, "Some good ones, I hope?"

That made her pause before answering truthfully, "Both good and bad."

The smile faded away. "I understand." He stood, then leaned in to take her coat from the back of her chair. "Come on. Let's go where we can really talk."

A wave of nervous excitement rushed through her, but she schooled her features to appear neutral as she got to her feet. "Lead the way."

Chapter Four

THE NOISE FROM the bar was instantly muffled when Sean closed the office door behind Cassie. He watched her as she made a cursory study of the small office before sitting on the far end of the worn couch, beside his coat. She held her pint with both hands, again resting it on her knee. Her manicured fingertips, polished in dark red, circled the rim of the glass over and over. She'd always been prone to fidgeting when uneasy, he remembered, and was glad to know he wasn't the only one feeling edgy.

He tried to appear nonchalant as he sat on the other end of the couch, careful not to let their feet bump or to touch her at all. But his eyes greedily drank her in. Her hair was so different that it still threw him. She looked so sleek and professional now. Her black turtleneck sweater looked soft, probably cashmere, and his fingers itched to touch her. She was still slender, but the full swell of her breasts distracted him. A memory of them, heavy and gorgeous as they filled his hands, flashed in his mind and sent a jolt straight to his groin. She made him crazy with lust, even still. He cleared his throat and made himself tear his gaze away.

She was dressed nicely, as if she'd met Bree straight from work. He felt scrubby in comparison, unshaven and wearing only a T-shirt and jeans. If he'd known his ex-girlfriend was going to show up in his bar, he'd have cleaned up some.

He finally allowed his eyes to rest on her face, again taken by how beautiful she was. A few years hadn't stolen from her looks, only added to them. Her skin was still perfect, and he longed to touch her. How many times had he held that face in his hands? His. She'd been all his.

Back then, she'd been pure sweetness and light. She'd openly adored him. He always felt invincible when she was around, her love for him sustaining and bolstering him. Now, she seemed closed off, and he knew he couldn't blame her. But he wondered if it was solely because of him, or had she changed?

She seemed unyielding, both in posture and in manner. And her dark eyes, which had always been so filled with warmth and affection when she looked at him, now reflected wariness as she regarded him. He hated that, but had to admit he understood it.

"Right. So," he began. "I'm still taking this in."

"Me too," she said.

He nodded. An awkward silence stretched for several long beats.

"Did you ever think of me?" she asked.

He blinked, taken aback by the question. "When? Over the years, ya mean?"

"Yes."

"Of course I did," he confessed. "Usually, at this time of year. Things around the city just brought it all back, ya know? Smells on a cold wind, Christmas time . . . you know why."

She nodded and took a sip from her glass. "Sure. The two Decembers we shared were so . . ." Spots of pink blossomed on her cheeks. "Forget it." She took a sip of her drink.

"I wish I could," he said thickly. "Forget it, I mean. But something always brings it back." He tried to get her to meet his eyes, but she wouldn't. "Did you ever think of me?"

"Of course. But less as time went by, thank goodness."

"If you thought of me at all, ya probably thought of me with anger, am I right?"

At that, her eyes lifted and met his, but she said nothing.

"I mean, that last email you sent . . . it was scathing."

"You called me, drunk, on Christmas Eve," she bit out. "Five months after you'd moved away. Rambling about how much you missed me. It was . . ."

"Honest," he murmured.

"Cruel," she countered. "Calling me like that, at Christmas, was just cruel."

He felt a chill skitter over him. "Jaysus, Cassie, I didn't mean to be."

"Yes, you did. You were cruel from the day you broke up with me."

"I know I was, but . . ." His breath felt stuck in his lungs. "Not that last phone call. That night, aye I was trousered, but I was trying to . . ." He shook his head. "Doesn't matter now. Anyway, the next day, you sent that email. Blasted me with both barrels. Made it clear you wanted me to leave ya be. Told me not to contact you again. I thought ya just wanted to forget I ever existed."

"At that point, I did." She looked at him from beneath the fringe of her dark lashes. There was a lot going on in her eyes, but he couldn't read her. Once upon a time, he used to be able to read her so well. Finally, her shoulders drew back as she cleared her throat and asked coolly, "Do you really want to go into all that right now? Because frankly, I don't."

"I don't either." He scrubbed his hands over his face and

leaned back a little. Another awkward silence stretched as they warily regarded one another. They sipped their drinks. Finally, she spoke.

"I thought you lived in Los Angeles," she said. "Why'd you move back here?"

"I didn't like it out there," he said plainly. "Totally different way of life. Which was good at first . . . because honestly, I was trying to get over ya and move on. But I was miserable." He took another long gulp from his glass. "Everyone out there's so phony. Plastic. The band wasn't taking off, we couldn't get a break . . . it sucked. After a while, I hated it. Even considered going back home."

"Back to Ireland?" she asked.

He nodded and rubbed the stubble on his jaw absently. "Then, about two and a half years ago, I came back to New York to visit Jimmy. His ma had just passed, back home. And being in the States when she passed, not being there for her, he was kind of a mess. Thought he could use a friend. And I was right. When I got here, not only was he falling apart, but the bar was going under too. He needed help. I knew I could give it. So I chose to come back here."

Her head tilted slightly as she regarded him. "Really?"

"It seems to have worked. We're here, right? Bar's thriving." He shrugged and added, "You help your friends. He needed help."

She seemed to take that in, then said, "You always did have a good head for business. Numbers. That came naturally to you."

He was surprised she recalled that. "Aye, that's true. So he partnered me in."

"You were always a loyal friend."

His mouth went dry. "Thanks, but I'm no hero or anythin'." He quickly stole a sip of beer. "It wasn't a hardship to make the move. I hated L.A., and I loved New York. I always did, and I still do."

She nodded. "So do I."

"Right. You never left Manhattan?"

"Nope. Did my graduate program at Columbia. Finished a bit early. Got a position at NYU. I'm an assistant professor. English Lit." She shifted the glass to balance on her other knee. "So yes, I've been here all along."

"Congratulations on all that," he said. "It's impressive. But I always knew you'd be successful . . ." He tried to smile, even as he thought, *That's why I let you go, Cassie. So you'd be free to spread your wings and soar.* "So, where do you live now?"

"In Chelsea."

"Nice area."

"It is. I like it. But my apartment's tiny, and I have a roommate. I never see her, though. She's in medical school at NYU. Crazy schedule." She ran her fingertip around the rim of the glass again. "And you? Where are you living?"

"Still down in the Village, same tiny apartment." He caught the surprise that flickered across her face. "Yeah, yeah. Only I live there alone now. When Jimmy moved out last year to live with his girlfriend, I stayed. Once he'd partnered me in to the bar, I was doing well enough that I didn't need a new roommate if I stayed there."

"Well, that's good." A small grin appeared as she said, "I remember Jimmy well, of course. So much fun . . . we had some great times."

"We sure as hell did," he said with a broad smile, warmed by her admission. It was one of the first positive things she'd said. "Now he's engaged to be married."

"Really? Wow. Good for him."

"Why 'wow'?" Sean wondered aloud. "You thought he'd never get married?"

"No, not really," she admitted. "He was always out for a good time. I never saw him as the marrying type. Then again . . . I thought you *were*." The grin evaporated and her eyes shifted back down to her drink as she whispered, "What did I know."

Sean's heart seized. A sudden rush of desperation flowed through him, searingly hot and urgent. He leaned in. "Cassie, I . . ." With frustration, he shook his head, pausing before throwing his cards down. But he felt compelled. "If you leave here tonight and never speak to me again, I need ya to understand something. I left you for your own good. I *meant* it when I told ya that. I thought I was doing right by you by letting you go."

The color drained from her face as she stared back at him. "And I told you that it wouldn't be like that. I told you *so* many times—I begged you to listen to me—"

"I know. But I couldn't believe it. I'd made up my mind that it was the right thing to do, and that was that."

"I remember very well," she murmured angrily.

"I was young and stupid and . . . well . . . insecure, I guess. Didn't want ya to end up resenting me . . ." He swallowed hard. "I couldn't even stay on the same coast as you once we broke up—that's why I moved so far away. I knew the band wasn't fantastic. But I needed to put real distance between us . . ." He glanced away as he revealed, ". . . so I couldn't come crawling back and beg ya to take me back. Because I wanted to, Cassie. So many times. *That's* why I called that Christmas Eve."

"No." She shook her head adamantly. "No. You were just drunk and lonely."

"You're right, I was drunk and lonely. But when I said I was sorry, when I said I wanted you back, I meant it. All the things I rambled on about that night, I meant them. But I'd done too much damage. You didn't believe me."

"That's right. How could I?"

"You couldn't, I know that." He sighed heavily, wretchedness squeezing his stomach again.

"I hated that you didn't come back right away. That fall..." Her dark eyes filled with tears as she looked at him. "I hated that you let me go; that you didn't fight for me, for us. You don't know how many times I wished you'd come back for me. Done or said something... anything to show I meant more to you than your pride." She sniffed back the tears that threatened. "And by the time you did, when you finally called *months* later, I didn't have any faith left in you. It was ruined. You ruined us." She took a deep breath, dabbed at the corners of her eyes, and whispered, "God, I can't believe I just told you all that."

He felt like he'd swallowed sawdust. He couldn't speak.

Luckily for him, she went on. "I'll tell you the truth. For a long time, I had this recurring daydream, that you'd just show up at my door..." Her voice broke and she sniffled, trying so hard not to cry. She looked away and shook her head. "Doesn't matter. Forget it."

Seeing how stark her sadness was—still, after all this time—made Sean's heart clench and his stomach churn anxiously. She still felt something, if just talking about it could bring her to tears. He saw it all over her face. *What did I do to this girl?* He tried to swallow back the lump in his throat, but it felt lodged there.

Her voice lowered back to a whisper as she confessed, "When we were over, Sean... I wasn't the same after."

"Me too, love," he finally managed, his throat still thick as he inched closer. "You weren't the only one." Slowly, carefully, he reached out and took her hands in his. She didn't pull them away. He caressed her skin with his rough fingertips and made sure she was looking at him as he said, "I just need ya to know it wasn't *you*. I loved you with all my heart. But I knew . . . I wasn't going to be . . . enough. You deserved more. That's why I felt I had to let ya go. You were an angel. You owned my heart."

The tears spilled over and ran down her cheeks as she choked back a sob.

"And I sure don't deserve your tears," he said, wiping at them gingerly. "Not after how I hurt ya. You didn't give up, you tried to fight to keep us together, and I . . . was insecure, and stupid."

She sniffed hard, swiped at her glassy eyes, and met his gaze head on. "You're right. You don't deserve any more of my tears. I don't want to talk about this anymore." She wiped her cheeks with the edge of her sleeve and lifted her chin. "It's pointless. The past is the past. You can't undo it." Drawing a shaky breath, her voice cracked as she added, "You didn't want me."

"Whoa, stop. I always wanted you."

"Every action you took showed me that you didn't."

"I—I know, but—" His hand scrubbed over his stubbled chin restlessly.

"You moved across the country to get away from me," she ground out. "I felt abandoned by you, with no hope that we'd work it out. Wasn't that your intent?"

"Kind of, but . . ." He raked his hands through his hair, his eyes wild.

"But what?" Her voice was hard now, and her face flushed with anger. "You made me promises, I believed them, and you broke every one. The one guy I thought would never intentionally hurt me? Hurt me the worst." She pulled her hands out of his and balled them into fists on her lap. Her glare was unyielding. "You tell me how I'm supposed to get

'You're wrong, I wanted you' from any of that. Why should I believe a word that comes out of your mouth?"

His brows creased as he tried to figure out what the hell to say. She was fired up now, and he didn't want to fight, but he wanted to make her understand. Suddenly, it was more important to him than anything had been in a long time. "Cassie, I—"

A hard knock on the door cut him off and made her jump.

"Ah fer Chrissake," he muttered. Then, loud enough to be heard, he shouted, "Not now!"

The door opened anyway. Jimmy looked down at him and asked with an edge, "Why's your sister tendin' bar?"

"She's doin' me a favor," Sean explained. "I won't be long."

Jimmy's eyes went to her and flew wide with recognition. "What the . . ." The blond Irishman's jaw literally dropped open in surprise. "Well I'll be damned," he breathed, staring at her. "Hello, Cassandra."

"Hi, Jimmy," she said in a soft voice. "Surprise."

"Got that right." He stared a moment longer, then said, "Sorry to interrupt." His chin tipped her way as he added, "Nice to see ya."

"You too," she said with a faint smile. The door closed and the room seemed too quiet. She wiped under her glassy eyes with her fingertips to make sure her skin was dry. After an awkward minute, she sniffed hard, stood up, and smoothed out her pants. She didn't want to look at Sean. It hurt to look at him. "I should get going."

"No, not yet!" he said urgently, springing to his feet. His deep blue eyes implored with her. "Not yet. Wait."

"You need to get back to work, and I need to go." As wondrous as it was to see him again, and to hear his heartfelt words and apologies, it was too much. She was still angry, it burned in her chest. She was completely overwhelmed. Blindsided. And she couldn't have those old wounds ripped open again. Even though he wasn't trying to do that, simply hearing him had that effect anyway. Her survival instincts had finally overcome the shock, and she wanted out.

But the way he was looking at her, with mournful tenderness and something close to desperation, clawed at her. Whether it was his need was to be understood, to be forgiven, or simply for her not to leave yet, she wasn't sure. Maybe it was all those things. She had no idea. All she knew was she had to get out of there. His presence had always been strong, but now it engulfed her. Consumed her.

"It was good to see you," she said, taking a deep breath as she recomposed herself and stepped away from him. A twinge of anger pierced her. Dammit, she'd all but fallen apart in front of him. She must've looked so weak. Not the image she wanted to present, or to leave him with.

It had taken her years to stop hurting over him. When the hot anger and deep sorrow finally left her heart, she went numb. She'd been okay with that; it was better than the pain. Now, she wanted to be stoic, the very picture of cool collection. She wanted him to know she was strong, she was fine, and she was over him. Because she was. She *was*.

Her chin lifted a notch and she flashed a phony grin as she said, "Take care, Sean. I'm glad you have the bar, and that you—"

"Would you let me take ya out?" he said, cutting her off. He stepped towards her. "To dinner? Or just a drink? Whatever you want. Please, Cassie. I know I have no right to ask, but I . . ." His dark blue eyes blazed with intensity as they swept over her. "I'd love to see ya again."

Half of her screamed to walk out and never look back, to never give him a chance to hurt her again. But the other half... ugh, he looked so sincere, so wanting... and so handsome. She was as attracted to him as ever, she couldn't deny that. He was still the most alluring, sexy, beautiful man in the world to her. Damn him.

"Just once," he murmured, pinning her with his stare. "Even just for coffee, a drink..."

"No," she said quietly. "I can't. I just can't."

His face fell, but he nodded.

"I'm sorry," she whispered.

"Don't be sorry," he said gruffly. "I understand."

They stared at each other in strained silence for a few moments.

"Right," he finally said. "Well. If you change your mind... ya know where to find me."

She had to snort at that. "I can't believe you've been in the city for two years and we never ran into each other."

"'Tis a big city," he said.

"Yes, it is. This proves it, I guess..."

His eyes speared her. She wished he'd stop looking at her that way. So mournfully. So wanting. His desire was palpable. His intensity hadn't diminished; she recalled the way she could feel her soul stir with just one of his deep, searching looks—the way he was looking at her right now. She had to turn away.

She reached for her coat. He quickly stepped forward to help her with it. As she fastened the front closed, his hands stayed on her arms. Her back was so close to his chest, she could feel the heat radiating from him. A buzz went through her, heating her blood. His breath was warm against her hair, and she had to close her eyes against the rush of feeling that surged through her core. Attraction, longing, desire, plain old lust... it stole her breath.

He whispered close to her ear, "I can't tell ya how glad I am that you walked into my bar tonight. Seeing you was wonderful." His hands ran slowly down her arms. "You're beautiful. Absolutely beautiful."

The butterflies in her stomach went crazy. "Stop," she whispered hotly, squeezing her closed eyes tighter even as her heart stuttered in her chest. "Stop being nice. I don't want you to be nice. It's easier when you're not nice."

"I'm sorry." His voice was rough, somber. "But I truly need ya to know, in case I never see you again, how sorry I am that I hurt you that way. I thought I was doing the right thing. But I could've handled it differently." He edged closer and kissed the top of her head. "I'm sorry, Cassie. Please say ya believe me."

"I believe you," she whispered, holding back her tears. *I will not cry*, she told herself. *I will not cry another tear in front of him.* "Okay? I do believe you, Sean."

He exhaled, and she felt the warm air against the side of her face. "Thank you. Thank ya for that."

They stood like that for a long beat before his hands fell away.

"I'm sorry," he said sadly. "I'm just . . . overwhelmed."

"Me too," she said. Her eyes opened and she turned to face him. He stared down at her with such passion it was almost a tangible thing. And God help her, the connection she'd felt with him was still there. They used to talk about it, their deep connection, how they were soul mates . . .

After it was over, when he broke up with her, when she fought for them and he still left, she was so angry at him. Soul mates didn't *leave*. Then she got angry at herself. Maybe it'd been a lie. A fantasy. She spent months speculating: maybe that "connection" was never there at all? Or she'd been the only one who'd felt it, and he'd been giving her lip service? She'd wondered if maybe she'd imagined it, idealized and romanticized it . . .

But no. She *felt* it, even now. She couldn't explain it, which was ironic since she was a professional woman of words. But it was there. Their connection had been real, she hadn't imagined it. It both soothed her mind and broke her heart all over again.

"What are you thinking?" he asked, tipping her chin up to look into her eyes.

She'd never tell him any of that. She covered, but with a different truth. "I always loved that you were so passionate," she said.

His hand lifted to touch her cheek and her breath caught. His thumb caressed her skin with such tenderness it made her heart squeeze. "Maybe . . . maybe someday you'll give me a chance to make it right. Take me up on that drink. Think on it?"

Her eyes fell away as her heart thudded in heavy beats. "I don't think so." She stepped back, away from him, to reach for her scarf and wrapped it around her neck.

"I don't care if it's days, weeks, months from now," he barreled on. "I want to see ya again. My invitation for that drink stands. Forever, if need be. Okay?"

Her throat felt too thick, and she swallowed hard to clear it. She just nodded.

His eyes flashed and a muscle jumped in his jaw. "Only a nod? Fine. I'll take it."

She went still; the air in her lungs felt stuck. The look in his blue, blue eyes was so raw. But she grabbed her tote bag, slung it over her shoulder, and played it cool. "This was . . . interesting," she said hoarsely. She cleared her throat. "I'm glad you're well."

He reached out and touched the ends of her hair. Then, before she knew what he was about, he leaned in and kissed her cheek. The touch of his warm lips and slight scrape of his stubble against her skin was like an electric charge, a jolt to her system. She jumped slightly, and his hand flew up to cup the back of her neck as he lingered there. He was so close, she could smell him again, that musky, enticing scent . . . feel his warmth . . . all she had to do was turn her head, and they'd be kissing.

But he stepped back. Those blues blazed as they swept over her face. "I'm not gonna lie, Cassie—I hope ya change your mind and give me a call. But if not . . ." His eyes softened, almost imploring. His voice dropped to a whisper as he said, "Happy Christmas, love."

"Merry Christmas," she said quickly, and walked out of the office before she did anything more that she'd regret.

She pushed her way through the crowded bar until she made it out the door. The cold air hit her like a slap, but she welcomed it. She needed a good slap. She'd been so close to changing her mind at that last second and saying yes to seeing him again. Which would have made her certifiably out of her mind.

She pulled her hat out of her bag, yanked it onto her head, and started to walk, weaving her way through people to head for the subway. The people and sounds were a blur around her. Her mind was still reeling. *She'd seen Sean.* And he'd been happy to see her, really happy. He'd apologized for hurting her and admitted he regretted losing her . . . said words she used to dream of hearing on long, lonely nights. He even wanted to see her again. He'd asked her out! He wanted to make things right . . . he'd almost kissed her . . . it was too much to absorb all at once.

Her world had turned upside down just by randomly walking into that one bar.

As she hurried against the frigid winds, a Salvation Army Santa stood on the corner, ringing his bell. She offered him a tiny smile, an automatic gesture.

"Merry Christmas!" he boomed jovially to her. "Watch for miracles!"

I think I might have to do that, she thought in wonder. *I think I might have just experienced a huge one, full of healing, and forgiveness.*

Chapter Five

"AND SO THIS is Christmas..." John Lennon's voice came through the tiny speakers in Cassandra's office. "And what have you done..."

She smiled to herself, but didn't lift her eyes and continued to read. One more student's paper to get through, and the final exams for her second class would be complete. Two classes down, one to go.

At least the holiday music station on Pandora was keeping her in good spirits. She'd made it through that morning's class in a bit of a daze. From the moment she'd woken up, her mind had been full of her encounter with Sean the night before. Luckily, the class was just review now that the papers were handed in, so she had the luxury of coasting on auto pilot. Good thing, too; she was completely distracted.

Did he have to look so good? And be as sweet and charming as ever? And apologize so earnestly for the heartache he'd caused her? And stand so close, drawing her in like a moth to a flame?

His eyes. Those deep, soulful blue eyes. She'd gone to sleep seeing them in her mind; they were the first thing she'd thought of when she'd woken up, and hadn't been able to stop thinking of them all morning.

"Happy Christmas!" John, Yoko, and the others shouted joyfully. Cassandra startled, realizing she'd daydreamed her way through the whole song. And hadn't finished that last page. Dammit. She cracked her knuckles and made herself focus. As she finished the last sentence on the last page, her stomach growled. A glance at the clock told her she'd have to get lunch soon if she wanted enough time to actually chew it before her afternoon class.

Her phone dinged with a text and she looked at it. Kara had written, *You saw Sean and didn't call me?!? How could you? Thank God Bree loves me more than you do. I NEED TO KNOW EVERYTHING!*

Cassandra laughed and texted back, *I'm sorry! Had my morning class, doing work now—finals start next week. Then I have another class this afternoon.*

You're dead to me, Kara wrote back.

LOL! I'm sorry, I'm sorry! Will call you tonight. Promise.

You better.

I will. How are you feeling, anyhow?

Elephant-like, Kara texted. *I'm so ready for this baby to come.*

Could be any day now, Cassandra wrote. *Careful what you wish for!*

Fine! I can't wait three more weeks. I'm huge and uncomfortable. And now that I'm on bedrest, I'm bored out of my mind.

Isn't Elena keeping you good company?

My sister needs some happy pills, Kara responded. *She's a bit of a grump.*

Cassandra laughed as she wrote, *Sorry. Dinner soon, the 3 of us? Maybe I can get Bree back into the city to join us and make it 4.*

We'll discuss it later, when you call me to tell me every single detail about your seeing Sean last night, Kara wrote. *Not being subtle. Call me later!*

LOL, I will! Love you. Hang in there.

Love you too. Bye.

Cassandra's stomach rumbled again, louder this time. "Lunch," she said aloud, and set down the thick paper. She'd write her comments and edits later. She was too hungry. The music went silent and the office was quiet for all of three seconds when her office phone intercom buzzed. "Hello?"

"Hi, Cassandra," said Tina, the English department's secretary. "There's a man here with your lunch."

Cassandra's brows furrowed. "What? I didn't order lunch. I was actually about to leave and go *get* some lunch. There must be a mistake."

"Um . . . I don't think so," Tina said. "He says it's for you. Seems adamant."

"I don't—you know what, I'll just come out. Be right there." She grabbed her keys, shoved her cell phone into the pocket of her gray dress slacks, quickly ran her fingers through her hair, and locked her office door behind her.

She didn't order lunch. She would've absolutely remembered ordering lunch. When she got out front, she saw that since she'd locked herself in her office only two hours earlier, Tina had strewn lights and tinsel around the room, and even had a mini Christmas tree with lights and ornaments on the floor beside her desk.

But what filled Cassandra's vision was the surprise guest standing there. Her stomach did a quick flip. "Sean? What—what are you doing here?"

"Hello there!" He grinned his killer grin, and raised the large white plastic bag he held. "I brought you some lunch."

She gaped, and her eyes flickered to Tina briefly before they went back to him. "How'd you know where to find me?"

"Wasn't too hard, love," he said.

"Really." She regarded him as she asked, "So, what—are you stalking me now?"

"Maybe a little," he said cheerfully, without a hint of sheepishness. "I'm thinking girl's got to eat. So, I brought ya lunch. Us, actually. Enough for two. Where should we have it?"

"I didn't say yes," she pointed out. "I didn't even ask you to—"

"But you've gotta eat, right?" His eyes twinkled with a combination of mischief and sass . . . and something else.

Her stomach growled as if on cue, loud enough for him and Tina to hear. His grin turned into a victorious smirk.

"See, you are hungry! I brought good food. You still like sushi, don't ya? C'mon, Cassie."

Tina's gaze flicked to Cassandra. "Cassie?" She tried to hide her amusement and failed. "I've never heard anyone call you that."

"With good reason," Cassandra ground out. Annoyed and slightly embarrassed at having an audience, she looked back to Sean. Big gorgeous jerk, standing there smirking and all sexy like that. In a royal blue pullover hoodie under his peacoat and jeans. The pullover brought out his incredible eyes. He didn't play fair. He never had. "Fine, come on. We'll eat in my office."

"Splendid," he said, his smile bright. Tina tried to hold back her giggle but failed.

✦ ✦ ✦

SEAN FOLLOWED CASSANDRA down the hall, glancing at the closed doors of other faculty members. He felt a strange, almost anxious twinge in his chest and marveled at the fact that he'd turn thirty-three in a few months, but still endured stirrings of unease in an academic setting. School had never been a welcoming place for him as a kid. Memories like that burrowed deep in one's psyche, and you couldn't get them out.

Now, he pushed them aside and let himself be hypnotized by the sway of her hips as she walked in front of him. Dressed in a simple black blouse, gray slacks, and black leather boots, she was the picture of a young professional. So different from the wild-haired girl who used to roam around the city with him in jeans and runners.

She still turned him on, no question about that. If she'd gained any weight since their days as a couple, he couldn't tell. The only stark physical difference was her shorter hair, currently pulled back in a small ponytail, revealing the nape of her neck. He'd spent hours nibbling on that sweet, smooth curve, making her purr and curl into him like a content kitten . . . his blood heated just remembering it.

At the end of the hall, second door on the right before the last, was her office. He noted the stubborn set of her jaw and the spots of high color on her cheeks as she pulled out her keys and had to grin. He'd surprised her, alright, and she was fighting to stay cool. He could see it all over her. And it tickled him.

"Why do ya lock the door?" he asked, leaning lazily against the wall.

"Um, so nothing gets stolen," she said as if it were obvious.

"But there's nobody back here."

"No, not at the moment . . ." She pushed the door open.

"We're alone, then?" He said it lightly, to tease.

But her face flamed.

His heart danced at that. *Score one for me.*

She walked into the office and plopped down in her leather chair. "Do you remember that I get cranky when I'm really hungry?"

"Aye, I do now." He closed the door and sat in the only other chair, a smaller cushioned one beside her desk. As he placed the bag on her desktop, he joked, "Better feed ya fast, then. You're getting crankier by the second."

"Well, I also don't like surprises," she grumbled.

"Even when it's sushi? Delivered straight to your office by a dashing Irishman?"

"Especially then."

He barked out a laugh and pulled the Styrofoam rectangles out of the bag.

As he also pulled two bottles of water out and handed her one, her mouth twisted. She was trying not to grin, but her dark eyes were lit up with humor. He winked at her.

"So what'd you bring me?" she asked, sitting back in her chair.

"Took a chance. I don't know what you like nowadays, but if memory served..." He opened the container he'd placed before her. "Eel and cucumber roll, spicy tuna roll, yellowtail. Is this okay?"

Her eyes widened a drop as she glanced at the sushi, then up at him. "Yeah. Yeah, that's what I like." She reached for a pair of chopsticks and snapped them apart. "Color me impressed."

He smiled, feeling like he'd won a small victory. "Great." He opened his own container. "Cheers. Enjoy it."

"How much do I owe you?" she asked.

His eyes flew to hers. "What? Don't insult me, love."

"But—"

"But nothin'. I bought and brought you lunch. My treat. End of story."

She nodded and said, "Thank you."

He watched as she popped the first piece into her mouth.

Her eyes closed in ecstasy and she let out the tiniest moan as she ate. It made his blood race, and he felt the stirring in his jeans.

"I was starving," she admitted, going for another piece. "Thank you, Sean. This was . . . kind of you."

"You're very welcome. Glad I caught you at the right time." He snapped apart his own chopsticks, briefly rubbed them together, and dug in to his lunch.

Her big brown eyes pinned him as she demanded, "Now tell me how you located me. For real."

"Like I said, it wasn't hard. Ya told me you taught English Lit at NYU . . . c'mon, love, you're on the bloody website. I called the department, spoke to the secretary, and made sure when you'd be here."

She nodded, accepting that. They ate in silence for a few minutes. She didn't seem angry at him, so that was good. But as he stole glances in between bites, he couldn't read her. Her eyes stayed on her meal. Was she glad he'd come or not?

"I had to see you again, Cassie," he finally murmured. "And I want to see ya some more. Have dinner with me tomorrow. Let me take you out."

She went very still. Even her mouth slowed as she chewed.

At her reaction, he stilled too. A rush of anxiety went through him and he asked, "Do ya really not want to see me again, after today? Truth."

She swallowed hard, fidgeting with her chopsticks. Then, she said quietly, "I kind of do want to. That's the problem."

"Why is it a problem?"

She didn't answer. She picked up another piece of sushi with her chopsticks and brought it to her mouth.

His heart felt stuck in his chest. "I'm just asking to take ya out to dinner, Cassie. Nothing more. Taking it slowly." A grin flickered. "I'm trying to, anyway. It's hard when you're so damn beautiful. It makes me want."

"You're dangerous," she whispered, her eyes fastened to his now. He saw the ambivalence there. Even a lick of fear, maybe. "You want truth? Here's a truth: my mind is screaming to not let you near me again."

His mouth went dry. He grabbed his bottle and gulped down some water. "I get that. But... what does your heart say?"

She sucked in a breath. "The last time I listened to my heart where you were concerned, I got demolished."

He sighed mournfully. "I know. But that was then..." He leaned in and covered her hand with his. "Give me a new chance now. That's all I'm asking for. A chance."

"A chance to hurt me again," she murmured, her gaze unflinching.

He winced. "No. A chance to try again. Starting with something small, like dinner."

"Why should I?" she asked. Everything about her seemed poised to defend herself: her posture, her expression, her tone. "Why should I let you back into my life, on any level?"

"Hopefully, because you feel the connection between us is still here," he said. "Just as much as I feel it, and did from the moment I saw ya last night." He squeezed her hand, caressed the back of it with his calloused thumb. Her eyes went liquid. "I could barely sleep, with the buzz of you in my head. Seeing you again, it was like... I don't know, a recognition? We're still connected. You know I'm right."

She frowned, her ambivalence clear as her eyes slipped closed.

He squeezed her hand again and said softly, "Look me in the eyes and tell me you don't feel it too, and when we're done with lunch, I'll walk out that door and leave ya be."

Her eyes opened, scrutinizing him. He could barely

breathe.

"Give me a chance, Cassie," he said. "And I'll romance ya within an inch of your life."

"I don't want fake, empty gestures," she replied, a trace of annoyance in her voice. "That's not romantic, that's not impressive—that's manipulative."

"I'm not trying to manipulate you. So they wouldn't be fake," he said firmly. "They'd be demonstrations, to show you that I'm willing to do whatever it takes to get to know ya again." His chest felt tight. "I just want to know ya again."

Still, she only stared back at him, those warm, dark eyes consuming him. He wished he knew what she was thinking. He understood her hesitation, but it killed him.

"I know I hurt you," he whispered. "You've every right to make me grovel. I'm doing it now. Because I want to see ya again, Cassandra."

Her face pale, she finally pulled her hand from his and picked up her chopsticks. She wouldn't look at him; in fact, her eyes avoided his now. His heart sank.

Well, he'd given it his best shot. He couldn't blame her. When he'd broken up with her, she'd tried to keep them together. She'd fought for them with everything she had. And that'd only made it worse for him, because the truth was he hadn't wanted to lose her in the first place. She'd begged him not to leave, and he'd left. Now he was begging her for another chance, and she wasn't having it.

He'd have to accept that and leave her alone from now on. To know she was out there, in the city, living her life without him in it, by choice. He glanced down at his lunch and his stomach churned with misery; his appetite was gone. Swallowing hard, he stayed silent. What should he do now? Get up and leave while he still had some dignity left? He had no idea. His gaze lowered to the floor.

"What time do you want to have dinner tomorrow?" she asked, as she carefully dribbled soy sauce on a piece of yellowtail.

His eyes snapped back up to her face. Elation rushed through him like a tidal wave, and he couldn't hold back his smile. "How does six o'clock sound?"

She peeked up at him from beneath her long, dark lashes, the hints of a grin lifting her lips. "Sounds fine to me."

"Fantastic." He sat back in his chair and smiled at her. "Excellent." The knot that had formed in his chest loosened, his stomach calmed, and he took a deep, cleansing breath. She was giving him the chance he wanted. Until she'd walked out of his office last night, he hadn't realized how desperate he was to try again with her.

A date? One shot? He was determined not to blow it.

Chapter Six

As Cassandra approached the arch at Washington Square Park, she saw Sean waiting there for her as promised. He leaned against the stone in the shadows, probably to shield himself from the cold gusts of wind, his tall, lanky frame clad in dark clothes. When he saw her, he straightened and smiled. She pressed her lips together to keep back the smile that threatened to take over her whole face.

Since he'd left her office yesterday, she'd thought of little but him. They had a dinner date. A real date. It was exciting and terrifying at the same time. Her friends had been vocal in their opinions on the subject, over the phone and through texts. Bree had been less than pleased, and insisted she make him work for every inch. Kara had cautiously encouraged her to give him this one shot. Jade had insisted he take her somewhere fabulous while he groveled. Elena had simply wished her luck.

She hadn't dared tell her mother, though. Cassandra suspected that if her mom knew she had even spoken to Sean, much less agreed to go on a date with him, she'd have beaten her with a wooden spoon. Joann Catalano Baines was fiercely protective of her family, and had a long memory.

It had taken Cassandra so long to let go of Sean. She'd thought they'd end up married. That wasn't an outlandish thought. He'd all but proposed on their second Christmas together. Standing in Central Park on Christmas Day, in the snow that night, on that tiny stone bridge, they'd made heartfelt promises to each other...

It'd taken her a long time to let go of the sorrow, the anger, the pain, and then the last wisps of dashed hope, before her heart finally settled into a flat, gray numbness, allowing her to move on with her life. She'd thrown herself into her graduate studies. Spent all her free time reading, studying, working, so she wouldn't have much time to date or to be lonely. She'd gone on some dates, had a few boyfriends... 'suitable' types, like she'd said to Bree. Upstanding, academic, dispassionate... and none of them touched her heart. She wouldn't let them. Getting hurt again was something she didn't care to repeat; being on her own was better.

And yet here she was, trying to ignore the way her heart was racing as she walked towards Sean in the park on a cold winter's night. She tried not to be moved by the way his eyes fastened to hers and twinkled with delight, or by the lopsided grin that spread on his face as she stopped a few paces in front of him.

"You came," he said, looking down at her. "I'm glad to see ya."

"You thought I wouldn't?" Her brows puckered.

"I'll admit it: I did wonder if you'd change your mind."

"I considered it," she revealed.

He blinked at her honesty.

She wrapped her arms around herself and met his gaze directly. "But if I make someone a promise, I keep it."

"Aha." A muscle jumped in his jaw. "Did ya come here to

punish me, then? I suppose I deserve it, but I figure if that's why you really accepted, I should know that going in."

His blunt assessment sobered her. "No, I didn't come to punish you," she said. "But I might let some cracks fly . . . like that one. Sorry."

"Forget it." His mouth twisted ruefully. "It's understandable. Besides, you always had a sharp tongue when pushed. Good to know some things haven't changed." He winked and offered her his elbow. "I'll take my chances. Shall we?"

She hesitated at first, then slowly slipped her hand into the waiting crook of his arm. With a smile, he nudged her and they started to walk.

"Where are we going?" she asked.

"Let's get a cab. It's freezing out. Your cheeks are already rosy, and mine are like ice."

"Okay. But you didn't answer me," she said, unable to repress a grin.

His smile went lopsided, deliciously teasing. "I didn't."

Though it was dark and cold, there were others milling about the park. No area in the city was ever really empty, something that was a comfort to Cassandra. She loved how Manhattan teemed with people from varied cultures and places. It fascinated her endlessly. And during the holiday season in particular, there seemed to be such an upbeat, almost magical feel in the air . . . everyone seemed happier. Whether it was an illusion or reality, she was never sure, but she felt it.

December had always made her feel twinges of melancholy, wistful for the future she thought she'd have with Sean and didn't experience. Now, walking arm in arm with him through the park where they'd spent so much time together back when they were a couple . . . it felt surreal. Like a dream. And just like a dream, it was thrilling, but left her vaguely uneasy, with the slightest sense of apprehension, nervous about how things were going to unfold.

When they got to the street, he lifted an arm to hail a cab, and a yellow taxi pulled up within seconds. He held the door open for her as she climbed in, warmth hitting her face. Sean slid in beside her, closed the door, and told the driver where to go. She knew they were headed down to the Village, but still had no idea where they were actually going.

She didn't care. She was too anxious and excited to care. And now, in the back of the cab, with the heat cranking warmth at them and the cabbie's radio playing *All I Want for Christmas (Is You)* by Mariah Carey, she became starkly aware of Sean's closeness. How his arm brushed against hers, how his long leg pressed against hers, how good he smelled. He'd shaved for their date, and the hint of his aftershave and his clean, smooth skin tantalized her. When his hand reached for hers, his skin was so warm . . . her heart stuttered in her chest as he slowly laced his fingers with hers and squeezed.

Her eyes raised to meet his. He looked back, unblinking, intense as usual. The look wasn't challenging, it was questioning. The back of the car suddenly seemed too small, such close quarters. The unexpected tender gesture plucked at her heart, she couldn't deny it.

"This damn song," he growled, low and bemused. "I can never hear it without thinking of ya."

"Seriously?" She stared at him in wonder.

"Oh, you bet." He looked slightly embarrassed. "Don't you remember that night . . . with that red nightie? How you sang this to me before . . ."

Her face flushed, probably the same shade as the negligee in question. "Of course I do."

"So do I, Cassie. Believe me." His eyes held hers. "I can still see you dancing for me. Your hair swaying everywhere, your skin, your goofy smile . . . how the night ended . . . I think of it all every damn time I hear this song."

She was dumbfounded. To think she'd had that kind of hold over anyone, for anything . . . she couldn't even fathom it. It was a heady, intoxicating thought. Empowering. Maybe he *had* missed her.

"Can I ask ya something?" His voice was still pitched low.

She nodded.

"Have ya . . . have ya had other relationships, since ours?"

"Yes." She caught a flicker of something in his eyes and wondered at it. Disappointment? Jealousy? She wasn't sure. Then, she couldn't help herself. "You?"

"Not really." He shrugged. "Dated plenty, sure. But . . . didn't want to get too involved." The taxi went over a pothole, lifting them in the seat as it bumped. His hand tightened momentarily on hers, an unconscious gesture of protection. "What happened with yours?"

"I'm sorry, with my what?"

"Your relationships. How many boyfriends have you had? That didn't work out?"

"Two."

He nodded and his eyes fell away as he asked, "Did ya love either of them?"

"No. They were nice, but they didn't . . . " Her voice trailed off. *They didn't compare to you.* She cleared her throat, trying to ignore the flutters in her stomach as he continued to hold her hand. "I guess when it came down to it, I didn't want to get too involved, either."

She stared down at their hands, intertwined like it was the most natural thing in the world. Deciding silence was best at that moment, she leaned her head back against the seat, hearing the rub of the synthetic leather seat by her ear. His eyes lingered on her, but he said nothing.

The song on the radio changed to Elvis Presley singing,

"I'll-a have-a aaa Bluuuue Christmaaaas... without yooo-ou..."

"I had an idea for something we could do after dinner," Sean said. "You up for it?"

"Depends what it is," she said warily.

He laughed, a full, rich sound. "So suspicious, ya are! It's something fun and easy. Nothing scary. Game?"

"Sure, I'm game," she said, so aware of how her hand felt in his, at how her insides warmed at the sound of his laugh. She'd forgotten what a delicious laugh he had. Like his voice, it was almost musical and made her feel swoony. She tore her gaze from his, but he didn't let go of her hand.

They looked out the windows at the scenery that passed as the cab headed down into the Village. Holiday decorations of all kinds lit the store windows and displays, adding cheer and vibrance to the city at night. A few minutes later, the cab pulled up to a small tavern.

Sean paid the driver and ushered her out, still holding her hand even when the taxi had pulled away from the curb. "Do ya know this place?" he asked.

"Never been here before." She glanced at the sign, *Mary's Pub*, and the subheading: "*Real* Irish food!"

"Ahh, then you're in for a treat," he said with a smile. "They've got the best shepherd's pie I've had in New York. Ya liked that a lot, ate it quite often back in the day. 'Best comfort food there is,' you used to say. So, I figured this place was a good bet for dinner."

Cassandra couldn't help but smile back. "You remembered that?"

"Cassie..." His bright blue eyes held hers as a gust of frigid air blew. The ends of his scarf whirled around, and the tousled ends of his honey colored hair that his wool hat couldn't contain twitched in the wind. "I remember everything.

The good and the bad, but it was mostly good. And most importantly, I remember you. Us." He squeezed the hand he held. "Why do you think I want another chance so badly? We were magic together. Ya don't forget things when they're magic like that. Some of those memories are some of the best ones of my life."

She couldn't move. His softly intense words and the emotion in his eyes were overwhelming. She shivered hard, and knew it wasn't just from the cold.

✦ ✦ ✦

DINNER HAD GONE splendidly, Sean reflected as he helped Cassandra on with her coat. For almost two hours, they'd talked, ate well, and finished a bottle of Merlot. They'd kept the conversation topics fairly neutral, with her talking about her graduate program and the classes she taught, and him sticking to tales of debauchery during his band days in L.A. and customers in the bar now who made him laugh.

She was . . . restrained at first. Two glasses of wine and time helped loosen her up, but she was more somber than he remembered. Maybe she'd become more serious through years of hard study and academia? Or, maybe she'd changed after he'd basically handed her heart back to her in pieces? He wasn't sure. Yet, he'd caught glimpses of the girl he'd known and adored. Her warmth, her good humor, her whip-smart mind, her sweet laugh and smile . . . the qualities that had initially drawn him to her were still there.

They'd both made a concerted effort to not bring up the past; an unspoken yet obvious agreement. The breakup was not discussed, and there had never actually been bad times between them. Not until he decided she'd be better off without him and left her for her own good. The pink elephant was definitely in the room, but neither of them wanted to address it on their first date. And that was fine for now.

The evening had been nice. Gone better than he'd dared to hope. He was grateful.

Now, as they buttoned their coats and headed for the door, he asked, "So, ya still game for the other thing I'd thought to do?"

Cassandra looked up at him, her cheeks slightly flushed and her eyes round, and he suspected she was a bit buzzed from the wine. "Yeah, I'm game," she said with an amiable grin. "I told you that before."

"Just checking," he grinned back. "Okay, then. Let's go."

Outside, the cold wind whipped their faces. They quickly pulled on their hats and gloves, tightened their scarves and coats, and Sean stepped to the curb to hail another taxi. This time it took a few minutes before one pulled up, and they rushed into the back seat of the warm, dark car.

"Bryant Park, please," Sean told the driver.

Cassandra's thin brows lifted in surprise. "Seriously?"

"I know, I know, it's cliché," he mock lamented. "But it'll be fun. Trust me." He watched her for a few seconds before remarking, "You're shivering."

"It was cold out there while we waited!" she said.

"It was," he agreed. He edged closer. "I'm cold too. Maybe we should huddle together for warmth. Ya know, body heat and all that . . ."

Her dark eyes flashed, but she said nothing.

Interesting, he thought. Slowly, he lifted his arm and wrapped it around her shoulders, then drew her into his side. "Mmmm. Cozy," he said softly, his lips against her temple.

She didn't pull away, but said, "Maybe too cozy."

"No such thing," he said. His heart started pounding in thicker, heavier beats. She was in his arms, against his body . . .

his reaction was visceral, immediate, and achingly familiar. His blood heated and raced, his jeans felt too tight, and his fingers itched to touch her. "I have to tell ya . . . you're more beautiful now than you were then," he murmured in her ear, pulling her even closer. "And back then, you were absolute perfection."

"I was not," she scoffed in a whisper.

"You were to me," he whispered back earnestly. "Always."

Her head lifted from his shoulder so she could look at him. Their eyes locked. She was right there; all he had to do was shift his chin and he'd be kissing her. Her luscious mouth and liquid eyes beckoned. He felt her warm, sweet breath against his face, saw the hint of longing in her eyes, and desire flamed in his veins, shooting through him mercilessly with renewed urgency.

"That's sweet of you to say," she whispered back. "You were to me, too."

He stared deep into her eyes, those bottomless dark wells, and lost himself. Slowly, with great care, he brushed his lips against hers. She gasped against his lips, but didn't pull away. His heartbeat took off, skyrocketing from the feel of her. Desire crushed him. He covered her mouth with his, kissing her deeply, his hand cupping the back of her neck to pull her closer.

Her hand came up to touch his cheek as her mouth opened for him. His tongue found hers; she tasted of wine and sweetness. Overcome, he groaned softly into her mouth as he kissed her, savoring her, sipping from her lips and caressing her face with his fingertips. Her arm snaked around his neck, holding him to her as she kissed him back. Liquid fire ran through him, pure heat. Her mouth was so soft, so warm . . . her tongue tangling with his made his mind go blank with want. His arms went around her, the kisses deepened, and the world fell away.

But there was a jolt as the cab came to a stop, and the driver said, "Sorry to interrupt, but you're here."

They pulled apart, their eyes locked as they both tried to clear the haze of lust.

"Jaysus. That was . . ." He trailed the backs of his fingers along her cheek. "I didn't realize 'til just now how much I missed kissing you," he said in a thick rasp.

"You're still great at it," she admitted, grinning impishly.

"Ha!" He smiled with delight as he pulled his wallet out of his pocket. "Glad to hear it!" He leaned in to smack a quick, light kiss on her lips and growled in a sexy tone, "You are too. And be warned: I'll be wantin' more of that before the night's through."

✦ ✦ ✦

HE HAD TO be kidding, Cassandra thought. Ice skating at Bryant Park? It was one of the most cliché things to do in New York at Christmas time. And yet, she was touched by the suggestion. Watching Sean lace up his rented skates with nimble dexterity, she bent to check her laces again. She wasn't great at skating, and hadn't done it in a very long time. The thought of falling on her ass in front of him held no appeal.

"I have an idea. Why don't you skate, and I'll watch you?" she asked.

He looked up at her from his seat, his marine blue eyes dancing. "You're not afraid, are ya, love? C'mon, now."

"I just don't feel like breaking anything so close to the holidays," she hedged.

"I won't let ya," he said, rising to stand. In the skates, he towered over her. He looked into her eyes and said, "I won't let ya fall, Cassie. I swear."

Her body hummed with a rush of emotion and adrenaline,

leaving her hyperaware of every muscle. "Yeah, well . . ." She got to her feet, wobbly and unsure. "I can't believe I let you talk me into this. I haven't done it in years. I'm an idiot."

A chuckle slipped out as he teased, "Ah, come now! It's goin' to be fun. Ya weren't that bad at this, if memory serves."

"Hopefully, my limbs will remember that too," she said, clinging to the railing as they headed to the small entrance. Sean laughed at her jest, then pushed off onto the ice. He did a half turn, graceful yet masculine at the same time, and her heart thumped madly. Did he have to look so good, no matter what he was doing? It was so damned distracting, especially while she was working just to stay upright.

"C'mon, Professor Baines," he called, doing another turn. "Join me!"

She stepped onto the ice and clung to the railing. "Getting there . . ."

An instrumental version of *Frosty the Snowman* played over tall speakers as she took a quick look around. The ice was crowded, and she worried not only about falling, but crashing into another skater. But there was Sean, grinning at her, looking confident and at ease, as always. He skated a few feet away, giving her time to acclimate, before gliding back to her side. "C'mere, Cassie." His eyes twinkled at her, and his handsome face was already ruddy from the cold. The ends of his hair poked out wildly from beneath his navy wool hat. "Push off now. Can't have a skate whilst clingin' to the wall, can ya?"

"Okaaaay . . ." She pushed away from the wall and, to her delight, stayed on her feet.

"There she goes!" he cried victoriously.

She skated a few paces while he stuck by her side. By the time they'd done one lap around the rink, she felt more comfortable. "I think I got this." She exerted some strength and skated away from him, shooting him a coy look as she did. His eyes sparked with mischief.

"Gonna make me chase ya, eh?" he joked.

"Damn right," she answered over her shoulder.

"I'll chase ya to the ends of the earth," he declared, following her with a cheeky grin. "Now that you're in my sights, love..."

"You're going to have to work for it, McKinnon," she said. She tried to skate away, but she was no match for him. He was at her side in a few strides, smiling wickedly.

"I know I'll have to work for it," he said. "But I'm not afraid of hard work. Especially where you're concerned, I promise. I'll do what it takes."

A lump formed in her throat. She murmured, "Don't make a promise you can't keep."

His grin faltered. "Never again," he swore quietly. They weren't only talking about ice skating anymore, and she knew he knew it. "I want this. I want a second chance with you."

"A second chance at what, exactly?" she asked. She stopped moving, and he stopped with her. They stood on the ice, people skating around them, staring into each other's eyes. "Tell me. I want to know. What are you looking for here, when you say you want another chance?"

"Another chance to be with you," he said, low and raw and honest.

"What does that *mean*?" she demanded. "To sleep with me? To date me? What?"

"Everything," he murmured. "I want a chance at having everything with you."

Her breath caught and her throat thickened.

"I haven't been able to stop thinking of ya since you walked into my bar," he admitted. His gaze was intense, too intense; she had to look away. Off to the distance, to the naked trees against the night sky, lit by street lights, black and stark and beautiful. He raised his hand to tip her chin back his way, forcing eye contact. "You're an amazing woman."

"So amazing you left me," she whispered.

His jaw tightened as he winced and his hand fell to his side. "I can't change the past. But I can apologize for it, over and over if ya need to hear it," he said. He leaned in slightly. "I have some hope. Because you didn't have to agree to come out with me tonight, but ya did."

"I don't trust you," she said. She saw him blink and jolt, as if she'd slapped him. "I don't trust you not to hurt me. I trusted you so blindly before, so completely, and I ended up regretting it. I can't let that happen again. I won't."

He nodded, absorbing her words. "I understand. But maybe ... in time ... with more contact, if ya let me, I can prove myself trustworthy again."

"How?"

"Time. It's going to take time. And I have the time." The faintest frown curved his full lips. "Unless this was a one shot deal? Tonight's date only? Was this it?"

"I don't know!" She edged back from him, shaking her head at herself. *Armor up, you idiot. Ignore that wounded look in his eyes. Armor up!* "Look, I'm here, right? I came out tonight, like you said. So, one step at a time. We'll see. Okay?"

His chin lifted and his deep blue eyes sparked with new determination. "Okay. More than fair. Thank you."

"Don't thank me," she snapped, feeling vulnerable and angry. "I have a feeling this is a terrible idea." She went to move away from him, but her skate caught in a notch in the ice and she stumbled. He reached for her and she shook him off. "I'm fine," she said, even as her face turned crimson. "I don't want your help. I don't need it."

"I know," he murmured.

She stopped cold, saw the look on his face, and sighed. "That was mean. I'm sorry."

He shook his head. "It's all right."

"No, I was a bitch."

"Because you're still angry at me. I understand, Cassie. Better than you think."

She bit her bottom lip and looked at him. "Then, why are you staying?"

"I told you. I want another chance." The corner of his mouth twitched. "I didn't think you'd make it easy for me. I knew that going in."

She couldn't help it—a grin popped onto her face. "Brave lad."

His eyes lit up and he grinned back. "Sometimes." He held out a hand. "C'mon, let's skate together."

Her heart skipped a beat and stuck in her chest as she stared back.

"Trust me," he said, so low and intense it sounded like an oath. His outstretched gloved hand hung in the air, waiting, as his eyes implored with hers. "Try?"

Slowly, she reached out and placed her gloved hand in his. His fingers closed around hers and he smiled, an expression of affection and relief. They started a new lap around the ice, with Perry Como's version of *Silver Bells* playing over the speakers and Sean holding her hand.

She stole a glance at him as they skated together fluidly. He was already looking at her, a glint of fierce tenderness in his eyes. *What did I just agree to?* she thought, half excited, half frightened. It made her heart flutter as she tried to remember how to breathe.

Chapter Seven

CASSANDRA ENTERED HER apartment late in the afternoon. It was empty, as it often was; her roommate basically slept there, and that was it. She dropped her filled tote bags by the small desk in the corner of the living room with a satisfied grunt. Her school work was finished for the semester, and she was thrilled. She wasn't planning to return to her office until after the new year. She had more writing to do—publish or perish, as the saying went—but she was giving herself off until the twenty-seventh. She needed a break. Time to let herself enjoy the holidays in full and recharge her mental batteries.

The past two weeks had gone by in a blur. Between final exams and seeing Sean again, Cassandra had felt as if her head was spinning. All the activity sometimes even made her feel disorientated and dizzy. Whose whirlwind life was she living? She'd been flat and dull for years. She hadn't realized just how much she'd shut down inside until Sean had come back into her life, all blazing color and passion and heart. She felt so . . . alive.

He was wooing her with everything he had, as he'd promised. And she was letting him. He took her out all over the city, for lunches, dinners, drinks, long walks. They went to a movie, they saw his friend's band play a show at Webster Hall, and they went to the Met for a whole Sunday. Slowly, cautiously, they were getting to know each other anew.

And while she still fought the doubts, she had to give him credit: he was being patient, persistent, and giving it his all. She recognized that. She knew he wasn't taking it lightly, this second chance to be in her life. If his words and actions were true indicators, he wanted to stick around. She found herself wanting to believe him. She found herself falling for him all over again, and she was fighting that with all her might. After all, she'd believed in him before, and look where that had gotten her.

This Friday night, there was the faculty holiday party. She'd go, of course, having to show face at the English Department's annual gathering. It would be nice, a pleasant evening at the Explorers' Club this year... but her mouth twisted as she remembered Oliver Pottson's words from this morning: "*So* looking forward to seeing you all dressed up for the party." She found him smarmy and pretentious. Sometimes the way he looked at her, or things he said, actually made her skin crawl.

Maybe... maybe Sean would go with her to the party? As she flopped onto the couch, she thought about asking him.

As if on cue, her phone pinged with a text. It was Sean. *Still on for tonight, right? Meet you here at the bar at 7:00?*

She smiled and typed back immediately, *Yes. Just got home. Going to take a shower and change. See you then.*

Splendid, he texted. *And thanks for the visual of you in the shower... I'm all turned on now...*

She laughed aloud and wrote, *You're so bad.*

I am! he wrote. *And you like that. And I like you. xx*

She smiled again and settled back into the sofa, sighing happily. He wanted her. He liked her. He cared about her. Even as they got to know each other again, some things were still very much the same. Back when they were together, he had always made her feel special, adored, cherished. And at ease. The easy familiarity between them was startling sometimes, as if seven and a half years hadn't passed since they were a couple.

It was almost *too* easy.

It unnerved her. She didn't want to just fall back into a pattern with him, picking up where they left off like nothing had happened. Too much had happened. And as much as she believed his remorse was true, she couldn't forget how deeply he'd hurt her when he'd ended it. She knew she had to let that go if they had any chance of a future relationship. But it was hard. Really, really hard. Just thinking back on those horrible weeks could still turn her stomach and form knots in her chest.

Looking back on it later, weeks after the breakup, she'd realized that Sean had been acting strangely since the night of the Columbia party in early May. She'd been invited to an orientation event at Columbia, for the graduate program she'd be starting in the fall, and of course she brought her boyfriend with her. She'd been so nervous over what to wear, finally deciding on a dark blue high-necked tank dress. Sean had looked handsome in a plain white button down shirt and navy pants. He'd even shaved, and bought a nice pair of dress shoes to wear, since his usual sneakers or army boots weren't going to cut it. She thought he looked gorgeous. But when they got to the party, he was the only one not wearing a tie. His pale cheeks had flamed with angry embarrassment as he apologized to her. She waved it off, swallowing her own unease to comfort her love.

They stood on the side for a few minutes, taking in the

scene. Holding his hand, Cassandra felt Sean's skin grow clammy, which it only did when he was nervous or upset.

"You okay?" she whispered to him.

He nodded curtly. "I'm fine."

She peered at him, but didn't get to ask anything further; a polished-looking woman in her late forties approached, introducing herself as Karen Weaver, one of the program mentors. Cassandra started to talk with her about the program, and Sean wandered off to give them space. Karen introduced Cassandra to several people in the room, and she got caught up in conversation. By the time she broke away to find Sean, two hours had passed.

And he was not in plain sight.

She looked for him in the hallway, the lobby . . . nothing. At the main entrance, as she wondered if he was in the bathroom, she spotted him. He sat alone on a bench under a tree, about twenty yards away, his back to her as he stared up at the sky. She rushed to him.

"Honey!" She flopped down beside him on the bench. "I'm so sorry, I—"

"Don't be sorry." His voice was flat, devoid of its usual merry warmth. "You had hobnobbing to do."

"I didn't realize how long I was away, though," she said, her hand rubbing his arm plaintively. "That was rude. I'm so, so sorry."

"I don't know why I'm here, Cassie," he murmured. "Why'd ya bring me?"

She blinked. "Because—because you're my boyfriend, and I love you, and I wanted to share this with you. For you to see where I'll be . . ." Her eyes swept over him. His jaw was set tight, his posture rigid. "You're really mad at me, aren't you."

"I'm not mad at ya." He rose to his feet and smoothed his hands over his long hair, which he'd carefully pulled back into a neat ponytail for the party. "I could use a drink, though. Some of the men here... they're pretentious arseholes." Finally, he looked into her eyes as he pressed, "Ya know that, right?"

Surprised, she just stared. "I... I thought they were nice enough... did something happen?"

A shadow crossed his face and he turned away. "You can go back inside, love. I'll just wait out here. Where I should."

Her gut started churning, blaring with intuition that something was very wrong. But she had to get back in to the party. She didn't want to make a bad first impression. She stood too and asked, "Come back in with me?"

He snorted. "I don't think that's a good idea."

"Why not?"

"You really don't know?" He faced her, standing close, his blue eyes blazing as they scanned her features. "I stand out like a sore thumb, love. I was gettin' looks. I'm not exactly professor material, ya know?"

She blinked again, thrown by his words. "What? What are you talking about? Looks from whom? I don't care if you're—I *like* that you're not professor material." She tried to smile, but her heart fluttered at the hooded look in his eyes. "You're Sean McKinnon, the hottest guy in New York. A killer musician, a sexy badass, and mine all mine."

His eyes pinned her for a moment. Then he turned away, murmuring, "We'd best get you back inside. Come, Cassie." He reached for her hand and led her back to the party without another word.

Something was different after that. She couldn't put her finger on it; it was just a feeling, a nauseating tug of intuition. Sean still spoke to her every day, and they made love almost every night... but he was off. He was holding something inside, she could almost feel it growing, like a cancer. He grew pensive, moody, with no apparent cause. But whenever she asked, he insisted he was fine.

She graduated from NYU two weeks after the party, with honors. Sean went to dinner with her and her entire family afterwards to celebrate. That night, they went back to his tiny apartment to make love, which he did to her with heartwrenching tenderness, possibly with more sweetness than ever before. An almost aching sweetness that mesmerized her.

She didn't know then, but realized later it was his goodbye.

When she woke up, she found herself alone in the bed. She wrapped herself in his royal blue bathrobe and padded out to the miniscule living room. He was sitting on the couch, in a white T-shirt and jeans, his head in his hands.

"Sean?" She moved towards him cautiously. "What's wrong?"

He looked up at her with a mournful, flat gaze. "I, ehm . . . we have to . . ." He shifted in his seat, then stood to face her. Taking a deep breath, he said, "I think we should break up. I'm sorry, Cassie. I've been thinking about this for weeks, and I just . . ." His eyes flashed with pain, but determination replaced the moment of weakness. "We should end this now. Go our separate ways. I think it's best."

She could barely breathe. Her stomach flipped over nauseously as a heavy chill skittered over her. "Wh-what? Where is this coming from?"

His eyes were sad, but she saw steel there. He'd made a decision, and when Sean set his mind on something, it was pretty hard to change it. "You'll thank me one day."

"Bullshit!" she cried. She stepped towards him, hands outstretched, and he stepped back to stay out of her reach. The rebuke felt like a punch in the stomach. "You love me, dammit!" Tears spilled from her eyes. "I know you do."

"God . . . of course I do," he whispered roughly, not

looking at her.

"Then why are you doing this?" She felt wild, suffused with angst that bordered on panic. "You love me, and I love you. Together forever, that's what you've always said. Or don't you remember?"

He winced, cringing visibly. "I remember," he whispered, his voice like gravel.

"On Christmas Day, late that night," she ground out between sobs. "On the bridge in Central Park, in the snow, under the stars."

"Stop, Cassie," he groaned, turning away to pace the small floor.

"Under the stars," she barreled on, "in the cold, you held my hands, looked deep into my eyes, and promised we'd be together forever. That we'd get married, and have children, and grow old together."

"I know what I said," he hissed miserably, stopping at the tiny table and gripping it until his knuckles turned white.

"That tattoo on your shoulder, you put that there for *us*," she cried, pointing at his arm. "Look at that Celtic knot, Sean, the one that has 'Together Forever' in Gaelic written along it."

"I'll see that the rest of my life," he growled. "Ya think I don't know it?"

"I thought you *wanted* to think of me," she croaked.

"I do!" he yelled, nearing a breaking point. "I—I did!"

"So that's changed, suddenly?" she choked out. "What, so you lied a minute ago, and you don't love me anymore?"

His head raised and he looked at her then. "No! No. I do love you!" He slammed a fist against the tabletop. "Dammit, you think this is easy for me?"

"I don't *want* to make it easy for you!" She started to sob through her words. "I'm going to fight for us until whatever has gotten in your head gets back out."

"It's not going to get out," he said, facing her. "I've been thinking about this for weeks. We're going to go in different directions now, and you're going to end up seeing me as dead weight. Resenting me. I'm leaving before that happens."

"That's crap! You've met someone else."

"Hell no!" he shouted back, indignant. "I'd never do that to you! I'd never cheat on you!"

She hated that the tears wouldn't stop, that she looked like a blubbering fool. But they wouldn't stop. "This doesn't make sense. Make me understand!"

"We just . . ." He raked his hands through his hair, the ends hitting the backs of his shoulders. "You're moving into a new world. I have to let you do that. I don't want to drag you down, Cassie. And I will. I know that. I saw it, at that party. You don't need some stupid guitar player hangin' 'round while you're doing all that book work. You need to be able to concentrate on your studies and focus. You need—"

"Stop telling me what I need and don't need!" she cried. "The only thing I need is *you*!"

He stopped in his tracks. "You're wrong," he said, his blue eyes spearing her. "Ya just don't know it yet. But I do."

"I won't let you do this," she said between sobs.

"Ya don't have a choice, love," he murmured hoarsely. "I'm goin'." He walked away from her, went to the bathroom, and closed the door behind him.

She stood there in utter disbelief, sobbing for almost ten minutes before she ran to the bedroom, got dressed, and fled the apartment.

They went back and forth for two weeks that way: her begging him in frantic phone calls to see reason and not end it, him insisting he was doing it for her sake and that it was over. They argued, they cried; she pleaded, he began to shut down. Then one night, he surprised her with a visit, showing up at her apartment. It was the first time they'd seen each other since the morning he'd dumped her. He looked like hell, which pleased her; she didn't want to be the only one suffering. She hoped he was there to say he'd come to his senses, that he was sorry he'd been such a fool, that he couldn't live without her and wanted her back . . .

But he came to tell her he was moving to Los Angeles in a week, going there with three of the guys in one of the bands he played with . . .

The phone rang, jolting Cassandra from her miserable reverie. She glanced at the caller ID. It was Bree. "Hey," she said softly.

"Hey yourself." Bree sounded glum.

"What's wrong?" Cassandra asked immediately.

"This whole mess . . ." Sabrina was going through guy problems of her own. "I want to fly away. Let's get on a plane. Tonight."

Cassandra smiled and settled deeper into the couch. She and Bree had played this game for years, whenever one of them was stressed out. "Where should we go?"

"Somewhere warm," Bree said, "and very far away."

"Um . . . the Bahamas?"

"Not far enough."

"Cancun?"

"Still not."

"Tahiti?"

"Bingo!" Bree cried. "I think we have a winner. Meet you at the airport?"

"You got it." Cassandra sighed. "What can I do?"

"Nothing. I'm just overwhelmed."

"Why don't you come into the city, I'll take you to dinner tomorrow night."

"I can't, but I wish I could," Bree said. "Thanks, though.

Raincheck?"

"Standing invitation."

"Am I being an idiot?" Bree asked.

Cassandra knew Bree was talking about Jake, her first love who'd recently reappeared in her life. "I don't think so. Am I being an idiot for dating Sean again?"

"Yes," Bree said without hesitation.

Cassandra laughed. "Then yes, you're an idiot too. So there."

"We're both so stupid," Bree said, laughing ruefully along with her.

"Looks that way."

Bree sighed, but it was lighter. "Thanks for the pep talk. At least I know I'm not the only idiot around. I feel better now."

"When I come out there for Christmas next week," Cassandra warned, "I'm going to smack you."

Chapter Eight

O'REILLY'S TAVERN WAS noisy with music and voices when Cassandra walked in at seven. She threaded her way through the bar, in between people who held their glasses and bottles and talked and laughed, looking for Sean.

"Can I get ya somethin'?" a girl at her side asked in a lilting Irish brogue.

Cassandra turned to look at the waitress, the pretty blonde from last time. Again she wore a red Santa hat, along with a red top and jeans, holding a tray. Cassandra found herself staring into deep blue eyes that were just like Sean's. "You're Sean's sister Anna, aren't you?"

The young woman smiled an easy smile. "Yes, I am. How'd ya know? The accent?"

"No. Your eyes." Cassandra smiled back. "I'm here to see him. I'm Cassandra."

"Oh!" Anna's eyes flew wide. "It's so nice to finally meet ya!" She gripped Cassandra's forearm and stared openly. "Sweet Jaysus, you're as gorgeous as he said ya are."

Cassandra blushed but had to laugh. "Um. Thank you."

"He's mad for ya. Ya know that, right?" Anna rambled

excitedly. "Since ya started seein' each other again, it's the happiest I've ever seen him. You're a right dear for givin' him another chance. He's a pain in the arse sometimes, but he's worth it. He's a good man, really."

Cassandra felt her mouth drop open.

Now it was Anna's turn to blush. "I said too much. I always do . . ." She shook her head and laughed wryly. "Don't tell him I said any of that, he'll skin me alive."

"It's nice to meet you too," Cassandra said, unbuttoning her coat.

"He's back in the office, I'll go get him for ya," Anna said, and hurried off.

Cassandra had to smile as she stuffed her gloves into her pockets. Sean's sister was a pip. Fiesty and open, much like him. But wow . . . Sean was the happiest that Anna had ever seen him? He'd talked to Anna about her? Hmmm. She removed her coat and shoved her hat and scarf into the sleeve to hold them there. She'd only just slung the coat over her arm when Sean appeared, taking it right off her arm.

"Hello, love," he grinned. His eyes danced as he looked at her, and he leaned in to drop a light kiss on her lips. "Here, let me have that. I'll take it back to the office for safe keepin'."

"Okay, thanks." Her eyes roamed over him. He looked particularly handsome in a dark cobalt button down and jeans. "I like your shirt. Did you dress up for me a bit?"

"I might have," he said, grinning his sexy, lopsided grin. "Ya like it?"

"I do," she said. "What's the occasion?"

"Well . . . you'll see in a bit." He winked and turned to point towards a tiny round table at the far end of the bar, up by the stage. "See that wee table? That's reserved for us. Go on and sit, I'll be right there."

She made her way to the table, catching snippets of conversations as she moved between patrons. The song over the sound system changed to John Mellencamp's rollicking version of *I Saw Mommy Kissing Santa Claus* as she took a seat. Her toes tapped in time to the song as she waited for Sean to return, which he did before the song ended.

"Alright, here we are." He placed a full pint of Guinness in front of her, then took the empty chair, his own glass in hand. She thanked him and took a sip, aware of his intense gaze.

"You look beautiful," he said. "I always loved when you wore red. It flatters ya."

She silently congratulated herself for remembering he liked when she wore red, and for choosing that top. "Thank you."

Suddenly, he was up out of his seat, leaning over her, a warm hand at the back of her neck as he kissed her. His mouth took from hers, long and sweet. "Mmmm . . ." he said against her mouth. "A beautiful woman who tastes like Guinness." He kissed her again, his tongue tracing along her lips. "I think I've died and gone to heaven."

She giggled, but her body was flaming from his words and his touch. Over the past two weeks, they'd gone on dates. They'd talked and learned each other anew, slowly gaining bits of trust back. And there had been kissing. Lots of it. But their physical interaction had been limited to kissing in public places. His hands sometimes roamed, but because they were out in public, nothing beyond a discreet caress here and there had played out. There was no doubt he wanted her. She could see it in his eyes almost every time he looked at her. She could feel the barely restrained passion in his touch, in the way he kissed her . . . sometimes he groaned lustfully into her neck as he pulled away from a kiss, and it made her go boneless. And he never pushed her, or made her feel pressured in any way. But . . .

The fact was, she was afraid to be alone with him. Because

she knew once they were alone, neither of them would be able to hold back. It'd be like a house on fire. It'd be full out torrid reunion sex. The emotional implications of that... she just wasn't ready.

Or, she hadn't been. Now, tonight, looking into his blue eyes lit with desire and sexy charm and sweet adulation, she knew she couldn't hold out much longer. And that she didn't want to.

On one of their dates, she'd gotten him to admit he'd dated a lot after they'd split up. "Lots of empty encounters," he'd said, looking away as he said it. He wasn't bragging, he was just stating facts. But he looked her right in the eye as he claimed that thought there had been a lot of girls, he'd never had feelings for any of them. "Not one, Cassie. Not one." That confession had softened the pang of jealousy that had twisted her gut, knowing he'd been with so many other women in one way or another. God only knew what seven years of experience with all those women had done to his already impressive bedroom skills.

She wanted to find out. She wanted his hands all over her body, to feel the length of his body aligned with hers... she wanted him to whisper in her ear the way he used to, feel his hot breath against her skin. During sex, his dirty talk used to spur her into incredible heights of desire, leaving her mindless; after sex, his sweet talk would make her swoon as he held her close.

Now, even though he was kissing her in the middle of a crowded city bar, need hit her like a heat flash. She wanted him. Right then. She couldn't deny it anymore, and didn't want to deny herself anymore. And if he wanted her even half as much as she wanted him... she shivered at the thought.

He pulled back and smiled softly. "Hey. What is it?"

"You," she admitted, looking deeper into his eyes. Her

fingertips traced the contours of his strong jaw, covered in soft golden stubble that just made him even more appealing. "You."

He stared at her for a few seconds, then reached for his chair and pulled it around the table. Turning her slightly in her seat, his legs spread wide so he could pull her in close, so close she could smell his musky, spicy scent. The intimacy of the position made her insides quiver.

"Me, eh?" His hands came up to rest on her shoulders. "What about me?"

She blushed and her eyes flickered away. "It's a secret," she whispered coyly, trying to distract him by turning it into a game.

He leaned in and kissed her, lingering on her lips, coaxing them open with his to touch his tongue to hers and make her melt. "Tell me," he murmured against her mouth.

She grinned and edged closer to seal her mouth to his. His hands moved from her face to thread through her hair, cradling her head as they kissed. Her arms snaked around his neck and the kisses deepened, simmering with heat.

"Tell me," he repeated with a sensual, crooked smile.

"I think you know," she whispered, playing with his ruffled honey brown hair.

"Oh, love, I'd never assume anythin' . . ." He nipped at her lips, the softest tug with his teeth that pinged low in her belly. "Tell me."

She pulled back just enough to look into his eyes. Their gazes locked.

"I want ya so bad, Cassie," he whispered. "So much. Tell me you want me too."

"I do." Her lips curled in a shy smile. "So . . . maybe later tonight . . . we can go somewhere . . . ?"

✦ ✦ ✦

SEAN'S BREATH STUCK in his chest and his blood raced as he stared into those warm, dark brown eyes he adored. "You sayin' what I think ya are?"

She nodded.

His heart skipped a beat or two. "Jaysus . . ." He cleared his throat and shifted in his seat. She was looking back at him, so beautiful, so sensual. It was all he could do not to drag her back to the office, lock the door, and take her on the couch this very minute. He willed himself to pull back, take his hands from her hair and lower them to hold hers. "If I'm goin' to take you to bed, and take that tremendous step, we have to talk about some things, love. It's too important."

Her face fell and her posture stiffened, and he swallowed back curses. "No, don't do that." He squeezed her hands. "Don't shut down on me. I don't want to go there either. I don't want to bring up the painful things again . . . but we have to. If we're going to move forward together, we have to close up that past, once and for all. Don't you think?"

She nodded as she stared at him, and he saw things shifting in her eyes. She was considering what he'd said, processing it. He knew that look, understood she was thinking it over, so he waited. Caressing her fingers between hers, never looking away, he waited.

"Can I finish my drink first?" she finally asked. "I have a feeling I'll need it."

"Aye, me too." He reached for his glass and clinked it to hers. "Sláinte." They sipped together. The song overhead changed to Paul McCartney's *Wonderful Christmastime* as the sounds of the bar around them—the chatter of customers, clinking of glasses—seemed to fade as she took in the way he was watching her.

"Can I ask you something?" she said.

"Sure."

"Do you, um . . ." A hint of color spotted her cheeks. Her head dipped a bit and her dark hair fell across her face. A self-deprecating grin flashed as she swept the lustrous strands back, then traced the rim of her glass with her fingertips. "Do you have plans this Friday night?"

He couldn't hold back a grin. "Well, I usually work on Friday nights, but I can skip out. One of the bonuses of co-ownin' the place. Why?"

"I have a holiday party to go to," she said. "I'd like you to come with me. If you want."

Warmth flowed through him, making his heart feel light. "I'd love to join you."

She smiled. "Great. Okay then. It starts at seven. It's a little dressy, though. Gotta dress up. Do you have a suit?"

"Of course I have a suit," he scoffed with mock indignation, but had to wonder if she was serious. "In fact, I have three, I'll have ya know. What do ya take me for?"

"Well, you used to not own even *one*," she said, lifting her glass. "Just checking."

He watched her sip her drink and said, "Fair enough. Yes, I have a suit, Professor Baines." Sean mirrored her action and stole a long swallow of his own Guinness. "So, a fancy party, eh? Where are we goin'?"

"It's the English Department holiday party," she explained. "My office party. NYU faculty and staff, that kind of thing. I'm sorry. It sounds lame. It will be. But it's the only kind of party I tend to have going on, so, you know . . ."

Something inside his chest went cold, turned leaden. He hoped it didn't show on the outside. "Ah. Well . . . are you sure ya want me at that?"

Her brows furrowed. "I guess I didn't sell it very well, did

I?"

"No! I mean, yes! It's not that you didn't sell it. I want to go with you," he said. "I'm just . . . surprised." He shrugged, feeling inarticulate. "Thanks."

She leaned in and pressed a light, sweet kiss to his lips. "Thanks for saying yes."

"We'll have a nice time." He grinned and kissed her, then said, "I'm goin' to play a set in a few minutes. That's why I grabbed this front table, so ya could sit nearby whilst I'm up here. Okay by you?"

"You're going to play and sing?" Her eyes lit up, and he caught the flare of excitement. "God, I used to love watching you. I'm psyched now."

"Good! Because after that . . ." He grasped her face with both hands and kissed her deeply. "I'm takin' ya home with me. And I'm goin' to love you all night long."

He heard her sharp intake of breath, felt her shudder beneath his hands, and smiled. His heart stuttered, then soared. He leaned in and stole a few more deep kisses.

But a few minutes later, as he prepared for his set, moving the stool and the mic that'd be aimed at his acoustic guitar, his mind reeled. An academic party. *Wonderful*, he thought dourly. *Just bloody wonderful.* That was exactly what had done his head in the last time. Did she not remember? Did she have no idea?

✦ ✦ ✦

CASSANDRA HAD ASKED him to accompany her to the orientation party. He'd been proud to walk in with her; she was easily the most beautiful girl in the room. But he hadn't worn a tie, and they'd quickly realized he was underdressed. The misery twisted his gut. He didn't want to embarrass her in any way, this was too important. First impressions were important.

But she'd brushed it off, not seeming to care. She only had eyes for him. The way she looked at him sometimes made him feel invincible, like a god.

But not in this room full of stodgy teacher types. Cassie was too wrapped up in her conversation with others to see the disapproving looks he caught from some of the prissy, proper men. Back in Ireland, as a kid, the middle of eight siblings, his family was not well off. His parents barely made ends meet, but there was love and pride there. McKinnons ignored the snobs who looked down at their worn clothes. The only place Sean had been made to feel like less of a person was in school. He hated school. He could never concentrate, and didn't do well. The letters may as well have been hieroglyphics sometimes. Frustrated, he acted out, as kids do. And got scolded for it by teachers, and then his father when he got home. By the time he was ten, he hated school and everything about it. It made him feel stupid.

The only classes he did decently in were math, art, and music. Music saved his sanity. When he was twelve, his older brother gave up the guitar and gave it to Sean, on a lark. But Sean taught himself to play, driven by pure love for it. The music teacher at school said he sang like an angel. That was the only course he could stand; he barely made it through high school. One teacher, his math teacher, finally helped him realize at fifteen that he not only had dyslexia, but ADHD too. It explained a lot, but it was too little too late. The damage had been done. Sean's grades were shite, and his frustration was boundless. After graduating by the skin of his teeth, he couldn't get out of there fast enough.

And now there he was, at some stuffy party for brainiacs, of which his girlfriend was one. He was proud of her, in awe of her academic success, really. He loved that she was brilliant. And he knew she thought he was smart as well, even if test scores had never proved it. But his intellect was nowhere near this kind of level. She fit in. He most certainly did not. Now, at this party, surrounded by teachers, the little boy in him who used to get frustrated and insecure and hated school was stirring from deep within.

He helped himself to another glass of champagne and moved off to the side, letting his Cassie shine. God, she was beautiful. Sitting on the sidelines and watching her was no hardship. He found a chair and sat against the wall.

But one man, with a tan linen suit and bow tie, came over to him. He'd been one of the people Cassie was deep in conversation with a few feet away. The small group was positioned so her back was to Sean, so she didn't see the approach. "Who are you?" he asked, looking down at him with an openly condescending sneer.

Sean bristled at his tone, but kept his cool as he gestured towards Cassandra. "I'm with my girlfriend. She's starting the program in the fall. Cassandra Baines."

"Oh." The man eyed her briefly. "Yes, she's lovely. Bright girl. Very bright." He turned back to Sean, eyed him again, and murmured, "Interesting match."

Sean blinked, then slowly rose to stand. "Excuse me?"

"You two seem . . . mismatched," the man said.

Sean's gut started churning. "Says you." He looked at this pompous arse, wondering what his angle was.

The man didn't blink and met Sean's gaze dead on. "How long do you think she'll stay with someone like you?"

A puff of air resembling a laugh of disbelief came from Sean's mouth. "Ya know nothin' about us."

"I've seen this before," the man sniffed. "You're her bad boy, sure. Good girls like to play when they're in undergrad. But even if you stayed together, how far in the program do you think she'll get with someone like you around?" His brow lifted arrogantly. "It's a highly competitive environment. I don't think you realize. She won't be able to get up the ladder with embarrassing dead weight holding her back. She needs a partner who is an active asset."

"You've got some nerve," Sean hissed. His blood raced through his veins.

The man sipped from his glass of champagne and shrugged. "You're out of your element here, is all. Just an observation. No offense intended."

It took everything Sean had not to slam this tool against the wall and pound him. He drew a deep breath. The words of a stranger wouldn't have cut so deep if Sean didn't suspect that . . . they might be true. The nasty bastard might be right. Sean had thought it to himself, but no one had ever said it out loud, much less so blatantly. His eyes narrowed on the man as he ground out, "When's the last time ya got laid, lad? Bet it's been a while. And the thought of a girl that beautiful and brilliant being with 'someone like me' must burn your arse, eh?"

The man snickered, a scornful sound. "If sexual power is all you hold over her? She'll dump you by Thanksgiving. Good luck with that."

"That girl you're talkin' about so disrespectfully," Sean warned in a low growl, "is the girl I love. So for her sake, I won't beat ya to a pulp right here and now. But you mind how you talk about her, ya hear me?"

The man leaned in and murmured, "I'm not talking about her with disrespect, my friend. I'm talking about *you*. And I think it's interesting that you counter my opinion with the offer of violence. You might want to think about the fact that violence and sex are the only assets you have."

Sean's hands curled into fists. "Get out of my face, ya miserable langer. And stay away from my girlfriend, or you'll be sorry you ever even looked her way."

The man raised his glass in a fake salute and walked away.

But Sean stood there shaking. So angry he could barely breathe. He needed to stay calm, for Cassie's sake. He'd never embarrass her . . . but *damn*. He needed air. Quickly, he left the building, bursting through the doors. Even as he sat on a nearby bench, his hands were still shaking and the pounding of his heart roared in his ears. What if that man was right? What if violence and sex *were* the only assets he had? What if Cassie's being associated with him would end up hurting her career one day? Or, even worse, what if she tired of him, found him lacking, and left him? He couldn't take that, it would kill him.

He had a lot to think about . . .

✦ ✦ ✦

"Sean? Hey. Earth to McKinnon."

He'd gotten lost in his miserable stroll down memory lane; he looked up to see Jimmy standing before him.

"Ya gonna play or what?" Jimmy said. "You've been standing there like that a while . . ."

"Shut up, I'm playin'." Sean raked his hands through his hair and shot a glance over at Cassie. She was sitting at their table, chatting with his sister and smiling. He busied himself with setting up. Music always soothed his inner beast.

Beast. He'd been a beast, breaking up with her seemingly out of nowhere, hurting her to make sure it stuck. He'd pushed Cassie away after that fateful party. Thought he was doing the right thing, for her sake—and maybe, too, for the sake of his own pride. He convinced himself of it, even as she begged him not to end it. He still didn't know, sometimes, if it was the dumbest, most destructive thing he'd ever done, or the best.

He'd hurt himself, but hurt her a million times worse. He'd

figured the least he could do for her was abide by her request in her blistering email and never talk to her again; to let her heal, let her move on. That was the last contact they'd had before she'd walked into his bar two weeks ago.

Now, finding her again felt like a miracle, a chance to start over and do right by her this time, and slowly she was letting him back in. So if she was willing to bring him into her academic world, wanted him to escort her to that faculty party? He'd swallow his ambivalence and do it in style, dammit.

Chapter Nine

CASSANDRA LET HER head fall onto Sean's shoulder. The back of the cab was warm, dark, and cozy as she gazed out at the passing scenery. Christmas lights twinkled everywhere she looked: the windows of stores, around lamp posts, hanging from awnings. The taxi driver, like many others, had holiday music on in the car. As James Taylor's *Have Yourself a Merry Little Christmas* played and she cuddled into Sean's side, she thought back on their night together.

They'd had a few beers, eaten dinner, talked, laughed, and enjoyed each other. She'd gotten to chat with Anna, who was fun and friendly. Jimmy had taken over all managerial duties so Sean wouldn't have to keep an eye on anything in the bar. Then, he'd gotten on that tiny stage to perform and stolen her breath. Watching him, hearing him play guitar and sing again, had been amazing. And since he'd made sure she was sitting right up front, he looked right at her as he sang. Some of the love songs were meant for her, it was obvious. He'd practically *serenaded* her. That had made her secretly swoon like a fangirl.

His tenor voice was more alluring than ever, his acoustic playing was strong, and his charisma while performing was off the charts. Add to all that his movie star looks ... he'd cast a new spell over her, one of seduction and admiration. She wondered if he had any idea how his talent, and his passion for music, affected her.

Here in the cab, his arm slid around her shoulders to draw her closer, he pressed his lips to her temple, and her stomach did a slow flip. He smelled so good, he felt so good, warm and solid ... it made her skin heat and her head swim. She wanted him so much. She wanted to fall into his arms, into his bed, shut out the world, and have him all to herself, body and soul.

"You're so quiet," he said, brushing her hair back from her face. He tipped his face so he could peer into her eyes. "Ya okay, love?"

"Very okay," she whispered, and pulled his head down to join her mouth to his.

He moaned softly into her mouth as the kiss flared, heat and desire rocketing as their tongues tangled and their mutual hunger escalated.

"Stay with me tonight," he whispered against her lips, sipping from them as his fingers played with her hair. "I want to make love to you all night. I want to kiss every sweet, sexy inch of ya ..." He nipped at her bottom lip, sucked on it. "... I want to touch every inch of your gorgeous body, pleasure you 'til you're mindless with it ..." Her breath hitched; he kissed her deeper this time. "... until we're both so exhausted, all we can do is fall asleep in each other's arms. And hold each other close as we do. Then, when we wake in the mornin', I want to do it all over again." He held her face in both hands.

She nestled closer, stroked his stubbled chin, looked into his beautiful blue eyes, and said, "I want all that too. *All* of that. All of *you*."

As she stepped into Sean's apartment a few minutes later, a

feeling like déjà vu washed over her. It looked different than it had seven years before, but enough of it was the same for her to feel strangely at home.

The old, beat up couch and chair had been replaced by a matching brown leather sofa and loveseat, the scratched wooden butcher block table by a glass coffee table. The art on the walls was all Sean: old album covers in frames, artsy posters, photos of Ireland. When she had been there last, it had been a mishmash of Jimmy's and Sean's things, careless and functional, two guys in their early twenties who shared space. Now, it was . . . cleaner, nicer, tasteful, more mature. It was a reflection of how Sean himself had grown.

"Does the place look familiar?" he asked as he laid her coat carefully on the loveseat.

"It does indeed," she grinned. "Only much nicer."

"I hope so!" he chuckled. He tossed his own coat and scarf onto the loveseat with less care. "I'm no reckless youngster anymore. Can't have the place lookin' like a college dorm room."

"Not if you want to impress the women you bring here," she teased. "Certainly not."

She'd meant it as a joke, but his expression sobered. "Cassie." He turned toward her with intent. "First of all, I haven't been with a woman in over three months, just for the record. And the second truth is, I've brought very few women here. Because . . ." He shrugged. "This is *my* space." His gaze narrowed on her, making the creases at the corners of his eyes deepen. "The only woman who ever felt to me like she belonged here was you."

His stark admission bowled her over. Her heart stuttered in her chest and her legs felt wobbly. "You don't have to say that because you think it's what I want to hear. I know there've been other women. And I've been with other men. I mean, come on, Sean. We broke up seven and a half years ago—"

"Aye, I know. But I don't want to think of ya with other men, I'll tell ya that. And I *did* tell ya there've been other girls. Just not *here*." He cleared his throat and rubbed his jaw as he looked at her. "Okay. No more of that tonight. Can I get ya a drink? Do ya want anythin'?"

"No." She stepped to him and put her hands on his chest, tipping her head back to gaze into his eyes. "I just want you."

"Jaysus . . ." His smile spread, slow and warm. "You know I want you too." His hands raised to sweep her hair back from her face. As his eyes roamed over her face, he caressed her cheeks with gentle fingers. His thumb brushed across her lips and her breath caught. "I need to hold you. To make love to you. To show ya how much I . . ." His eyes held hers in one of those soul-searching looks that made her blood pound and heat surge through her body. "Christ, there's so much . . ."

"Shhhh," she whispered. "Just show me." Her fingers traced over his lips. "Take me to bed, Sean, and show me."

His eyes flared, sparking with desire. He took her by the hand and led her to his bedroom. She went gladly, her heart racing with anticipation as her body tingled with need and lust and want.

His room was small, as she remembered, and the queen sized mattress took up most of the space. He went to turn on the light, but she stilled his hand. "Look," she said, gesturing towards the window. The apartments across the narrow street had decorated for Christmas, to the point of overkill. So many colorful lights hung and shone that they all lent their light to Sean's bedroom. Red, blue, green, white. . . "I can see you just fine," she whispered. "It's pretty."

"Not nearly as pretty as you," Sean smiled back. "I can see you too. It's certainly festive . . ." In a quick move, he reached to the bottom of her V-neck sweater and pulled it up, over her head, letting it drop to the floor. "But even by the lights, you're wearing too much. I want you naked, Cassielove. It's been so long since I've gotten to look at you. . ."

He let his eyes roam over her, taking her in. "Sweet Lord, you're so beautiful." The sight of her standing before him in the dim light, her delicate soft skin revealed to him, her heavy breasts encased in a lacy red bra, set his pulse skyrocketing and made his blood rush hot through his veins. "And you wore all this red for me, ya vixen."

She grinned at him, a spark of pride and seduction in her dark eyes.

His hands caressed her shoulders and slid down her arms as he pulled her close. Covering her mouth with his, his hands moved up to caress and squeeze her breasts through the lace, eliciting sighs from her that made his insides melt.

She unbuttoned his shirt, spreading it wide and slipping it off over his broad shoulders. But he felt her stop moving and pulled back. She was staring at his body.

"What is it, love?" he asked.

Her eyes skimmed over him. "How many tattoos do you have now?" There was surprise and laughter in her voice.

He grinned at her as he replied, "Seven, total." He reached out to unhook her bra and slowly slide the straps down her arms. She let it fall to the floor and met his gaze before he lowered his head to suckle one breast, then the other. Her head fell back as she arched into him, wanting more. They moved to the bed and fell onto it, wrapping themselves around one another, curling in tight, caressing and stroking and kissing. His teeth scraped her sensitive skin and she moaned.

Shifting to lie on top of her, he said, "I hate to let go of these perfect breasts, but I have to if I'm goin' to get your pants off." She giggled as he made short work of her jeans.

"I only see four tattoos," she said. "This one, of

course . . ." Her fingertips traced the large one on his right shoulder, the one he'd gotten for them, to proclaim his love for her. The large, intricate Celtic knot with *Together Forever* written in Gaelic. She'd been by his side the whole time, sitting with him in the tattoo parlor down in Alphabet City for hours. "But these . . . are new." She touched the other tattoos on his left bicep and wrist, then the one on his upper chest.

"Not new to me, but new to you, sure. Do you like them?" His brow furrowed as he gazed down at her. "Or you're saying it because ya don't?"

"I like them. A lot," she admitted. She bit down on her lip for a second before adding, "They're hot. *You're* hot. And you know it."

"I know no such thing," he quipped, but his insides warmed at her admission. Her fingers ran over the planes of his chest, his arms, his sides. "I love the feel of your hands on me," he said into her neck, dropping kisses everywhere his mouth could reach. "I missed that."

She smiled. "I missed touching you too." Her head craned, searching. "Where are the other tattoos?"

"The others are lower, love. One's round my left ankle, one's on the right calf . . ." His thumbs softly stroked her nipples. They pebbled beneath his touch and he watched her eyes darken with desire. "And one tat . . . well, you'll have to strip me naked to find that last one. It's in a strategic spot, ya see." His grin turned wolfish. "Down on my hipbone. I'd love for ya to trace that one with your tongue . . ."

"Sounds good to me," she murmured wickedly, reaching for the button of his jeans.

He rolled off her to lie on his back for easier access. She leaned up on one elbow as her fingers danced across his pelvis, playing with the trail of hair that led from his navel down into his boxer briefs. Her fingers teased along the length of his bulge in slow, deliberate strokes and he sucked in a sharp breath. When she did it again and looked right into his eyes, he groaned as his body shuddered. "You're killin' me."

Smiling, she undid the zipper and pushed his jeans down. He helped her, shoving them off his long legs. "My turn to look at you," she said, as her eyes, then her hands, swept over his body. A wistful look crept onto her features. "This was *mine*."

"Can be again," he whispered, pushing her hair back. "Just need to say so . . ."

Then she said, "What you said before, that you haven't had sex in three months?"

He just looked at her and nodded, trying to remember how to breathe as her hands continued their exploration across his belly and palmed his erection again.

"It's been much longer for me," she admitted, her voice dropping to an almost shy whisper. "It's been over a year and a half."

He blinked at that in surprise. "What? Seriously?"

"I was busy with coursework . . ." The corner of her mouth lifted wryly. "I wasn't dating anyone. Didn't have time for casual sex. That's what I told myself, anyway." Her eyes lifted to meet his and her hands stilled. "But really, I just didn't want meaningless sex. It held no appeal for me. So . . ." She shrugged, a glimpse of her vulnerability lancing his heart.

He reached up to cup her face in his hands. "It won't be meaningless tonight," he promised in a husky whisper. His heart thudded against his ribs. "For me, nothing with you has ever been meaningless. Ever." He stroked her soft skin, trailing his fingers down her neck, her shoulders, and she sighed with pleasure. He kissed her again and pulled her close, intending to kiss her senseless.

She pressed the length of her body against his. He was so

hard that it was bordering on discomfort being restrained, and he pushed his briefs down to let his erection spring free. She smiled and wrapped her fingers around it, stroking him firmly, and he couldn't hold back the rough groan that ripped from deep in his throat. Suddenly, they were kissing like their lives depended on it—grabbing at each other, pushing away the tiny remainders of clothing until they were naked and close and entwined . . . his hands and mouth possessed her, until her sighs turned to guttural moans, until her moans turned to pleading whispers.

"I need you inside me," she begged, writhing beneath him. "Now. Please, Sean . . ."

He reached for the condoms he'd left on his night stand and quickly got one on. She was so wet, so ready for him. He looked right into her eyes, so warm and wanting as he pushed in slowly and entered her body. They both shuddered and moaned together at the feel of it. He held still for a moment, staring down at her, wanting to memorize every detail. "Ah, I missed you, love."

"God, I missed you too," she gasped. "I missed us . . . like this . . ."

His hips rolled, thrusting deep and smooth, earning another raspy moan from her. Her eyes slipped closed as she undulated beneath him. He kissed her mouth, her jaw, her neck as he moved with her, breathing in her scent, licking and tasting her skin.

"Oh God, Sean . . ." She arched her back, grinding her hips against his as she pulled him in even deeper. Her legs came up to wrap around his hips and he thrust hard, again and again, watching her face as he moved inside her.

He was home. Being inside her, making love to her, was like coming home.

In each other's arms, she was everything he remembered

and more. She was beautiful and flushed with passion and moaning his name... he lost himself quickly, gave his mind over to sensation, to the blinding heat and intoxicating pull as their bodies rocked together. When he thrust faster, harder, her moans turned to urgent cries until she broke apart beneath him, crying out his name as she clung to him and her body bucked and shuddered. He couldn't hold back, emptying himself in a thunderous release deep inside her, holding her tight... loving her, loving her, loving her.

The Christmas lights from outside painted their naked bodies in glowing colors as they held each other. When he got out of bed to dispose of the condom and wash up, he slipped into the kitchen. He brought back a bottle of Cabernet and one glass.

"Share the glass with me?" he said, climbing back into bed and into her waiting arms.

"Of course." She smiled the lazy, content smile of a woman well satisfied.

He returned the smile as he poured some wine and offered it to her. "Sláinte, love."

She took a few sips, then held the glass out to him for his turn. He took it but leaned in first to lick her lips and kiss her.

"You're bloody amazing," he told her. "Ya know that?" He drank some wine.

"In bed?" she asked, arching a brow.

He laughed, choking on the Cabernet, sputtering and coughing and making her laugh too. She grabbed the glass to keep him from spilling it all over the blanket and put it on his night stand.

When he could breathe and speak again, he said, "Aye, in bed, but I meant in general."

"You're pretty amazing too." She settled herself against his chest, in his arms. They kissed for a long while before she murmured, "I need to say something." She shifted so she could look into his eyes as she spoke. He braced himself. "These past two weeks, we've talked a lot, I've listened, I've thought, and I've decided..." Her expression softened and her eyes went liquid. "I want to try again. I want to be with you. Date only you. Do you... want that too?"

"I want that more than anything in this world," he breathed, unable to believe what he was hearing. "And I swear, I'll spend the rest of my days making up for what I did to us."

"*No*," she said firmly. "No. That's part of what I'm getting to here." Even as his brow puckered in confusion, she pressed a kiss to his lips. "We've both changed, and grown. Hopefully, we've learned from the past. But I don't want to stay in the past. I want to move forward. And we can't do that if I keep reminding you how you hurt me, and you keep apologizing. I forgive you, Sean." She held his face, cradling it in her soft hands, looking deep into his eyes. "Now you need to forgive yourself too. And we have to leave all that behind."

Something happened that hadn't happened in many years. He felt his eyes burn and sting as they welled up. "I don't know if I can. Not completely. I don't know if I ever will..."

"Forgive yourself," she demanded in a whisper. "It's time."

Good Lord, he couldn't cry. He hadn't cried since he'd gotten her scathing email telling him not to contact her again, and he realized there was no hope for it, he'd really lost her. Yet here she was, forgiving him, and insisting they had to let it all go. "I don't deserve ya," he whispered thickly.

"Yes you do," she said. "And I don't ever want to hear you say that again."

His eyes travelled over her features, her beautiful face, and he said, "Ya know... maybe there's a few things I should tell you now. So you understand better... because I never did.

And maybe it's time I did, so you'll understand why I say things like you deserve better than what I can give you."

"Sean," she protested, "Stop that."

"Hear me out, love." He shifted away so he wasn't holding her, but could look into her deep brown eyes and have that lock. "It's about school and childhood," he began. "And how those affected the choices I made years ago. You deserve to know the whole of it."

Her eyes were wide now, and her body motionless as stone. "Go on, then. I'm listening."

He swallowed hard. *Already opened the can o'worms*, he thought. *Can't go back now. Just tell her.* "Cassie, you know I have ADHD. We talked about that a bit in the past, remember?"

"Sure," she nodded, her brow creasing in confusion.

"I never let on how much it affected me growing up," Sean said. "I never told ya how hard it was for me as a kid . . ." He softly stroked her arm, slow caresses, up and down. "Hey, they didn't know I had a legitimate issue. Everyone—my parents, my teachers—just thought I was a troublemaker. School was a bloody nightmare. I all but failed out."

"I'm very sorry to hear it," she said with empathy. "I've heard stories like this before, adults who had ADHD as kids but went undiagnosed. I'm sorry you had such a rough time."

"Thanks. But I'm not tellin' you this for sympathy. I'm tryin' to explain . . ." He sighed. "You were born smart. So wondrously brilliant. I admire that, ya know."

"Thank you," she said demurely. "Of course, it's not anything I ever had a say in. Lucky enough to be born smart. I . . ." He saw the light bulb go on, the flicker in her eyes that maybe, because they were so deeply connected, she knew where he was going with his tale. She sat up in bed and said pointedly, "Lots of ADHD kids are the brightest in the class. You're smart too, Sean. You are."

"I know. Well, I know that *now*. As for brightest in the class? I always had a head for numbers, that's for sure," he said. "But it didn't help with grades, or bein' able to focus, or doin' what the teachers say. I got in a lot of trouble, love." His voice lowered to barely a whisper. "Like, my father beratin' me at home 'cos I couldn't sit and do my homework, like my brothers and sisters. Or like the teachers whapping at me with rulers and erasers, 'cos I wouldn't stay still and all that. Everyone yellin' at me ... belittlin' me ... I hated school. *Hated* it." He glanced at her almost sheepishly. "So, when I got older, I got away from it. Away from that whole bloody town. I moved an *ocean* away. And then ... " He tried to grin, but it faltered. "Then I went and fell in love with a brainy, book-lovin' girl who loved school more than anythin', so much that she wanted to be a teacher. A *teacher*." His eyes speared her. "Irony much?"

✦ ✦ ✦

CASSANDRA STARED AT Sean in utter shock. His strong jaw was tight, his brows furrowed. He was obviously both relieved to tell her this and anxious at the same time. But she couldn't wrap her head around it. "Why didn't you ever tell me any of this before?"

"C'mon, Cassie. I barely made it out of high school and never went to college; you finished every semester with honors and graduated at the top of your class." One of his hands released hers to rake his fingers through his hair, but the other held onto her tight. "I didn't want ya to think I was a moron. Or maybe that you were ..." He shrugged, but his eyes locked with hers. "... well, datin' beneath ya. I often wondered if ya thought that, deep down ... I wasn't enough. Not for the long haul, anyway."

"Never," she said, spitting it out vehemently. A chill skittered over her. "Not once."

He nodded. "Thank ya for that."

"You don't have to thank me. It's the truth. It's just a fact. And frankly, I'm a little insulted that you'd think that of me."

"Cassie, it wasn't about you. It was about me." He slanted a sideways glance. "My whole youth, I kept hearing what a bad kid I was. Out of control, wouldn't pay attention, wouldn't focus . . . bad stuff. And when people tell ya something all your life, it's hard to stop thinking of yourself that way, even if in your heart ya know it's not true."

She gazed at him, this charismatic, talented, passionate man, and wondered how rotten his childhood had been that this was at his core. And she wondered how she thought she'd known him better than anyone in the world, and this was the first time he'd revealed these things to her. Had she ever really known him at all?

Sadly, she murmured, "So . . . school must have been incredibly difficult for you."

He blew out a disgruntled huff of air. "We had no money, my family. My sisters and brothers, they were all bright, all did fine in school. I was the standout. Being the fourth of eight kids, they all thought I was just acting out for attention. It wasn't 'til I was fifteen that a school counselor took the time to help me and diagnosed me with ADHD. And . . . well, I never told ya . . ." He looked directly into her eyes and took a deep breath. "I'm slightly dyslexic, as well. I do all right . . . but I am. It's harder for me, reading. Your specialty. Your *passion*."

She jerked back as if he'd pushed her. Things clicked that never had before, and the realization shook her to the core. "I . . . I just . . . why didn't you ever tell me any of this? My God, Sean—how could you not tell me these things?"

"Pride," he murmured, his gaze unflinching. "Simple pride.

And fear of rejection."

Her heart ached. She didn't know what was worse: that he'd ever been made to feel lesser by anyone, or that he'd felt the need to hide it from her all this time. Then something else occurred to her. "Why are you telling me this now?"

"Because, Cassie. We . . . took this step. You let me make love to you. You let me in." He watched her nervously. "So I wanted to be honest with you. I keep asking you not to hold back from me. I wanted to . . . reciprocate." His fingers trailed along her jaw as he added, "Fair's fair."

She could see the anxiety in his eyes, and it made her heart melt. "Then let me tell you something important too . . ." She nestled close to him, feeling his solid warmth. Her mouth brushed his with a slow, sweet kiss before she whispered, "I don't care about any of that. I mean, I hate that it affected you so . . . but I don't care, because I love you."

His eyes pricked, burning as he stared. "Ehm . . . say that again?" he whispered thickly.

"I love you." She kissed him. "I want you, Sean McKinnon, and I love you."

"God, I love you too," he breathed. "So much." He kissed her passionately, crushing her body to his.

"So, Irish. What are you doing for Christmas?" she asked when he stopped long enough to come up for air.

"Not much actually, Professor. Anna and I are volunteerin' at a soup kitchen during the day, then might be goin' out for dinner."

"That's wonderful that you two are doing that," she said. "The volunteering, I mean. But after that, why don't you both come out to the island?" She smiled warmly. "Have dinner with us instead."

He knew she meant Long Island, where she'd grown up, where her family still lived. That she wanted him there was huge, not lost on him. "What, at your parents' house?"

"Yup." Her dark eyes danced. "We always do Christmas Eve at Aunt Enza's—that's Bree's mom. Between Enza and my mom, they pull off the whole Feast of the Seven Fishes Italian extravaganza. But on Christmas Day, we have a smaller dinner at my parents' house. Just them, me, my younger brother, and my dad's sister and her family. About ten of us. We'd have room for two more. I'd love for you to be there."

"Wow." He shifted to look at her better. "That would be like announcing to the world that we're back together."

"Well, aren't we now?" she asked.

He smiled and kissed her lips. "Yes. Yes we are."

"Then come to my parents' for Christmas dinner. Bring your sister. You can both sleep over there, plenty of room. And we'll all go back into the city together the next day. Okay?"

"I'll tell her. I think she'd like that." Sean hugged her tight and whispered, "And I'd *love* that. But ya best warn your parents I'm back for good, if ya haven't already. Your dad never frightened me, but your mom . . . she might try to beat me."

"She might. Her wooden spoon is legendary." She laughed and added teasingly, "Are you scared?"

"Terrified. But you're worth it." He kissed her again, and again. His hands were all over her warm, soft skin. He couldn't get enough of her, and started to make love to her once more. She was right there with him, luscious and hot and ready to go again. In his head, he sent silent prayers of gratitude to the skies . . . and hoped things would be as good as they seemed to be.

Chapter Ten

SEAN FUSSED WITH his tie in the bathroom mirror. Jaysus, he hated suits. He'd gotten a haircut that morning, making his unruly hair behave a bit, and shaved his face clean. He'd chosen his best suit, the black Armani, and a festive tie in shades of grey, black, and red. He loved the way Cassie's eyes had lit up when she saw him all dressed up, and that had almost made it worth it. But he still hated wearing such restrictive, stuffy clothing, and always had.

They'd gotten through the first hour of the party already. Some of her colleagues were nice, friendly, and talkative. Some were plain boring, or pretentious. That's what he'd expected, and that's what he'd encountered. But Cassie had told him they didn't need to stay long. That she couldn't wait to get him home to get the suit off him. His mouth quirked as he recalled the look in her eyes as she'd said that. He'd been entertaining similar fantasies all evening; she looked absolutely delectable in her long black velvet dress. His hands had played along her back all night, enjoying the feel of her body encased in the soft, plush fabric.

The door to the men's room opened and a tall, skinny man

entered. His dark hair was peppered with gray, and he wore a navy suit and bow tie. Sean gave him a flick of his chin, a curt nod of acknowledgement before turning back to the mirror for a last once-over.

"Don't think we've met," the stranger said. "Oliver Pottson, department chair. And you are . . . ?"

Aha. The one Cassie told him about. He was a tool, he could tell. "Sean McKinnon." He held out a hand and Pottson shook it. "I'm here with Cassandra Baines. My girlfriend."

"Oh. I see." Pottson's pale green eyes slid over Sean in open assessment. Based on his frown, Sean gathered the guy didn't like what he saw. "She hasn't mentioned you."

Something hummed in Sean's gut, but he ignored it. "We only got back together recently."

"Back together? As in, you dated before?"

"That's right." Sean turned to face him full on. The guy was only two inches taller than him, but looked like he could blow away in a strong wind. He reeked of pretentiousness, and he looked just plain nasty, a hard edge to his scowl and a mean glint in his eyes. Suddenly, Sean wanted to take his bow tie and shove it up his arse. "Ya know, Mr. Pottson, I didn't know department heads kept personal tabs on their professors."

"Well, she's only an assistant professor, actually," Pottson corrected him. "And that's *Doctor* Pottson."

Sean let a lazy grin cross his face. *Smug bastard. How about Wanker Pottson?* "I know Cassie's an assistant professor. She's only twenty-nine. She's damn impressive if you ask me. But a little young for you, no?"

Pottson's brows lifted haughtily. "I think Miss Baines is extremely impressive. But young for me? What exactly are you implying, Mr. McKendrick?"

"McKinnon," Sean said tightly. "And I'm implyin' that for her department chair, you seem to be overly concerned with her personal life."

"You're out of line," Pottson snapped. "I've been keeping a close eye on her because as head of department I'm invested in her professional future. I think I have a right to be concerned if she's going to be distracted by a volatile personal life. I'm . . . well . . . mildly surprised that she brought a date to the party tonight. I thought the only relationship she had was with her career. You've been together long?"

"Not this round. But before, the first time, yes. We were very serious a few years back. I'm lucky we found each other again." Sean cocked his head. "But I have to ask again, how's that your business?"

Pottson cleared his throat. "I was simply making conversation."

"Uh huh." *You're a langer*, Sean thought. *A pompous arsehole. Watch my woman all you like. She's back with me now.* "Anything else you want to ask me before I get back to my girlfriend?"

Pottson's pale eyes narrowed, like a shark going in for the kill. "You've been back in her life for what, a few weeks, I take it?"

"Aye."

"Do you know who she dated before you, Mr. McKinnon?" Pottson asked, silky-voiced. "Someone who owned enough property to make up a city block. He took her to Europe, sent flowers every week. Interesting comparison between the two of you."

Something like dread unfurled in Sean's gut, twisting it into knots as the cold harshness of it crept up into his heart. But he ground out from between clenched teeth, "You go to hell."

Pottson laughed softly. Sean wanted to hit him so much it was hard to hold back.

"You have no idea what Cassie and I have meant to each other," Sean growled. "You can take shots at me all ya want.

Doesn't mean anythin'. You're one step short of a stalker, if you've been keeping that close an eye on her." Sean's hands balled into fists.

"I'm no stalker, Mr. McKinnon. But I know Professor Baines a little better than you do, apparently. She'll get bored with someone like you a lot sooner than later. And then she'll find someone who'll give her what she's looking for. Deep down, I think you know I'm right." His thick brows lifted as if to punctuate the point, and he left the restroom.

Sean's blood raced through his veins and roared in his ears. He stood still, closed his eyes, and took a deep, calming breath. *Bastard. That bloody creepy bastard. I should've beat him senseless.*

But he couldn't help but think back to a similar party, years before. How one toad's cutting words had hit all Sean's buttons, shaken his doubts loose, and started him on the path to misery. He couldn't let that happen again. But Jaysus . . . he needed a drink. Shoving hard at the door, he barreled out of the restroom and back down the hallway.

The dark, wood paneled room at the Explorers' Club was filled with people talking, glasses, soft music. Sean grabbed two glasses of champagne from a passing waiter's tray. Lit candles and strung garland made it almost feel like an old-fashioned Christmas; it made him recall his grandparents' small house back in County Cork. He and his family lived in County Kildare, but they went to his ma's parents' every Christmas when he was young. His sweet grandmother had loved garland, and red ribbons. The house had been filled with them.

Sean surveyed the scene before him. Pleasant enough. He didn't hate being here, as he'd thought he would. Or, he hadn't before that chat with Pottson. He downed the contents of one glass until it was empty, then set it down on a nearby table. From the tall, narrow windows, he could see that a light snow had started to fall outside, the crystal flakes flowing on the wind. It was pretty, picturesque. *Her last boyfriend owned enough property to make up a city block...*" He scrubbed his free hand over his face in frustration.

Looking around, he located Cassie across the room, talking to another woman and three men in a small circle by the fireplace. The crackling flames danced on her pale skin, backlighting her as she laughed at something someone said. Affection and pride swirled inside: she was his woman. If... he could keep her. The little gnats of doubt buzzed around inside his head. He tried to shake them off as he crossed the room to join her.

"Hiya," he said at her side, handing her the glass of champagne.

"There you are!" Her smile could have lit the room as she turned to him. "Oh, thank you. My glass was empty, how'd you know?" She kissed his cheek before stealing a sip of champagne.

"I need to talk to you when ya get a minute," he whispered in her ear.

She pulled back to look at him, her brows puckered. "Everything okay?"

"Aye, sure. Just saying. It can wait."

"No. Now, I'm curious." She turned to her colleagues and smiled sweetly. "Will you excuse us?" And with that, she grasped Sean's hand and pulled him out of the party, down the hallway to the small but impressive lobby. High ceilings, marbled floors, art on the walls and priceless artifacts in glass cases... a different world from what he was used to, that was for sure. He glanced at her as she stood before him. *She belongs here. Look where I'm from... and look who she is.* He hated to think Pottson could be right.

"So talk to me," she said. "What's up?"

Damn. He didn't want to do it right then. "You look beautiful tonight, ya know."

"Thank you. So do you. Now stop stalling."

"I, ehm . . ." How could he phrase this properly? To tell her he'd just had a similar experience to the one he'd had before, and warn her about her arsehole boss, and ask her what he meant to her, all without sounding like an ass?

"Sean?" She stared at him expectantly.

"Sorry, I just . . ." He dragged a hand across the back of his neck, trying to form the right sentences. Taking her hand, he pulled her to sit with him on a velvet chaise. "You . . . don't know how desirable you are, Cassie. You don't. You never have. But there's a history of your being around men, who are pompous and jealous. Who apparently think a man like me shouldn't have any claim to ya."

Cassandra's mouth literally dropped open as she gaped at him. "Wh-what? What on earth are you talking about?"

"It's true, love. One of those tools got to me before, got in my head, years ago. And I listened to him instead of you, and I ruined everything," Sean said brusquely. "Tonight, some langer who seems to think he has rights to you just came at me."

"*Who?*"

"Yer man Pottson. Bloody wanker."

She scowled at the mention of his name. "Oh, God. What happened?"

"He wants you," Sean said flatly. "That was clear."

"You've got nothing to worry about. I would *never* . . ." Her voice dropped so it wouldn't carry. "God, Sean, I told you, he skeeves me."

Sean had to grin at that. "He should. He's skeevy."

"But he *is* the head of my department. He could make things very difficult for me if he chose to. So I just try to be polite, keep things light, and not make waves."

"That's sexual harassment," Sean ground out.

"That's real life," Cassandra said flatly. "Hierarchy, politics—it happens all the time."

"Are you kidding me?" Sean blinked. "Ya know what? I may not have a fancy degree, but I run a business, and sexually harassing employees isn't okay by me. I've seen it in bars and clubs, other places. You think because Pottson's got a bunch of letters after his name, that makes it more acceptable somehow? It isn't, Cassie."

"You don't know how it is," she said, a sharp edge to her tone. "You don't know the ins and outs of academic life, you don't—"

"Don't go there," Sean warned, feeling the knot return in his gut. "I know enough to know sexual harassment is never okay. Don't treat me like an idiot for not playing along with his shit. And don't sound like one by insulting me."

She flinched as if he'd slapped her. "I wasn't insulting you!"

"Really? Think back on what you just said to me, darling. You were patronizing me."

"I was not!" she cried. "You just don't understand—" She jumped to her feet and stared down at him. He rose slowly, staring back.

"Go on. Say it again," he murmured in a dangerous tone. "Tell the dumb bar owner how he's not smart enough."

Crimson bloomed on her cheeks. "That's *not* what I meant. What did he say to you? Will you tell me what happened, please?"

Sean couldn't rip his gaze from hers. Did she realize what was going on here? Because suddenly, he sure as hell did, and he didn't like it one bit. "He informed me that in comparison to all your previous dates—the rich, educated, and powerful—that a boy toy like me won't last long. You'll tire of me. He's been watching, so he knows."

"He said *what?*" Her face blanched of color, the hot pink draining from her cheeks.

"Aye. Not to worry, though. I put him on notice."

"You did? Oh God, what'd you say?" she asked anxiously. "You didn't do anything... say anything... that could, well..."

He peered at her, frowning. "That could what? Protect you? Defend you? He's a langer."

"I know that, but Sean, he's my boss. You can't—I mean, I have to—"

"*You* have to, Cassie. I don't. I don't take crap from anyone. And I can't believe I'm hearing that you would." Sean raked his hand through his hair, swore under his breath, and started to pace.

"I don't! But I don't have to rock the boat, either," she said. "There's a middle ground."

"No there isn't. Not on something like this."

"That man is my boss and I want to be tenured one day," she said harshly. "So if he said something that—"

"He was rude, condescending, pandering, and obnoxious. He thinks he has rights to you. He's lucky I didn't plant him in the wall." He stopped pacing and speared her with a look. "Cassie. Are you upset with Pottson, or me? Because right now, I'm not sure."

"If you attacked my boss, I have a right to be concerned," Cassandra said.

"Aha. That's bloody great." He suddenly felt like he was on a speeding train and didn't know how to stop it. Didn't know where the brake pedal was. He raked a hand through his hair in distress. "You know what? He was an arse, I shot back and stood up for us, and suddenly I feel like *I'm* the one being questioned here."

"What? Just wait a minute—"

"Pottson's a bloody langer. Just like that snake at Columbia years ago, the one who got to me," Sean went on, spiraling out of control. "But things were different then. I was insecure and young and stupid, and I couldn't get past it. He made it sound like I was a dumb loser who'd hold ya back if I stayed with ya. I thought I'd end up embarrassin' ya somehow. *That's* why I broke up with you, you know."

"Are you kidding me?" Cassandra's heart felt like a cold rock in her chest, to match the lump in her throat. She swallowed to dislodge it, but it didn't work. Finally she croaked, "You had that little faith in us? In *me*?" Nausea roiled in her stomach. "So you quit before I could fire you."

He winced but murmured, "When ya put it that way . . ."

"Oh my God," Cassandra hissed. Her heartbeat raced and her face felt hot. "You made my choices for me."

Sean nodded, but said nothing. Still as stone, the pain in his eyes spoke volumes.

Her head was spinning. She didn't know whether to laugh, shout, or cry. Overcome, she raised her hands and slammed them against his chest, a hard shove that sent him flying back. "How dare you have so little faith in me! How dare you make my decisions for me and hurt me like that!" She tried to keep from yelling, but she felt wild. "For years, I felt like I didn't measure up, like I'd done something to make you want to walk away from me . . . and all this time, it was you. *You* didn't feel like you measured up."

He looked her in the eye and said with soft sorrow, "That's right. You're right." His admission came so softly that it ripped at her heart. "Only I never meant to make you feel that way."

"How could I *not*?" she cried. "You dumped me! Without any good reason, with just obnoxious platitudes about how it was best for me and that I'd thank you later."

"Cassie..." He stared at her woefully. "The other night, you told me to forgive myself, and I told you it was very hard for me to do that. Now you know why."

She pushed her shaking hands through her hair. Somewhere in her clouded mind, she realized it wasn't just her hands that were shaking, but her whole body.

"And while we're at it," he continued, "you said you'd forgiven me for hurting you. But right now, it doesn't sound like it. It sounds like you're still fiercely angry at me."

"Well, right now I am, yes!" She felt her self-control slipping away at lightning speed. "If you'd told me *any* of these things back then, it would have made sense when you broke up with me. I would've understood what was driving you. We could have talked about it, I would've..." She wanted to punch him. She wanted to cry. "You know what? I can't go there now. I can't. So just tell me, did you do anything to Oliver tonight I should know about?"

"Like what?" Sean asked, affronted.

"I don't know. Something that could jeopardize my position here? Or my career?"

"Is that all you care about?" he hissed, eyes wide.

"No! But Sean, I've worked damn hard to get to this juncture. For years. You've been back in my life for a few *weeks*. So I'm sorry, but I have a right to know, or to be upset, if you said or did something—"

"You're unbelievable!" he cried. "You care more about your job than about us!"

"No," she said, "but I do care about both. I don't have to apologize for that."

His blue eyes flashed, indignant, taken aback. "After everything we've done to get to this place, where we were together, trusting again..."

"You want to talk about trust now? You sure? Because after what you just told me, if you'd trusted me in the first place, back then, you would have come to me. I would've been able to make you see that guy was just a jerk, we would've had a good laugh, and that would've been it."

"A good laugh?" He stared at her.

"No one could have taken me away from you. Except for you. And you did. *You* did that."

He whirled away, scrubbing his hands over his face before turning back to her. "I thought I didn't deserve you then, don't ya get it? I didn't see what someone like me had to offer someone like you, in terms of a real future. I wasn't enough for ya then. I just . . . want you to be sure I'm enough now." He swallowed hard, his deep blue eyes pleading. "How did even we get here? I just wanted to tell ya that Pottson mouthed off, that he's hot for ya and he's a creeper, and you're comin' at me! And we're arguin' about the past, and trust, and everything—what the hell . . ." He stood there staring at her, searching. "Would you rather be with someone different? Is that what this is really all about? Because God knows Pottson and all those other guys can give ya things I can't."

Heart pounding, she gaped at him with a mixture of horror and sadness. "You still don't get it," she whispered hotly, shaking her head. "I don't care what you, or any other man, has to 'offer' me. I don't need anything. I take care of myself." A dull throbbing ache started to pound in her head, but she stood her ground. "I don't need you. But I want you. You were always enough for me, then and now." Her eyes burned and filled with tears, even as she took in the shadowed look on his face. "That's why I let you back into my life. But if you still don't know that, if you're still unsure of that, even now? There's nothing I can say to make you believe it. It's a lost battle." The tears spilled over onto her cheeks.

"Cassie..." He reached out to her, but she backed away. "I'm sorry, but after what you said—"

"No. Just stop." Pushed to the limit, her mind started to shut down. She wanted escape. Shaking off his hands, she backed away. "I can't do this again," she croaked. "I can't keep fighting for us... and I can't build a future with a man who doesn't trust me enough to let me in. You don't."

"I do trust you! That's why I told you all these things! I won't leave you again. Is that what you're waiting for, for me to leave?"

Her bottom lip trembled. "Maybe I still don't know for sure. Maybe you're right, I haven't really forgiven you."

The desperate glint in his eyes relayed frustration and a hint of fear. "Ya know, I think this talk got thrown way off track. Can we please go somewhere more private and talk this through?"

She shook her head, swallowing a sob. "I'm done talking. I'm... done. I can't put myself through this again. This was a mistake after all." Turning her back on him, she started to walk.

He caught up to her in a few long strides and grabbed her arm, whirling her around to face him. "Don't you dare leave this way," he said, his breath coming in hard gusts. "Don't walk away, Cassie. Let's talk this out."

"I've heard enough for one night." Shaking her head violently, she ground out, "Let go of my arm."

"Please, Cassie. You want me to beg? I will. Don't leave like this, please. We—"

"Everything all right over here?" A gray-haired man in a suit was there, eyeing Cassandra with concern. Two security guards stood a few feet behind him, watching.

Sean released her arm. "We're fine. She's fine."

Swiping the wetness from her cheeks, Cassandra said

quickly, "We're fine. I need to get back inside to my faculty holiday party."

"Don't go," Sean pleaded in a hot whisper.

"Why not? You did. My turn."

His eyes widened like she'd struck him. "Please... it broke us both when I went running scared. Don't you do it now."

"I'm not running scared," she exclaimed.

His gaze sharpened. "The hell you're not. That's exactly what this is."

Her breath caught and she blinked at him. She couldn't think straight anymore. "Goodbye, Sean. Merry Christmas," she blurted, and practically ran back into the party room.

Sean stood rooted to the spot, staring after her in disbelief.

"You need me to call you a cab?" The gray haired man's voice was softer than before. Sean turned his head to look at him and saw sympathy in the older man's eyes.

"No," he whispered. "Just need my coat, and I'll be goin'."

Three minutes later, he was outside, trudging through the snow in his dress shoes. He knew he should hail a cab, but on a snowy Friday night, he'd have just as much luck by starting to walk home. He didn't care that it was a far walk from midtown to the Village. He didn't care about anything. The snow fell around him, the Christmas lights sparkled in every window, people rushed by him, and he didn't care.

Chapter Eleven

CASSANDRA SAT BY the large bay window of her parents' living room, curled into the end of their plush sofa. She drew her legs up against her chest and wrapped her arms around her knees as she watched the snow fall lightly outside. She was tired; it'd been a long few days.

After bolting away from Sean at the party, she'd gone straight to the ladies' room and bawled her eyes out, hiding there until she could recompose herself enough to slip out and go home. Around midnight, she'd fallen into a restless sleep, but was startled awake by the ringing of her phone. Kara had gone into labor, at last. When the call ended, she saw that there was a waiting text from Sean, sent while she'd been asleep.

> *I hate that we fought like that. I'm going mad. I can't sleep. I'm sorry, Cassie. I'm sorry for all of it. Just don't shut me out. Please. We need to talk. I love you.*

Her stomach churned and she tossed the phone onto her bed. She had to get to the hospital for Kara. Her friends needed her. That was all she cared about at the moment. She spent the rest of Saturday and part of Sunday at the hospital.

Sean tried to call again, two more times, and the texts came every few hours. He was climbing the walls, not hearing from her. She knew it was unfair, that she was being petulant . . . but she realized he'd been right: she *was* running scared. She'd been so taken aback by what he'd told her, and so afraid of getting hurt again, she was the one who'd run this time. And since she didn't know what to do about all the feelings swamping her, she was all too happy to dive into Auntie mode for Kara.

On Monday, she and Elena helped Kara and the baby get home from the hospital. There, along with Bree, they spent the day packing up everything to get the new mother and child out to Aunt Enza's house. Enza had insisted they stay with her for a week or two, being the baby's honorary grandmother, and Kara had gratefully accepted the invitation. Elena helped Cassandra and Bree load up their cars, and they caravanned it out to eastern Long Island.

For three days, Sean kept texting and trying to call. Cassandra ignored him. The texts went unanswered, and she let his calls go to voice mail.

She knew how ironic it was. She'd desperately wanted him to fight for her all those years, to not let her go. Now he was doing exactly what she used to wish for, but she was too overwhelmed, hurt, and scared to accept it. The pain was ruling the roost for the moment, despite her happiness about her new niece and the general flurry of Christmas excitement. Going back to her parents' house for a few days was another good escape. She wanted to be inaccessible; she needed the space and time to think.

She hated to admit it, but she'd had to face the fact that Sean was right about a few things. She had treated him as if he wasn't part of her world, therefore unable—or not smart enough—to understand how things went.

And she hadn't fully forgiven him for the past. The second

their stability as a couple had come into question, she'd thought he would bolt for the door. She hadn't had faith in him, or forgiven him. He'd been right about that too.

So even if she was angry, she knew he had a right to be also. She had to talk to him sooner or later . . . but she just . . . was it pride holding her back? Fear? Both? She wasn't sure, and until she was, she was going to stay incommunicado.

The only thing she knew for sure was that she was hopelessly in love with him, the one constant throughout their tangled history. She knew he loved her too. She believed that. But was love enough? Could they make it actually work? Or had Sean been right the first time when he'd ended it, afraid their worlds were too different after all? She just didn't know.

"It's pretty, isn't it?" Her mother, Joann, sat beside her on the couch and looked out at the snow falling. Dusk had set in already, turning the snow-covered landscape a soothing shade of blue.

"Beautiful," Cassandra replied. "I've always loved the snow."

"Have you talked to him yet?"

Cassandra looked back out to the snowfall. "No."

"How many days has it been now? Four?"

"Five."

"So I take it you disinvited him and his sister for Christmas dinner?"

Cassandra cringed. "Um, I didn't . . . but I guess at this point, that's understood."

"Know what? I don't understand any of this," Joann said flatly. "Call him. Text him. You have to talk. You can't just not answer him and hope he'll go away. It's not fair, when he's been trying so hard to reach you. Ignoring a problem doesn't get it worked out. You're more mature than this, or so I thought."

"Wow, Mom, don't hold back," Cassandra griped sarcastically. She stared at her mother. "I thought you hated him."

"I'm not a fan," Joann hedged. "Not after how he hurt you. But this time around, from everything you told me... from what I can see? This one's on you, sweetie."

"Me?" Cassandra sat up a little straighter. "How is it on me? He didn't trust me enough to tell me so many things—things that ended up splitting us apart. How do I know that won't happen again?"

"You don't. That's the risk you take." Joann crossed her legs and shifted where she sat. "Let's not do this right before we go to Enza's, okay? I don't want to argue."

"I don't either. I just..." Cassandra glanced back out the window, watching as the crystalline flakes fluttered through the evening air. "What if he was right, Mom? That deep down, I thought he wouldn't fit into my world and I didn't even realize it?"

Joann pulled her into a hug. "It's going to all be okay. I know it."

"How do you know?"

"Because you're a strong, smart woman. And because it's Christmas. Wonderful things happen on Christmas. I believe in that."

"I used to..." Cassandra sniffled. Her voice dropped to a quavering whisper. "I want to believe, Mom."

"Then believe. Decide to believe. Faith is a choice. The only one who can choose to take that leap of faith is you." Joann pulled back to look into her face. "Right now, we have to get to Enza's, make and eat a ton of seafood, and celebrate with all our loved ones. And I need to meet that new baby! My honorary granddaughter!" She smiled warmly. "It's Christmas Eve. Let's go be merry."

Cassandra nodded, hugged her mother once more, and headed for the upstairs bathroom. She grabbed her cosmetics bag from the drawer. As she quickly touched up her makeup, she thought of Sean, and everything her mother had said.

Decide to believe. Faith is a choice.

She and Sean had found each other again. He'd pursued her, tried to make up for the lost time and hurt feelings, and show her how much he cared... told her he loved her... trusted her. He trusted that they'd work as a couple and that she'd stand by him. That was why he'd come to her about Oliver, already so on edge, and...

Oh God, she'd let her own insecurities take over and she'd pushed him away—almost mirroring what he'd done to her years ago. Suddenly, she understood his actions in a new way. And realized that the first time, he'd been wrong, but this time, she'd been wrong.

She pulled her phone out of her pocket. No new texts, not for two hours. The last one from him said: *I can't bear this. I hate that we're not spending Christmas together. I miss you so much it hurts. I love you, and I won't give up until you talk to me again. I won't give up on us. Le chéile go deo.* xx

Le chéile go deo—Together Forever.

She'd read that last text ten times already. His love and sadness were palpable.

I won't give up on us.

Faith is a choice . . .

Faith. Take a leap of faith. It was Christmas, after all. If you couldn't take a leap of faith on Christmas, when could you?

"Cass?" Her mother's voice boomed from downstairs. "We're leaving, let's go!"

"Coming," Cassandra called back. There was no time now. She'd call him later, if it wasn't too late. And until then, she could try to piece together what she wanted to say, something meaningful, something coherent beyond: "I'm sorry, and I want to work this out, and I love you too."

Chapter Twelve

HOURS LATER, WELL after ten o'clock, Cassandra stared out the car window into the darkness, feeling her heavy eyes droop. Christmas Eve at Aunt Enza's was always magical. This group of friends *was* a family, the family the moms had chosen and made themselves. And now, it was growing, with the new generation. Bree's daughter Charlie had cooed so much over Kara's brand new baby girl, it melted all their hearts. Cassandra, Elena, and Bree had helped cook, while all their brothers and fathers talked and played cards. They'd all exchanged gifts. They'd laughed and eaten and sung Christmas songs and eaten some more. It had been a lovely, memorable Christmas Eve.

The only thing missing had been Sean. He should have been there with her, laughing with all the men, kissing her under the mistletoe... she wondered what he'd done that evening instead.

Next to her in the back seat of their parents' SUV, Darren nudged her. Now twenty-six and a good six inches taller than her, her little brother had grown from an annoying kid into a kind, quiet man. "You're falling asleep. Here." He offered her his shoulder. "It's gotta be more comfortable than the glass."

"Thanks." Cassandra let her rest on his shoulder and exhaled a soft, relaxed breath. Enza's house was almost an hour's drive from their house, and her father hadn't gone above forty miles an hour. The snow was falling so lightly it was almost invisible, but it still fell, and the roads were icing up, while on the radio Bing Crosby crooned about a white Christmas . . .

"Cass." Her brother's voice broke into her thoughts, and she startled. "Hey. We're home."

"Okay . . ." She rolled her head, stretching out her neck muscles. "How long did I sleep?"

"Maybe forty-five minutes," Darren guessed.

"I am so ready for bed," Joann yawned.

"Wait. Someone's at the door," her dad said. He stared out the windshield, face crinkled as he tried to see in the dark. "There's someone there, on the porch."

"What?" Joann said nervously, peering out the snowy window. "Are you sure?"

"Looks like it," Roger said.

Darren pulled on his hat. "I'll go look. You all stay here."

"What are you, crazy?" Joann said. "We're not letting you go out there!" She looked at her husband. "Should we call the police?"

"Why don't we see who it is first," he said. "Could be someone we know."

Cassandra squinted, trying to see the stranger on their front steps. The twinkling white lights her father had hung revealed a shadowy figure . . . *No. No way.* Her breath caught and stuck. She could make out a distinct shape: a guitar was slung over the stranger's back. "Oh my God. It's Sean."

"What?" Joann yelped. "How do you know?"

"His guitar," Cassandra said, scrambling to pull on her hat

and gloves.

"Oh, Good Lord," Joann murmured.

"Are you sure that's him?" Roger asked.

"Yeah."

Before her parents could say another word, Cassandra exited the car and slammed the door behind her. Tiny snowflakes bit at her face, the cold wind and adrenaline rush combined waking her up completely. She trudged through the snow, up the driveway, to the front porch. Sure enough, under the awning, sitting in a chair, was Sean. He rose to stand as she made her way up the steps to face him, looking at her with a mixture of trepidation and hope.

"It is you," she said, staring at him. Her breath came out in tiny white puffs.

"I had to see you," he said quietly.

"How long have you been sitting out here?" she asked.

"Maybe an hour," he shrugged. "I took the train from the city, then a cab from the station. I mean, I had your parents' address, but no clue how to get here, so I let the taxi driver do it for me."

"You've been sitting here for an hour?" she exclaimed. "In the snow? My God, Sean, you must be freezing!"

"I'm fine, love," he said, but she saw how red and ruddy his fair cheeks were.

"Yeah, right. You—ugh, come inside," she insisted, fumbling for her keys in her bag.

"Cassie," he started earnestly.

"Wait, we'll talk. But we have to get you warm first, my God . . ." She found her keys and opened the door, pulling him into the house. Then, she turned to the car and waved for her family to come too.

Sean placed his small black duffel bag and guitar case against the wall. They stood in the foyer and faced each other.

Beads of moisture that had been snowflakes clung to his tousled hair, the dark gold stubble on his square jaw, his long eyelashes. He looked so sweet and so handsome in his wool peacoat, herringbone scarf, and thick knit hat that she wanted to grab his face and kiss him . . . but she quickly realized he was shivering and trying not to show it.

The rush of love that washed over her threatened to drown her. It was all she could do not to throw her arms around him. Instead, she shook her head at him and muttered, "You're insane! You could have gotten frostbite out there!"

"Don't care," he said through slightly chattering teeth, his eyes bright. "I'd've waited all night for ya."

Her nerves were like livewires, jangling and electric. "I'll get you some whisky," she said. "And a blanket. We'll wrap you up in it, on the couch, and my dad will start a fire in the fireplace. We'll get you warm, okay?"

But he grabbed her arms. "That all sounds fantastic. But Cassie . . ." He pulled her close, looked into her eyes, and said, "Listen to me. You can't leave me. Please."

"Sean—"

"I love you." His deep blue eyes were intense as they seared into hers. "I love you more than anything in the world, Cassandra Baines. Ya hearin' me?"

Her bones melted at the earnest tone of his voice. "I love you too," she whispered.

His breath caught and his eyes searched hers. "I wasn't sure anymore. I mean . . . Jaysus, ya wouldn't answer me. Not a bloody word."

"It's been a crazy couple of days," she told him, dodging. "Kara had the baby. On Saturday. I've been with her most of the time."

"That's great, I'm happy for her. But ya could've texted back," he said softly. "You didn't because ya didn't want to."

She sighed. "You're right. I . . . well, I had a lot to think about." She gave him a gentle look and touched his stubbled chin. "But the one thing I knew, have always known, is that I love you. That has never changed, and never will. I'm sorry I hurt you at the party, and I'm sorry I didn't answer your texts."

"It's okay. We're talkin' now." His still-gloved hands lifted to cup her face. "I love you so much. I've been a bloody wreck without ya." He lowered his head to brush a tender kiss against her lips, sweet and intoxicating. Lingering, he sipped from her lips, savoring her. "We need to talk, we need to fix this . . ."

"Let's just get you warmed up first, okay?"

The sound of footsteps and voices came behind them as her parents and brother entered the house. "What on earth were you thinking?" Joann chastised Sean as she walked in.

"That I needed to talk to your daughter." He couldn't help but grin, that lopsided grin that Cassandra adored. "It's good to see you again, Mrs Baines. You're lookin' well. Happy Christmas."

"Happy Christmas to you too. You're a loon." She shook her head at him, then said, "We brought home plenty of leftovers, are you hungry?"

"No, I'm fine, but thank you for asking. A drink would be good, though, gotta say."

"We'll get you one." Cassandra's dad strode across the room to shake his hand. "Been a long time. Merry Christmas, Sean."

"Same to you, sir."

Cassandra watched as Sean chatted briefly with her parents and her brother, as she tried to slow the racing of her heart. He'd come for her. He'd waited in the damn snow, in the dark and cold, on Christmas Eve, for her. Her heart felt ready to burst out of her chest.

"Why don't we let them be alone," Joann suggested. Darren scooped up some of the bags of food Enza had sent home with them and carried them off to the kitchen.

"Dad?" Cassandra asked. "First, can you build us a fire?"

Within a few minutes, Roger had flames dancing and crackling in the fireplace, Joann had made a pot of tea and brought out some of Bree and Enza's pizzelle cookies, and Darren put a glass of Irish whisky in Sean's still-cold hands.

"Thank you all so much," Sean said. He sat on one end of the couch, Cassandra at the other, as he looked up to speak to her family. "Thank you for your hospitality, for not calling the police when ya saw some guy lurkin' on your porch, and for lettin' me warm up inside."

"It's the Christmas spirit," Darren joked. "Well, I'm going up to bed. I know it's early, but I'm wiped." He dropped a kiss on his mother's cheek, then shot Sean a look and asked, "See you in the morning, I guess?"

"I'll go set up the guest room for you," Joann said.

"Mom . . ." Cassandra said in a quiet but firm voice. "Not necessary. He'll be staying with me, in my room."

A momentary flicker of surprise skittered across Joann's face. Sean's eyes rounded and sparked. But Roger's brows creased hard, making Darren snort and chuckle.

Cassandra rolled her eyes. "I'm almost thirty," she said. "Give me a break, okay?"

Joann shrugged. "Okay." She tugged on her husband's sleeve. "Let's go."

But once Sean and Cassandra were finally alone in the living room, an awkward silence fell over them. She watched his eyes canvas the room, coming to rest on the tall Christmas tree that stood proudly in the corner.

"That's a beautiful tree," Sean said. "Your ma did all that?"

Cassandra nodded. "She decorates the inside of the house, Dad decorates the outside."

"Well, they both did a beauty of a job. The place is all decked out like a Christmas picture postcard." He looked around the room again and said, "I remember this house well."

"You should. You were out here for dinner with me at least once a month."

"And how we went to the beach in the summer, every other weekend. We had good times there."

She nodded. "We did." Her eyes roamed over him again. Unruly hair, gorgeous face, hot body in an ivory wool fisherman's sweater and dark jeans. She wanted to crawl into his lap. Memories of when she had before swamped her. "We had a lot of good times together."

"And I want to make more," he said in a fierce whisper. "I love you, Cassie. I've been dyin' for the past few days, thinkin' I lost you again."

"I'm sorry for that." She stared down at her hands. "I just wasn't ready to talk. I am now. I'm sorry for the past few days, Sean."

"I can tell you are, so it's all right..." He stared at her. "But what now?"

"Well... to start... if we're going to be together," she said quietly, "you can't keep things from me. Stop being a martyr, and stop shielding me. If I'm going to be with you, I need to know there's *nothing* you hide from me, even the not-so-pretty things."

"I swear it, I won't do that again. Besides, ya know it all now." His eyes warmed. "And ya still love me anyway."

"Of course I do," she said. "I don't want someone perfect. I don't expect you to be perfect. I love you for who you are."

"I get that now." He grimaced and looked down into his glass. The bronze liquid shimmied as he turned it in his hands. "It took almost losing you again to realize... I'm sorry I pushed you away. It won't happen again."

"Good. I hope so. I'm trusting you."

His eyes held hers. "Do ya, Cassie? Do ya trust me? Truly?"

"I do now." She reached for his hands. "Because you're a deeply good man. We've learned from our past, I think. We can do anything together. I've been thinking a lot these past few days. I was unfair to you. But I need you to understand what a leap of faith it was to start seeing you again. Why I flipped so fast the other night when things started going wrong. I was scared. You were absolutely right when you said I was running scared." Her dark eyes pinned him. "But I'm not anymore. You've proved yourself to me that I could trust you again. I believe you're truly sorry for the past. I know now that you did love me back then, even though you screwed it all up. And that our connection was real."

"Of course it was real," he blurted. "Ya can't fake feelings like this." He gestured between them with his hand.

"I agree." Her fingers continued their gentle exploration, tracing along his jaw, his lips, and he grew still. "We found each other again. So . . ." She drew a deep breath and her voice dropped, turning quiet and solemn. "I'm here. I'm in this. We love each other. We want to be together. I want to move forward with you, not stay stuck in the past." Her hand raised to touch his cheek. "So I am. I'm done with holding on to that. Because we're moving forward now, and I believe you won't do anything like that again. I believe in you, Sean. In *us*." Her hand stilled and her voice thickened as she revealed, "I'm taking the leap of faith. I'm choosing it. I choose us."

His eyes widened, then liquefied as he leaned into her palm, nuzzling it. "I believe in us too." He leaned in to kiss her lips, a feather's touch. "A leap of faith . . . sounds like a Christmas kind of thing."

"It does, doesn't it?" she smiled.

Sean caressed Cassie's hair, her face, unable to believe the waves of emotion that were cresting through him. "I love you. So much."

"Then kiss me," she smiled sweetly.

He drew her into his arms, but then, sooner than he really wanted to, he pulled back. "Wait here a second, all right?" Clearing his throat, he stood and walked out of the room, returning with his guitar and his duffel bag. "I have a few things for you, love. Didn't think I'd come all this way on Christmas Eve without a gift or two, did ya?"

He retook his seat at the end of the sofa, then pulled his acoustic guitar from its black fabric case and onto his lap. "Well..." He plucked a few strings, doing a quick tuning. "Okaaay. Right. This is first." He smiled at her as he started to play softly.

Cassandra immediately recognized the song; her breath stuck in her lungs and her throat sealed up. Sean started singing, a slow, sweet version of *All I Want for Christmas*. It had always been her favorite Christmas song. She'd even sung along with it for him, their first Christmas together, dressed in a red nightie she'd bought just for him. When the song was over, he'd peeled her out of it and they'd made love for the first time.

For the years since, she'd always thought of him when she'd heard the song and it had made her heart squeeze. But tonight the lyrics seemed more poignant than ever before. His smooth tenor voice caressed the notes, his melodious playing was perfect... her eyes filled with tears as he serenaded her with this most special song. His singing it to her was a Christmas gift, the most heartfelt one he could have given her.

"Make my wish come true," he sang, looking right into her eyes. "All I want for Christmas... is you."

Tears slid down her face, tears of joy and love and the

relief of knowing faith and forgiveness at last. They were meant to be. They were soul mates. She'd taken a leap of faith, and the Universe had answered her with a resounding affirmation.

When the song was over, she took the guitar from his hands and placed it gently on the floor beside him. "That was wonderful," she whispered, wiping her cheeks dry. "Thank you so much for that."

"I'm glad you liked it." He kissed her lips with gentle tenderness. "And it's true. All I want for Christmas is you, Cassielove."

"Me too."

"I'm here. I'm still a bit cold, but I'm here."

She hiccupped a watery giggle. "Come here and let me warm you up then." She straddled his lap, her legs sliding around his hips and her arms cradling his shoulders as she smiled down at him. His hands ran up her thighs, then her back, as her fingers tangled in his hair and they kissed.

"Happy Christmas, love," he whispered against her lips.

"Mmmm. Merry Christmas." But then he pulled away. Cassandra stretched out on the sofa as she watched him burrow through his duffel bag. "What's so important?" she teased. "What's more important than loving me senseless, Irish?"

"This." He cleared his throat and ran his hands through his hair before turning back to her. Already on the floor, on his knees, he moved to her side . . . and watched her eyes fly wide as he held out the small black box.

"Oh Sean," she whispered. New tears welled in her eyes as she stared at him.

"I loved ya so much I think the Universe conspired to bring you back to me. In time for Christmas. So I could echo the things I said to ya on Christmas night eight years ago . . ."

He held her free hand with his free hand and repeated some of the words he'd uttered that fateful night. "I love you, Cassandra Lynn Baines. I want to spend the rest of my life with you, and stand proudly by your side. I want to make your world half as bright as you've made mine. You're the only woman I've ever loved. Do me the honor and marry me."

"Yes," she whispered in a rush of heat, her dark eyes shining. "Yes, Sean, I'll marry you. I love you so much."

Smiling, he slipped the engagement ring onto her finger and whispered, "Le chéile go deo, Cassie. Together forever."

The End

Goodness and Light

A New York Christmas Story

Patty Blount

Dedication

To my niece, Jennifer, with the hope that she realizes her dreams of becoming a writer.

Acknowledgements

For everyone impacted by the events of September 11th.

I have to send buckets of chocolate kisses to Jeannie Moon, Jolyse Barnett and Jennifer Gracen—my writing partners on this series. It was Jeannie's idea to write the Christmas in New York series and I wasn't sure I was up to the challenge but these incredibly talented authors convinced me to try. So glad I listened to them.

Hugs also to everyone at Tule, especially Lilian Darcy, for her sharp editorial eye and her sense of humor. If you fall in love with Lucas—as I have—it's due entirely to Lilian's insight.

Enormous thanks to my family for putting up with me during the intense schedule.

Finally, a special thanks to the city of New York, a light that will always shine.

Chapter One

NEW YORK NEVER changed. Elena Larsen stood beside her friend's Zipcar and took a good look around. The crowds, the traffic, the smell of street vendor chestnuts floating on the cold December air. It was all exactly the way she remembered.

"Laney, I am so glad you finally joined us this year." Cassandra gave her a reproving look.

"*You're* glad?" Elena laughed. "I single-handedly saved the economy. My checkbook will never recover." From the car, she hauled two shopping bags that strained their handles.

"Hey, it's Christmas. 'Tis the season for checkbook abuse." Cass walked around the car and grabbed her in a tight hug. "If you let another decade go before visiting us again, I will hunt you down and kill you."

Elena hugged back but made no promises. New York may have been home at one time, but now it held only bad memories.

"I have to run. Give Kara a kiss and a belly rub for me, okay? Bye!" With one last wave and a blown kiss, Cass was back in traffic, a cab driver offering his opinion of her driving with a raised finger and a blare of his horn. Cassandra Baines was the quintessential New Yorker—a study in contradictions, a mix of urban polish and take-no-crap attitude. Kara, Elena's sister, was even more so. Elena had no doubt attempting to rub her sister's pregnant belly would get her hand slapped—which, she concluded with a wry grin, was probably why Cass had suggested it. She shook her head with a laugh. Damn, it had been good to see her—really good. *Thirteen years is too long for friends to go without real, face to face contact,* Cassandra had scolded her when she'd first seen her. Elena tamped down the guilt that flared in her gut—she'd *had* to leave.

She simply couldn't bear New York City after that day.

She hefted her luggage—a huge suitcase on wheels and a small laptop bag—over a patch of snow and did her best not to look south.

She looked.

And realized she'd been wrong. New York *had* changed.

The spire of One World Trade Center glinted in the sun and she felt a tug on her heart that she'd never expected to feel. She hadn't been in Manhattan since she was fourteen years old and despite the scar on the skyline, there was something here that still whispered *home*.

Elena stood and stared and was abruptly bumped from behind. Unbalanced by the bags clutched in her hands, she couldn't stop the fall, and landed in a heap in the same mound of snow she'd tried to avoid. "Hey—" she protested, but a strong voice overpowered hers.

"Hey! Watch it!" A man shouted at the guy who'd shoved her, but it did no good. The obnoxious guy never looked back. The stranger bent to her, held out a bare hand. "Are you okay?"

Elena looked up into the face of the man who'd come to her aid. Dark hair curled over the edges of a knit hat, framing dark eyes that glinted with annoyance and concern. His cheeks were ruddy from the frigid air and his mouth, just the shape of it, made her own drop open with a little gasp.

Oh, wow.

She watched, hypnotized, for a long moment until that mouth curled. "Miss? I'll ask again, are you okay?"

Elena gave herself a little shake and nodded. "Yeah, I'm fine, just—just really pissed off."

The stranger grinned and Elena's breath clogged in her lungs. His mouth was enticing when it was pressed into a tight, annoyed line but when he smiled, it was damn near lethal.

When he smiled, something changed.

Fluttered.

Clicked.

She shivered and shook off the sensation, placing her gloved hand in his without thinking. Suddenly, she was upright with no memory of how she'd gotten there. Her rescuer was large.

Tall.

Broad.

Yet she felt completely safe in his hands. She blinked and swayed, and he shifted his hands to her shoulders. A delicious warmth spread over her.

"You're sure you're not hurt?"

She jerked, nodded. "No. Uh, yes, I mean I'm good." *Jeez.* She couldn't remember how to form words. His smile was intoxicating. Perfect teeth, just the right shade of white between *loves coffee* and *Osmond cousin* bracketed by honest-to-God dimples—the last time Elena saw dimples this cute, a boy had smiled at her only to vanish into the crowd gathered to honor the victims lost on September 11th. She thought he was an angel who'd stopped her from doing something even worse than what had already happened. He'd tucked something into her hand, something that caught the sun, a bit of light that cut through all that darkness.

A snowflake. A crystal snowflake ornament. She'd kept it all these years and still wasn't sure if she'd imagined the boy who'd given it to her. The man in front of her wasn't him—couldn't be him—he wasn't as tall for one thing. Looking up at that boy had put a crick in her neck. But he sure reminded her of him. Oh, she could happily spend the rest of her life staring at this man's smile.

"Miss?" He shifted, obviously uncomfortable with her scrutiny and she crashed back to the present, mortified that she was still holding him.

"Oh. Sorry."

She hurried to pick up the shopping bags and when she reached for the luggage handle, he shook his head. "I'll help you."

"It's okay, I can manage." She gave it a small tug.

"I'm sure you can. But I'll help you anyway. Where do you need to go?" He tugged back.

Frustration, embarrassment, and just plain anxiety at being back in New York frayed Elena's last threads of patience. "I said I can manage. Thanks for your help. I can take it from here."

The man studied her. She studied him back. He was big—easily six feet with broad shoulders and narrow hips. He wore a dark jacket with a scarf looped around his neck. To her total surprise, he laughed and held up his hands in surrender. "Obviously, you're a native New Yorker home for the holidays." He handed over her bags.

Home.

The word stabbed through her heart and she rubbed her chest where the wound still stung. They'd left home not long after the towers fell and moved to Virginia, where the house was nice enough, if you liked old Victorians. And she supposed the Georgia house had charm. The Florida house was big, even had a pool. But her dad never stayed long in the jobs that took him and what was left of their family from state to state. Maybe that was why all those houses had felt more like hotels than home.

No. No, that wasn't why.

It was because her mother wasn't with them. She was lost here, in New York—a whisper on the wind that blew across lower Manhattan.

Her grave.

Elena forced a smile. "Yes." She turned to leave.

"I'll walk you to where you're going."

Elena shook her head. "Thanks, but I'm here." She jerked a thumb at the building behind them. "My sister's place."

Another grin. Impossibly, it was more devastating than the first one. "Merry Christmas." He extended a hand. "I'm Lucas but everyone calls me Luke."

His attitude, the twinkle in his eyes, his smile, his dimples. Jeez, they could melt the snow under her feet, or under her – Oh God. She quickly dusted snow off her butt, feeling her face burn when his grin grew wider.

"I like your hat," he offered. "My mother would have loved that."

Loved—past tense.

Elena couldn't miss that. Her eyes snapped to his, held there, and yes, if she looked closely, she could see sadness under the twinkle. Courtesy demanded that she acknowledge his statement, but self-preservation compelled her to avoid it. Elena never spoke of her mother and the attack that killed her and did her best to not think of it. Discussing *his* mother would send her right back into that dark place she'd spent thirteen years clawing her way out of. Instead, she thrust out her hand, clasped his. "Merry Christmas to you, too. Thanks for rescuing me."

It couldn't have been warmer than twenty-five degrees and he had no gloves, but somehow, their brief connection shot a jolt of heat through her system.

When she failed to offer her name, Lucas shoved his hands back into his pockets and asked, "Can I give you a hand getting inside?"

"Um, no. I've got it. Thanks again." Elena took a definite step back.

The move made his hands come up, surrender-style. "Not a line, not a ploy, I promise."

"No, I didn't think it was. I just don't want to keep you from wherever you're going. You've already done a lot. Thank you."

"What's your name, pretty lady?" He angled his head and her mouth opened all by itself because her brain was completely entranced by that smile.

"Elena."

"Elena. Nice meeting you. Merry Christmas again."

"You, too. Merry Christmas."

She wheeled her suitcase and hefted her shopping bags through the door of her sister's building. When she looked back, the man with the supernova smile was gone and she sighed in relief.

And, maybe, just a little disappointment.

But mostly relief. She wasn't here for a holiday fling even if the guy did have the most amazing smile she'd seen in a long time. She pressed the buzzer for 4D.

"That you, Laney?"

"It's me."

"Yay!"

The buzzer sounded and Elena shoved open the inner

door that led to the elevator, which smelled faintly of garlic from someone's pizza delivery. When the doors slid open on the fourth floor, Kara stood there with open arms.

"Laney! Oh, God, thank you so much for coming!" Kara folded her into a hug.

"Ow! I just got kicked." Elena couldn't resist. She reached out and patted her sister's round tummy.

Kara winced. "Uh, sorry about that. Milk Dud's happy you're here, too."

Elena's lips twitched and a laugh bubbled out. "You don't seriously call my niece or nephew Milk Dud, do you?"

"Yes. I do."

Elena bit back her mirth when Kara whirled around and tried to stalk back into her apartment. At nearly nine months pregnant, the best she could manage was a fast shuffle. Elena followed her into the apartment and gasped. "Kara! This place is gorgeous!"

Kara grinned and put her hand over her belly. "It's amazing, right? Steven and I found it on our first day, after we decided to move in together." When her grin faded, Elena wanted to hunt down Steve Orland and peel the skin off his body for hurting her big sister.

"Have you heard from him?"

"Not since the stick turned blue, when he told me we'd both be better off without him." Kara said with a sad shake of her head. "But he does send money. Every month. Like a freakin' utility payment."

"Aw, honey."

Kara shook her head again, waved a hand. "No, no, no. Not going to cry one more tear over him. Come on, let me show you around."

The apartment had two bedrooms, each with its own bath, an efficiency kitchen that was separated from the living room by a breakfast bar, and a great big closet roomy enough to sleep in. Huge floor to ceiling windows graced every room, though the windows in the second bedroom were safety-gated. That room was already painted a soft green with stuffed animal critters happily romping over an entire wall behind a half-assembled crib. Beside the crib, there was a rocking chair next to a tiny table and bookcase, ready for story time. Boxes of baby equipment were stacked in another corner. An air bed was spread out on the floor, waiting for Elena.

"Oh, Kara, this is beautiful. Milk Dud's going to love this room.

Her sister beamed and her eyes misted. "I hope so. I can't wait for this baby to be born." And then she winced, put a hand to her back.

"You look really uncomfortable."

"Oh, God, I really am." They left the nursery and Kara shuffled back to the living room, carefully lowering herself to the sofa where a book of baby names waited with sticky notes marking a dozen pages. "The baby's low and if peeing every five minutes wasn't torture enough, I now have sciatica—which is why I just couldn't do the big Black Friday shopping thing."

Elena hadn't done their big Black Friday shopping thing in years, but said nothing. She stared at her sister's round tummy, searched for a change of subject. "By the look of you, I'd swear you love being pregnant. I always thought that glow stuff was bull but you've got it."

Kara smiled. "I guess I kind of do, even though I haven't seen my feet since the summer." Her smile dimmed. "Tell me the truth. Do they hate me?"

Elena's eyes snapped to Kara's. "Of course they don't. Enza even sent leftovers for you. They're all worried about you. And two of them are plotting revenge against Steve on your behalf."

Her sister laughed. "Let me guess. Aunt Enza and Bree?" Sabrina was one of the quartet of daughters all born the same year to former sorority sisters who'd met decades earlier at Bucknell University. Elena had been born two years later, but the girls—Sabrina, Cassandra, and Jade—had widened their circle to include Kara's little sister. Aunt Enza—Vincenza—was Sabrina's mother and because their own mother had called her *sister*, Elena and Kara would forever call her *aunt*. Now a hot-shot attorney, Enza could freeze, melt, or cut you with a single look. Elena bit back a grin. She sure as hell wouldn't want to be in Steve Orland's shoes when Enza finished torturing him but she'd make popcorn and grab a chair to watch while she did.

"I'll call them," Kara promised. She put a pillow behind her back, settled in, and held her book out to Elena. "What do you think of this name?"

"Um. Hmm. Walter Larsen. It's um, well—"

"Old-fashioned." Kara sighed. "What about this one?" She flipped to another marked page. "I kind of like Octavia."

Elena pulled the book gently from Kara's hand. "Kara, do you not remember elementary school at all?"

Another sigh. "Oh, God, you're right. They'd torment her, call her Octopus." Kara's face wobbled and she burst into tears. "What am I doing, Laney? I can't even pick out a name for this baby! I'm already a terrible mother."

"No, that's not true." Elena winced in sympathy. "Come on now. You have plenty of time. Lots of people don't name their babies until they're born. Ask Bree, she'll tell you the same thing."

"No, she won't. Bree's a great mom." Kara sniffled and grabbed a tissue from the box beside the sofa.

"And you will be, too. I know it."

Kara reached over, squeezed Elena's hand. "Damn hormones. I go off like a firecracker now. I left work—doctor says I have to take it easy and I have so much to do, Laney. The crib and diapers and a name and—"

"Then it's lucky I'm here."

"I'm *so* glad you are." She blew her nose.

"Okay, then. You just sit there with your feet up and give the orders."

Kara clapped. "Yay! First, tell me about the cute guy you were chatting up outside." At Elena's shocked face, Kara laughed. "I had my nose pressed to the window. I couldn't see much of him, but the look on your face was priceless."

Elena shot her sister an exasperated look. "Oh, what look? There was no look."

"There was most definitely a look." Kara pointed to the table near one of the windows. "Your first duty is to retrieve the phone I left way over there."

Elena fetched the phone and sank to the sofa beside her sister. Kara thumbed through her photos and showed Elena the picture she'd snapped earlier. She and Luke of the Radiant Smile were both crouched, hands extended for one of the bags. Too bad he was facing away from the camera. That smile would have been nice to see again.

"And there it is again." Kara clapped her hands and grinned.

"Will you stop? There is no look."

But there was. In the picture, Elena's eyes were aimed up at Luke and her mouth was open in a wide smile she didn't remember forming. She didn't just look surprised. She looked... well, like a kid on Christmas morning.

She slapped the phone to the cushion between them and leaped to her feet. "I'm going to get these bags unpacked and then cook you and Milk Dud a fantastic dinner." She flashed

Kara a bright but fake grin and disappeared into the second bedroom.

The second she shut the door, Elena's grin faded. Kara had been right; there was most definitely a look. With his mega-watt smile and twinkling eyes, Luke had made a hell of an impression. But that wasn't all. Luke *reminded* her of things she'd tried so hard to forget.

Tried, but never would.

Chapter Two

LUCAS ADAIR STRODE down the street, picking his way over icy patches and the occasional pile of unshoveled snow, still thinking about the blonde he'd just helped. He'd noted the building number, intending to find her again. He usually took the PATH train to lower Manhattan but today, something had urged him to get off and walk part of the way, to soak in some of the holiday cheer infecting the city. And then, some dick had to go and ruin his plan by shoving the blonde.

That girl. Damn. She was a sweetheart, the kind his mother would have been conspiring with her mother to set them up. She was gone now, his mom, one of the thousands lost in the horror that was September 11th. She'd had time to call home and leave a tearful message of goodbye.

He was one who played back that message.

Over and over and over.

Dad was already at work—on his Con Edison service crew. Lisa was away at college. Mean old Mrs. Fisher, his math teacher, had stepped out into the corridor for a hasty conversation with another teacher. When she came back into the classroom, she'd not only forgotten the trig problems on the board, she was crying tears the entire school had been sure her species was incapable of shedding. Lucas knew something was up. Something big. He didn't find out what until the principal's voice, tight and choked, crackled over the PA system, announcing that two planes had struck the twin towers and that we were under attack.

Attack.

The word had hung there, the PA system still hissing and crackling. And in that brief moment of silence before chaos erupted, he had time for one heart-stopping thought.

Mom.

She worked in 2 World Trade Center. They'd had a hell of a fight the night before about his laziness, his lack of interest or pride in anything. He'd mouthed off to her and she'd slapped him, hard, across the left cheek. He'd stalked off and gone to bed, cursing her until he'd fallen asleep.

Students screaming, crying and even fainting hauled him back to the moment. He sat there, his books still open to that stupid trig problem, when the sensation of a hand touching that same cheek sent a cold shiver skating down his back.

And he *knew* she was gone.

He stood up, bolted from the school and ran home, shouting for his mother the second he opened the front door. Nothing but the beep on the answering machine responded. He didn't want to press that button, didn't want to confirm what he already knew. But he had to hear her voice.

Hey, it's me…um… a plane crashed into my building…I'm okay…but…but…oh, God! There's a lot of smoke and fire and nobody knows where to go. The stairs are blocked. They're trying to get help but—I'm sorry. David, I love you. I've loved you since we were eighteen years old and wouldn't trade a minute of our life. Lisa, Lucas, I love you both so much. You two are my dreams come true. Don't roll your eyes, Lucas, it's true.

He'd had to squeeze them shut because he *had* rolled them just like she'd known he would.

I love you always and know you'll—

Her words were cut off by the sounds of shattering glass and an unearthly groan. People screamed and then the call disconnected. He'd played that tape a second time, a third time, a hundredth time, so many times.

His dad had found him sitting on the floor with the answering machine in his lap and his hand pressed to his cheek. Could anyone have gotten out? Escaped the collapse of all that steel and concrete? Hours later, while the world watched and waited for survivors to be pulled out of the wreckage, he sat with his hand still pressed against his cheek where the sensation of that phantom touch still lingered.

Somebody bumped him and he jolted out of the past, surprised to find his eyes damp.

"Sorry."

He waved off the woman's apology with a scowl. It was his fault. He was so caught up in memories, he wasn't paying attention to where he was going. He didn't have time for this. He had several projects at work quickly approaching their due dates plus the September's Families Guild holiday event scheduled for December 20th. With the holidays added into the fray, his frustration levels were at a personal all-time peak. There was no room on his to-do list for obsessing about the past.

It was something about that woman's smile. He knew she was important. He wasn't sure how yet. A horn honked and he sidestepped a slow-moving couple. Al, his closest friend, would insist meeting this woman was a sign. If Lucas hadn't been in such a bad mood, he wouldn't have needed an infusion of holiday cheer. And then, he wouldn't have decided to walk. Oh, yeah, it was a sign. His grin flashed for a brief moment and a woman walking past him faltered in her steps. He quickly lost the smile his mother had always called his secret weapon, and tried—in vain—not to feel that pang just under his heart every time he thought of her – her fear and her love in the moments right before she died.

At the corner, he waited for the light to turn green, hands deep in his jacket pockets, trying not to regret giving away his gloves to that homeless kid. Then again, that jolt of current, that sizzle of heat when he'd shaken pretty Elena's hand would have been obscured if he'd kept them. He could almost hear Almir saying, "Could be another sign, Luke!" Hell, she even wore a pin on her hat kind of like the ornament he'd given away.

Damn it, would he ever forget about that stupid ornament?

The smile twitched when he remembered just how furious Lisa had been to learn he'd given it away. He hadn't thought—he'd simply reacted. And he knew Mom would have done the same thing had she—

The grin completely disappeared when it struck him how completely moot that thought was. If she hadn't been killed, he wouldn't have had the crystal snowflake in the first place and there would have been no reason to give it away.

He looked up, up, up, shielding his eyes from the sun and stared at the tip of the Freedom Tower, feeling the same sense of pride—of love—he'd felt since the first time he'd been down here. He'd been sixteen years old then—braces on his teeth, acne marring his face, and a body like a puppy's—all paws.

They'd looked for her, of course. Hospitals, churches,

shelters. When the hours became days and the days became weeks, hope that she'd somehow gotten out faded and died. Mom was gone. And when the unspeakable pain of that fact dulled slightly, he'd learned to see—and appreciate—the acts of kindness humans managed to perform in the face of it. No, not the country's leaders because it was expected from them, but from the people who lived and worked right here. The tireless sifting from the first responders, the generosity of store owners who handed out water and shoes and towels, the looks that passed between complete strangers that said *I know. I know how bad it hurts.*

He didn't remember September fading into October or even November that year. Suddenly, it was December. Christmas time. His mother's favorite season. They'd decorated the house the way she loved it best. And then, one of those kind strangers invited them to Ground Zero for a special Holiday Remembrance for just the families of those lost.

There were thousands of them.

He'd had to wear a suit, which sucked, but he'd gotten to meet the mayor, which didn't. All the family members were encouraged to bring something, some small token that belonged to the people they'd each lost. Lisa had pressed one of his mom's Christmas ornaments into his hand that morning. Mom had collected them. This one was a crystal snowflake dotted with rhinestones. He'd gripped it tightly for hours—the train ride down from Newburgh, the taxi ride to the site, the long walk down the ramp to the pit.

That was where he saw her.

A girl—thirteen, maybe fourteen years old, standing on the ramp all alone. She had long wild blond hair that gleamed like the sun itself. But that wasn't what grabbed his attention. It was her eyes. Huge brown eyes filled with worse things than the pain they all felt. Hers held fear. Hatred. Guilt.

He'd recognized all three.

Her thin shoulders shook under the strength of it. He watched that storm in her eyes grow and grow and felt fear build inside him. He knew he had to do something—anything—to show her that she wasn't alone. He'd said something to her about light. *There's still light in the world.* Or something lame like that. And pressed his mother's snowflake into her hand, smiled down at her, and when some of that terrible grief left her eyes, he felt something—something so huge, so deep, so real—he'd never told anybody—not even Almir and God knows Al knew more about him than anybody else did.

It was too personal.

The girl had disappeared into the crowd and he never saw her again. He wished he had. He wished he'd kept the stupid ornament, when the darkness crept in and nearly blinded him.

The light turned green and he strode down the street to September's Families Guild, where he volunteered his time and considerable energy to helping families like his cope with their losses. He'd stayed close because New York was where his family had always lived—and now, died. For Luke, it was critical to never forget, to never let fear swallow him. He lived in Hoboken now, in a condo with a view of Manhattan that made his breath catch every time he looked.

He opened a door, stepped inside the main office for the SFG, the same group responsible for organizing that first Holiday Remembrance back in 2001. Over a dozen years later, the annual Remembrance was an event that celebrated life instead of mourned it and that was a mission Luke could get behind. He was on this year's planning committee and with just a few weeks to go until the big event, operating on nothing more than coffee fumes.

"Hey, Therese," he called out to a girl in Goth gear running off copies.

"Luke." She blew black bangs out of her eyes. "Bad news. Kara Larsen is out. Doctor says it's time for her to park it until the little rugrat pops out."

Luke groaned. "Crap. I was really hoping for another week or two." He thought of the dozen or so tasks on their to-do list and tried not to run screaming for a cruise ship heading to the tropics. "Is she okay?"

"She's fine. The baby's low—"

He shot up a hand. "I don't need the play-by-play."

Therese smirked. "Sciatic pain. Trouble walking."

"Good. Great," Luke said with a sigh of relief. "Okay, where's the RSVP list? I'll work on those damn seating charts. Can you order-"

"Already did."

"You're awesome." He grinned and Therese rolled her black-rimmed eyes.

SFG had dozens of volunteers who worked on various projects designed to aid families who'd suffered losses during the attacks. Luke was the chairperson for all things related to the annual Holiday Remembrance. Every year, he promised himself this would be his last. And every year, he found himself raising his hand to volunteer for next year's. His committee consisted of ten volunteers—nine now that Kara was out.

He strode into a tiny office, jerked his head in greeting toward his group. "Any reply from the mayor's office yet?"

"Yeah. He's a yes, but has to leave by nine for another engagement."

"Another engagement?" Lucas cocked a hip and stared at Jenny, the youngest member of his committee, who squirmed under his glare, gripping a steno pad like it was Captain

America's shield. Lucas forced himself to smile though his jaw was tightly clenched. "Fine," he said with forced patience. "We'll move his speech to first."

"Um, we can't. We have the keynote first."

"Right." Lucas shrugged out of his jacket with a loud sigh. "Okay, let's get the schedule up on a white board and see where we can shuffle."

Several hours later, Luke's eyes felt like they'd been thoroughly sandblasted. He'd managed to finalize the line-up of speeches and finished the seating plan. He clicked the send key on his computer and shot the seating plan to the other committee chairpersons. The venue the SFG had selected for this year's event was just a few blocks away, the Skyline Hotel. Their Grand Ballroom could comfortably seat four hundred guests. SFG had sent out this year's invitations in October with a November RSVP date, starting a wait list after they'd received four hundred confirmations. The room was located on an upper level and had a breathtaking view of the September 11th Memorial.

"I'll be glad when this is over." Luke kicked back in his chair, shut eyes he was sure were bleeding, and thought about reheating another pizza slice in the tiny microwave but couldn't summon enough energy.

"Few more weeks, Luke, and you can fly to Tahiti, kick back with a drink with an umbrella in it, and rub oil into some woman's back." His best friend, Al, laughed, clicking through the file Lucas sent, looking for any stray typos.

"Oh," Luke said on a moan. "What I wouldn't give to do that right this minute."

"Hey, Luke. Sleep on your own time. This lady claims her sister sent her to help."

Luke pried his eyes open at Therese's voice and found her standing beside *her*—the hot beauty he'd met earlier. The pretty

Elena. He jerked, gasped.

"You should go home. You look like crap," Therese remarked.

Luke shot her a wry smile. "Thank you. Thanks a lot. I'm Luke. Lucas Adair." He extended a hand toward the pretty blonde. When her eyes fixed on the scar that rode the entire side of Al's face, he quickly added, "This is Almir Suliman."

"But you can call me Al." He stood.

"Hi," she replied, shaking their hands. "I'm Elena. Elena Larsen."

"Kara's sister?" Al frowned. "We just heard she's under doctor's orders to say home."

"Oh, she's fine. The doctor doesn't want her walking far. That's why I'm here—she sent me to help."

Luke smiled a wide slow grin. "Did she now?" *Merry Christmas to me.* "God bless her." He dragged over a chair, all but shoved her into it. Elena's eyes darted to his mouth and her face went slack for a moment. When she shook herself, as if out of a trance, Luke swallowed his grin. He knew that look. Oh, she liked him, he was sure of it. There was something electric in the air between them, something he intended to pursue.

"Are you hungry? We've got some pizza left—" Al waved a hand toward a pile of pizza boxes.

"No, I'm good. Just had a huge meal."

"Excellent. Well, we've got programs to finalize, a menu to confirm, favor bags to stuff, decorations to arrange—"

"Whoa, whoa!" Elena held up both hands. "One thing at a time." Her eyes, brown to contrast with the blond hair, looked horrified.

"There's a lot of work to do," Luke said, annoyed.

"And I just got here. I don't know anything about everything you just said," Elena protested.

"Don't worry. We'll teach you." He went to the door, cupped his hands to be heard over the din. "Everybody, drop what you're doing. Let's get the favor bags started." That was an easy, though time-consuming task. He strode to a conference room whose enormous table was littered with boxes in assorted sizes and stared at the piles of donated favors. They needed to fill four hundred bags.

A chorus of groans went up as Luke's committee dragged their feet to the large conference room.

"Wow," Elena said, ogling the contents of the room. "That's a lot of swag."

Curious eyes swung toward Elena so Lucas raised his hands to shush the room. "Everybody, this is Elena Larsen, Kara's sister, on loan to us for the duration."

"Did Kara have her baby?"

"Is she okay, we heard—"

Lucas let out a shrill whistle to quiet the group. "Kara did not have her baby yet. She's on doctor's orders to rest so Elena is helping out. Save your questions for later. I want to get this moving."

"Um, sorry, boss, but I've got to get home." Therese shook her head.

Luke glanced at the watch strapped to his wrist and cursed. "Okay. Fine. Who's walking with Therese tonight?"

When nobody replied, Lucas pointed a finger at a husky guy barely into his twenties. "Jason. You do it. Anybody else need to leave right this minute? Figure out who's walking with who. Nobody—"

"Walks alone." The group finished for him in unison.

Lucas laughed, shook his head. It took about ten minutes for the goodnights, but soon, the room had been reduced to just five people.

"Hey, Elena. I'm Debbie." A tall woman smiled. "Who did

you lose?"

When Elena's face lost its color, Lucas shot Debbie a look and strode over to the table in the center of the room, hoping a fast change of subject would help. "We've got everything arranged in stations. Over here, you've got your empty tote bags." Luke showed her the flattened gift bags in silver bearing the SFG logo. "Open the bag, start here, pull one of each from these piles until you make it all the way around the room. Then, put the full bags here, on this cart." The cart was a big rack on wheels and should hold a few hundred bags.

"Aye, aye, Captain." Al bowed and added a little wave of his hand. Lucas swallowed the curse he would have shot back had they been alone.

Elena's beautiful brown eyes went round as she scanned the huge conference room. "Okay. Let's get to it." She grabbed a bag, gave it a snap to open it, and started her circuit around the table, filling the bag as she went. She finished it off with a wad of tissue paper and put the finished bag on the first shelf. "That's one. Only three hundred and ninety-nine to go."

"That's the spirit." Luke held up his hand for a high five. When the same sizzle shot up his arm, he entertained a brief fantasy of swiping everything off the long table that filled that the conference room, laying Elena over it, and kissing every inch of her body.

"Luke?"

He jerked when Al's hand waved in front of his eyes. "Oh, uh, sorry."

"You okay?"

"Yeah. Fine." He avoided Al's gaze and got to work.

✦ ✦ ✦

ELENA HAD A moment of panic when Luke got lost in his own

little world. Was she safe with him, a man she'd known for a grand total of twenty-seven minutes? But when he'd smiled that panty-dropping grin of his, she forgot what she was supposed to be afraid of. *Don't stare at the smile.* It was a freakin' weapon of mass seduction, she concluded. How there wasn't a deli counter take-a-number system outside his door, she had no idea.

Favor bags. Right. She grabbed two more bags, snapped them open and filled two at once. When she'd made it all the way around the table, she found Al watching her with a gleam in his eye.

"I've got an idea," he began. "I'm getting punchy and want to go to bed, so let's make this a race."

"What kind of race?" Debbie crossed arms over her impressive chest.

"Just a little contest. Let's see who can fill the most bags in an hour. Winner buys the loser a cup of coffee."

"Pass." Elena was too tired to race and definitely not interested in coffee.

Al laughed. "I figured the ladies would cave. There's no beating me." He thrust both hands in the air, champion style.

"Please." Elena scoffed. "It's not like bag stuffing requires any degree of strength or agility. I can stuff just as well as you can."

"Guess we'll never know." He taunted. Beside him, Lucas smiled and shook his head and she almost forgot what they'd been talking about.

"Okay, fine. Let's just do this." Damn it, she had to stop looking at the Smile. It was making her do all sorts of things not in her nature. Feel all sorts of things she didn't have time to feel.

Al took out his phone, set the clock for thirty minutes. "Ready? Annnnd go!"

Debbie raced to the box of flat bags, took out two, looping them onto one arm. Elena grabbed four bags and did the same thing. They circled the table, scooping favors into each bag.

"Good idea, Al." Lucas elbowed his friend.

"I thought so." Al crossed his arms. "Think we should fill a few bags of our own?"

Elena cleared her throat.

Loudly.

"Okay, okay." Lucas laughed. He stepped behind Elena, grabbed several bags and snapped them open.

"No fair! You copied my idea."

"Anything goes, baby," he shot back, snatching Greyline Tour Bus tickets from her hand, tucking them into a bag on his arm.

She got even at the box of pens from a lower Manhattan business by blocking him with her body. He tried elbowing her out of his way, but she held her ground until he bodily lifted her up and behind him. "Whoa, whoa, you're a cheater!"

Laughing, he tried to block her from accessing the box of passes to the *Intrepid Sea, Air, and Space Museum*. She knew she couldn't possibly lift him out of her path, so she squeezed his biceps, not expecting to feel such…such definition. Her mouth went dry.

At the first touch from her fingers, Luke froze and his eyes slipped shut. So caught up in the magic of that simple touch, neither of them said anything until Al cleared his throat and said, "Uh, guys?"

Luke's eyes snapped open and he shot up both hands in a T-shape. "Time out! Personal foul," Lucas objected.

"Anything goes, baby," she gleefully reminded him.

The timer went off and Elena nearly flushed as red as Debbie's sweater when she looked around to find Debbie and

Al sitting with their feet up. Her eyes darted to Lucas, but he only shrugged and grinned. "Come on, loser. I owe you coffee."

But Elena shook her head. "I really hate coffee," she admitted. "How about hot chocolate, instead?"

His smile widened. "I make the best hot cocoa ever poured."

At Debbie's audible gasp, Elena's faced heated and she had to look away.

Lucas just kept right on grinning.

He wasn't giving up that easily.

Chapter Three

"So, Elena. How long are you staying in the city?" Al asked from his side of the corner booth in a nearby diner.

Both women sat opposite the men. Lucas used the opportunity to study Elena Larsen. Brown eyes that contrasted with the sleek blond hair that just skimmed her shoulders, lush lips he couldn't wait to kiss—

He jerked out of his fantasy and Al looked at him. "What's wrong?"

Shrugging, Luke reached for the little basket of sugar packets and tried to stop staring at Elena.

"Until the end of January. I can work remotely until after Kara's baby comes. She's due soon so I thought I'd help her get settled since she's alone." Elena's mouth went flat.

Debbie nodded. "We heard something about Kara's boyfriend being out of the picture. What kind of guy does that?"

Elena said something and raised her cup to her lips. Luke's stomach tightened when his eyes locked on her mouth. Her lips were perfect and for a moment, he had this fierce wish to be the cup. He managed to focus on the last part of Elena's sentence—something about the baby's crib.

"Wait, why can't you build it?"

"We have to get special tools. Like a special screwdriver."

She held up her hands to shape something that looked kind of angular. And then he got it. "Ah. An Allen wrench. I've got a set of them. I'll lend it to you."

Al cocked his head. "Or, you could just build the crib, Luke."

Elena's gaze bounced from Al to Luke. "You could?"

With a deadly glare shot at Al, Lucas finally nodded. "Yeah. I can come by tomorrow, if that's okay."

Elena blinked and shook her head. "No, don't worry about it. We'll figure it out."

He sighed and then his hand squeezed hers. "Elena. I know Kara's having a rough time and this is something I can do to make it a little smoother. Okay?"

Elena studied him for a moment and he only barely managed not to squirm under her intense stare.

"What?"

She flushed, lowered her eyes. "I'm sorry. I'm just not used to people like you."

Luke's eyebrows lifted at her direct attack and he might have asked what she meant by that remark, but decided he really didn't care that much.

Al, however, did. "People like him? What does that mean?"

"Al." Lucas put a warning hand on Al's shoulder, but he shrugged it off.

"No, Luke, I want to know what the hell that means."

"Forget it. It doesn't mean anything." Elena waved a hand impatiently.

"Elena, you just met us, but let me tell you something. Lucas Adair is the best man I know."

"Oh boy." Luke's head dropped. "Say goodnight, Al."

Elena leaned back and bit her lip. "I'm sorry. It's just people never do stuff for nothing, you know? Everybody always wants something."

Luke frowned. "That's awfully cynical in someone who's—what? Twenty-five?"

She snapped up straight. "I'm twenty-seven."

He stared at her for a moment and then slid out of the booth. "The offer stands," he said without smiling.

"I'm sorry, you guys," she muttered.

Al sighed. "I'm sorry, too, Elena." he patted her hand. "He's my closest friend and I don't like to see him unfairly judged. Give him a chance, okay?"

"Understood." She raised both hands, rubbed her face. She'd never intended to insult anybody. "So what's the story?" At their blank looks, she elaborated. "It's Friday night. You guys are all single, right? How come nobody's cell phone is buzzing with invitations and booty calls?"

"Just got dumped," Debbie admitted, brushing dark hair out of her eyes.

Oh. She hadn't considered that. "Ouch. That sucks."

Debbie sipped from her cup, gave her half a grin. "She said I wasn't serious. And she was right. I'm *not* serious. Life's too short not to have some fun, you know?"

She? Oh. Oh!

Well, Elena knew all about the caprice of life. But having fun? No. No, that wasn't possible these days. Her eyes tracked Lucas, who'd walked across the diner to chat with the server. The server was now looking at him like he'd just walked out of a flying saucer.

"What's up over there?" She jerked her chin at the drama.

Al followed her gaze and grinned. "Like I said. He's the best guy I know."

At her blank look, Debbie provided the details. "Luke is all about the random acts of kindness, you know? He's probably picking up the tab for somebody. Who do you think it is?" She turned to Al.

Al scanned the diner. "That old lady by the window."

"Uh uh. I think it's the couple in the corner."

Elena's belly did a little roll. "He pays for people's meals? That is so sweet."

"Yeah, but don't make a big deal out of it, okay? It weirds him out."

How could she not? It *was* a big deal. Lucas Adair was a good man. Saving her from thugs, building cribs, volunteering hours—Lucas had gotten under her skin in a matter of minutes. She watched the server approach a young couple in the back of the diner. They couldn't have been out of their teens. The server pointed at Lucas and the couple grinned and waved.

He should have a good woman—not somebody who sucked the happiness out of everyone around her.

You ruin everything, Laney!

If she had a dollar for every time Kara or her brothers had said that, she'd be living on a private island.

When Lucas returned to their booth and sat down, she hid her face in her cup, refusing to look at him.

"So where's home?" Al finally asked when the silence grew long.

"These days, it's Florida. We moved soon after—" Abruptly, she clamped her lips together. She would not speak of that day. She simply would not.

But they knew.

"I lost my brother that day," Debbie revealed. "Al lost his dad. Who'd you lose?"

"Guys. Enough." Luke's voice was a whip.

"No, no. It's okay." Elena took a deep breath. It was kind of nice talking to people who didn't just feel sorry for her, but were dealing with the same pain themselves. "I lost my mom."

"Oh. You and Luke have something in common. He lost his mom, too."

That cracked the shields around Elena's heart. Elena slid Luke a glance over the rim of her hot chocolate. He was potent, like the coffee he drank. There was simply no diluting him. Dark hair that begged for a woman's fingers to rake, those eyes with the crinkles at the corners. And the—

No! Damn it, not the smile. But it was a flash of teeth and then it was gone. He sipped from his cup and abruptly, the grief descended on Elena again.

"How do you all stand being here?" she whispered.

Al smiled for a second and then turned to stare out the window. "I can't leave. My dad's spirit is out here, somewhere. I can't leave that—him."

Elena frowned. "Spirit? You believe that stuff?"

Al gave her half a shrug. "Sure. Not like a ghost or anything. Just little things. Signs, you know? I like to surround myself with them."

Signs. That sounded a lot like faith that Elena no longer had. "Well, that's all that matters," she offered in her best noncommittal, not judgmental tone.

He nodded. "Kara told me your mom worked for Burke & Kirkpatrick. Yours did, too, right, Luke?"

"Almir. Leave it alone," Luke warned.

Elena's blood chilled. She hadn't known that. How could she? They'd just met. "Your mom worked for Burke & Kirkpatrick?" Had they been friends? Had her mother told his mother all about her and her wild mood changes and all the crap she'd dished out on a daily basis? Had her mother told his mother what Elena's last words to her had been? She rubbed her chest, where the guilt still burned.

Luke nodded again. "Yeah. They were risk managers in the same department. I work at Burke & Kirk now, too. In IT."

He sipped more coffee, as if it were the most natural thing in the world to discuss their mothers in the past tense. She put her back against the seat rest, stared out the window, and let her cocoa go cold. Her hand kept creeping back to her chest, rubbing the ache.

"So, what kind of work do you do that you get to work remotely?"

"I'm a technical writer. I write instruction guides and help systems."

"Oh, you're in IT, too?" Al's grin got wide and just a little bit wicked. "Luke's head of development at Burke & Kirk. Lucas, you have to try out some of those software developer pick-up lines on someone who gets them."

"No."

Elena's lips twitched and she groaned just for form. Inside, she was grateful for the change of subject. "Okay. Gimme one. Let's see what you got."

"No."

"Come on, Luke! Don't be such a dick." Al elbowed him.

"No. And don't call me a dick."

"Please? I want to hear these, too." Debbie patted the table between them.

"Okay, okay. You asked for it." Luke rubbed his hands together and gave Elena a smoldering look, dropped his voice down an octave. "I hope you're broadband, baby, because I really want high-speed access." He wiggled his eyebrows.

Elena rolled her eyes. "That's terrible."

"Yeah, man, that was awful," Al agreed.

"I warned you."

"Come on, do another one," Debbie said.

Elena put out a hand. "Please don't use the obvious puns on *RAM* or *motherboards*."

Lucas looked at her sideways. "Please. This isn't my first program."

She snorted and let him continue. Luke took her hand and leaned in real close. "Baby, you overclock my processor but trust me, there's no part of my body that's micro or soft." He delivered the final words with his eyes locked on hers.

Elena stared into his dark eyes and felt herself melting, weakening, and might have leaned over the table to fuse her mouth to his had Debbie not burst into laughter, breaking the spell. She laughed, too, to hide her growing discomfort.

Luke stared at her, his dark eyes strangely guarded. She stopped laughing when the waitress dropped two bills on their table along with a snarky comment about starting a collection, and saw Luke's face redden. He squirmed, swallowed hard, abruptly grabbed the two scraps of paper and headed to the register.

When he returned to their table, she avoided his gaze, busying herself with hat, gloves, coat, and purse. The man—with his volunteer efforts and enthralling smile and kindness to strangers—nobody could be this good, she decided. Maybe it was all just a ploy. Maybe he was nothing more than veneer. Well, she had neither the time nor the interest in diving beneath that surface.

She shoved her hand through the shoulder strap of her bag and extended it in farewell. "Well, thank you for the cocoa and the company. I suppose we'll see you at the Remembrance event—assuming Kara doesn't go into labor, of course."

"Nice meeting you." Debbie held out her hand.

Luke put up his hands. "Whoa, whoa, whoa—did you hear what I said earlier? Nobody walks alone."

Here we go. "Look, Lucas. I'm sure you're a great guy, but

I'm only here for a few weeks and I've got a packed schedule with work, shopping, building the crib for Kara's baby, not to mention all the details we still need to finalize before the big night. I appreciate the attempt, but I'm just not interested."

Beside her, Al and Debbie exchanged a knowing glance.

The smile—that patently potent source of power—fled. His eyes cooled and his shoulders straightened. "Never said I was interested, Elena. All I said was nobody walks alone."

She bit her lip. "I'm sorry, I didn't mean—"

He turned his back and strode to the exit.

Uncomfortable, the remaining three followed.

"Damn, it's friggin' freezing out here," Debbie complained. "No gloves again, Luke? Who got them this time? Homeless guy? Some kid on the subway?"

Lucas didn't respond. Elena glanced up at him, saw the tight expression on his face and didn't press. The wind was biting so they walked in silence at a fast clip, exchanged terse goodbyes with Al and Debbie at the subway station and said nothing more on their brisk walk back to Kara's building.

"Goodnight, Luke. Thanks again." Elena opened the door and turned back to wave.

Big mistake.

In the glare of a streetlight, she instantly saw that Lucas wasn't quiet because she'd turned him down. No, Lucas was quiet because he was pissed. A slow and steady rage had been bubbling beneath that veneer of his—his jaw was so tightly clenched, she marveled that his teeth hadn't cracked under the pressure. Guilt burned in her gut. With a resigned sigh, she started her apology. "Luke—"

"'night," he said. Hard to have been more brief.

"Wait!" She called when he strode away. He halted, but didn't turn. "I'm sorry. I didn't mean –"

"Don't sweat it," he cut in. "Players like me just move on

to the next name in the contact list, baby."

Okay. She had been a bit presumptuous on that point. "I apologize for making—"

"Noted. Goodnight." He turned, waited for her to enter the building.

His icy tone shot straight through her and all she could think, all she could see, was that she'd made him stop smiling. She wanted to apologize, wanted to throw her arms around him and beg his forgiveness, do whatever it took to put the light back in his eyes, but before she could, he stepped in front of her, shoved open the door to Kara's building, practically pushed her inside, and was gone.

Elena watched him stalk down the block, unable to deny the terrible feeling deep in her heart that she'd just lost a precious gift.

Chapter Four

LUCAS STEPPED ONTO the train, found a seat and shifted in annoyance when something stabbed his butt. Someone had left a—a seashell on the PATH train?

He cast his eyes to heaven and sighed heavily. "Really?" He picked up the shell, stared at it for a long moment and finally tucked into his pocket with a small smile.

The ride wasn't long and soon he was jogging the few blocks to his condo. He unlocked his door and managed not to throw his keys at the wall. The nerve of that woman—all but accusing him of being a player. Hell, he could have stolen half a dozen kisses tonight while they'd stuffed those prize bags but hadn't attempted one because his mother had taught him to respect women, not play with them. Then, he got insulted anyway.

He was better off, he told himself. She had some serious baggage. And, as she'd so clearly outlined, she wouldn't be here that long. He locked the door, stripped off his outer gear and hung it in the stingy closet in the hall, slamming the door behind him. He stalked into his bedroom, stripped to his boxers and flung his clothes across the room, which made him feel only marginally better. Okay, so maybe he did have ulterior motives—he liked her, found her attractive and smart and interesting. She seemed like a nice person he might have wanted to spend time with. It was Christmas, after all. He flipped the covers over and flopped into bed, gave the pillow a punch or two and groaned.

The baby's crib.

The hell with it and her. Let her build it herself. He fell asleep, doing his damndest – and failing miserably – to dream about anything except tiny babies trapped in collapsing cribs. At seven AM on a Saturday morning, he stalked back to his closet, opened the bright red toolbox he kept high on a shelf, and found himself staring at his Allen keys, right on top.

Okay. Fine.

He'd build the damn crib and make a fast retreat before things got weird. He would be pleasant around Elena for Kara's sake.

He grabbed his phone and sent a text message to Kara, inviting himself over as soon as she was up to it. To his astonishment, she texted back immediately.

I'm up. I haven't slept in a month.
Come over whenever you want and
I'll make you breakfast. You rock!

Thirty minutes later, Lucas was standing outside the door to Kara Larsen's building. She'd been volunteering with the SFG for years, but for some reason, he'd never been the one who'd walked her home. He pondered that for a minute. Al would say he obsessed over it, but he preferred *pondered* because it implied a certain detachment. It wasn't like he really believed it was one of Al's irritating signs.

She buzzed him inside and he stepped out of the elevator,

surprised to find her waiting at the door to her apartment.

"Hey, Kara. How you feeling?"

She rolled big brown eyes so much like Elena's and shot him a wry grin. "About as good as I look."

"Well, you must feel amazing then."

"Sweet talker." She waved a hand, stood aside to let him in. "What's this?"

"The firehouse was selling them so I picked one up for you." He held out the fragrant wreath he'd just bought on his way from the PATH station to her door.

"Lucas! Thank you. I haven't had the energy to do anything for Christmas."

Luke propped the wreath against a table, dropped his toolbox beside it, and led Kara to the sofa. "Lie down." When she had, Luke covered her with the blanket folded over the back of the sofa and grabbed a dog-eared copy of a baby name book. "Wow. You've got a lot of potentials here."

"Yeah, but nothing that sings, you know?"

"Do you know what you're having?"

Kara shook her head. "No, I want to be surprised. I pick up the phone a dozen times a day to call my doctor and ask, but then I remember how few surprises like that there are in life, you know, where both possible options are equally good?"

Luke thought about that for a moment and nodded. "I never thought about it like that, but you're right." He looked around. "So where's the crib?"

Kara bit her lip. "Um, about that. I was so excited about you building the crib, I forgot that my sister's sleeping in that room."

Luke's mood chilled. Elena. Right.

"What do you think of Stella?"

"Who?"

Kara laughed. "Not a who yet… I mean for the baby."

"Um, Stella?" Lucas immediately thought of a lifetime of Stanleys shouting that name and shook his head. "No."

"Crap," Kara sighed and covered her face with the book. "Why is this so hard?"

Lucas had no answer for her. He pointed to a closed door. "Is it okay if I wake her up?"

She peered out from behind the book and waved a hand. "Yeah, go ahead. She's got plans today. She promised me Christmas cookies." Kara rubbed her belly in anticipation.

His lips split into a wicked grin. This was going to be fun. He grabbed his toolbox and headed for the closed door.

Chapter Five

"GOOD MORNING, SUNSHINE! Time to greet the day!" A cheerful voice cut into the dream she'd been enjoying—the very hot dream about a guy with a brilliant smile wearing nothing but a Santa hat—

Wait.

The voice had *not* been her sister's.

Elena jack-knifed upright, heart hammering at her ribcage, and found Lucas Adair in her bedroom. "What? What happened? Where's Kara?"

"Whoa, whoa, whoa! Take it easy. I'm here to build the crib so I need you to vacate the room."

Elena pressed a hand to her chest, tried to quiet her racing heart, and narrowed her eyes. "You want me to leave? At—" she tapped the cell phone she'd left beside the air mattress—"eight o'clock in the freakin' morning?"

Luke stared down at her, no twinkle in his eyes and no smile on his lips. "Just get up so I can put the damn crib together and get out of your life."

Elena rubbed sleep from her eyes and sighed. "Lucas, I am so sorry about everything I said last night. If you'll let me, I'd like to start over."

He considered that for a minute. "I'll think about it. If you spend the day with me."

"Why would you want to do that?" She looked at him sideways.

He crouched down, dropped the toolbox and rubbed his chin. "Damned if I know. Come on, give me a chance."

She flopped back down on her air mattress. "Fine. I'll see you in an hour or two."

"Oh, no you don't." Luke punctuated his comment with a rip of the cap on the air mattress and in seconds, Elena's comfortable bed sagged to the hard floor.

She snapped aside her blanket and stalked around him to the apartment's single bathroom, across the hall.

"Good morning! How come you didn't tell me—"

Elena slammed the bathroom door on her sister's greeting and took care of business behind the locked door. When she emerged a few minutes later, Elena was astonished to find Kara in the kitchen cooking breakfast.

"What the hell are you doing?" she demanded.

"Good morning to you, too." Kara put a cup of instant cocoa into Elena's hands.

"Kara, what is *he* doing here?"

"He texted me this morning about the crib. And look!" She clapped her hands and pointed to a wreath lying against the end table. "He brought a wreath. It's totally Christmas now."

Elena smelled the evergreen and her stomach kinked. It *did* smell like Christmas, just the way she remembered it. How could Kara be so damn cheerful about that? Christmas hadn't been worth celebrating since they were in high school.

"Laney? Oh, honey, I'm sorry."

Elena blinked, found Kara standing beside her looking all

glum, and her guilt levels shot to redline. "No! No, it's okay. I just got scared, you know? Strange guy in my room, startling me out of a sound sleep—"

"Laney, you met Luke and spent hours working with him. He's certainly not a stranger. Besides, he told me you *asked* him to do the crib."

Elena's eyes narrowed. "Oh, did he?" She moved to the pan her sister had already buttered, and cracked some eggs into it, determined to put some food in her sister's mouth so she'd stopped talking about Lucas.

Kara didn't notice her sarcasm. She was still gushing about him. "…and everybody at SFG will tell you he's a great guy. And, he's single."

"So ask him out if he's so wonderful," Elena mumbled.

Kara's jaw dropped. "Not me, you nut. You."

"Not interested."

"Oh, Laney. You are *so* interested, it hurts." Kara shook her head. "Come on! I know he's the guy who picked up your bags yesterday. Remember that look?"

Elena slammed a drawer shut. "Kara. There was no look. I'm here to help you through this pregnancy, not be on the next episode of The Bachelor, okay? Give it a rest!"

There was silence for a long moment.

"Yeah," Kara finally whispered. "Yeah, okay."

Elena didn't dare look at her sister. She heard Kara shuffle back to her spot on the sofa and cursed silently. She'd promised herself this visit, this Christmas would be different. No flipping out. No angry outbursts. She'd promised she'd be here for Kara and the baby. Here they were, not even twenty-four hours later, and she'd already snapped. She cut the heat under the pan, stalked back to the bathroom. She needed a shower. A hot shower to soothe her frayed nerves and then she'd apologize to her sister. Make things right.

Do what she'd promised her she'd do.

All this tension—she knew it was her fault. Knew it, but hadn't the first clue how to stop it. She turned on the tub, tested the water, switched it over to shower. Maybe it was because Kara was older, Elena supposed. She'd *adjusted*. She'd *moved on*. Elena hadn't, and couldn't see how she ever would.

No, she decided, shampooing her hair.

No, it was more than that.

Kara's relationship with Mom had always been easy. Fun. They'd been best friends. Elena had always been the one in the way. Her mother's eyes had never crinkled at the corners for her but they had for Kara. Kara was a different person. Mellow. Easy-going. Nothing bothered her. Nothing upset her. But Elena? Elena could burst into tears or laughter and back again at a moment's notice.

You ruin everything, Laney.

Kara's favorite words. Elena must have heard them a thousand times. The first time she'd heard them, she'd been about eleven or twelve. Mom had taken them to the mall to buy Kara a cell phone. They'd looked and looked and Elena had helpfully compared all the features and picked out the best phone in the bunch. It came in purple—*purple was her favorite*—with a slide-out keyboard so she could text all her friends.

But then Mom had said only Kara was getting a phone that day. It wasn't fair—just because she wasn't in high school like Kara didn't mean she wasn't *special* too. High school was still years away. And when Kara pointed to the pretty purple phone that should have been hers and even stuck out her tongue behind Mom's back, Elena had snapped.

In front of about a thousand people, she'd stamped her foot and screamed that it wasn't fair that Kara *got* everything and *got away* with everything but all Elena ever *got* was yelled at. Mom had hustled them out of the cell phone store, called her bratty, selfish, and spoiled, and they'd left the store empty-handed. Back in the car, Kara cried. *I won't be able to text Bree and Jade and Cass because of you! You ruin everything, Laney.*

She finished her rinse, turned off the water and wrapped herself in a towel.

Kara had never questioned Mom. When Mom had wanted something done, Kara had done it, no questions asked.

Elena had been all about the questions. She'd loved Mom, more than anything—she loved her. But Mom had been so strict about every little thing and sometimes—okay, all the time—Elena had fought for more.

I hate you for this! I hate you so much and wish you'd drop dead!

She squeezed her eyes shut, tried to breathe over the fire in her chest, and put the memories firmly out of her head. When she emerged from the bathroom, dressed for the day, a coat of makeup for protection, she found Lucas in the kitchen frying eggs.

"Where's Kara?"

"Gone."

"Gone?" Panic rose in her throat. "What? Where? She's not supposed to walk—"

"Relax. She didn't. Someone named Cass showed up. They left about five minutes ago. Something about cookie day."

"Oh, Christ, she can't do that." Elena scrubbed two hands over her face. "Aunt Enza's cookie days are marathons. She could pull a muscle. She could end up in early labor!" Where was her cell phone? The phone beeped as soon as she picked it up.

> I'm fine. Thought we could both use some space. I'll be home tomorrow. Still love you.

She called Kara. "Kara, honey, I'm so sorry."

"Laney, stop. It's my fault. I shouldn't have invited you

here. I know how you feel about Christmas and New York and Mom and I just needed you because I was stupid and in love and got pregnant and now I've blown it! I'm sorry," Kara cried.

Elena grabbed a paper towel off the rack over Kara's sink. "No, *I'm* sorry. I don't know what's wrong with me. I shouldn't have yelled and I'm sorry." She wiped her eyes. "You're not stupid. You trusted somebody and he hurt you. *I'm* the one who ruins everything, remember?"

"Laney, sweetie, please. I *need* you to be part of my baby's life. Without Mom—oh, Laney, I miss her so much. I want to be the kind of mom she was and Laney, I..." Kara's voice trailed off for a moment. "I don't think I can do that alone. Please, *please* tell me you'll forgive me and stay?"

"Forgive you?" Elena swallowed hard. "No, no, there's nothing to forgive, Kara. Nothing! I'll apologize to your friend. Luke's been nothing but sweet to me and I dumped all my issues on both of you. Please come back."

She'd do anything—even do Christmas with all the trappings if it would make Kara smile. Anything except the *stay* part.

"Oh, Laney."

Elena heard static.

"Elena, can you hear me?"

Cassandra had her on speaker.

"Yeah, hi, Cass."

"Listen. I'm taking Kara out to Long Island so Aunt Enza can spoil her for a day. She needs it and so do you. Walk around the city. Cry. Scream at Ground Zero. Get it out of your system. When I bring her home, I need you to have your head on straight."

"Okay. I will. I'm sorry, Cass."

✦ ✦ ✦

LUCAS WATCHED ELENA end the call and toss the phone on the sofa beside her. He'd heard nearly every word the sisters exchanged before Elena hid in the bathroom, and applauded Kara for not putting up with it. But now, he could see the misery on Elena's face and wasn't sure what he'd walked into. He considered making up some excuse, making a fast exit.

And then she looked up at him with those big soft eyes.

"Lucas, will you sit down for a minute?"

Well, there went his shot at a fast exit. He regarded her for a moment and nodded, then sat beside her on the sofa, putting his toolbox on the floor beside the table.

"I owe you an apology. I—well, I have a hard time with people."

"Could try being nice." The retort danced off his tongue before he could think twice.

Elena flinched. "Like you?"

His face clouded. "I'm not nice."

She looked at him sideways. "Oh, please. According to the SFG crew, you walk on water."

He considered telling her his darkest secret—the secret that proved he wasn't nice at all. Instead, he held up his hands. "Look. I don't know what Al and Therese and Debbie told you last night. I bought a couple of kids their lattes. Big deal."

Elena opened her mouth only to shut it before she pissed him off all over again. "Thanks for building the crib. I owe you one for that and I'm about to ask you for another favor. If you don't mind joining me while I run errands, I'll make you dinner."

"Dinner, huh?" He blinked down at her in surprise. "Must be a hell of a big favor."

She huffed out half a laugh and shrugged. "Depends on your perspective. I—I—" To her total mortification, tears she couldn't stop dripped from her eyes and her mouth just wouldn't close. "I don't want to make my sister cry again. I want to make things right and I don't know where to go for all the stuff I need and even if I did, I'd be too scared to do it alone."

Luke rubbed his jaw, studying Elena. Scared, huh? That explained a lot. Actually, it explained everything. She'd left New York soon after her mother's death and had avoided coming back.

He remembered one day, soon after he'd met Almir, when they were walking downtown and Al had smiled and pointed across the street. A big tough muscle-bound guy had gotten off a Harley-Davidson to help pick up the food that some piss-ant kid on a skateboard had knocked out of an old lady's grocery bag. "Sometimes, we're afraid of the wrong things."

He'd thought about that for a long time and decided Al was right—sometimes grunge has a silver lining and sometimes solid gold is just painted lead. Maybe Elena just needed help knowing where to look.

That, he decided as he stood up and held out a hand to her, he could handle.

✦ ✦ ✦

THEY BEGAN WALKING toward Church Street. The air was brisk and the day was bright. Lucas slid on trendy black glasses and his hat, and took her gloved hand in his, guiding her gently over patches of ice and little piles of snow that had gone gray from car exhaust.

"You sure you don't mind walking?" he asked while they waited to cross a street. "We could take the subway."

She shook her head. "I hate the subway." She worried that he'd heard the note of fear in her voice and wasn't letting go of her hand because of it. Damn, even through her gloves, she felt how cold his hand was. She sandwiched his between both of hers, rubbed briskly, and was rewarded with a quick grin—still devastating despite its brevity.

They turned a corner and she skidded to a halt. Her jaw dropped and she pointed across the street. "That's not—"

"Hook and Ladder 8? Sure it is."

She slapped his arm. "Come on! It looks just like—"

"Because it is."

Her eyes popped and her jaw dropped. "Get out!"

Lucas raised his eyebrows. "So you're a fan?"

"Are you serious? I've seen that movie a hundred times." She stared at the famous *Ghostbusters* firehouse. "I had no idea it was a real fire station."

"And you call yourself a New Yorker." Luke shook his head and took out his phone. "Stand there and smile." Elena did a game show hand gesture. He snapped a picture and handed her the phone. "Here. Put your number in so I can send you that."

They walked on. It took no more than twenty minutes to reach the baby shop. Elena examined all the crib sets before picking out one that would be a perfect match to the wall art Kara had in the baby's room.

"Okay, baby bedding—check. What's next, boss lady?" he asked with a grin as they walked down the street.

When the Salvation Army volunteer they'd just passed called out a happy *thank you*, Elena halted in the middle of the sidewalk. "Did you just—"

She slid him a look, about to rib him, and remembered Debbie had said Lucas hated people knowing about all his good deeds. "Just what?" he asked, his voice as cold as the temperature.

"Never mind. Come on." She shook her head. "Let's forget the groceries. I'll pick up just what I need for cookies and we'll order something in."

He frowned down at her. "You're in a hurry."

"I am," she admitted like she'd just been caught robbing a bank. "I feel sick about making Kara cry. I want to make it up to her before she comes home. I want to buy her a tree and a star for the top, and lights, and everything that goes on trees. I want her and everybody else to stop hating me."

Lucas abruptly tugged her to a stop and turned to face her. "Nobody hates you."

I hate you! I wish you'd drop dead!

She put her hands over her ears, but that did nothing to stop the echo of words shouted a long time ago. She wanted to crawl into the sewer because he was wrong—people did hate her. In fact, she hated herself.

You ruin everything, Laney.

"Before, when you said I'm not nice. You're not wrong," she admitted. "I was a real brat when I was a kid and this morning's little incident proves I still am." She wished her mom were there to tell her it was okay, that she knew Elena didn't mean what she'd said, that she knew Elena was sorry.

He moved closer, his hands squeezing her shoulders. "I'm willing to amend that assessment."

"Seriously?" She stepped closer, put a hand on his chest. "You'd do that?" When he nodded, she clapped and flung her arms around him. "Oh, thank you, Luke!"

Lucas Adair may very well be too good to be true, but he made something deep inside her believe in magic.

Chapter Six

"WHERE DO WE start? Where do city people buy Christmas trees?" She put her hands on her hips and looked up and down the street.

When Elena Larsen wasn't being deliberately aggravating, Lucas decided she was sweet. And beautiful. He looked at her with a wry smile. "You act like you haven't—" And his laughter faded when the truth struck him between the eyes. "How long has it been, Elena?"

Her face went flat and the light left her eyes. "I haven't done Christmas since my mother was killed. I avoid the city, the holidays. My friends. Kara came back here for school but—" She held out her arms. "This city…for me, it's death and, and destruction and hate and—" She broke off, shook her head and lifted a shoulder. "They don't understand. Our friends are mad at me, she's mad at me—"

"I get it." He stopped her with a touch to her cheek. He sucked in a deep breath and got ready to step onto shaky ground. "Pain, grief—they're isolating things, you know? They're so huge, they eclipse everything and make you think nobody else feels what you feel, but that's wrong. Everybody does, Elena. Everybody. When I figured that out, when I finally talked about it, things—"

"Got better?" she asked with a roll of her eyes and Lucas understood she'd heard this before.

For a long moment, he considered lying and finally shook his head. "No. Not better. Just less huge, you know?" When she looked at him sideways, he shrugged. "Honey, it's like a club that should never have members but it does and membership means there's a certain amount of…of common ground." He finished with a wave toward the Freedom Tower.

She let out a long sigh. "I'm trying. I really am."

He put down the shopping bag and took her in his arms. "Elena, I know you are. I think it's incredible—*you're* incredible—that you're here now and trying to do things for Kara."

To his surprise, her arms circled him and she put her head on his shoulder. "For all the good that's doing," she murmured into his jacket. "I *hate* that I made her cry."

Lucas held her a moment longer, the old familiar fury straining the leash he'd kept it on for the last decade. He pushed it away and tried to focus on her, instead. There was something about her…something almost familiar in a way. She smelled like vanilla and he thought of the Christmas cookies she'd yet to bake. She felt warm and comfortable in his arms. His arms tightened around her because he wanted to make her laugh, make her feel safe. He wanted that like he wanted his next breath.

Al would insist it was a sign, he concluded. But then again, she wasn't staying. She'd been clear on that. So what kind of cosmic practical joke would point him toward a woman who would leave as soon as they got comfortable around each other?

So you have to work at something for once.

He went still. He could *swear* the voice in his head was his mother's. Every muscle in his body tensed and he brushed it aside. Instead, he made a decision. Made a *wish*. He pulled away from Elena, cupped her face and leaned back so he could see her. "Okay, new plan. What is the happiest memory of Christmas you have?" She frowned and tried to look away, but he wouldn't allow that. "Tell me."

She took a deep breath, laughed out a cloud of vapor. "Baking, because Kara sucks at it. Baking cookies was the one thing I shared with my mom."

He could work with that.

"Well, that and watching sappy movies," she added.

"Cookies. Movies. And hot cocoa. Pretty sure I mentioned I make the world's best hot cocoa." He smiled slowly, pleased when her eyes focused on his mouth.

Her lips curled. "The *world's* best? Come on."

"Okay, okay. *Widely admired*? How about *damn good*?" He delivered the last with a little tickle, happy when she squealed and wriggled away. "Here's what we're gonna do. I'll hail you a cab and you go back to Kara's, start those cookies. Leave the tree to me. With luck, we'll get it all done before Kara's back. Deal?"

She looked up at him with such an expression of hope in her eyes, his breath caught. She was all bundled up in her coat, a scarf wrapped around her neck, wearing her hat with the tiny wreath pinned to it, and it suddenly hit him like a falling brick that she could be his.

If he could convince her to stay.

When she was all entranced by the magic of Christmas trees newly decorated, he'd invite her to shop with him to put presents under it. He'd make her his famous hot cocoa. He'd show her Radio City and Rockefeller Center. He'd take her through Central Park in a carriage. He'd prove to her that New

York was still New York—even with its scars.

She nodded. "Okay."

He smiled—full wattage. His mother had called his smile his superpower. She'd sure paid enough for it—first braces, then a crown for a tooth he'd chipped playing hockey. It was now photospread-perfect and he hoped it wouldn't fail him now. Elena was special—he wasn't sure how yet—but now that they'd returned to civility, he was determined to find out.

He stuck two fingers in his mouth and let out a shrill whistle that had a cab pulling over in seconds. "Anything you want me to add to my list?"

Elena shook her head. "Nope. I'll head over to the market, grab my list of ingredients—oh! Milk Duds. I need Milk Duds." She laughed at his confused look, climbed into the cab, settled her shopping bag beside her. "It's what Kara's been calling her baby bump."

"Milk Duds. Okay. See you later." He ran a thumb along her jaw, waited for another smile and closed the cab door, then waved as the cab merged back into traffic, before he began to jog down the street, prepared to find the tallest, lushest tree he could afford.

✦ ✦ ✦

"THANKS FOR THE assist, Al. Couldn't have done this alone." Lucas held out a hand to his friend.

"No problem, man." Al returned the grip. "So...do I get fed or what?"

Lucas laughed. "I have it on good authority that there will be cookies."

They wrestled the tree through the outer door and Lucas pressed the buzzer for Kara's apartment.

"Hello?"

"It's Lucas and company."

There was a laugh and then the inner door buzzed. The two men shoved their greenery into the elevator and squeezed in after it.

"Press 4."

"Press—are you insane? I've got a tree branch itching to take out an eye."

"Pansy." Lucas shifted the tree, Al grunted, cursed. He managed to press 4 and hold his breath.

"You so owe me for this."

"Yeah, yeah. Quit bitching and heft." When the door slid open, Lucas all but tumbled out of the elevator at Elena's feet.

"Is that a tree or the whole damn forest?"

"Little help here?" Al's muffled voice called out from the elevator.

When Elena looked startled, Lucas quickly added, "Oh, that's Al. He's helping."

She laughed. "Hey, Al!" Elena peeked inside the elevator, saw nothing but evergreen and a few hands.

"I smell the cookies." Luke patted his stomach.

"Two batches done, a third in progress. Come on in. I'll fix you guys a plate."

Elena tried to grab the tree trunk but Lucas thrust a couple of bags at her instead. "Tree stuff." He grinned and followed her inside Kara's apartment, Al trailing behind with the top of the tree. "What's this?" He glanced into bowls of red and green batter.

"Rainbow cookies."

"I love those," Al moaned. "Promise me you'll save me a few."

Elena smiled. "Deal."

Lucas moved to the wall of windows in the living room, cut the twine off the tree with a pocket knife. "Okay, I'm thinking right here, in the center."

"Oh, that's pretty." Elena pressed her hands to her mouth, her eyes wide. "It's beautiful. And big. Very big."

"It's perfect. Come on. Let's get it in the stand."

With a grunt, Al tilted the tree upright in front of the window while Lucas rooted around in the bags for the stand he'd bought. It took a few minutes of grunting and hefting and adjusting, but the tree was soon secured in its stand.

"Perfect. Okay, time for cookies, then we'll hang the tree lights." He unwound the scarf from his neck, shed his jacket, tossed it on the sofa. Al did the same.

Elena crossed to the counter that separated the living room from the kitchen, grabbed a spatula and slid fragrant sugar cookies onto a plate, then put it on the table by the sofa.

"Oh, wow." Al shut his eyes as he bit into a cookie, while Luke shoved one in, too.

When there was nothing left but crumbs, the guys unwrapped several boxes of light strands and began winding them around the tree while Elena refilled the plate.

"Now this," Al said with his arms spread, "is a beautiful tree."

"It is, it really is." Elena covered her mouth. "I hope she likes it."

The tree was a fragrant spruce that just skimmed the ceiling. The lights twinkled around ornaments and little baby booties and socks and t-shirts Elena had taken from the chest of drawers in the second bedroom where the crib was now beautifully dressed and waiting for its tiny inhabitant.

"Have you guys seen this?" Al held out Kara's baby name book to Luke.

"I know my name."

"Not the name, smart ass, the meaning."

Luke humored his friend. "*Light giving*. So what?"

"Elena, look at yours."

She took the book, flipped to the girls' name section. "*Shining light*."

"I repeat, so what?" Lucas spread his hands.

Al rolled his dark eyes. "Your names mean the same thing. Don't you think that has to mean something?"

Lucas snorted out a laugh. "*Something*. Look, Al. Elena's already said she's only here for a few weeks. We're just hanging out. No pressure." He looked to her for confirmation. When she nodded, he sighed in relief.

Because he *was* relieved, he told himself.

Al looked from Lucas to Elena and back again. "Yeah. So. It's late—" Al stood up, stretched.

"It's six-thirty."

"—and I've got stuff to do, so I'm gonna just hit the road, ice this newly acquired hernia and—" he started moving toward the door.

"Al, stay. I'm making dinner."

"—finish that book I'm supposed to read for my book club. Goodnight!" He opened the door and with a wink, was gone.

There was a moment of silence as Luke and Elena looked at the door and then at each other and then burst into laughter, collapsing on to the couch together. When she caught her breath, Elena met Luke's eyes and asked the question burning a hole through her head. "Do you believe all that sign stuff?"

Lucas knew a set-up when he saw one. He shrugged. "Sure. But not to the extent Al does."

Elena's forehead puckered. "What kind of signs?"

He turned, pulled a leg up on the sofa. "Things that remind me of my mom." And he didn't like the look on her face so figured a change of subject would be really helpful right about now. "Come on. Let's get that dinner going."

She managed a tiny grin and nodded. In Kara's kitchen, they diced up onions and peppers and whipped up some spicy fajitas they ate sitting on the floor in front of the coffee table. Lucas snatched the remote control and scrolled through the movie options.

"Oh, this one's great!" He cued up A Christmas Story, settled back next to her. "If Milk Dud's a boy, would you let him have a Red Rider BB gun?"

"Are you kidding? He'd shoot his eye out."

Lucas laughed. "You're such a mom."

"I am not! I'm an aunt—or about to be."

He scoffed. "Come on, admit it. You're gonna spoil him rotten."

She shook her head. "Nope. Not me. I'm a hard-ass."

His eyes immediately skimmed down her body, stopping at her butt. It didn't look hard at all. It looked soft and incredibly sexy. "What do you think the baby is?"

Elena swallowed some water and thought about that. "I think it's a girl."

"A niece. Bet you can't wait to play Barbies with her."

Elena made a face. "Oh, hell no. I hated Barbies. No, I can't wait to show her baby's first computer. We need more women in IT."

"No argument here." Luke put up his hands. "Want to know what I think?" He put down his fork, skimmed his thumb along her jaw. "I think you'll be the best aunt a baby's ever had."

Elena's eyes went soft. He took her glass, put it on the table, moved closer. "Want to know what else I think?" He swept her hair behind her ear, cradled her face. "I think you're beautiful and incredibly loyal to brave a city you're so damn afraid of just so you could be here for your sister." Her tongue darted out to lick her lips and Lucas didn't think—couldn't think anymore. He leaned in, drew her closer, his fingers sifting through the soft silkspun hair, his mouth just a breath from hers. "Elena." He hovered, shaking from the effort to wait, just wait for her to catch up to him.

She said nothing.

But she did grab him by the hair and angle his mouth to fit perfectly against hers and suddenly, Lucas was the one who had to catch up. He moved his hands down her hair, her shoulders, her back, up again, his fingers searching—mapping—memorizing—all her lines and curves. She smelled like sugar cookies and vanilla and in his arms, something in his heart whispered, *this woman*. Her hands fisted in his hair and she gasped into his mouth and if that wasn't a sign, he was dead. With his tongue, he touched, teased, tasted, and tempted. He'd wanted a kiss, just one kiss in the glow of the Christmas tree lights, but now he knew that wouldn't be enough.

But it had to be.

Unless he could convince her to stay.

Chapter Seven

WHEN THEY FINALLY separated, the pure joy she saw on his face sent her into a full-scale panic.

When was the last time she'd brought legitimate *joy* to somebody? When she arrived at Kara's door, it was relief, not joy on her sister's face. And being with Bree and Aunt Vincenza—there'd been exasperation covering the happiness at finally having her at their table after all these years. Damn it, when was the last time? She couldn't remember. Had there ever been a time when she hadn't sucked the joy out of souls wherever she went? Hadn't she done that just this morning, made her pregnant sister cry? Hadn't she made her own mother cry the day—

"Hey, hey, hey, what's wrong?" Lucas frowned, brushed her hair from her face.

"Don't do that. No. No, please don't do that! Please, don't." Elena clutched him tighter but he firmly held her away.

"You didn't say no—"

"No!" She took his face in her hands. "You're sad. Please, please don't let me make you sad. I make everyone sad and I don't want to do that to you."

Luke's forehead smoothed and his hands came up, cupping her face. "Then don't," he said with a shrug and a grin, like it was easy as walking.

She wrapped her arms around his neck, tucked her face into the curve of his shoulder and whispered, "I don't know how."

He murmured into her hair. "Want lessons?"

She knew he was kidding, but clutched at his words. "Yes! Yes, I need lessons. I want to be like you, Lucas. I want people to be happy around me. I want people to say things like Al said about you—'*Elena's the best woman I know!*'"

"Stop, Elena." His hands cruised up and down her back in a gesture that soothed and stirred her. "I was teasing. I'm no expert, believe me."

She straightened her spine, pulled away, trying not to shiver from the lack of contact with him. She backed away, curled herself into the corner of the sofa, pulling up her knees and avoided those intense eyes. "Of course. I—I'm sorry." Her face burned. She searched for a quick escape. "Oh, I didn't realize it had gotten so late. I'm sure you have things to do so, um, thank you. For today." She stood up, waited for him to grasp the hint.

He stretched out on the sofa. "Sit down, Elena."

Sit down? She couldn't possibly stay in the same room with him and not die of embarrassment. She jerked around, grabbed the cookie plate, fled to the kitchen to scrub off its pattern. Seconds later, his hands clamped down on her shoulders, tried to tug her back against his chest, but she stood stiffly at the sink.

"I'd apologize, but I don't fully understand what's wrong."

"Nothing's wrong."

He thrust out a hand to kill the water. "Look at me, Elena."

Oh, no. No, she couldn't possibly do that.

He cursed, spun her around and hunched down so they were eye to eye. "I. Wasn't. Sad."

She wished she could believe that.

"Elena, I kissed you. You kissed me back. Maybe I shouldn't have done that—or maybe I should have asked first—but I'm not sorry I did it. I'm only sorry that you are."

Her jaw dropped. "What? No! No, I'm not sorry we kissed. I promise you, I liked it." What did a body look like after it died of embarrassment? Did the skin keep the fiery red flush she knew covered her from toe to hair follicles?

His hands loosened on her shoulders and he pulled her closer. "Glad to hear it. I have one more theory." He kissed her, right under her ear, where her pulse beat so fast and so hard, she was certain he could taste it. "I think you're out of practice." He dipped lower, this time, kissing along her jaw, and her bones melted. "Need to try again." His lips were there, right there, just a whisper away from hers and she swore her tongue tingled in anticipation. "This time, don't think. Just feel."

His lips landed, devouring hers like she was his first meal after a fast. Everything about him charged her senses. His scent—evergreen, the clever fingers roving over her body, heating her through her clothes. His hair, all that thick dark hair, was soft and silky under her fingertips. He shifted, moved his hips between her thighs, his hands on her bottom keeping her there—right there, where all that power surged.

He was, she concluded, the penance for her sins. Life, karma, fate—whatever you called it—it obviously had a sick sense of humor. It dropped the perfect man right into her hands—a guy whose smile was almost radioactive, a guy who bought dessert for teenagers and volunteered hours of his time to charities like SFG—and she could never keep him. Didn't deserve to keep him. And even as he pulled things from her she didn't know she could give, she knew she'd have to say goodbye to him and add that pain to the list she'd begun the day her mother died.

✦ ✦ ✦

LUCAS STRODE THROUGH the frigid night air, hands in his pockets, mind still swirling with thoughts of Elena.

The look on her face after he'd kissed her—damn, he'd never get it out of his head. Her eyes—those enormous milk chocolate eyes of hers spilled all her secrets. There'd been fear. Desire. Those he knew. But there was more... something he couldn't pinpoint—words spoken in a language he hadn't yet mastered. It was there, right at the front of his brain, but just out of reach. Whatever it was, it was something familiar. Something he *knew*. More like resignation. And when she started babbling about not being sad, it was all he could do to not jump on top of Kara's kitchen counter and shout it was the best kiss of his life.

His steps faltered. The best kiss of his life... yes. Yes, he decided. It definitely was. Until the second one. A laugh tumbled out of his mouth. Al was always lecturing him about his sexual habits. Thought it was terrible that his encounters were nothing more substantial than casual hookups or friends-with-benefits, blah, blah. Al said when a woman finally came along who Lucas could fall for, it would be like getting kicked between the eyes by a Rockette in tap shoes.

He found a seat on the PATH train and rubbed his forehead. When the significance of that gesture dawned on him, he muttered a curse and slouched low in his seat, thinking about his mother's snowflake. Part of him wasn't entirely sure if the reason he kept volunteering at SFG wasn't to find that girl—

some pathetic attempt to use crystal snowflakes as a pair of glass slippers. God knew he was no prince, especially after what he'd done—

He snapped upright.

The look in Elena's eyes... he finally recognized it. It was the same look he used to wear until Al helped him deal.

Guilt.

✦ ✦ ✦

EARLY SUNDAY MORNING, Elena headed off to do the rest of the grocery shopping she'd planned to do the day before. The weather was bright but cold so she burrowed deeper into her coat, tugged her hat low over her ears and started walking, excited to finish her errand so she could see Lucas later. The sun caught the spire on the new One World Trade Center, a spear through the clouds, and for one very long minute, she couldn't breathe, couldn't think, couldn't move.

"Elena?"

She whipped around, found Luke's friend standing behind her.

"Oh, hi, Al."

A smile and a nod. "You remembered." He stepped closer, cupped his hands and blew on them. "You okay? You're not lost or anything, are you?"

She'd been lost for many years now. "No, no. I'm right where I am supposed to be." On the edge of Hell.

"Me, too!" Al said, his face bright.

She smiled tightly. "Well, great. I should get going. See you at SFG."

He pulled an old, beat up baseball card out of his pocket. "Look what I just found." He smiled at it like a proud new father at a baby.

Elena stared at the card. "A baseball card."

"My dad loved his baseball cards. Kids today don't care about collecting baseball cards—I sure didn't. So what are the odds of finding one of these on a street nowadays?"

Elena glanced at the trash that lined the street, awaiting pick up, and figured those odds were pretty damn good. "So you're saying this is a sign from your dad?"

Al shrugged. "I like to think so. What about you? What kind of signs remind you of your mom?"

The look on her face when I told her I hated her guts. Elena shook her head. "The usual."

"No, I mean what were the things that made your mom happiest?"

Playing along, Elena thought for a moment. "Well, she loved to play cards. And she had an addiction to Nestle Crunch Bars."

"There you go. Look for those signs. You'll be surprised how often you'll see those signs when you actually look for them. What else?"

"Jeez, I don't know. Oh! She loved to bake. I used to help her bake Christmas cookies. And architecture. For some reason, she was always reading books on architecture, even though that wasn't her field." Elena turned slightly, looked up at One World Trade Center.

He turned, faced the same direction and stared out at the new building, the one designed to honor the country and its victims. "It's beautiful, isn't it?"

Her eyes snapped to his. "Beautiful?" How could a structure that was essentially a grave marker be beautiful?

"Well, yes. It's full of symbolism."

Impatient, Elena nodded. "It's 1776 feet tall, yes." She'd heard all about the tower's design.

Undaunted, Al continued. "With the spire. Without the

spire, it's 1368 feet tall, the same height as Tower 1 before it collapsed." He waited, but she said nothing. "And look there, at the top? That's called a square anti-prism."

She blinked, waited for him to make his point. "So?"

"You know what a prism does, right? Splits up light into its colors? So maybe, an anti-prism does the opposite."

Elena thought about that. "It...sucks in color?"

"Exactly." Al's grin widened and then he turned back to face the building. "Our new tower is a nexus of color and light. I think that's a fitting tribute to all those we lost—and maybe to someone who loved architecture?"

"Come on. It's just the by-product of all those politicians debating," she argued.

"Probably," Al admitted. "But so what? It doesn't matter *how* you explain it. It only matters because it matters to you."

She blinked, thought about that for a moment and gave up. She'd already spent a ton of money on therapy and she really didn't need more even if it was free. "Thanks, Al, but I think I'll just stick to not thinking about it."

Al laughed. "Jeez, you sound just like Lucas. No faith. You two are hand-picked for each other. Where is he anyway? Are you meeting him?"

She shook her head. "Not until later. He had to do a breakfast thing this morning."

Al's eyebrows shot up. "He told you about the soup kitchen? Whoa, he really does like you."

Elena's heart fell. All Lucas had told her was he had a breakfast thing. Soup kitchen? Of course. He was probably up at dawn, serving breakfast to dozens of homeless people while she—oh! She shut her eyes and let go of the dream she was hardly aware she'd been nurturing. She was a fool. She'd known all along that Lucas was simply too good for her. What the hell was she doing?

"Uh oh. He *didn't* tell you about the soup kitchen, did he?" Al turned.

"It's fine. Don't worry about it. I really have to go." She walked briskly away.

"Elena. Elena, wait!"

She walked faster, dodging the lighter-than-usual pedestrian traffic on the sidewalks and tore the stupid hat with its stupid wreath off her head after a third person wished her a Merry Christmas. It wasn't merry. It hadn't been merry since she was fourteen. Her eyes blurred and she blinked furiously, annoyed with herself. It was that kiss, that soul-touching, toe-curling, life-changing kiss. Just thinking about it put a hitch in her stride.

It was her own fault. She'd been enthralled by his smile from the second she'd seen it. She kept telling herself she was leaving soon, so stay uninvolved, keep things casual but did she listen? No, she kissed this man with the beautiful smile, beautiful eyes, and beautiful heart like she actually deserved some of that beauty for herself.

It was so ludicrous, it was laughable.

She unzipped her purse, found her phone, tapped out a quick message.

> L., thanks for all your help yesterday but I think I need to focus on Kara right now. I'm leaving soon and don't want to start something with you I can't finish. Thanks for understanding. Merry Christmas. E.

Yes, laughable.

She tugged a tissue from her coat pocket, and wiped her eyes.

✦ ✦ ✦

LUCAS SHOVED HIS phone back in his pocket with a curse.

"Careful, man. You might scare away the customers." Chuck Garrison crossed his arms over his barrel chest and studied Lucas carefully. "Woman trouble?"

Luke pulled the candy cane from his mouth and snorted out half a laugh. "Yeah."

Chuck blew out a loud sigh, tore the paper hat off his head. "Man, that is discouraging. Guys like you have trouble with a woman, there is no hope for short and pudgy guys with an adorable sense of humor like me."

"Come off it, Chuck." Luke rolled his eyes. "You're the married deacon of a church with three kids."

"Oh. Right. All hope was lost years ago." He tugged off his formerly white apron, balled it up. "Wanna talk about it?"

Luke shot him a yeah-right look. "No. I want to hit something. Hard. You okay by yourself? I'm going to the gym."

"Yeah, sure. Go. And good luck with your lady."

His lady. Outside Trinity Church, with the frigid air hitting him like a bucket of cold water, Lucas couldn't stop thinking about Deacon Chuck's words. Lucas didn't do relationship—no girlfriends, no involvements, no relationships.

No meaning.

His lady. Damn it, no. He had no claim on Elena Larsen. Okay, so they'd shared a kiss or two. And yes, it had damn near stopped his heart. That didn't mean—

Ah, hell.

Yes, it did.

Without the fury pushing him, his restless mind kept replaying everything that had happened the day before. He hadn't said anything rude—though there were a few opportunities he'd let fly by. And she hadn't pissed him off.

Much.

The kiss—she'd assured him it wasn't the kiss. So what the

hell happened?

His phone buzzed again. He pulled it out, tugged off his gloves, and checked the ID. "Hey, Al."

"Luke, I'm sorry, but I think I messed things up for you with Elena. Have you talked to her today?"

Lucas came to a screeching halt in the middle of the sidewalk. "You spoke to her? When? What did you say?"

"I saw her about an hour ago. Down near Fulton. She said she had to buy groceries."

Lucas shut his eyes, prayed for patience. "I mean what did you say to upset her?"

"Nothing! We were standing on the street, looking up at the new trade center. I mentioned some of the symbolism—"

"Oh, please. Not more signs."

"I know, I know. But she seemed interested in all of that. It wasn't until I mentioned the soup kitchen that she got weird."

"Why the hell did you tell her?"

"That was an accident. She said you had a breakfast thing, so I thought you'd told her you served breakfast over at Trinity. I misunderstood."

"Okay, forget it. What did she say?"

"That's just it. She didn't say anything. She just took off. Looked like a kid who just found out the truth about Santa."

"Thanks, man. I'll take care of it."

"Good luck."

It made sense. An hour ago was about the time he'd gotten her text message. Lucas shoved the phone back in his pocket and took off at a run. Woman thinks she can just kiss him to within an inch of his life one day and walk away the next? They'd just see about that. If she thought he'd hit the streets just because she sent him off with a text message—

He skidded to a stop, pulled off his hat, dragged both

hands through his hair. At a slow walk, Lucas pondered his options. Walk away. Confront her. Move on. He could call Jill or—or what was that redhead's name? Alison. He could put Elena firmly out of his head. Yes. Yes, that was a good plan. This way, there'd be no drama.

He hated drama.

He turned away, took one step and found Elena standing there, watching him, with that same haunted look in her eyes, the same look that used to be in his and sometimes, still was.

She turned and ran.

Chapter Eight

HER JAW FELL open.

She turned a corner and there he was.

Saint Luke.

Her heart tore down the center. She couldn't—she simply couldn't deal with any more of this—this *taunting*. She was sorry! Deeply, irrevocably sorry. But it did no good. Her mother was gone now—there could be no forgiveness, no forgetting.

Her sin had festered—a dark spot on her soul—for over a dozen years and it had gotten worse, not better. Here she was, back in New York where she swore she'd never go again, falling for an angel with a glowing smile instead of wings who helped people in distress. Slowly, she put down the grocery bag in her arms and watched Lucas.

Suddenly, his gaze snapped to hers and for a brief moment, she wondered why he looked so sad. Then she ran—left the bag of groceries where she'd plopped it—and ran. Ran to Kara's building, grateful that the elevator was waiting when she reached it.

It was one small thing that went in her favor.

She let herself into Kara's apartment, fell back against the door and tried to still her racing heart. When she could move without shaking, she searched for her sister, found the apartment empty.

Kara still wasn't home.

Elena sighed, stared at the baby's crib, all ready for baby's first nap. There would be a little life form inside that crib in a few weeks. A life its grandmother would never get to see because she'd been stolen from them, and its father would not see by choice. Her hands curled into tight fists and she breathed through the pain in her chest.

Abruptly weary of the signs and the guilt and the pain—of damn near everything, Elena nearly crawled into her air mattress, wishing Kara were home so they could just lie next to each other the way they used to when they were little and scared of thunderstorms. But the buzzer sounded.

Slowly, she headed to the wall buzzer and pressed it. She knew it was Lucas and accepted her fate.

Her earlier text message was a crappy way to say goodbye to somebody. She owed him an honest conversation. She opened the apartment door, waited for the elevator. She could hear it, the *ding* it made as it passed each floor sounding like the fall of a gavel in her sentence. When the doors slid open, she straightened her spine, and prepared to tell the most incredible guy in the world she couldn't see him again directly to his face.

✦ ✦ ✦

LUCAS COUNTED THE floors, not sure if he should confront Elena or kiss the breath out of her. The elevator finally slid to a stop and he shoved out of it while the doors were still opening, her bag of groceries clutched in his arms. She was waiting for him braced for battle, her back straight, her chin up—and misery filling her eyes.

Ah, hell. Confrontation wasn't gonna work.

"Elena, are you okay?"

"I'm fine," she said, avoiding his gaze.

Oh, sure, and the Brooklyn Bridge just came up for sale. She blocked the door and he concluded kissing her wasn't the right decision either so he merely walked right past her, into Kara's kitchen, and began unpacking the bag. His eyebrows shot up when he saw almost a dozen empty Nestle Crunch Bar wrappers and scooped them up. "Did you eat all of these by yourself?"

She snatched the wrappers from his hands, stuffed them into the tiny trash can Kara kept under her sink. But she didn't answer him. Instead, she moved beside him to unpack the rest of the bag. Milk, bread, eggs, toilet paper, a whole chicken, flour and sugar.

And a Queen of Hearts, torn and filthy.

Her face was pale and her chin quivered. He watched her as she carefully and deliberately put all the perishable food in the refrigerator and all the dry goods in a cabinet. And then she carefully and deliberately folded up the paper bag and tucked it in the cabinet under Kara's sink.

She lowered her head to the counter with a sob and he swore he heard his mother's voice scolding him. *Lucas Alexander Adair! Help that girl.*

I'm trying, Mom, he wanted to shout back and wished he had a clue what to do to make it better.

Just listen.

He scooped Elena up at the knees and took her into the living room. He sat in the middle of the sofa, cradling Elena in his lap, running his hands down her hair to soothe. "Talk to me. Tell me what's wrong."

"The signs, Lucas. They're everywhere." She clutched him,

shaking.

He swallowed a curse. He would *kill* Al first chance—abruptly, he refused to finish that thought. Damn. He shook it out of his head and sighed heavily. "Right. You were talking to Al. I'm sorry he upset you."

"No. I'm sorry." She shook her head, wiped her eyes and shifted, moved away from him. He recognized her move to the opposite end of the sofa as an attempt to put distance between them.

He met her eyes head on, refusing to hide the pain he hoped she could see in them. He needed her to know she could—she *was*—able to hurt him. "You keep saying that and then keep right on doing the things you're sorry for."

She blinked, surprised, and he knew she hadn't considered that. That gave him an idea. But first, he needed the details. "Tell me about the candy wrappers. Why did they upset you?"

Elena covered her face for a second. "They were my mom's favorite thing. She used to keep bags of them hidden all over the house." She managed half a laugh over her tears. "When we moved the first time, away from the city, we found a bag stuffed inside the vacuum cleaner attachments case which is funny because we *never* would have looked there."

Lucas listened but didn't say anything.

"I saw Al on my way to the market and he told me how he loves to be here because his father sends him signs. He showed me this baseball card and—" she trailed off, shaking her head. "I thought he was nuts and then I went to the market. Nestle Crunch Bars were on sale—two for a dollar. Right at the freakin' entrance. I walked by them. Coincidence, I tried to tell myself."

He nodded, his lips twitching into a smile. "Yeah. Felt the same way when Al did this with me."

"I wandered around the store, found the Queen of Hearts

stuck to the milk carton." She demanded with a swish of an arm. "I mean, who delivers milk to the markets of New York City with a deck of cards in his pocket?" She curled her legs under herself, wrapped her arms around them. "I got chills, Luke. I didn't finish my list—just got the hell out of there. And on the walk home, picked up wrapper after wrapper after wrapper."

She looked at him, all enormous frightened eyes and he felt a pull on his heart.

"What about the Queen of Hearts?"

Elena managed half a smile. "My mom loved to play cards."

He nodded and drew in a deep breath. "You know what my mom loved?" He shifted closer, put a hand in his pocket and pulled out a seashell, dropped it into Elena's hand. When she sent him a questioning look, he only shrugged. "I don't get it either, but she loved seashells. Every trip we took, she bought a seashell." He smiled, rolled his eyes. "Really drove my dad nuts. *You can get one for free on the beach! Why do you have to pay for a damn shell?*' She got them from the beach, too. Our house has dozens of seashell projects she made over the years—picture frames, lamp shades. I found this one on the train, right after I walked you home the other night."

Elena's eyes went round. "And you think it's a sign?"

He opened his mouth and abruptly clamped his lips together.

"What?" She pressed, but he only shook his head.

He'd nearly told her about the snowflake ornament he'd given to a frightened little girl. He would never tell her, not now. Not after learning how much this talk about signs upset her. He moved closer. "Elena, what if Al's right? What if the baseball cards, the seashells, the candy wrappers—what if they all really are signs? I don't think that's a bad thing." He took the seashell, studied it. "It makes me...warm inside, I guess, knowing she might still be with me."

What little color there was in her cheeks fled and her jaw dropped. Slowly, mechanically, she shook her head. "No. Oh, Lucas, no!"

He wrapped his arms around her to soothe, to comfort. "Shhh, baby, shhhh. Tell me."

Elena shuddered and pulled away. "It means she's still punishing me, Luke. Still mad at me. It means she's in Hell—and so am I."

He thought about that. "Why would she punish you?"

Because she'd disobeyed. Because she'd done exactly what her mother told her not to do. Because she'd ruined everything. She shifted, turned away. "I...I can't talk about this, Luke. I'm sorry. You should go."

Not gonna happen. He lifted her face to his. "You believe in that? Hell, I mean."

"Yes. No. Jeez, I don't know what I believe anymore." She scrubbed her hands over her face.

A new thought arrowed straight through his heart. "You...you think *I'm* part of this... this punishment? Is that why you sent me that text?"

Elena leaped to her feet. "You—you really need to leave."

He stood, waited for her to face him. "Answer me."

"Luke, please," she whispered.

"Not going anywhere until you answer me."

She shut her eyes and nodded once.

He stepped closer. "You're wrong. You're a gift, Elena."

Her eyes snapped open.

"Elena, from the second I saw you get out of that little Zipcar the other day, I've wanted to get to know you. Spending yesterday with you, putting up this tree? That was the most fun I've had in a long time." He brushed the hair behind her ear, cradled her face in his hands. "Al is my closest friend but he drives me crazy with all this crap about signs. It makes him happy so I go along with it. But not this, sweetheart. Not you. I can't walk away from you just because of some—some silly superstitious crap."

She stared up at him, at that bright smile, those dark glittery eyes, and felt the pull deep in her gut. He slid his hands into her hair, his thumbs drawing circles along her face.

"I know you're leaving soon. But we have the next few weeks to make this the best Christmas either of us has had in years." He ran his hands down her back, subtly pulling her closer. "I want to get to know you better. I want you, Elena, and I'm pretty damn sure you want me, too." His hands settled on her hips, stirring up a storm of desire. "Let's forget all about Al's signs and just—just have some fun together. Spend time with me. We'll tour the city, watch silly holiday movies—you and me."

You and me.

Luke's words spun Christmas magic inside her and Elena found herself nodding, pressing closer to him until his mouth was on hers again. Their first kiss nearly melted a hole through her chest but it was nothing but a distant memory—a pale impersonator of the kiss he gave her now. He tasted like candy canes and sugar cookies and when his hand brushed along the sides of her breasts as he banded his arms around her body, she felt like a Christmas gift—wanted and precious and wrapped in bright ribbons.

✦ ✦ ✦

"YOU CAN DO this, Elena." Lucas tugged on her hand.

She swallowed hard and stepped down to the subway entrance, clutching his hand tightly in hers.

"The subways are the best way to travel around the city. Sure, they can be dangerous, but you're not alone, so your odds of getting into trouble just drastically fell."

Her hand tightened even more, but she nodded and barely three minutes later, the train arrived and they stepped aboard. She gripped his hand for the entire trip and when the train finally reached Penn Station, only then did she release all the breaths she'd been holding. He took her to Macy's at Herald Square, where Elena bought gifts for Milk Dud and Kara, and—when Lucas wasn't looking—for him. After that, he took her to the top of the Empire State Building where the cold and the view were equally breathtaking.

They walked uptown along Fifth Avenue, stopping to look in store windows from time to time. He wanted to take her skating at Rockefeller Center but the lines were too long so instead, he tugged her into a store that sold nothing but Lego blocks. When his eyes went round at the sight of a Lego replica of the UN building, Elena took out her credit card and bought it for him on the spot. In return, he led her to a bakery and bought her a trio of the biggest cupcakes she'd ever seen.

Burdened with shopping bags filled to bursting, they walked down Fifth Avenue and Elena's phone buzzed.

"It's Kara. She's home," Elena said, reading the text.

"We should head back." Lucas put down one of his bags, stuck two fingers in his mouth and whistled for a cab. Once they'd climbed inside, their bags safely tucked between their legs on the floor, he wrapped his arms around her and held her close. "Thank you," he murmured against her neck, where he kissed her.

Elena's pulse leaped and her eyes fluttered shut only to pop wide when he lifted icy cold fingers to her face. "Lucas! You're practically hypothermic!" She grabbed his hands and rubbed them briskly between hers.

He grinned. "Cold hands, warm heart."

Elena stripped off her gloves and dove into one of her Macy's bags. "I should have given these to you as soon as I bought them." She tore the tag off a pair of black leather gloves lined in cashmere and handed them to him.

"Whoa, fancy." He slid his hands inside, gave them a flex. "Better?"

"They're perfect, Elena. Thank you." He studied his hands in the black leather. "I promise not to give these away."

Elena looked at him sideways. "You give away all your gloves?"

Lucas lifted a shoulder. "Maybe."

Elena stared at him for a long moment. He really was too good to be true. And—at least for the moment—he was hers. She shifted, took his face in her hands and kissed him full on the mouth, took the kiss slow and deep. When they pulled apart, the bright and hopeful expression on his face pinched her heart. "I'm sorry." She moved away.

"I'm not."

She snorted. "I'm serious, Lucas. I'm only here for a few more weeks. I have no business starting something with you."

He shifted in his seat, faced her. "I'm a big boy," he began and his words almost made her blush. "Come on. Let's go make your sister and Milk Dud some dinner."

Something inside her, some chain that weighed her down, broke free at his words.

She tried not to take that as a sign.

Chapter Nine

"**H**I, GUYS!" KARA said brightly from her favorite spot on the sofa. The baby name book was now accompanied by a legal pad, on which dozens of names had been scrawled and crossed out.

Elena rushed across the apartment and folded her sister into a hug. "I'm so sorry."

"Me, too." Kara sniffled. "Is that what this is for?" She waved a hand to the huge tree in front of her window.

Elena shook her head. "This? This is Christmas. The baby's crib, though? That's an apology."

Kara's eyes went round. "The crib? I didn't go in the other room. Oh, Lord, haul me up. I need to see." She held out both arms. Luke laughed, took one arm while Elena took the other. Together, they helped Kara reach her feet, followed her into the bedroom. "Laney, oh wow, this is adorable." She brushed a hand over the blanket, the crib bumpers. "It matches the walls perfectly." She turned, caught Elena's hands. "Thank you."

"I'm so glad you like it."

"I love it. And—" She winced, put a hand to her side. "I think Milk Dud does, too."

Elena's hand followed her sister's. She gasped when she felt the baby kick. "Whoa! Doesn't that hurt?"

Kara shrugged. "When the baby hits my kidney or liver, yeah. Otherwise, no. It's pretty cool." And then her face crumbled. "Oh, Laney." She fell into Elena's arms. "There's a little human inside me and Mom isn't here to see it—him—her."

Elena swallowed hard, squeezed her eyes shut and held her sister as tightly as she could given the swell of baby between them. She opened her eyes when Luke's hand squeezed her arm.

Not your fault, he mouthed.

But it was.

"Come on now, no tears. It's Christmas time." Lucas rubbed Kara's back. "Let's make some dinner. Elena and I got dessert, so I hope you're hungry."

"Like pretty much all the time." She patted her belly. "Milk Dud is a bit of a pig."

"Hmm, well, the little Milk Dud is gonna love these." He tugged her back to the living room, pulled a container from one of their bags and opened the lid on one of the monster cupcakes he and Elena had purchased earlier. "It may need to thaw out for a while. It's damn cold out."

Kara's eyes popped and she shuffled to the kitchen for a fork. "I don't care how cold it is, I'm eating it. So what else did you two do today?"

"Lucas took me to Rockefeller Center, the Empire State Building, and a Lego store."

Kara's face softened. "Lucas, you really are a saint for showing my baby sister a fun time."

But his face clouded. "No. I'm really not." He sat down on the sofa on the cushion opposite Kara's favorite spot and grabbed her TV remote. "What do you ladies say to watching a

Christmas movie?"

"Yes!" Kara clapped. "When we were little, we used to do this all the time—spend an entire weekend watching all the holiday classics. Laney used to love those clay cartoons, remember?" She lowered herself to one of the kitchen stools.

Elena merely grunted.

"But I love the comedies."

Luke's eyebrows climbed. "*Christmas Vacation?*"

"Yes! Hell yes! That one's hilarious."

While Lucas selected the channel, Elena busied herself in the kitchen, prepping the roast chicken, only half-listening to Kara babble. She slid the chicken into the oven and then switched to mixing hot cocoa.

"I got your message. How's Bree doing? Did you see *him*?"

"See him?" Kara fanned her face. "I met him. The man is totally P.D. and Bree still gets The Look at the mere mention of his name. But don't worry, she'll be fine. Aunt Enza and Uncle Ed are all over him."

Elena laughed and quickly shot a glance at Lucas, who was also entirely P.D. – panty-dropping – but she did not want to explain that to him.

She'd die of embarrassment.

"Need help?" His deep voice made her jolt.

"No, I'm good," she lied.

His eyes narrowed, but he didn't press her. "Let's watch the movie, okay?"

Elena breathed a sigh of relief and grabbed two cups. Kara took the third and they rejoined Lucas at the sofa, settling in to watch the movie while the chicken roasted.

But Elena couldn't stop thinking about Bree. After all these years, to have to face the father of her child, the man who'd left her and never looked back. Kara was right, though. Aunt Enza would twist the balls right off Jake Killen before she'd let him hurt Sabrina a second time.

The pang of pain that twisted in her gut made her wince. What would Mom think of Lucas? Would she warn her to be careful, or welcome him to the family? She sipped her cocoa, tried to imagine having a conversation with her mother that didn't end with raised voices and stomping feet.

"So what's P.D. mean?"

Elena choked on her cocoa and Kara laughed like a hyena.

"It's—" Kara started, but Elena slapped a hand over her sister's mouth.

"It's an inside joke. If we tell you, we'd have to kill you and Kara's in no shape to be disposing of bodies."

Luke rolled his eyes. "Be serious."

Kara bit her hand and Elena yelped. "Hey!"

"Oh, come on, Laney, tell him! He's P.D, too, so he should know what it means."

"Don't. You. Dare."

"Laney, it's—"

"I mean it, Kara. Tell him and I'll reveal your middle name."

Kara's face dropped. "You wouldn't."

"I totally would."

Pouting, Kara let her head fall against the sofa cushion. "You ruin everything, Laney."

The words were said in jest, in fun, but they burned like acid. Elena's entire body tensed and she leaped up, hid her flaming face in the oven, pretending to check the chicken. The opening credits to the movie began and Kara laughed at the part when Santa Claus gets electrocuted by the exterior lights, but Elena stalled.

Get it together, she warned herself. She'd vowed not to mess up anymore. She shut the oven door, sat between her sister and her—her—

Just what was Lucas Adair, anyway?

Elena did her best to enjoy the movie but it wasn't possible. With Lucas sitting next to her, she had to keep reminding herself to watch the movie rather than him. When Kara and Lucas laughed, she tried—oh, she tried to join in, but her heart screamed that she had no right to fun and laughter. She'd lost that right the day she'd cursed at her mother. Sometime during the movie's botched sledding attempt, the oven timer dinged. They paused the movie, plated up roasted chicken and potatoes and gravy and watched the rest of the movie while they ate. She watched Chevy Chase explain Santa Claus to a little girl and made a wish. She wished for a life without guilt in it, a life where she'd never said hateful things to her mother on the day before her death. She wished for something she could look forward to, find comfort in—or someone.

Someone she could hold on to.

She made the wish the same moment Lucas shifted his hand across the sofa to squeeze hers, all but stopping her heart. He couldn't have known. It...it simply wasn't possible for someone to know exactly what she'd been thinking. She couldn't breathe, she couldn't understand, she couldn't accept all this talk about signs. There was only one sign—the hole in her heart where her mother should have been. It was the only thing that was real. And damn it, it hurt.

Lucas shot her a quick smile and that hole in her heart filled—just a little bit, but it filled. It wasn't the same as having Mom back, or having her forgiveness. But it was something. She took a deep breath, held it and squeezed back. He shifted, raised his arm, invited her in.

She moved into the circle, cuddled closer, careful not to disturb Kara, who'd fallen asleep. "Look at that," she whispered to Lucas, pointing to the ripple that moved under Kara's belly.

"Whoa," he whispered back. "She was kidding about the kidneys and the liver, right?"

Elena snorted. "I hope so."

On another deep breath, she smelled his soap or deodorant or cologne—she wasn't sure which—and it curled her toes. "Elena?" His fingers drew circles on her shoulder and she felt the heat even through her sweater.

"Hmmm?"

He pressed warm lips to that spot just under her jaw. "Tell me what P.D. means."

"Not a chance in hell," she murmured.

The Griswolds were choking down dry turkey when Luke laughed, making his chest rumble. She thought about moving, about reaching forward for her cup of cocoa but his arm tightened around her.

Instead, she watched the movie.

And laughed, too.

✦ ✦ ✦

WHEN THE MOVIE ended, they left Kara to put in a few hours at SFG, working on the program for the Remembrance event. It was quite late when Lucas walked Elena back to Kara's apartment, leaving her with a slow hypnotic kiss and a warm grin.

She wasn't sure which one was more potent.

She floated through work on Monday, taking conference calls and answering emails in the same spot where she'd snuggled with Lucas the night before. He called her on his lunch hour. She texted him on hers. After work, she met him at SFG and with the entire team's help, they produced the table and seat cards, programs and menus. On Tuesday, he sent her a text that said, "Al would pass out." Attached, there was a picture of a store window with oversized playing cards arranged in poker hands in the window. She laughed and showed Kara the picture, determined not to suck the joy out of it for either of them. Wednesday night, he took her on a carriage ride around Central Park. Thursday, they cooked dinner together for Kara, who was unhappy that her latest appointment with her obstetrician revealed she would probably go past her due date. On Friday, he took her to Radio City for the Christmas Spectacular.

They spent their days sneaking in quick phone calls and text messages and their evenings either cooking dinner or grabbing take-out before heading to SFG to put all the finishing touches on the Remembrance event. They wrapped presents, tucked them under the tree in Kara's living room, mailed Christmas cards, and watched movie after movie.

And on Friday before the Christmas show, she looked at her face in the mirror and finally admitted there was a Look. It happened whenever Kara mentioned Luke's name.

"Ah ha! There it is again." Kara clapped her hands in delight. Elena's face burned.

"Okay, okay, you win. There's a look. Happy now?"

Kara considered that for a moment. "You guys haven't, um, you know—"

"Kara!"

"Well, have you?"

"Not that it's any of your business but no. We haven't."

"What are you waiting for?"

Elena shrugged. "I haven't invited him here because that's just wrong. And he hasn't invited me to his place."

"Huh. Okay, look. You're gonna need to speed things up a bit."

"Kara, no. Just…no. It'll happen when the time is right."

"With that attitude, this baby will graduate high school

before you two—"

"Kara!"

Kara nibbled on a nail and gave Elena a slow look of assessment. "You could put more effort into it—maybe a low-cut top or a short skirt."

"Or just tell him I'm ready."

Kara looked horrified. "Where's the fun in that? You should leverage the season, you know? Tie a red ribbon around your goodies or—"

"Answer the door wearing nothing but the wreath he bought you."

Kara blinked. "Um, that's good. That's really good."

"Kara, for Pete's sake! I know what to do."

Kara laughed and shrugged. "Okay, so you could just invite yourself over to his place and ...stay."

Elena shook her head. "I can't leave you for the whole night. What if you go into labor?"

"I'll call Cass."

That could work. And, Elena had to admit, she was desperate to be with Luke. The way he kissed her, the way he looked at her, the way he made her feel—being with Lucas would be amazing, she was sure of it.

"Call him," Kara demanded.

Elena thought it over for exactly two seconds and then grinned. "Okay." She grabbed her phone, dialed Luke's number.

"Hey, pretty lady. What's up?"

Oh. She coughed. "Um. Well, Kara's making plans with some of our friends to come over, spend the night with her. And I was thinking..." *Cough.* "Um. Well, maybewecouldhaveourownsleepover," she finished on a *whoosh* of courage.

There was only silence.

"Luke?" She glanced at the phone, saw that the call had

not dropped. "Are you there?"

"Yeah," he responded, his voice suddenly deeper. "Are you saying what I think you're saying?"

"Yes."

"You're sure."

"Yes."

"You're—"

"Lucas." She cut him off. "I just gave you the mother of all signs."

"You sure did." He laughed and she felt all her tension disappear. "Okay, so you're saying you've got an empty expansion slot and want me to fill—"

"Lucas!"

"Okay, okay. I'll see you in a little while. You know, we could skip Radio City and just—"

"Say goodbye, Lucas."

"See you soon, pretty lady."

She ended the call, glared at her sister who was choking on laughter.

"Smooth, Elena. You should write a blog."

"Yeah, yeah, yeah. Go call Cass."

When her sister disappeared into her bedroom, Elena collapsed onto the couch. Crap, that was a freakin' train wreck. Seduction wasn't supposed to be so... so gut-wrenching. It should be effortless. Easy. Right.

Her cell phone pinged. She tapped the screen, read a text message from Lucas.

Saw this, had to share ;)

Attached was a picture of a guy wearing a Trojan soldier costume, crossing a street. It took her a full minute and then she burst into laughter, texted back.

It's a sign. You'd better stock up!

Her phone buzzed immediately.

Count on it.

Still laughing, Elena went to find her sister. "Did you call Cass? What did she say?"

Kara dropped her phone and patted the bed, her eyes dancing. "Laney, listen to this! Cass saw *him*."

It took her a moment. "Him?" And then, Elena's eyes popped and she sat beside her sister on the bed. "Sean? She told you she saw Sean?"

Kara nodded. "Yep. They met at a bar."

"Here? In New York?" Elena covered her mouth with both hands. "Oh, wow. This is huge."

"I know. She'll be here tomorrow. She's gonna tell me all about him. I get the feeling she wants me to talk her out of it." Kara nudged Elena with an elbow. "So? How did it go with Lucas?"

Elena felt her face go hot. "I shocked him. I totally shocked him. His voice got all low and raspy, Kara."

"No way."

"Then he texted me a picture of a Trojan and—"

"Oh, my!"

"Not that kind of Trojan." Elena pulled out her phone. "Here. Look."

"Oh. Oh, that's okay, then." Kara winced, put her hand to her belly. "Milk Dud's working out again."

Elena touched the side of her sister's stomach, felt a very definite jab. "Holy crap, are you having a Rockette?"

"I don't know but I swear, the baby was literally jumping on the bed last night. I can't lie on this side anymore."

Elena couldn't help but giggle.

"Stop laughing and pull me up. I'm stuck."

Elena laughed harder.

Soon, Lucas was at Kara's door and when he saw Elena, his eyes running up and down her body, he used that same deep raspy voice. "Again, I have to put this out there. We can forget about Radio City tonight—"

But Elena was already shaking her head. "Cass can't come until tomorrow. I really have to be back here tonight, Lucas."

He grimaced. "You're trying to kill me, aren't you?" He pressed a hand to his heart, patted it. "Okay. I'll have you back in plenty of time to say goodnight."

To her amazement, Elena loved the Christmas Spectacular, from the toy soldiers to the living nativity—it was all a feast for her eyes, but it was the giant snow set that reminded her so much of the snowflake a special boy had given her. She left Radio City feeling light and full of joy. They passed a sidewalk Santa and Elena pressed some cash into the man's kettle, her face heating at the look of joy on Luke's face.

Joy. She'd done that. She'd put that look there.

They said goodnight at Kara's door and Elena could taste the barely restrained patience in Luke's kisses. "Tomorrow," she said.

"Tomorrow," he grinned and she had to have just one more kiss.

✦ ✦ ✦

THE NEXT MORNING, Lucas arrived at Kara's door bearing a bag of bagels and containers of juice. He wore his new gloves, and black sunglasses tucked into the zipper of his jacket. Elena's heart did a long slow spin.

"My hero!" Kara teased. "So how are the SFG plans going?"

"Just about done." Lucas clapped once to emphasize the statement. "Thank you both. I wasn't sure we were going to pull it all together, with all those last-minute adjustments, but we're in great shape." He turned to Elena. "You'll be my date, right?"

Elena had to fight the urge to kick the ground like a ten-year-old. "I didn't want to go and had no plans to go." His smile dimmed and she quickly added. "Until I met you."

He turned up the power to full wattage and there it was again—that clutch in her heart.

"Awww," Kara teased and dove into the bag, pulled out bagels. Elena popped straws into the juice containers. The buzzer rang. Juice squirted from Elena's container.

"She's here!" Kara clapped and then grabbed a paper towel while Elena buzzed Cass up.

"Kara." Lucas took her hand. "You sure you're okay with this?"

Kara turned, put her hand on his cheek. "Whose idea do you think it was?"

He snorted. "Damn if this isn't the strangest conversation I've ever had." He lost the grin, got serious. "I won't hurt her."

Kara pinched his cheek. "If I even suspected you might, we wouldn't be having this conversation."

"Fair enough."

A few minutes later, a force of nature strode into the apartment—Lucas recognized her as the driver of the Zipcar. Cassandra Baines—one of the Circle. She tugged off a pair of gloves and immediately exclaimed, "Look at you, mama! You can't possibly get any bigger. How excited are we getting?"

"*We* are not getting excited, *we* are getting bat-shit terrified."

"Oh, stop." Cassandra waved away Kara's admission. "You're going to be a great mom."

Elena cleared her throat. "Cassandra Baines, this is Lucas Adair. Luke, this is the infamous Cass."

He dialed down the smile power to about sixty percent and held out his hand. "I've heard a lot about you."

"Oh! Well then, I'm sorry." She snorted and fell to the sofa. She rifled through her handbag, talking while she searched. "I've heard all about you, too." She winked at Elena. "Which is why I bought you a gift. Ta da!" With a flourish, she pulled out a small bag and handed it to Luke. To Kara, she stage-whispered, "You were right. Completely P.D."

He peeked inside it and flushed crimson. "Ah, thank you."

"Cass, tell me you didn't." Elena glared at her friend. They'd just met and she was already teasing him? Cassandra let out one of her trademark bawdy laughs. If Elena knew Cass, she had a pretty good idea what was in the bag.

"Oh, I did and you can thank me. Tomorrow. Now get lost."

Elena kissed Kara goodbye, gave Cass's hair a little tug, grabbed her overnight bag and walked to the door, where Lucas already waited, his face still red. As soon as she opened the door, he stepped out, halted, and turned around. He grabbed Cassandra's bag and shoved it into his jacket pocket.

"Thanks for the gift." He grinned full power and shut the door, but it did nothing to muffle the howls of laughter on the other side.

✦ ✦ ✦

LUCAS TOOK ELENA on the PATH train to Hoboken, anticipation all but *killing* him. She'd looked amazing last night but this morning, wearing plain jeans and a sweater, she damn near stopped his heart. He searched her eyes, kept looking for signs of doubt, anxiety, fear—but they were clear and bright.

That was a good sign and later, he'd ask her if she'd spend New Year's Eve with—

Good sign? Hell. Al was rubbing off on him. No plans. She was going home after the holidays. She'd been clear on that from the beginning—no strings, just a holiday—

No.

He reached over, gave her hand a quick squeeze and she smiled and just like that—he fell like a house of cards. He loved this woman, loved her from the center of his soul and had absolutely no intention of letting her leave New York, or him. If he couldn't convince her to stay for the sex, he'd win her over with his hot cocoa recipe.

His hands shook as he unlocked his front door, stepped aside to let her enter first.

"This is beautiful, Luke," Elena said when he shut the door.

"Thanks. I like it."

She wandered around his living room, stopping at the windows to soak in the incredible view of the city, before turning to admire the space. He'd painted one wall a bold red. In front of it stood the dark leather sofa his sister gave him when she redecorated. It faced a sleek fireplace. Above it, a guy's best friend—his flat screen TV and surround sound system. He'd left the windows uncovered because the incredible view of Manhattan was part of the purchase price of the condo. Right now, that view was blocked by a huge tree, bigger than the one he'd bought Kara. He wouldn't admit it, not even to Al, but pulling out the collection of ornaments meant something to him.

His mother had started it for him the year he was born. Every year, he carefully wrapped each ornament to protect and preserve it—especially the two crystal snowflakes he had left from the set of three he'd sacrificed to cheer up a heartbroken little girl. Every year, when he unwrapped them, he remembered exactly when he'd received each one. Like the smiley face ornament—she'd bought him that after he'd broken his arm and was convinced he'd ruined Christmas for everyone.

He took off his hat and gloves, unzipped his jacket, tossed everything on one of two chairs that flanked the Christmas tree. "Let me take this." He helped Elena off with her coat, piled it on top of his and set her bag down at the foot of the stairs.

"One bedroom?"

"Three." He walked toward her with a grin. "I'll give you the tour in a few minutes. But first, there's something I have to do." He took her hand and led her to the kitchen. Elena ran her fingers along gleaming black granite counters while Lucas opened one of the white cabinets and took out a pan. "Have a seat. I'm going to make you a cup of my as-advertised, world-famous hot cocoa."

She raised her brows. "Oh, right. The world-famous, widely admired, best-you've-ever-had hot cocoa. Is there like a money-back guarantee or something?"

He shot her a glare. "Tough lady. Jeez, it's pretty damn good, okay?"

"Okay, hot shot. Go for it." She smiled back and he was surprised to discover he enjoyed the comfortable banter that they'd developed ever since they'd agreed to stop obsessing over signs. She seemed easier around him, less—well, awestruck and damn if admitting that didn't make him feel like a dick. He knew the SFG crew had been telling stories about him. Hell, the way Al talked, he saved kittens from trees and widows from evil evicting banks. The thought made him laugh.

✦ ✦ ✦

"WHAT IS GOING on with you?" Elena angled her head, smiling at him. "You've been lost in your own thoughts all morning." He'd been quiet, but fixed on her like a hunter on prey. Yet she found it easy to be with him. When had that happened, she wondered? True, he was hotter than a tropical sun but Elena had grown to appreciate Lucas for the man he was behind the nuclear smile. The way he thought about her and Kara, doing things for them before they'd even asked.

He only shrugged, piercing straight through her with another of those intense looks, then got busy, so she sat at a stool and watched him move around the space—easy, competent. He had great hands and as she watched him break a huge slab of dark chocolate into small chunks, couldn't help but imagine those hands on her.

All over her.

And when he held up one of those hands to lick chocolate off his fingers, she couldn't help but imagine his tongue, too.

She bit her lip and fanned her face. He poured milk into the pan, added brown sugar and stirred, the muscles across his back and shoulders rippling under his Henley shirt adding more fuel to her hyperactive imagination. Her mouth watered—whether it was from the way those muscles flexed or the delicious scent filling his kitchen, she couldn't be sure. He moved to another cabinet, took out a tiny bottle of vanilla, and stirred a spoonful into the sweet milk. From the stainless steel refrigerator, he removed a plastic container, pried off the lid, stuck a finger in it and slid it into his mouth.

Whipped cream. Sweet Lord, he made his own whipped cream?

"Come here," he said in that same deep voice that curled her toes. On autopilot, she joined him at the stove and he put a whisk in her hand. "Stir the milk for me. Just like this." He stood behind her, put his hand over hers, guiding her motion and she was hot, much too hot to drink hot cocoa. While she stirred, he slowly added the chocolate chunks and a pinch of salt. "Don't stop."

Stop? She wouldn't dream of it.

Her eyes tracked him. He moved to a cupboard over the sink, pulled out mugs and put them beside the stove, leaned over and inhaled deeply. "Smells good, right?"

Elena couldn't talk, she couldn't possibly make a sound that would be anything but a moan right now, so she only nodded. He cut the heat, carefully poured the thick sweet chocolate into the mugs and then spooned on a heap of cream. She took one cup and lifted it to her lips but he stopped her.

"Wait. Garnish." With a grin, he sprinkled some of the chocolate dust still on the cutting board over the cloud of cream. "Now it's ready."

She kept her eyes pinned to his, blew softly across the top, and sipped. Yes. Yes, oh yes, he was right, it was the best cup of world-famous, widely admired, damn good cup of cocoa she'd ever had. This wasn't a drink, this was an *experience*.

Lucas grabbed the second mug, sipped and nodded in approval. "It's good."

Good? It was nirvana. He watched her over the cup's rim, watched her watching him. When he licked a tiny bit of cream from his lips, she put out a hand to steady herself and he grinned.

He put his cup on the counter, took hers and did the same. He skimmed a finger along her jaw, heard her swallow hard and stepped closer. He stared into her eyes for a long moment. "If you changed your mind or just don't want to, I—"

She shook her head, hooked one finger through his belt loop and tugged him toward her, touched her mouth to his and heaven help her, she nearly exploded. Mouths fused, they fell against the refrigerator, then another counter. Lucas boosted her up, stepped between her legs, and pulled back to study her with hooded eyes. Slowly, he moved closer, pressed his lips to her throat, his hands skimming over her breasts.

"Elena. You feel so good."

No, oh, no, no, no, he had that entirely backwards. *He* felt good. His hands on her body felt good, his lips on her skin felt good. She moaned—a long breathless sound – and felt him smile against her mouth. For a moment, a precious moment she wished she could preserve forever like a flower pressed in a book, she felt the hole in her heart close up—the place where the guilt had roots. She felt no anxiety, no worry, no fear, no grief—only him and the warmth he brought her.

His mouth came back for more and she knew he could taste the chocolate and cream on her tongue, lapping at it like a cat. His hands moved under her sweater to cup her breasts, tease more groans out of her. She melted into him, her hand pressed to his heart. He smelled like sugar and chocolate and her body coiled, tightening in anticipation while his body vibrated under her hands.

"Lucas," she murmured, running her hands up his arms and into his hair. "What's wrong? You're shaking."

✦ ✦ ✦

LUCAS KISSED HER once, twice, tried to calm his galloping heart. Words danced on his tongue—words he wanted to shout from the top of a skyscraper, words it was way too soon to say. He smiled and shook his head. "You. You're killing me." He leaned in, kissed along the curve of her neck.

Elena's hands settled on his chest, pushed gently. She looked up at him, confusion and disappointment in her eyes. "Do you not want to—"

"No! Hell, no." He stepped closer. "I mean yes. Hell,

Elena, I want you so badly, I can't talk straight."

"I want you, too."

Do you? he wondered for a moment as the panic clogged his throat. She was his. At least for today, she was his and if he couldn't yet tell her what she meant to him, he'd spend all day and all night showing her. "Come to bed with me, pretty lady." He held out his hand, smiling when she took it.

He led her to the stairs and halted. "Hang on." In the jacket he'd flung to the living room chair, he found the bag her friend Cass had given him, then all but dragged Elena upstairs to his bedroom. He up-ended the contents of the bag onto the bed.

Condoms in every possible variety rained down and Elena gasped. "I'm going to *kill* her."

"Later. You have plans now." Lucas leaned down, bit her ear and she groaned for him. "Close your eyes and pick one."

With a laugh that was mostly a sigh, Elena did.

"Ribbed. Excellent choice." Luke peeled off his shirt and Elena's mouth fell open. He figured that was a good sign. Slowly, she traced his pecs, followed the line of hair that dipped below his belt, and made his stomach quiver with her bold fingers. He slid his hands to her waist, peeled her sweater up, up, up and over her head. His breath caught at the sight of her. He dipped his head, pressed his lips against her heart, happy to feel it thundering, determined to make it his.

"From the first second I saw you, I've wanted to do this," he murmured, kissing his way down her rib cage. He popped the clasp on her bra, drew it slowly down her arms, then the fly on her jeans, and tugged the pants off her hips. He dropped to his knees, took off her shoes one at a time, pressing kisses along her belly as he slowly tugged down her panties. When he stood, he lifted her right out of the pants that pooled at her feet. She gasped, and her eyes went wide. Still holding her, he captured her mouth, kissed her fast and hard.

He kissed her like she was his first drink of water after crossing a desert. He sat on the edge of the bed, cradled her in his arms and kissed her over and over again—slowly. Deeply. Elena was naked in his arms and he tried to slow down, to keep a tight rein on his control. He fisted a hand in her hair, pulled her head back so he could see her face with her eyes closed, her mouth swollen. His other hand cupped her breast, teased the nipple, made her breath hitch. The sound inflamed him and he had to taste. He bent his head, took her into his mouth and when her back arched and her nails dug into his flesh, he half-feared the top of his head might launch into orbit if he waited any longer.

He shifted, laid her on his bed and stripped off jeans and underwear in one smooth motion. Panting, enjoying the way her eyes raked over him, he was sure his skin blistered from the heat of that look. He tore open the packet of the condom she'd picked, rolled it on and met her on the bed, pressing his center to hers.

"Tell me again, Elena." He took her hands, raised them over her head, threaded their fingers together. "Tell me."

"I want you, Lucas."

With a prayer of gratitude, he sank inside her and groaned. "Elena." He held himself still, wanting—no, *craving* the feel of her body tightening and moving around him. She lifted her legs, slid them along the back of his calves and wrapped them around his waist, her hips rising up, urging him on. He moved and her moan made his eyes roll back. Instinct took over—he forgot his routine, forgot his damn name. She was all that mattered, all that there was. He let go of her hands, used his to cruise up and down her body, some primal part of his brain categorizing her responses—the spot behind her knee, the crease of her thigh, and oh, *there*. Right there.

His pulse pounded. He wanted all of her, all there was, so he gave, gave all he was until she tightened around him, exploding with a scream. He kept moving, kept up until she stilled and sighed out his name.

Only then did he follow.

Chapter Ten

ELENA STRETCHED AND sighed, a long low sound of satisfaction, and then wrapped her arms around Lucas, burying her fingers in all that thick hair—currently splayed on her chest. Still connected, they lay catching their breath, Lucas rubbing his thumb along the curve of her breast. She was—was—wow. There were simply no words, she decided.

"Elena," he whispered, his voice a breath in her ear. That was all he said. Only her name, but it made her heart do a slow somersault. Her body still quivered from what he'd just done to it. After a few minutes, he lifted his head and kissed her, a sweet touch of lips that opened a new wound in her heart, one that made her wonder if leaving New York—leaving *him*—was really such a good idea after all.

She reminded herself she couldn't keep him. But damn it, she wanted to pretend she could, even if only for tonight, so she tightened her hold.

He kissed her again, then shifted to leave the bed, striding to a door that led to his bathroom. While he was gone, she tried to put her feet back down on solid ground, but it wasn't possible. The earth was still moving. She shifted to her side, burrowed deeper into his bed, tried in vain to shove away the guilt.

"You're thinking."

Her eyes snapped open. Lucas stood in the bathroom doorway, comfortably naked, watching her. The sight of him made her mouth water and her body want—and the guilt grow. Elena shifted again, this time, to find her clothes.

"No. Don't do that." He moved quickly, pulled the shirt from her hand, turned her to face him. "We've still got a bag of condoms to work our way through."

She managed to laugh though her eyes stung. "Okay if I use your shower?"

Lucas cursed and lifted her off her feet, tossed her back to the bed. When she moved, he climbed in with her, pinned her.

"Lucas, let me go."

"Uh uh. Talk to me."

Elena rolled her eyes. "Is that what I'm here for? To talk?"

He stared down at the sarcasm on her face, swallowed his retort when he saw the misery beneath it. He rolled off the bed, dragged on his jeans and left the bedroom. He headed downstairs, hoping that a few minutes alone would help her settle. In the kitchen, he put the hot cocoa mugs in the microwave, gave them a zap and sat at a stool to sip his.

He was completely adrift here. No program, no flowchart to step him through this. He was in love with a woman who had one foot on a plane.

A few minutes later, she joined him. She'd pulled on his shirt and it was the sexiest thing he'd ever seen in his life. "Oooo." She smiled brightly and grabbed the hot mug. "Thanks."

Frowning, he angled his head and stared.

"What?"

"That's my question." He spread his hands, waited for her

to say something. Anything. "What the hell is going on with you?"

"Nothing."

"Oh, come off it, Elena!" He shoved back from the stool, prowled the kitchen. "We should still be upstairs, enjoying round two and pillow talk, not standing in my kitchen, about to have our first argument."

Her smile froze, then faded. She whipped around, stalked to the stairs.

"Where the hell are you going?" He followed.

"Away from here. From you."

Like hell she was. "Yeah, that's the crux of the issue, isn't it? You don't want me."

"I just had you." She whipped back around to face him. "I called you, remember?"

With all the force of a two-by-four to the face, the reason why Elena was freaking out struck Lucas. "Yeah." He moved in front of her, blocked her path. "I remember. It was nice."

Okay, it was a cheap shot. Desperate times.

Her face went red and for minute, he thought his understatement would keep her fighting, keep her *here*. But she edged past him. Faster now, he kept talking. "Being with you today cemented something I've known since the day I met you but figured you don't want to hear." Her movements were jerky, rushed, and he knew he had seconds before she was gone so he blurted it out, the timing be damned. "I love you. Damn it, Elena, I love you!" He shouted the words, frustration shredding what restraint he had left.

She spun around, the steel in her brown eyes wavering. Her jaw fell open, and with a violent shake of her head, she stepped back—stepped away from him. "Well, stop."

He almost laughed. He stepped toward her until he was a breath away. "I'm so damn in love with you, it hurts. And you know it. In fact, I think you feel exactly the same way and *that's* why you're picking a fight. You can't allow yourself to love me because it takes courage for that—courage you don't have." Her eyes blurred and he kicked himself for making her cry. When her hand crept up to rub that spot on her chest, he lost what little hold on his temper he'd had left and let out a stream of curses. "I'm begging you, Elena, *please* talk to me!"

For one full minute, she glared at him, chest heaving, and then her knees buckled. She fell to the floor, a sob shattering the echo of his demand. "I can't stay! Don't you understand that? I cannot stay here."

He forced himself to stay exactly where he stood. "Why? Tell me why, damn it."

"Because!" She buried her face in her hands and folded over while the grief finally—blessedly—escaped. "I thought I could do this but I can't. I don't want to think about it. And being here forces me to—Oh, I can't!" She pressed both hands to her chest and rubbed and his heart cracked in two. Slowly, he crouched beside her, pulled her into his arms.

"Baby, I know it hurts." He put his hand over hers, rubbed gently. Her hands came up to clutch his. "But it wasn't your fault. Why do you feel so guilty?"

She shook her head. "It *was* my fault."

He shifted her weight, stood up with her in his arms and sat on the sofa, cradling her against his chest. "Tell me."

"I was such a brat, Lucas." She whispered into his shoulder. "My mom—she was great but I never appreciated her. Ever. We fought all the time. She picked on everything—and boy, did I give her a lot to pick on. I wore nothing but black, my hair was a nest, I had a bratty attitude to pretty much everybody and my grades were pitiful. Whatever we did— shopping trips, dinners out, holidays—they typically ended with us fighting and Kara saying, 'You ruin everything,

Laney.'" Her voice cracked.

Understanding dawned. "She said that when we watched that movie. That's why you fled to the kitchen. But she was kidding, wasn't she?"

Elena nodded. "Yes, but the words, Luke. They're like a scar, you know?"

"Go on. Finish it."

She sucked in a deep breath. "I finally found a boy I liked. I cut class to be with him so we could—Well, Mom found out. She told my dad. She grounded me and I—damn it, Lucas." She covered her face as heavy sobs broke free. "I told her I hated her guts. I told her I hated her guts and wished she'd drop dead." Her words were almost impossible to understand through her sobs. "That was the last thing I got to say to her. And she died, she died believing I—"

She couldn't get the rest of the words out. She sobbed out a dozen years of guilt onto his bare chest and the weight of it stabbed straight through him. He held her, rocked her, until she emptied—dimly aware of the tears falling from his own eyes, of the guilt carved into his own heart.

When her sobs quieted, he started to shed it. "You think I don't understand, but I do. The night before…my mom and I also had a big argument. She kept saying how lazy I was. How I took no pride in anything I did, no interest. I said something disrespectful—and she slapped me."

He didn't even notice his hand come up to touch his cheek.

"That morning, I was in school when we found out about the attack. I ran all the way home. She left us a message. She told us she loved us. And she would love us for always." His voice thickened but he pushed the words out. "I never told anybody this—not even my family." He glanced at his hand, surprised to see it was already rubbing his cheek and managed a small smile. "She touched me. I felt her—right there, in math class, when the principal announced that the towers fell. A hand cupped my cheek and rubbed it and I swear to you, it was her. I stood up, ran home, and found a message she left on the machine." His smile bloomed. "She loved us, Elena. Even me. They were her last words—not our stupid fight, not how mad at me or how disappointed in me I knew she was. She forgave me because—" He had to stop, swallow hard. Swallow again. "Because she was my mother and she knew she was going to die and—" His voice broke but he shoved through it. "And that's what moms do."

Elena only stared at him and his smile faded.

"But I didn't believe that. Didn't trust it—any of it. I convinced myself I dreamed it. Made it all up and then did something so despicable, it makes me sick." He buried his face in his hands and groaned.

He heard her take a breath to say something but before she could speak, he cut her off with a joyless laugh. "Just listen. I'm not exaggerating." He pulled in a deep breath for courage. "After she died, the rage—I swear, Elena, it was so huge, it had its own heartbeat. I spent about a year walking around like a—like a lit fuse, pissed off and ready to brawl with anybody who looked twice at me—and some who only looked once."

Her hands, still clutching his, squeezed gently—a show of support that gave him a glimmer of hope.

"One day, I saw this guy who just looked wrong to me. Suspicious—like a terrorist. I started in on him, he got up in my face and next thing I know, I'm in handcuffs and covered in his blood. I fractured his skull, Elena. I beat him almost to death—and I think I would have if somebody hadn't stopped me." He dropped his head back, squeezed his eyes shut. He hated remembering this part—hated that he was capable of hatred, of violence—of being the very thing he despised most.

"I was arrested, charged with assault, attempted murder."

She shifted. He lifted his head, met her gaze, thumbed away the tears that still shimmered on her lashes.

"All I kept thinking was my mother was right. She was right and I hadn't listened to anything she'd taught me. She'd have been so disappointed. She *forgave* me before she died and I went and —" He couldn't say it. Her arms came around him, stroking his head.

"The guy I hurt testified in court—he described every word, every punch. I puked right there in front of the judge. They had witnesses, they had evidence—they could have given me the harshest sentence, put me in prison."

"But they didn't. You're here," she whispered.

"Only because my victim asked for leniency."

Through his tears, he flashed her favorite smile. "He told the judge that he understood my actions had been based on fear, that he could see the remorse and regret in my eyes and asked if instead of a prison sentence, the court would order me to volunteer my time with an organization that promotes healing. The judge agreed and at seventeen years old, I started working with people who were just like me. Suffering, dealing with loss and unimaginable fear."

He shifted across the sofa, Elena pressed to his side. "Few months later, he came in to see how I was doing. And I lost it. Just went down to the floor and sobbed like a baby about how sorry I was. He taught me how to find the love and joy in life again. It was always there...I just didn't know where to look."

He tucked a finger under her chin, lifted her face to his. "Elena, every time I see him, that guilt's there. But he taught me how to redirect it. Make it useful. Constructive. Something that's not based on fear and hate."

"So all your good deeds—"

He waved a hand. "Just a way for me to channel my guilt,

to wish I could go back and, and not have tried so damn hard to deny what that touch to my face really was." He stood up, crossed to the huge window and stared down at the city – always busy, always so alive. "I have a lot of regrets, Elena, but that one's the hardest to deal with."

She was silent for a long time and he hoped she was considering everything he'd told her. He almost flinched when her hand touched his back. He turned, folded her into his arms and held on, held tight.

"Oh, Lucas. I'm so sorry. Every time you did something I thought was too good to be true, all I could think was there was no way I could possibly hold onto you, when I'm not good." Her voice was rough.

"You *are* good, honey. You came when your sister needed you."

He felt the sob build inside her and tightened his arms. "Listen to me. You and me? We were both just being the cliché teen. Believe me, I know how much it sucks that we didn't get to fix things but you have to let it go so you don't become me."

She huffed in frustration. "Hell, Luke, it's not that easy. I push everyone away. I hardly talk to my closest friends and my sister—I've done nothing but make her cry."

He lifted her face. "They don't know, do they? What you just told me?"

When her face crumbled again, he had his answer. "You have to tell them, Elena. You have to trust them. From everything you've told me about your circle, I have to believe they'll all rally around you."

She shook her head. "They'll hate me."

He sighed, shifted her again until they sat face to face. "Elena, the guy I beat up said something I never forgot. He said, *darkness cannot drive out darkness: only light can do that. Hate cannot drive out hate: only love can do that."* He waited a beat for that to sink in. "Recognize it?"

She shook her head.

"Dr. Martin Luther King said that. And it hit me like a steel boot to my head that I *was* hate—I'd let it fill every cell in my body. That was the day—the moment when I promised myself I'd spend the rest of my life looking for the light and if I couldn't see it, I'd *be* it, even when I couldn't feel it. You look at me like I'm some sort of perfect being, but I'm not. I'm not a hero, Elena. I just believe in trying, that's all."

Slowly, she shook her head, her eyes never leaving his. "You're wrong, Luke. You are good. You are so, so good." She leaned in, forgot why she had to protect her heart, forgot why she needed to leave, forgot it all except the compulsion to comfort him. She pressed her mouth to his—a sweet, gentle whisper of lips that moved him.

Broke him.

On a gasp, he pulled her to him, kissed her with all that he was. "Stay. Stay with me. Love me," he whispered against her lips, already pulling her toward him.

"Yes," she whispered, overcome.

They spent what was left of the day making love, whispering in the growing darkness, healing each other. Lucas turned on the Christmas tree lights, grabbed some pillows and blankets and they made love on the floor in front of it.

✦ ✦ ✦

IT WAS DARK when they separated, stretched out on the sofa with nothing but the tree lights to see by.

Lucas kissed her hair. "Al is a hundred percent convinced that my mom is working with yours to set us up."

"My friends are just as bad—Cass and her bag of presents,

Kara arranging our dates." Frustrated, Elena sighed heavily. "Don't you wonder maybe all these signs are some kind of, I don't know, an illusion?"

"They led us here, didn't they?" He countered with a sweet smile.

Maybe they did.

It hit her then with all the force of a two-ton blast.

His smile. *That* smile.

"Hey, hey, you okay? You look like you just saw a ghost." Frowning, he tilted her face up to his.

Not a ghost. An angel. "Lucas, I need to tell you a story so you can tell me I'm not completely insane."

Still frowning, he rolled to his side and propped his head on his hand. "Tell me."

She swallowed hard once, then twice. When she could talk, she blurted out the first thing that hit her—that mattered to her. "The way you smile at me. Oh, Luke, I love it, love it so much. It—you—remind me of this boy I met. It was the first Remembrance event."

"I remember it. I was there."

She squeezed her eyes shut, shook her head. "Standing on the ramp, leading into the pit. I was staring down, down into that pile of rubble and thinking about… about the darkness and the destruction and there was this boy, a boy who was so, so tall. He smiled at me and put something in my hand." She was rambling now because the more she talked, the more she knew she was right. "He had terrible skin and braces on his teeth and he was the most beautiful boy I'd ever seen and he saved me and I think I always knew and that's why I was so afraid—I think he might be you and I—I just don't know what to do with that."

Luke's dark eyes, round with shock, closed. "What did this boy put in your hand?" he whispered.

"A snowflake. A crystal snowflake."

He made a noise like he was choking and her eyes snapped to his in alarm. But his no longer held any light. He got up, walked to the tree and pulled off an ornament and held it out to her. She knew without looking what it was. A cold dread grew and spread and sucked all the hope from her like a collapsing star. She forced herself to face her sentence. She looked down, saw a snowflake ornament identical to the one that a beautiful boy had given her all those years ago. The one that even now was carefully wrapped in the bottom of her suitcase.

His voice sounded miles away. "...part of a set. There'd been six—my sister has three but I only have two. I gave away my third back in '01, at the first holiday event to this girl who looked like she wanted to jump into the pit at Ground Zero."

She didn't move—she couldn't. Oh, the pain was vicious. She could barely hear his words over the blood rushing in her ears. She stared at the crystal snowflake—saw but refused to believe. Lucas—he—ah, hell, he was the boy who'd—who'd *saved* her. Could fate be this cruel? She turned and looked at him—truly looked. The braces were gone, the pimples were gone. But that smile was the same—how had she not seen it?

"Why?" She croaked out the question.

"I needed her to know there was still light in the world. She was so lost and I was afraid...afraid she was going to do something terrible. I told her—you—to hold it up to the light," he said, still looking at the ornament.

Elena said nothing. She remembered doing just what he'd said and the snowflake in her hand caught the light, sparkled and shimmered. And while she stared at it, he'd disappeared and she'd thought she'd imagined him, thought he was an angel sent from heaven to stop her from doing the most selfish thing she could have done. She'd *hated* that boy for saving her—for years, she hated him, when the pain in her chest grew to unbearable levels. And yet she would pull that crystal snowflake out from its box and stare at it until she could get her bearings once again, and it worked every time.

Lucas was that boy—her angel. Her savior. But as the years piled up, she'd cursed him for making sure she could never forget, never close the hole, the gaping pit in her soul, never get a moment's peace from the words she'd screamed in a child's temper tantrum.

She lifted her eyes to heaven and cursed her mother for punishing her like this.

She turned and fled upstairs for her clothes.

Lucas watched her run, his heart in splinters.

Chapter Eleven

LUCAS WAS A smart man.

When Elena went white and turned for the stairs without a word, he knew—knew as sure as he knew his own name that even though she had the crystal snowflake he'd given away all those years ago, even though she was the girl he'd spent the last thirteen years worrying about, even though she was the woman he loved, she would only ever see this as a sign she'd been damned.

Instead of bringing them together, that stupid snowflake would be the wedge that split them apart.

He didn't have a clue how to stop her, how to convince her she was wrong.

He crossed to the sofa and sat, his hands curling into fists when the ceiling over his head creaked. It took her a few minutes and then she was back, dressed. She grabbed her outer gear and her bag and without a word, moved to his door.

A tidal wave of panic rose up in him. "I always figured I'd find that girl with my snowflake someday," he began. "Al's signs drive me nuts, but deep down," he slapped a hand to his heart. "Deep down in here, I *believed*, Elena. I believed if I kept looking, one day I'd find that girl and she would be in my life. But that's impossible now because you refuse to *see*. You want me to believe my mother hates me and is punishing me—punishing us—and I *can't* do that. She *forgave* me, Elena. I *won't* believe she sent you here to punish me. I called you a cab. You can wait for it on the curb. Want the rest of that cocoa to go?"

It was cheap and childish but damn it, he was raw and he'd needed to make her hurt the way he was. When she flinched, he figured the barb had hit the target. And then he cursed himself for hurting her, cursed her for hurting him.

She opened the door.

He threw her another spiteful parting shot. "I want the snowflake back. Since it's clear it and I mean nothing to you, I want it back."

She nodded, refusing to look at him. He watched her shoulders move like she had to force them to hold her body up. Finally, she turned. "I'm—"

"Do *not* say you're sorry or I will lose it, I swear. If you were sorry, you'd stay. We've already established that you're scared so you go on back to Kara's, eat some cookies and curl up in a ball. After you tell your circle what's been going on with you all these years—after they tell you what a *coward* you are, give me a call. Maybe I'll pick up." He stood, stalked to the door, cursed when she stepped back and through it. He wanted to grab her and shake her senseless and because he knew, too well, what could happen when he let his fury rule him, he slammed and bolted the door between them.

And threw his fist at the wall beside it.

✦ ✦ ✦

KARA AND CASSANDRA were waiting for her at the door.

"Laney? Lucas called us. I'm so, so sorry, honey."

When Elena didn't—couldn't—answer, it was Cass who wrapped an arm around her, and took her in. The tears fell and the sobs shook her body while her sister and closest friend held her, rocked her, murmured soothing words to her.

It was a long time before she could talk. And when she started, she couldn't stop. She told them all of it, every unbelievable, heart-shattering word.

"It was him?" Kara whispered, her own eyes damp. "You're positive?"

"Kara, he has the other snowflakes and besides, he *knew*."

"Knew what?" Cassandra prodded.

Elena straightened up, wiped the tears off her face, and prayed for courage. "Knew what I was thinking. I never told you this—I never told anybody this, but that day, walking down the ramp to the pits, I thought about—" her voice cracked. "Thought about—"

"No." Kara's eyes popped.

"I thought about throwing my leg over that rail and—"

"No, damn it, Laney, no!" Kara cried, grabbing for her, but Elena leaped up and walked away, to the tree Lucas had found for her—for them.

Cass cleared her throat. "Laney, honey, I know—we all know how hard it was to lose your mom, but you have to know she'd have hated—"

A laugh bubbled up from her chest—hysterical and raw and not the least bit joyful. "Oh, that's not all of it."

Kara grabbed her phone. "I'm calling the girls. I'm calling Gigi and Enza and Joann, too. You need help, sweetie. You—"

Cassandra gently took the phone from Kara's hand, shook her head. "No. No, Elena doesn't need to be smothered right now. Laney. Tell us all of it. Tell us why."

Elena's knees went weak. She sat on the floor, right by the tree, and just stared at all the lights and ornaments. There was one ornament not on that tree. It was wrapped in a box and hidden deep in her suitcase. "Curtis Fox. Curtis Fox is the reason why."

Kara cursed. "For heaven's sake, Elena."

"I remember this guy. You were in—what, ninth grade?" Cass put in.

"Tenth. I was head over heels for him. We cut class to—ah, you know."

Kara made a sound that made her disgust clear.

"Mom found out, grounded me. We had a huge fight. I told her I hated her guts. That I wished she'd drop dead."

When neither girl said anything, Elena added the last straw. "That was the last thing she heard from me before she died." The silence pressed on her like a weight. She stared at her sister, at her friend.

Waited for it.

Braced herself for it.

"Well?" she demanded. "Say it."

Kara and Cass exchanged a look. "What, honey?"

Elena blew hair from her eyes. "*Laney, you always ruin everything.*" She waited a beat, her heart thundering in her ears. "I've heard those words so many times and I've been waiting, just waiting, for you guys to say it now—now that you know."

It took her a few minutes but then Kara gasped. "Oh no, Laney! This is why you stayed away—because you were afraid of some stupid bratty *I told you so* I said when we were little?"

Elena flung up her hands. "It's not just the words, Kara. It's the look. Every time I ruined something special you and Mom had going on, you said that and looked at me with all this pain and disappointment and I swear, that hurt more than anything. And every time, I swore, I vowed I wouldn't be bad again and somehow, I always was."

Kara shook her head. "You were a kid, honey. Challenging

and difficult, but a kid. None of us blame you for what happened to Mom."

"Maybe not. But how can you not blame me for letting her die angry?"

Kara bit her lip and Elena knew she had no words to explain that away because it was true.

"Elena," Cass finally said. "I still don't understand why or how this affects you and Luke."

At the mention of his name, her tears began all over again. "Because of the signs. She's punishing me. She's punishing me and I deserve it, I deserve every bit of it, and I'm sorry! I'm so, so sorry, but I'll never get to tell her that. She'll never forgive me."

Why hadn't her mom found a way to speak to her—to forgive her—like Luke's had? She'd had a moment, a second, really, when she'd thought he was right—that finding each other so many years later was a sign. But when he told her how certain he was that he'd felt a touch on his cheek, she knew it was nothing more than wishful thinking and she had to leave. Immediately. It was the hardest thing she'd ever had to do. And even Lucas—who understood more than anyone ever had—looked at her with that same expression of disappointment and fury she'd experienced most of her life.

You ruin everything, Laney.

She sobbed until she fell into an exhausted sleep, only dimly aware of Cassandra and Kara trying to comfort her.

✦ ✦ ✦

THE NEXT MORNING, Elena woke to a rude nudge. "Get up."

She bolted upright to find Cassandra standing over her with her arms crossed and her face tight.

Blinking swollen and hurt-filled eyes at her, she groaned

"What?"

"I said get up."

"Cass, for the sake of my sanity, leave me alone."

"Read my lips." She leaned closer, her expression fierce "No. Way." Elena's lip quivered and Cassandra sighed. "Oh, Laney. You've had way too many years to deal with this alone. Now, you're going to have to deal with all of us."

All of them? Wonderful. Elena scrubbed her hands over her bleary eyes and climbed to her feet, found the whole crew gathered in Kara's living room. Strong and steady Sabrina sat next to Elena's hormonal and broken-hearted sister, both of them wearing similar expressions of outrage and pity. Elena snapped up both hands and shook her head. "No. I cannot do this right now."

"I repeat, you have had too many years. Sit down." Cass ordered.

"I have to pee." Elena practically ran to the bathroom, locked herself in, trying hard to calm her shattered nerves. She could hear all of the girls whispering about her. When she heard Bree ask if there were razor blades in the bathroom, she flung the door open and stepped out, concluding it was easier to just rip off the bandage and get it over with.

"Okay. Say what you need to." She walked to Kara's kitchen, sat on a stool and faced her executioners.

"Honey, what do you think we're gonna do—beat you?" A voice said from the phone in Bree's hand.

Elena jerked. "Damn it, you called Jade, too?"

"Of course we did." Cassandra folded her arms. "When one of us is hurt, all of us bleed."

Kara put up a hand. Jade's question deserved an answer. "Is that why you never said anything?" she asked quietly, her eyes as red and swollen as Elena's. "Because you thought we'd slap at you?" Her tone held pain. "Is that what you really think of us?"

"Kara." Bree shook her head, a warning. "Laney, when I found out I was pregnant, do you remember what happened?"

Elena nodded, unable to look at her.

"Did anybody make me feel like crap? Did anybody say any of the things I was so afraid they'd say?"

"No," Cassandra cut in. "I'd have kicked their butts if they'd tried."

Elena looked from face to face. They didn't understand. They didn't get it. Getting pregnant was a beginning, not an end. It resulted in something happy—Charlie, Bree's daughter.

What Elena had done was permanent.

Irrevocable.

Unforgivable.

"Show of hands." Elena thrust her own into the air. "How many of you told your mom you hated her before she died?" When no hands joined hers, she nodded bitterly. "So please don't tell me you understand."

Bree looked away, pressed a hand to her mouth. But Jade voiced her opinion, her anger loud and clear through the tiny speaker on the cell phone. "You're wrong. You're so wrong, Laney. We know you. We *know* you. We know you loved your mom. We know and so did she."

Slowly, robotically, Elena shook her head, pressed her hands over that dark and cold hole in her chest, but it grew and expanded and spread and she knew she couldn't hold it in, couldn't hold it back. "But she didn't!" The words exploded from her on a sob that scraped her raw. "I never got to tell her, to apologize for all my stupid tantrums and rudeness and disobeying."

The girls folded her into their arms, stroked her hair until she quieted. Bree pressed a box of tissues into her lap and then fetched her a bottle of water, while Cass covered her with a blanket. But Kara crossed her arms over her round belly and sat in the farthest corner of the sofa.

"I'm so mad at you, Laney. All these years, you stayed away. All this time, wasted. Why didn't you tell us? Why didn't you *trust* us?"

Elena lifted her heavy head. "Trust? You think I didn't *trust* you?"

"You obviously didn't." Kara rubbed her belly, avoiding Elena's eyes.

"No. No, that's not why I didn't tell any of you."

"Then why?" Kara demanded, her voice thick.

It took her a long moment, but Elena finally found the words—or maybe, just the courage to say them out loud. "The look on your face is burned into my brain—it haunts me, Kara. It tortures me."

"*My* face?" Kara repeated.

Elena nodded. "Mom and I never got along but you and Mom were best friends. I saw the same look on your face every time something happened in your life—graduation, moving here, the baby—you miss her and it's my fault she's not here with you right now. If she hadn't been so upset with me, maybe she wouldn't have left for work so early—" Elena pressed both hands over her ears.

When she raised her eyes, she found all of the girls were crying.

"Oh, Elena, you poor kid." Bree opened her arms, but Elena only shook her head. She didn't deserve their kindness now. But Bree folded her up in a hug anyway.

"Elena, you're wrong." Kara struggled to her feet, turned her sister to face her. "I love you. I don't blame you for any of it. Do you understand?"

Elena managed a nod, though Kara's words did little to lighten her burden.

"Mommy adored you, Laney. Yes, you argued a lot, but you were a kid. That's what kids do. Look at me and Daddy. He's mad I got pregnant, mad I moved back to New York, mad I went to NYU instead of Bucknell. I've said a ton of things to him when I was angry that I didn't mean."

At that, Elena lifted her head. Kara and Dad didn't get along at all. Why had she never noticed that before? "Yeah, but he didn't die the day after you said them." Elena slipped from her sister's arms and fell back to the sofa.

Kara angled her head. "No. No, he didn't. But he loves me, Laney. Even if I do press his buttons, I know he loves me just like I know Mom loves you."

Elena shook her head. "No. She died hating me and still hates me, if all of these signs are real."

"Laney, the only one who hates you is you." Jade's voice on the speaker phone made her jump. "Nobody else. You need to put that aside. Everyone in this room loves you. You told us Lucas loves you. All these signs you told us about—Elena, I think you're right and they're real—"

Elena folded her arms over her middle and gasped.

"Let me finish," Jade continued. "I think they're real and tell me your mother loves you and forgives you. She can't be here, but she found a way to connect you with someone who will love you, Elena. Someone who can understand exactly what you feel. Why aren't you all over that?"

"Because—because he's the best man I know." She flung out her arms, let them fall. "And me? I'm nothing but a black hole who sucks the happiness out of everybody around me. I can't—I won't do that to him." She stood up, headed to the second bedroom. "I'm going to pack."

Kara's head snapped up. "Are you serious? I have a week left and you're just gonna walk out on me, too?"

Elena paused, but never turned around. "You're both

better off without me around—all of you are."

In the baby's room, Elena gasped when her words punched her. She'd just said the same thing to her sister that Steve had when he left Kara.

Oh, hell. She really was heartless.

Chapter Twelve

ANOTHER STORM HIT New York on Sunday night, dumping a foot of snow over the city and canceling all flights out of town. The SFG holiday Remembrance was in five days and though Elena had no intention of going, she'd hoped to be out of the city well before the event. She was still getting emails about last-minute finishing touches and couldn't face the committee. Couldn't face Lucas. And damn well couldn't face her sister.

They'd shared the apartment in a silence colder than the December weather. On auto-pilot, Elena made Kara meals, did her laundry, fetched her mail, and cleaned her home around conference calls with her project teams and her manager. She couldn't get Lucas off her mind and she couldn't talk about him without someone willing to talk to her.

None of the girls were speaking to her at the moment. She'd hoped to stay with Cassandra, but Cass had left before she'd finished packing. Even Jade, the friend who knew her the best, wasn't responding to her texts.

On Tuesday, Kara had another appointment with her doctor. Elena accompanied her but might as well have been invisible. Kara ignored her, refused to let her come inside the examination room, said not a word on the way home. Elena got her settled with her baby name book and escaped to the cold gray streets for some alone time.

She shoved her hands in her pockets and walked down West Street with no particular destination in mind. She ignored the biting cold, stepping over mounds of snow. No matter how long she walked, Lucas haunted her. A man huddled in a doorway, his fingers almost blue. She peeled off her gloves for him. A woman slipped and fell on ice and she hurried over to help her up. She'd never noticed before, never noticed the people around her suffering. She'd been too focused on her own suffering to care. Close to tears, Elena suddenly found herself walking through the September 11th Memorial grounds.

"Oh!" The gaping hole in her heart twinged and though the pain took her breath away, she couldn't turn away. She walked toward the fountains, something she couldn't name pulling her closer and closer to the bronze plaques that surrounded the holes left behind when the towers fell. On the North pool, she found it two panels over from the corner.

Marie Elise Larsen

She pulled her gloveless hands out of her pockets, traced her mother's name in the icy metal, and whispered, "I'm sorry. I'm so sorry, Mom." She reached out both arms, stretched herself over the bronze plaque and cried until a hand on her back made her jolt around in fear.

"Miss, I'm sorry to bother you, but um, well, here. I thought you could use these."

Elena blinked hot tears from her eyes and found a man standing behind her, clutching a wad of tissues. She narrowed her eyes, examined the dark face, the scar that marred it from cheek to temple.

"Al?"

"Elena!" Luke's friend smiled at her. "I didn't realize it was you. But please, take them anyway.

"Oh. Um. Thank you. Thank you very much."

Al smiled and shook his head. "It's no trouble, believe me. I always bring a pile when I visit."

Frowning, Elena asked, "You come here a lot?"

"Oh, sure. I come all the time. It makes me feel closer to him." Al stared out over the pool. "My dad."

"I'm sorry." She stared into the pool, where ice hung from the sides.

"Which one is yours?"

Sniffling, Elena pointed. "This one. She was my mom." Her voice cracked.

"I'm sorry, too," he said, and then pointed to another name about a yard away. "This one's mine." The name read Fahran Suliman.

"I'm sorry," Elena returned the sentiment with a gulp. Hollow words to match the hollow feeling in her chest, but what else was there? "Al, can I ask you something?"

When he nodded, she waved her numb hands over the memorial grounds. "How do you stand it? Doesn't it make you remember? Doesn't it make you sad?"

He studied her for a long moment and finally said, "You're shivering. Let me buy you a cup of coffee and I'll tell you."

Elena considered his offer for a moment. She wasn't ready to face Kara—not yet. And she didn't want to be alone, either. "Okay. Thanks."

"Here." He stripped off his gloves and handed them to her. "Put them on," he ordered when she started to refuse.

She tucked her hands into the warm leather and managed a

smile. "Thanks."

Al led her to a small coffee shop right outside the Memorial, where a small sofa sat near one window, Christmas songs filled the air, and a smiling barista greeted them from behind a counter. Half a dozen people sat around the shop, wrapped presents in shopping bags at their feet. "Hot cocoa?" he asked with a wink and her face fell.

No. No hot cocoa. Not ever again.

"Tea, please. Honey and cream."

His smile evaporated. Nodding, he got in line while she found an empty table. She put his gloves neatly on the table and used the tissues he'd given her to blow her nose, mop her eyes.

"Here you go." He put a steaming cup of water on the table and handed her a small plate that held her tea bag, a few thimbles of cream and packets of honey. She fussed over the drink, her numb fingers making her fumble.

"My dad," Al began and Elena's movements went still, "worked as a trader. They found his wristwatch and his briefcase, but not him," he revealed and Elena gasped. At least, her family had been able to bury her mother.

"What did you do?"

"Eventually, we buried those things." He sipped his coffee. "The truth is, he's buried somewhere under those pools and when I come here, I feel him with me."

She played with her empty cream cap. "Do you really believe that stuff?"

"What stuff?"

"Life after death. Heaven. All those signs." She spread her hands.

"I do. It all helps me cope." He took another sip. "You should talk to Luke."

At the mention of his name, Elena's eyes welled with fresh

tears. Al gave her hand a squeeze.

"Elena, you're asking me if there's a God, if there's a Heaven, if there's a life after this one, and I can't answer that. Nobody can. It's either something you believe in or you don't." He played with his cup. "I'm not very religious. I was raised Muslim and there are some things that even I—with my lack of faith—believe."

At her blank look, he elaborated. "I believe in *people*, Elena." He turned to stare out the window, at the Memorial just a block away. "Hundreds—thousands of people worked incredibly hard through unimaginable conditions to make sure those who are still here are honored and respected and never forgotten. *Darkness cannot drive out darkness: only light can do that. Hate cannot drive out hate: only love can do that.* I believe in the people who believe that."

She stared at him. "Martin Luther King."

"You know it?" He smiled, pleased. "When I come here, that's what I remember. It helps erase the images of horror I used to see every time I shut my eyes."

At her look of disbelief, he laughed once. "Every time I come here, somebody smiles at me or gives me a hug or stuffs tissues into my hand. Every time I come here, I feel connected, Elena. I feel like I'm part of something that's bigger than the hate that almost killed me." He tapped the scar that rode the side of his face.

"Killed you?" She frowned, raised her cup and then froze when the truth smacked her across the face. *I fractured his skull, Elena. I beat him almost to death...*

She shook her head. Lucas couldn't have done that, he was good and kind. *You look at me like I'm some sort of perfect being, but I'm not. I'm no hero, Elena. I just believe in trying, that's all.*

"Oh, Al, I'm sorry. I'm so sorry." She pointed to his scar. "You're the one he almost killed."

Al blinked. "He told you."

"Most of it," she admitted. "He never said it was you, though."

"Don't be mad at him for that. That's my fault. I hate talking about it, remembering it."

She continued to stare at Al. "You...you forgave him," she said with a shake of her head.

"Because I can't stand the alternative, Elena. He was consumed by guilt and pain and I had the power to end that for him."

"But you're friends, aren't you?"

"The best."

"How? How do you look at him and not hate him?"

"Because I know him." He grinned, a brilliant flash of white teeth. Al's smile was almost as beautiful as Luke's, she thought with a pang of guilt. "He devotes himself completely to leaving the world a better place than he found it. It's not just lip service, you know? Most of us, we go through life oblivious to the people around us—their needs, their sorrows. But not him. He sees what the rest of us don't."

She squeezed her eyes shut. Hadn't she just told herself the same thing?

"He's a good man, Elena," Al said quietly. "The best I know."

She squeezed her eyes harder, but the tears fell anyway. "I know," she whispered. "Too good for me. I won't ever—" She bit her lip, shook her head.

Al angled his head. "Ever what?"

"Be good enough for him," she admitted.

He snorted, put his cup down, and laughed out loud. Elena lifted wounded eyes to his.

"I'm sorry, I'm sorry, but you just said the same thing *he* said to me not even a week ago. Damn, you two are the perfect match."

A tiny wisp of hope caught, held.

Soberly, Al angled his head. "Elena, what happened that has you both so miserable? He's not talking."

She lifted a shoulder, sipped the tea she didn't want. "He...he said he's in love with me."

"And why don't you think you deserve that love?" he asked without hesitation and she fumbled her cup, spilling some tea. She grabbed napkins, blotted up the spill.

Al covered her hand. "Elena. Tell me."

"I'm...I'm not...a good person." When he said nothing, she felt a dam burst inside her and everything rushed out—all the pain and sorrow and guilt. "I was horrible to my mother, Al. I said unforgivable things to her and never got a chance to tell her I was sorry. She died believing I hated her."

His chair scraped the floor when he left it to come around to her, fold her up in his arms. "I'm so sorry—all the times I told you about signs—you think it means she's punishing you?"

She shook, determined to stop the flood of tears—would she ever dry up? She nodded against his shoulder. "The playing cards. The candy wrappers. The stupid snowflake! It's her, Al. I didn't believe it, not at first, but how can I not? She grounded me the night before she died and she's still punishing me now. Every day of my life, I remember what I did, what I said and Lucas? He's just more punishment."

Al was quiet for so long, Elena wondered if she'd upset him, too. She picked up her heavy head, turned bloodshot eyes to his and shrugged. "So, thanks for the tea. I should probably get going." To where? She had no idea. She stood up but he shot out a hand, stopped her.

"What if you're wrong?"

She blinked. "What?"

"I said, what if you're wrong? What if everything that happened—your sister's baby, meeting Luke, the snowflake, all of it—what if it's not punishment, but pardon? What if your mother's trying to tell you she knows you're sorry and that it's okay, she forgives you? Doesn't that change anything?"

She blinked at him, unable to grasp the words. "Why? Why would she do that after what I did?"

Al rolled his eyes. "Because she's your mother, Elena. She knows you. She knows you best."

She couldn't take any more. She simply couldn't hear one more word. She turned and ran into the cold dark night.

✦ ✦ ✦

WITH AL'S WORDS echoing in her exhausted brain, she ran blindly and saw a church across the street. What if Al was right? What if all these signs really were signs Mom forgave her and she'd—and she'd just made the second biggest mistake of her life?

She crossed the street and climbed the steps, hesitated at the door. She hadn't been in a church of any sort for well over a decade and felt like the biggest hypocrite alive walking in now, but she had to know.

She pulled on the door, but it was locked tight. A bitter laugh escaped her lips. "Figures." She rattled the door one more time and sank to the cold granite steps in defeat, and prepared to do something she'd never done, even when things were at their darkest.

She prayed.

"Okay, God. Okay. I'm here, right outside your door and I don't know what to do, where to go, how to fix everything I broke. If you and Mom are sending me signs, send me one now and I promise I won't ignore it."

She waited. And waited some more. Her hands were numb and she was so damn tired, she could barely keep her head up. She forced her head up and blinked a few times. Suddenly, she saw a man stride by. He wore a hat like Luke's, a jacket like Luke's, even a scarf looped around his neck like Luke's.

"Lucas!" She leaped to her feet, chased the man in the hat. "Lucas!" It took her half a block to catch up to him. When she grabbed his arm to stop him.

"Can I help you?" Annoyed, a stranger glared pointedly on her hand on his arm.

"Sorry. I thought you were someone else." It wasn't him. Disappointment cut through her like a rusty knife. She turned away. This was pointless.

"Hope you find him."

She'd managed two steps before he called her. "Hey! You dropped something." The strange man picked something up from the ground.

In his hand, he held her MetroCard from her first visit to Luke's place. She stared at it, that tiny bit of hope catching into a flame. This was it—this was the sign she'd prayed for. The certainty—the faith—filled her with warmth. She grabbed the card and pressed a noisy kiss to the stranger's cheek. She took off at a run. "Thank you!" She called back over her shoulder.

Elena ran all the way to the PATH entrance, waited impatiently for the train. By the time she arrived at Luke's door, it was late. She pressed the buzzer, waited some more.

There was no answer.

The flame of hope that had sustained her during her dash from Manhattan to Hoboken sputtered, died. Slowly, she walked back to the PATH station and waited for the next train back to the city.

So much for signs.

✦ ✦ ✦

LUCAS TAPPED HIS glass on the bar. The bartender promptly poured him a few more fingers of—what the hell had he been drinking? Right. Whiskey. His phone buzzed in his pocket for the hundredth time that day. He glanced at the screen.

Elena.

I'm sorry. Please pick up. Please.

Did she think he was he a moron? An idiot? Did she really expect him to just pick up the phone, and what—talk about the weather like nothing was wrong, like she hadn't shredded his heart to ribbons? He wished he could crush the damn phone to powder and deliberately loosened his hold before he did. He gulped his drink, felt his head spin and figured it was time to cool it. Not like it was helping him forget a damn thing anyway. He thought about calling Al, but didn't want to ruin his friend's evening. He took out his wallet, handed his credit card to the bartender, settled his tab. He'd called in sick that day, but tomorrow, he would put Elena Larsen firmly out of his mind and get back to work.

He stood up, tugged a black hat over his head, zipped his jacket and stared at the warm leather gloves Elena had bought him. He stuffed them back in his pocket. He'd rather freeze than use them and would give them away as soon as he found someone who needed them. Back outside, where the temperature had dipped below freezing, his breath visible as he walked home, he accepted that it wasn't possible to drink Elena off his mind. She'd permanently etched herself on him—heart and soul. He wished he'd seen the sign for it because Christ, he'd have run the opposite way if he'd known how much it would hurt.

A horn blared and he hustled out of a car's path, slipped on ice and fell on his bottom. Cursing until he lost his breath, he managed to drag himself back to his feet, annoyed because apparently, even his ass wasn't safe from the pain of losing Elena. He limped home, halted when he caught a glimpse of a red hat heading into the PATH station. He stood and watched for a moment and finally turned away.

It couldn't be Elena.

No use hoping it was.

He turned up the walk to his door, unlocked it, and in the swath of light carved into the dark when he opened it, he saw something on the icy path. He retraced his steps, slowly bent his aching body and picked up a key.

He'd never seen the key before but somehow, he knew it was Elena's and the thought gave him comfort.

Chapter Thirteen

"ELENA! WHERE THE hell have you been?" Kara demanded.

Sniffling, Elena stood in the doorway, her hands numb. "Kara," she began, but couldn't hold it together long enough to get the words out. "I lost my key."

Kara wrapped her arms around Elena. "Oh, honey, you're frozen to the bone. Come on, Laney. Come with me." She led Elena into the bathroom, began filling the tub with steaming hot water and bubble bath. "Where are your gloves?" She unzipped Elena's jacket, tugged it off.

"I gave them away."

"Gave them—why would you do that?"

Elena's face crumbled. "I saw a homeless person and—and it's what Lucas would have done."

Kara pulled the hat off Elena's head. "Get in the tub, stay in until you're not cold," she ordered.

Elena stripped down, stepped into the tub and sank under the hot suds. A few minutes later, Kara knocked and stepped in with a bowl of hot soup. Elena took it with a tired smile.

"Kara, if you still want me, I'd like to stay. I'm sorry I took off."

"Of course I want you! Laney, for what it's worth, I think you're wrong. I think Mom forgave you. I think Mom forgave you the minute it happened. I haven't even met my child yet but I can promise you this. Nothing this baby does or ever will do could ever make me hate him or her. She was our mom, Laney. Of course she forgave you. Of course."

Elena said nothing for a long moment. Al had said the same thing. She hoped Kara was right. She hoped they both were right. She really needed that.

"Kara, you're gonna be a great mom."

Kara beamed, squeezed Elena's shoulder.

"Oh, Kara! I love him. And I think I made a terrible mistake. I don't think I can fix it."

Kara took the bowl, put it on the toilet tank. "The only mistake you made is not trusting the people who love you." She smiled. "And as one of those people, I'm telling you that we've already forgiven you for that."

Elena sank deeper into the bubbles. "He won't talk to me. I've called and sent texts, but—"

"Laney, give him some time."

"I went back to his place today, but he never answered the door."

"He probably wasn't home."

Elena shrugged. Maybe he wasn't. "I also went to the memorial. I saw Mom's name."

Kara's lip trembled. "Oh, Laney."

"I even prayed. I haven't done that since I was fourteen."

Kara sat on the side of the tub. "Did it help?"

"I didn't think so at first. And then, I saw a guy I thought was Lucas, so I chased him, but it wasn't. As I walked away, the guy said I dropped something. It was my MetroCard, Kara. He held it out to me and I thought, it was a sign."

"So you thought it meant you were supposed to go see him?"

Elena nodded. "I think I guessed wrong. He wasn't even home. I suck at seeing signs."

Kara shook her head. "Oh, stop being so dramatic."

"Kara, seriously. I need to fix this."

"Okay." Kara grabbed a towel, unfolded it. "Dry off and get dressed. Let's brainstorm."

✦ ✦ ✦

ELENA AND KARA spent a few hours coming up with ways to find Lucas, get him to listen to Elena's explanation.

She texted him. He didn't reply. She left voice mails. He didn't call back. She spent hour after hour at SFG, but he never showed. She rode the PATH train alone to Hoboken three nights in a row. He never answered his door.

"Kara," she said on Thursday morning over bowls of oatmeal. "Do you really want to go to the Holiday thing tomorrow?"

"Laney, trust me. He wouldn't miss that. Not after all the hours we all put in."

"It feels wrong. I don't want to use a solemn occasion like that for me, you know?"

Kara nibbled a fingernail. "I see your point. Okay. We'll go and if you see him, you just smile. Even if he looks angry, smile. Don't make a scene or do anything that detracts from the solemnity."

Elena nodded. "Agreed."

"Okay, what's your schedule like today? I've got an OB appointment this morning."

"I've got a progress review call at nine and after that, I'm free." Elena took the empty bowls to the sink, squirted some soap into them and ran the water.

"Great." Kara heaved herself off the stool. "Elena. I'm going to ask my doctor to induce. I just can't stand being pregnant anymore. I want to see my baby. I want to get started on our new lives."

Elena pulled in a breath, nodded. "Okay. Let's get dressed. We'll see what your doctor says."

Kara nodded, eyes wide and scared. Elena watched her shuffle across the apartment and into her bedroom. When the door shut behind her, Elena let out the sob she'd been trying to swallow.

"Please. Please, Mom. I need another sign. I don't know what else to do. I don't know."

✦ ✦ ✦

ON THE SATURDAY before Christmas, Elena stood in Kara's bathroom, threaded a chain through Luke's snowflake and looped it around her neck. In the mirror, her face was pale despite her makeup and her eyes reflected the churning in her gut. She stared at the ornament Lucas had given her when she was fourteen years old, standing on the ramp that led to her mother's—and *his* mother's—tomb. She wasn't entirely sure why she'd kept it all these years. It was a three-inch-high bauble in plastic and crystals and rhinestones and—and—oh, it was the most beautiful thing she'd ever seen—right up until the day she'd seen him smile and she was suddenly certain *that's* why she'd kept it. It, like the boy who'd pressed it into her hands, was *light* itself—the only spot of it she'd been able to see in a world that had turned ugly and hateful overnight.

Her lip trembled and she battled to hold on to the slim strand of hope the ornament represented.

She wore no other jewelry with her simple black dress and

hoped the snowflake would speak—loudly—for her. She hadn't seen Lucas all week.

I love you, he'd said.

And instead of responding in kind, what had she done? She'd fled. She'd been a coward.

She left the bathroom, joined her sister in the living room. "Okay. I'm ready."

Kara looked up from her always-present baby name book. "Oh, Laney. You look amazing."

Elena's hand fluttered to the ornament hanging over her heart. "I hope this works, Kara. I don't know what else to do to get him to talk to me."

Kara closed her book. "Laney, he's hurt." At Elena's wince, she quickly added, "Don't give up. He'll talk to you when he's ready."

Elena nodded, managed a tiny smile. "I hope so. I really do. He's it for me, Kara. I never saw him coming, but he's the one." Tears stung her eyes so she carefully rubbed beneath them and moved to grab their coats. "Are you sure you're up for this?"

Kara maneuvered herself off the sofa. "Definitely. I haven't been out of the apartment for anything other than OB appointments in weeks." She stood in the light of the Christmas tree by the window and Elena could only stare. She wore a simple pair of black pants with a sparkly top in a deep Christmas green but didn't just glow—she shimmered with the kind of inner light Elena was now convinced only pregnancy could create.

They made their way to the elevator and into a cab, Kara holding Elena's hand. Elena stared out the window at twinkling lights strung in apartment windows and smiled to herself. Funny how all she could see now was light. The cab slowed as it approached the hotel and three cars ahead, Elena saw Lucas step to the sidewalk. He wore a tux in classic black with a straight tie, something pinned to his lapel—she couldn't tell what. Her stomach dropped when a woman in a gown stepped out of the cab after him, followed by an older man.

His family, she realized, a wave of relief flooding over her.

Someone stopped to greet him and his teeth flashed for a split second, but even from inside her cab, she could tell the smile never reached his eyes. Not for the first time, her heart clenched at the realization that she was the reason why.

Her own cab pulled to the curb. She got out, turned back to help her sister. When she looked up, Lucas was gone.

"I'm okay, Laney. Go after him."

"Are you sure?"

"Definitely. Go."

Elena hurried into the hotel lobby as fast as her strappy heels would allow. The lobby was a sea of people in red, green, silver, gold and an awful lot of black. She wasn't one for making wishes, but damn it, she wished he'd look her way. Suddenly, the crowd parted and there he was, not ten feet in front of her.

"Lucas!"

He froze.

She held her breath.

He turned.

She smiled.

She poured everything she had—everything she was—into that smile.

She moved. Walked to him, held out her arms.

His jaw tightened and he turned.

She stood, alone, arms spread.

Empty.

The crowd closed in and Elena made her way out of the main path, trying to hold in her tears.

"Elena! Elena!" Kara waved from across the grand entrance. Elena hurried to her side, helped her check their coats and assisted her into the elevator that took them to the ballroom, where a throng of people were looking for their table assignments. She guided Kara into a chair at table four, where an elderly couple beamed at her baby bump and engaged her in conversation.

She sat next to Kara, her eyes scanning the banquet room, transformed to look like a winter wonderland. White lights twinkled from every column and wall in the huge room. From the ceiling, decorations dangled. Snowflakes. She shut her eyes with a wince. People greeted each other with quiet hopes for a healthy new year since *happy* seemed far out of reach. Elena smiled and nodded at the greetings aimed at her, but she wasn't listening. She was searching for Lucas.

She finally spotted him at the bar and hurried to join him. "Luke."

He whipped around, his dark eyes snapping with suppressed rage. They glared holes through her for a moment and then narrowed at the ornament suspended around her neck. His jaw tightened when she touched his arm. On his lapel, a picture of a pretty dark-haired woman was pinned.

His mother.

"Please. Just give me a minute."

He took her elbow, gripped it hard, moved her to the corner of the bar. "I don't want to hear a word you have to say."

"Even if that word is love?"

He snorted out a bitter laugh and shot her an icy glare that made her shiver. "I already know you love me, Elena. You run from everybody you love."

The barb stung. "I know I hurt you, but please listen. You were right—"

He waved his hand, an impatient slash through the air. "You have something that belongs to me."

"You gave it to me." Her hand fluttered to the snowflake around her neck, covering it protectively.

"I gave it to a little girl who needed it. The woman in front of me doesn't, so I want it back."

She flinched at the pain she heard in his voice and with shaky hands, reached up to unfasten the chain. "I'm sorry." She whispered, holding it out.

He snatched the snowflake from her hand, his mouth open to deliver one more parting shot when Kara shouted her name. Elena whirled, found Kara standing near their table, clutching her belly. "Kara?"

"Laney! My water. It just broke."

Panic paralyzed her and she could only stare, mouth gaping, as people closest to them jumped into action. A cell phone was suddenly thrust into Kara's hand so she could phone her doctor. The venue's maitr'd organized a cab. Luke held out his hand but Elena couldn't figure out why.

"Coat check, Elena. Give me the coat check ticket."

Coats. Yes, they would need their coats. She fumbled with her little black evening bag, managed to find the ticket. Lucas snatched it and strode away. She finally remembered how to move and joined Kara.

"Are you having contractions?"

"Only one so far. We have plenty of time." But Kara's eyes were huge with fear.

"Luke's getting our coats. You'll be fine, Kara. You'll both be—Kara? Kara!"

Kara's face scrunched up and a gasp fell from her lips when the second contraction hit. Lucas jogged over, coats in his arms. "Kara," he said. "Come on, honey, do the breathing they taught you."

Right, the breathing! Elena kicked herself. She tugged on her coat, held Kara's out for her. "Two contractions in five minutes?"

Kara nodded, panting.

"We should probably hurry." Elena took Kara's arm, started for the main doors to the banquet room.

"Oh, God." Kara clutched Elena's hand.

"I got you." Lucas scooped Kara up at the knees, strode out of the room, into the elevator. Elena had to hustle to keep up. He strode down the steps and across the main entrance, where a cab was already waiting and tucked Kara carefully into the backseat. Elena climbed in after her and turned to thank Luke, but he firmly shut the door between them, his mouth a tight, bitter line.

As the taxi drove off with Elena's hand pressed to the glass, Kara whimpered. "I'm so sorry, Laney. I'm so sorry."

Chapter Fourteen

IN THE EARLY hours of Sunday morning, in a labor room at New York Presbyterian Hospital, Elena helped her sister grunt and sweat and push her daughter into this world. Baby Girl Larsen arrived with a full head of dark hair and weighed in at a healthy seven pounds even.

Elena cut the cord and as she looked into her niece's blue eyes, felt her heart go *splat* for the second time that month. She snapped pictures as a nurse cleaned the baby, fastened hospital ID bands around her tiny ankle and wrist and grinned proudly when she got one of her own. She attached the images to a text message announcing "Milk Dud's a girl!" to everyone in their circle including Lucas and because she was in a forgiving mood, shot one over to Steve Orland, too.

He might be an ass, but it was Christmas time and the man deserved to know he'd just become a father.

Her dad and brothers replied in seconds, promising they'd book the next flight. Aunt Enza said she'd be there with the gang in tow the minute visiting hours began.

The nurse changed Kara's bedding and gown and Elena brushed her hair and got her comfortable. After mommy and baby had tried their first nursing session, Kara yawned loudly and handed her baby to Elena. Elena cradled the baby in the crook of her arm. "Look what you made, Kara. Mom would be so freakin' proud of you." Elena's voice cracked.

"Oh, Laney, I'm so glad you're here."

"Me, too." Elena smiled. "Me, too," she said again. "I'm so sorry for everything." The baby let out a tiny squeak and both sisters gasped in wonder. "She's absolutely perfect, Kara."

"Laney, look. The sun's coming up."

Elena walked the baby over to the window that overlooked the city. A layer of snow covered the rooftops and the first rays of the sun shattered the darkness. "Look, baby. There's a great big world out there and I know, believe me, I know it can be scary, but all you have to do is look for the light and you'll be just fine." Her voice broke but holding that brand new life in her arms, she couldn't be sad—not all the way.

"Call him. Call Lucas again."

Elena turned away from the window, but kept her eyes glued to the precious bundle in her arms. "Later. I'll call him later. And I'll keep calling him until he talks to me. I'm not giving up, Kara. He said he's in love with me and he needs to know I'm in love with him, too. He needs to know I'm staying in New York, I'm staying with the SFG and I'm staying with you."

Kara gasped. "Are you serious?"

"Completely."

"Lucas changed your mind?"

Elena laughed once and thought about that. Nobody can change a mind that refused to be changed. "No. But he definitely helped."

"So what did?"

"Your room number." Elena looked up, found Kara recording her with her cell phone and adjusted the baby so the camera could capture that adorable little face. "When they directed us into this room, I couldn't believe it. Six eighteen, Kara."

It took her a second and then Kara gasped. "Mom's birthday!"

Elena nodded and shrugged as the tears rolled down her cheeks. "It's a sign, Kara. It's Mom's way of saying she was here with you—with us and that she loves us. I never would have connected that—wouldn't even have noticed that—if I hadn't met Lucas." She carefully put the baby into her little plastic bassinet. "Kara, do you think there's still hope?"

Kara tapped her phone, saved the video, and nodded. "There's always hope, honey." She shifted over on her bed. "Come on. Let's shut our eyes for a while, okay?"

Elena smiled and slid beside her sister just the way they used to when they were little and thunderstorms pounded their house. They slept soundly for several hours until a nurse came in with Kara's breakfast tray. Elena stretched, smiled, and looked at the baby, snuggled in her tiny bed next to them. She felt… she couldn't find the words. Content. Light. Maybe even happy.

How was that possible?

Later, when visiting hours began, Cass, Jade, and Bree rushed in with balloons, flowers, presents wrapped in pink and red paper. Their moms, Aunt Vincenza, Aunt Joann, and Aunt Gigi—the women who'd stepped in—stepped up—when Kara and Elena lost their mom, followed behind.

"Awww, she looks like Marie," Aunt Enza said in a voice thick with tears, as she stared at the baby in Kara's arms.

"You think?" Kara smiled at her daughter. "I only see Steve."

"Look at all that hair! That's totally Marie." Enza ran her hand over the baby's head where a tiny pink bow held up a tuft of hair. Elena grinned wide. Mom's hair had been thick and straight. When Elena was little—well before she'd discovered the joys of the Brazilian Blowout—she'd wished for straight hair that gleamed like her mom's but she'd been cursed with her father's wiry mess. It looked like her niece would be spared that nightmare.

"Let me see! All I see is blanket," Aunt Joann complained. She peeked over Enza's shoulder and squealed.

"Oh, she's beautiful!"

"Good job, mama," Jade added.

"Kara, honey." Aunt Joann cupped Kara's cheek. "I am so proud of you and know your mom would be, too."

Kara's face wobbled and Aunt Gigi rushed over to fold her up in a hug. "Shh, shh, shh, baby, we've got you. You're not alone. You're never alone."

"Oh, Aunt Gigi, it hurts," Kara whispered. "I hate that my daughter will never know my mom. But I'm so glad, so incredibly glad she'll have three grandmas."

While the moms cooed over Mom and Baby, Elena glanced at Cassandra. She stood just a little apart from the group. Elena put a hand on her shoulder. "I'm so sorry, Cass." But Cass only shook her head.

"Not needed, Laney. Everything's just the way it's supposed to be."

Not everything, she thought when Cass sent a wistful look toward the baby.

"So what's her name, Kara?" Bree asked.

Kara bit her lip and hesitated a moment. "Um, well, I've been going through that stupid book for weeks and there's one name I like. I hope you guys like it."

"Just tell us." Jade danced up on her toes.

"Okay. It's Nadia Marie."

Elena eyes filled. "Oh, Kara."

"What? What? It's horrible, isn't it? I was afraid—"

Elena shook her head violently. "No. It's the most beautiful name ever."

Aunt Enza carefully held up baby Nadia for everyone to see. "Welcome to the world, Nadia Marie. You are going to be so loved."

A sniffle from the bed had all the girls smothering Kara with hugs. Elena watched them and knew with absolute certainty she couldn't leave these women a second time.

"It means *hope*."

At the sound of that deep voice, Elena's heart stopped then took off soaring. Slowly, she turned to the door, found Lucas standing there with an enormous Teddy bear—both of them in Santa hats. He had a growth of stubble that only seemed to magnify the potency of his smile, and the sparkle was back in his eyes.

The hope she thought had died warmed her all over. She took a step, wanting to wrap herself around him and never let go. "Lucas, I—"

He stopped her with a raised hand, and stepped into Kara's room. "I know."

"How? How do you know?"

He put the bear on the bed by Kara's feet and held out his cell phone. "When I woke up this morning, I found a present waiting for me." He cued up the video Kara had taken early that morning and pressed Play. The whole room fell silent when Elena's voice, cracking with emotion, filled it. *It's a sign, Kara. It's Mom's way of saying she was here with you—with us and that she loves us. I never would have connected that—wouldn't even have noticed that—if I hadn't met Lucas. Kara, do you think there's still hope?*

Elena looked up at him, at Kara, her heart bursting.

"Her name means *hope*, Elena." And he smiled that breathtaking, joy-giving, world-brightening smile of his and she knew. She understood what he was saying.

"Oh," she said on a breath. "It's a sign." She turned to Kara. "Did you know that? Did you pick Nadia because it means *hope?*"

Kara said nothing, just smiled. Lucas reached out, squeezed Kara's hand and pecked her on the cheek. "Thank you. Can I—would it be okay if I held her?"

"Absolutely." When Kara nodded, Aunt Enza carefully transferred the baby into Luke's arms.

Baby Nadia opened her eyes, blinked, and started to cry, but Lucas was having none of that. "Oh, no, no, don't do that." And then in a soft voice, he sang. *"Said the night wind to the little lamb, do you see what I see?"* Baby Nadia quieted and just stared up at him, eyes locked on his mouth, entranced by the sounds he made. When he finished, she gave a huge yawn and closed her eyes. Elena's heart swelled with love and she wished she'd snapped a picture.

Her phone pinged. Kara held up her own with a wink and Elena snorted out a laugh.

Bree nudged Cass. "You were right. That's a total panty-dropping smile."

"Panty-dropping?" Luke's eyes popped and then narrowed at Elena. "Is *that* what P.D. means?" And then he laughed. Elena felt a rush of love so strong, she wrapped her arms around Lucas and the baby and in front of her sister, her best friends—her circle—she whispered, "I'm sorry, Lucas, so sorry for not telling you I love you, too. I'm so in love with you. I'm staying right here and I hope you can forgive me for running. I tried to find you, to tell you—"

"I know." He touched her face, wiped away a tear with his thumb. "I found your key to Kara's place in front of mine. I knew you'd been there. And I read all your texts. I know you love me." His face lit up with joy and Elena gasped. It was the one gift she'd never expected to receive. "You told me why Al's signs freaked you out. I should have been patient, should have given you time and I didn't. You should have been able to trust me and I let you down. Damn it, Elena, I'm sorry. Please say you forgive me."

"Yes, yes, only please promise me you'll smile at me like this for the rest of my life."

His eyebrows shot up and he grinned, just a little bit wicked. "If that was a proposal, Miss Larsen, you need to work on your technique. This," he said, pulling a box from his pocket, "is how you propose."

As the girls all gasped, Elena's mouth fell open and words clogged in her throat. When her knees buckled, he laughed. "Elena, you're my loop condition, you orient all my objects and I can't compile without you." When she rolled her eyes and giggled, he turned serious. "Marry me, Elena. Make me part of your life."

Part of it? He was the center of it, the sum of it, the whole of it.

He flipped open the box. "This was my mother's." He held baby Nadia in one arm so she slipped the ring on her finger herself. Lucas took her hand and kissed it. "A perfect fit."

Laughing, crying, she squeaked out four words. "Must be a sign." And then the hole in her heart filled with warmth as her sister, her friends, and her aunts hugged her, congratulated her. She would tell Lucas all of it later—about her doubts and how Al and the girls had helped her see things from a different perspective. She would devote her remaining days to looking for the light in the world. With a bundle of hope in their arms and love surrounding them, she drew Lucas closer and kissed him slowly, sweetly, knowing that with him in her life, she'd never be afraid of the dark again.

Epilogue

ON NEW YEAR'S Day, a fire burned in the fireplace, Christmas carols played on an iPod, and laughter rang out from every corner of the huge Gervais home. Outside, snow fell softly, turning the view from the rear window into a greeting card. Elena snuggled on the enormous sectional sofa, idly playing with the ring Lucas had put on her finger the day Nadia was born—one that had once belonged to his mother. He sat beside her, watching Bree's daughter, Charlie, hold the baby, a pillow tucked under her arm for extra safety. Kara dozed on the other end of the sofa, exhausted by her first weeks as a mommy. Aunt Enza had insisted Kara and Nadia stay with her until Kara was recovered, a decision little Charlie had treated like an extra Christmas gift.

"Support her head, Charlie," Bree reminded her daughter for the umpteenth time.

With an exaggerated eye roll, Charlie groaned from the chair opposite the sofa, a pillow tucked under arm. "I *know*, Mom."

"I know I say this every year but this was a good Christmas," Cassandra said.

Jade gave her a wide smile. "Santa sure delivered this year."

"Brought us everything we always wanted," Bree added, sipped her wine.

Charlie looked up. "Mom, are you ever gonna have another baby?"

Bree coughed and sputtered on the wine she'd just swallowed. All eyes shot from Charlie to Bree and back again. Time seemed to stop and wait while she thought of a response.

"Well, sweetheart, that's something to think about. It's a big decision."

Charlie smiled. "I hope you do. Babies are so cute."

Beside Elena, Lucas hid a grin and she was suddenly consumed by thoughts of their own babies. What would they look like? Would they have their Daddy's bright smile? She couldn't wait to talk to Luke about it because Charlie was right.

Babies were so cute.

Jade stared into the fire. "Do you guys believe in magic?"

There was a long moment of silence. "I do now," Elena said, catching Luke's hand and earning one of those quick heart-pumping grins. "It's people. People bring magic to the world."

"And happily-ever-afters to girls haunted by their pasts." Cass teased Elena.

Elena looked at her sleeping sister and thought about that for a moment. "Not all of us. Kara needs a happy-ever-after."

"Kara got a happy-for-now," Bree said. "Trust me," she added with a smile aimed at her daughter.

"Well said, Bree." Jade raised her glass.

"There's always next Christmas," Cass reminded her.

Elena gasped. "Oh, can you picture Nadia? She'll be walking by then, getting into everything."

"She'll understand a lot more by then. Family. Friends. Love." Bree sat back, crossed her legs.

Elena gripped Luke's hand and smiled. Christmas always used to fill her with dread and now, she couldn't wait. "To next Christmas." She touched her glass to Jade's.

Their hearts full, the friends lifted their glasses in a toast as the lights twinkled on the tree and snow fell softly outside.

The End

About the Authors

Jeannie Moon has always been a romantic. When she's not spinning tales of her own, Jeannie works as a school librarian, thankful she has a job that allows her to immerse herself in books and call it work. Married to her high school sweetheart, Jeannie has three kids, three lovable dogs and a mischievous cat and lives in her hometown on Long Island, NY. If she's more than ten miles away from salt water for any longer than a week, she gets twitchy.

Visit Jeannie's website at JeannieMoon.com

Jolyse Barnett may not be able to cook to save her life, but she can whip up a delicious romantic tale. She discovered the joy of playing with words at a young age, filling notebooks with poetry and stacks of pink diaries with her teenage angst and dreams. After she graduated from high school, she developed a more practical side. She earned her degree in Writing (Of course!), fell in love with her best friend (Yes!), and now lives her own happily-ever-after (Yay!). She enjoys a fulfilling day job and explores the world one vacation at a time with her two children and real-life hero.

Visit Jolyse's website at JolyseBarnett.com

Jennifer Gracen hails from Long Island, New York, where she lives with her two sons. After spending her youth writing in private and singing in public, she now only sings in her car and is immersed in her passion for writing. She loves to write contemporary romance for readers who look for authentic characters and satisfying endings. When she isn't with her kids, doing freelance proofreading, or chatting on Twitter and Facebook, Jennifer writes. She's already hard at work on her next book. Jennifer is a member of the Romance Writers of America and is active in the Long Island Romance Writers, as well as being a member of CTRWA.

Visit Jennifer's website at JenniferGracen.com

Powered by chocolate, **Patty Blount** is a hopeless romantic who frequently falls in love with fictional characters, only to suffer repeated broken hearts when the story ends, kicking her back out into the real world. Goodness and Light is her first contemporary romance for adults—to date, three of her novels for teens have been published, with a fourth expected in 2015.

Visit Patty's website at PattyBlount.com

Thank you for reading

Christmas in New York

If you enjoyed this book, you can find more from all our great authors at TulePublishing.com, or from your favorite online retailer.

Made in the USA
Charleston, SC
01 December 2014